The Story of the Grail and the Passing of Arthur.

by
HOWARD PYLE.

NEW YORK:

Dover Publications, Inc.

Published in Canada by General Publishing Company, Ltd., 30 Lesmill Road, Don Mills, Toronto, Ontario.

Published in the United Kingdom by Constable and Company, Ltd., 3 The Lanchesters, 162–164 Fulham Palace Road, London W6 9ER.

This Dover edition, first published in 1992, is an unabridged republication of the work originally published by Charles Scribner's Sons, New York, in 1910.

Manufactured in the United States of America
Dover Publications, Inc., 31 East 2nd Street, Mineola, N.Y. 11501

Library of Congress Cataloging-in-Publication Data

Pyle, Howard, 1853–1911.
   The story of the Grail and the passing of Arthur / by Howard Pyle.
      p.   cm.
   Summary: Follows the adventures of Sir Gerwaint, Galahad's quest for the holy Grail, the battle between Launcelot and Gawaine, and the slaying of Mordred.
   ISBN 0-486-27361-X
   1. Arthurian romances. 2. Grail—Legends. [1. Arthur, King. 2. Knights and knighthood—Folklore. 3. Folklore—England.] I. Title.
[PZ8.1.P994Su 1992]
[398.22]—dc20   92-29058
                                                  CIP
                                                      AC

Foreword.

✠   ✠

IN this volume there follows the fourth and last series of those histories relating to the life and to the kingship of Arthur, King of England.

In this it shall first be told how it befell with Sir Geraint; then it shall be told how the Holy Grail was achieved by Sir Galahad, the son of Sir Launcelot; and then it shall be told how King Arthur passed from this life, and how, after doing battle right royally for his crown and having overcome his enemies, he was slain by one of them whom he had wounded to death.

Much in this is sad, but much is not sad; for all endings are sad, and the passing of any hero is a sad thing to tell of; but the events and the adventures and the achievements of such a man are not sad. Thus it is here said that much of this is sad, but much is not sad.

Now I have for seven years been writing these four books, and in them I have put the best that I have to say concerning such things. Wherefore I now hope that you may like that which I have thus written, for if you do not like it, then I have written in vain; but if you do like these narratives, and the several various incidents in them recounted, then you put the seal of your approval upon my work, and my reward is full.

Know you that it is a very glorious thing for any man to achieve the approval of others; for all men write for approval, and all would win approval of their fellows if they were able to do so; wherefore, it is my strong hope that you may set the seal of your approval upon these books.

Be it said that some things in these histories are not recounted in other histories of this momentous reign, but that most of the things that I have written are recounted in such histories, and all those things so recounted I have told to you as they have been aforetime written by other men. In this I have shaped them and adapted them from the ancient style in which they were first written so as to fit them to the taste of those who read them to-day.

And I thank God that He has spared my life to finish this work, and also I hope that He may spare me that life still further, to achieve other works which I desire to undertake. But nevertheless it would have been a great regret to me to leave these books unfinished. For I have made a study of this history and have read much concerning it; wherefore, it was my earnest wish to finish that which I had begun if God would spare me my life to do so. This He has done.

So now I take leave of you upon the threshold of this book, and bid you godspeed in reading it. And the first of these adventures that you shall read shall be "The Story of Sir Geraint," which was the first time written in the ancient Welsh, but which is here re-written for your delectation in the manner which I here set it forth.

Contents

PART I

THE STORY OF SIR GERAINT

Chapter First

Chapter Second

Chapter Third

Chapter Fourth

Chapter Fifth

Chapter Sixth

PART II

THE STORY OF SIR GALAHAD

Chapter First

Chapter Second

Chapter Third

Chapter Fourth

Chapter Fifth

Chapter Sixth

PART III
THE PASSING OF ARTHUR

Chapter Fifth

Chapter Sixth

Chapter Seventh

Chapter Eighth

Chapter Ninth

Chapter Tenth

LIST OF ILLUSTRATIONS

xi

The Story of the Grail and the Passing of Arthur.

 ir Geraint, Son of Erbin

Prologue

UPON a certain time, at Michaelmas tide, King Arthur held a high hunting near to his court at Carleon-upon-Usk. Upon the morning of the day appointed for this hunting, all the attendants of the King were gathered in the courtyard of the castle ready to depart. The King cast his eyes about him, but he did not see the Queen near at hand. Quoth he, "Where is the Queen this morning, that I do not see her here?" One replied to him, "Lord, she is yet abed and asleep; shall we go wake her?" The King said, "No, if she would rather sleep than hunt, let her lie abed."

King Arthur proclaims a hunting.

Then another said, "Lord, Sir Geraint is not here either. Shall we call him?" King Arthur laughed. "Nay," quoth he, "let him also lie abed if he be drowsy." Therewith they took horse and rode away into the dewy sweetness of the early morning; the birds chaunting their roundelays and the sun bathing the entire earth as in a great bath of golden radiance.

Anon and after they had thus all departed, Queen Guinevere bestirred herself and awoke, and she said to her attendants, "Where is the King?" They say to her, "Lady, he hath ridden into the forest with his court." At that the Queen was vexed, and she said, "Why was I not awakened?" They say to her, "Lady, the King forbade that you should be disturbed." "Well," said she, "let that be as it may, but I shall yet go to view the hunting." So she arose and clad herself in a robe of sea-green taffeta, and she belted herself with a belt of gold, and she had her lady to enmesh her hair in a net of gold. And after she had broken her fast, she and her court took horse, and rode forth to the woodlands to find the King and his court.

Now as the Queen and her ladies and their attendants wended onward in a sedate and quiet fashion, they were presently aware of one who came riding after them at a hand gallop. Then the Queen drew rein, and said *Queen* to her attendant ladies, "Who is yonder gentleman who *Guinevere and* follows us at a hand gallop?" One of her attendants said, *her attendants* *ride into the* "Methinks, Lady, yonder is Sir Geraint." The Queen said, *forest.* "Yea, it is indeed Sir Geraint," so they all drew rein and waited until Sir Geraint overtook them. Then the Queen said to him, "Sir Geraint, I am glad that thou too art a sluggard, for now, as a penance, we shall hold thee in attendance upon us." "Lady," quoth Sir Geraint, *They meet Sir* "that is no penance but a pleasure, for what pleasure could be *Geraint.* greater than to wait upon you and your court upon so fair and sweet a morning as this?"

"Sir," said the Queen, "that is very well said. Now I bid you to ride beside me, and so together we will seek the King."

So Sir Geraint rode with the Lady Guinevere in that wise, and as they rode they discoursed together concerning many things of interest.

Now as they ambled thus through the forest they presently perceived a small company of riders who came the other way through the checkered lights of the woodland.

The first of these riders was a very strong, powerful and lordly knight in armor. Beside him rode a fair lady clad all in scarlet, and following after these two there came a deformed and crooked dwarf clad in green. And the dwarf sat perched upon a great tall horse like a toad upon a mountain.

Then the Lady Guinevere said, "What company is yonder?" But no one could answer her question. Then the Queen said to one of her damsels, "Go, maiden, and ask the dwarf who is the knight whom he follows."

So the maiden to whom the Queen spake made forward to meet that party, and she accosted the dwarf, saying, "Sirrah, I pray you tell me, who is the lordly knight whom you follow?" The dwarf said, "I will not *The maiden* tell you, for it is not needful that you should know." The *bespeaks the* maiden said, "Then, since you are so ungentle to me, I will *dwarf.* e'en go and ask the knight his own name. For I do not think he will be so discourteous as not to tell me his name and his degree." The dwarf said, "I forbid you to do that, and I will not permit you to ride forward, for my lord is of such quality that the likes of you are not fit to speak with him." And when he saw that the Queen's maiden was of a mind to follow the knight, he catched the horse by the bridle rein and forced it backward so that the maiden was in danger of falling.

Then the maiden said, "Let go thy hold upon my horse!" and when the dwarf had released her she drew rein and returned to the Queen complaining of the discourtesy of the dwarf, and saying, "Lady, yonder is a most rude and uncivil atomy, for he forbade me to speak to his master, and when I would have done so in spite of him he catched my horse by the bridle rein and forced him backward so that I well-nigh had a fall."

The Queen frowned and was very much displeased, and she said, "Sir Geraint, go you and find for me who is yonder knight." And Sir Geraint said, "I will do so."

So Sir Geraint rode down to where the others were, and he followed after the three until he had overtaken them. Then he rode up *Sir Geraint* to the dwarf and he said, "Sirrah, tell me the name of yon- *bespeaks the* der knight." The dwarf said, "I will not do so, for it is not *dwarf.* befitting that I should speak his name to you."

Sir Geraint said, "Then I will ask for myself." Therewith he set spurs to his horse and drove forward toward the knight. But the dwarf, seeing his intent, spurred his horse across the way, so that Sir Geraint could not pass. And he cried out, "Sir Knight, forbear, for you know not what you do."

Sir Geraint said, "Sirrah, bear back!" and therewith would have over-ridden the dwarf. Then the dwarf, in a rage, rose in his stir- *The dwarf* rups and smote Sir Geraint in the face with a whip which he *strikes Sir* held in his hand. And the whip struck Sir Geraint across *Geraint.* the cheek and the eyelid, so that a great red line immediately started out across his face.

Then when Sir Geraint felt the smart of that blow he was filled with rage and he turned upon the dwarf, clapping hand upon his sword. But he straightway withdrew his hand, saying, "Sirrah, this shall be a sad day for your knight!" Therewith he turned his horse and rode back to where Queen Guinevere was waiting for him. Then he said to her, "Lady, I could not learn the knight his name, but if I have your leave I will follow after him, and when I come to some inhabited place I will purvey me armor, and then I will compel him to return to you and to tell you his name, and to ask pardon for the insult which his dwarf offered your maiden."

Then the Lady Guinevere beheld Sir Geraint's face, and the weal where the dwarf had struck him, and she cried out, "Sir Geraint, what ails your face?" Sir Geraint said, "The dwarf smote me with a whip." The Queen said, "What did you do to him for that blow?" Sir Geraint replied, "I did nothing to him, for I will deal with the knight who is his master, and not with him." "Sir," said the Lady Guinevere, "you did right in that matter. So I pray you to follow after those people and to do as you are able with the knight who is the master of the dwarf."

Sir Geraint said very proudly, "I need no revenge for the blow of such a mannikin, but I would fain compel this knight to come to you, to disclose to you his name, and to ask pardon of this maiden for the discourtesy of his attendant." The Queen said, "Go; follow him."

Sir Geraint departs after the knight. So Sir Geraint departed after the knight, and the lady, and the dwarf, as the Queen bade him to do.

So begins the Adventure of Sir Geraint, concerning which you will learn much more if you will read this narrative to its conclusion.

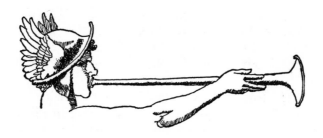

PART I

The Story of Sir Geraint

HERE beginneth the story of Sir Geraint, which same hath been noted in many ancient histories of the reign of King Arthur, and which is here inserted because it belongeth to the story of King Arthur at this place, as follows:—

nid and Geraint in the garden:

Chapter First

How Sir Geraint followed the knight and the lady to whom the dwarf belongeth. How he lodged in a ruined castle, and how he found armor to wear.

SO Sir Geraint followed after that knight and the lady and the dwarf, and they led him at first toward Camelot. Then they turned aside and led him in another direction. For, by and by, they came to a cross-road and they turned into it, and later they came to a high ridge of land that overlooked a valley. And the valley was spread out beneath them, meadow and dale, woodland and fallow, as though it had been carved very minutely in ivory or in some sort of wood, very hard and fine, and so exquisitely and wonderfully modelled that it was as though a man might have covered it with the palm of his hand.

Then, after awhile, they quitted this open ridge of land and entered a woodland. Here they beheld no other thing than trees and green leaves, for all else was shut from sight. And no other sound disturbed the ear saving only the sweet song of the woodland birds, chaunting their pretty roundelay. Anon they descended from these places, and so at last came to a high-road that led beside a wide and brightly shining river, where slow-moving barges and quick wherries drew silvery threads across the smoothly mirroring surface.

Thus, by highland and lowland, by farm and woodland and waterway, the knight, the lady and the dwarf travelled for all that day; and for all that day Sir Geraint followed patiently after them.

So toward eventide they came to a town set on a hill. And overlooking the town was a high grey castle, and there was a wall drawn all about the castle and the town. And over against the town and the castle and set up on a hill opposite to them was another castle, very ruinous and neglected.

The knight, the lady, and the dwarf entered the town, and Sir Geraint followed after them. And he followed them through the streets, and *The knight* everywhere he beheld great crowds of people, and his ears *enters the town.* were confused by the constant and continuous sound of laughing and chatting and calling of voice to voice. For all these people cheered and applauded the knight with his lady and the dwarf, when they entered the town—crowding after them and about them, seeking to touch the knight or his horse. And everywhere the lights of forge fires were burning, and the bellows were blowing, and the anvils were ringing with the continual beating of hammers upon armor. For all the town was in a bustle and uproar, as though preparing an army for battle.

Meantime the knight, the lady and the dwarf made their way through the throng and the turmoil, which every moment became greater and greater about them. For the street was presently full of people, and other people appeared at the windows and looked out and down upon them as they went forward upon their way. And some waved scarves and others cheered, and everywhere there was an uproar around about that place.

Then Sir Geraint said to one who was near to him, "I prithee, friend, *Sir Geraint in-* what is all this bustle and noise and what does it all por-
quires concern- tend?" Quoth he to whom Sir Geraint spoke, "The Sparrow-
ing the knight. Hawk! The Sparrow-Hawk!" and hurried away.

Then Sir Geraint queried of another, "What is all this to do?" Quoth he, "The Sparrow-Hawk, good friend, the Sparrow-Hawk!" and he also hurried away.

Then there came by a stout red-faced man, and of him Sir Geraint asked, "What is all this noise and bustle? I prithee tell me." Quoth the fat man, "The Sparrow-Hawk, good sir, the Sparrow-Hawk."

Then Sir Geraint was angry, and he reached down from his horse and caught the fat man by his collar, and held him fast. And he said, "Sirrah,

I will not let you go until you tell me what is the meaning of all this tumult. Who is yonder knight, and whither goeth he?"

"Hah! Sir! Do you not know?" said the fat man. "Yonder knight is the Knight of the Sparrow-Hawk, and he goeth to the castle where he shall lodge until the battle of to-morrow."

"Well," said Sir Geraint, "that is something to know. Now I bid you tell me where I may find lodgings in this town and where I may find arms wherewith a knight may arm himself." *Sir Geraint inquires concerning lodging.*

Quoth the fat man, "There is no lodging to be had in this town at such a time as this, nor are there any arms to be found at any place. But if, fair sir, you will cross the valley, to yonder ruined castle, you will doubtless find lodgings for the night, and maybe you may find arms, and to-morrow you may behold the Knight of the Sparrow-Hawk overthrow in the lists all who come against him."

Then Sir Geraint, seeing that the three whom he followed were now at the ending of their day's journey, let go the man, who immediately ran away into the crowd that still followed after the knight, the lady, and the dwarf.

So Sir Geraint drew rein and he turned his horse and he quitted that town and crossed over the valley to the ruined castle upon the other side as he had been advised to do.

As Sir Geraint drew near to the castle, he was aware of an old man who walked along upon the parapet of the wall. When this old and reverend man beheld Sir Geraint, that he approached, he descended from the wall and he came down to the gate and there met Sir Geraint. And Sir Geraint beheld that the old man was *Sir Geraint approaches the ruined castle.* tall and lordly in his appearance and that he had a noble and stately countenance. But Sir Geraint beheld that he was clad in poor and simple garments, grey in color, and patched in places, and worn and threadbare at the seams. Sir Geraint said to him, "Sir, I pray you tell me—shall I find lodgings at this castle for to-night? And *He bespeaks the old man.* I pray you also tell me if you know where I may procure a suit of armor fit for me to wear?"

Quoth the old man, "Fair Sir Knight, it hath been long since any of your quality hath been to this place. For this is a poor and ruined house of a poor and ruined man. Ne'ertheless, such as it is, you are welcome hither. I pray you come in. As for armor, I have every belief that I shall be able to supply you with the same, provided you will accept that which is old and out of date."

Thus saying, the old man took the horse of Sir Geraint by the bridle and he led it into the courtyard of the castle, and when he was come there he set his fingers to his lips and whistled very loud and shrilly. Anon a side door of the castle opened and there came forth a maiden both young and graceful, very tall and slender. And she was clad in a plain blue garment, straight and slim, and girdled with a girdle of blue leather. Her hair was plaited and twisted, and was without any net or ornament of any sort. But Sir Geraint looked at her very searchingly, because it appeared to him that this was the most beautiful young maiden whom he had ever beheld in all of the world.

When the maiden had come to them the old man bade her to take the horse of Sir Geraint to the stable and to see that it was fittingly groomed and cared for.

Then Sir Geraint would have protested at this service, but the old man said, "Sir, I pray you to let be, for we have no servants in this house, and we deem it a shame for a guest to do himself his own service. Wherefore my daughter shall find it a pleasure for to serve our guest."

So Sir Geraint dismounted from his horse and the maiden led it away *The maiden* to the stable. Then the old lord took Sir Geraint into the *stables the horse* castle and he conducted him to an upper room wherein he was *of Sir Geraint.* to lodge. And he prepared a tepid bath for Sir Geraint, and he brought him a loose garment, faded in color but trimmed with fur that had once been handsome and of rich texture, and the garment was very soft and comfortable.

Then the old man called to his wife and he gave some money into her hand, and he said to her, "Go down into the town and procure the best that you are able with this money, for it hath been·many days since we have had a guest of so much worth and nobility as this gentleman appears to possess."

So the old gentlewoman went down into the town, and after a little she returned again with a porter bearing a great hamper of food.

Meanwhile, whilst this food was preparing for supper, Sir Geraint and the old lord of the castle walked in the garden talking together.

Sir Geraint inquires Quoth Sir Geraint, "Sir, I pray you tell me several *concerning the knight* matters. First, I pray you tell me of this Sparrow-Hawk *of the Sparrow-* *Hawk.* concerning whom yonder place appears to have gone mad?"

"Messire," said the old lord, "I will tell you. Some years ago I was the earl and overlord of yonder town. But my younger brother undermined me with the inhabitants, and lately he hath gathered all of my power into his hands. Wherefore he is there, lodged in all splendor, and I am here, as thou seest.

"Now you are to know that my brother hath a mind to assemble a court of very worthy knights about him. Wherefore he hath had made a sparrow-hawk of pure silver which same is mounted at the top of a silver staff. For this sparrow-hawk many knights have come jousting; for what knight soever gaineth it and keepeth it for three years in succession, that knight shall be known as the Knight of the Sparrow-Hawk. Wherefore many have contested for it.

"For two years now a knight, hight Sir Gaudeamus of the Moors, hath overcome all who have come against him, and if he overcometh all the knights contestant again for this year, he shall be acknowledged as the true Knight of the Sparrow-Hawk."

Thus spake the old lord of the ruined castle, and when he had done Sir Geraint said, "Sir, with that armor which you say you *Sir Geraint* have, I think that I myself will contend with that knight to- *asks for armor.* morrow day. So I pray you to let that armor be sent to my room, where I may have it to hand when I want it."

Quoth the old lord, "Messire, I have, as I told you, such a suit of armor, but it is of a sort that I know not whether you will wear it or not, for it is old and beaten; but if so be you are not ashamed to wear such ancient armor, I shall be glad to purvey it for you."

"Sir," said Sir Geraint, "I give you high thanks. And now come I to another matter. A short while ago I saw a maiden whom I thought was the most beautiful that ever mine eyes beheld. Now if that damsel hath no knight to serve her, I pray you tell me if I may fight for her sake to-morrow in the field of the Sparrow-Hawk?"

Said the old man, "Sir, that maiden is my daughter and my only child. Her name is Enid. If so be she shall accept you for her knight, then shall I be more than glad for her to do so. But I will send her to you, and you may break that matter to her yourself."

With this, the old lord took his departure; anon came Enid the Fair into the garden where Sir Geraint awaited her, and when he beheld her coming, his heart was very glad. So she came to him, and he took her very gently by the hand, and he said to her, "Lady, here am I, *Sir Geraint be-* a knight of King Arthur's Round Table and of his Court. I *speaks Enid the* am of good repute and I believe am not altogether unworthy *Fair.* of my belt and my spurs. You, I think, are not more than twenty years of age, and I have nearly twice those years, yet I find that I have great pleasure in gazing upon you. Now I pray you, tell me if your heart may incline unto me sufficiently to suffer me to be your knight in the tournament to-morrow day. For I purpose then to endeavor for this Sparrow-

Hawk, and I have no lady whom I might consider as the lady of my heart upon such an occasion."

At this address Enid was very much astonished and abashed. She uplifted her eyes and looked at Sir Geraint very steadily for a little. And she beheld that he was tall and powerful of frame and that he possessed a strong and very noble face. Wherefore her heart went out to him and she said, "Noble Lord, it will give me great pleasure to accept you for my knight champion, if it so be that one of your high nobility and splendid distinction shall regard my poor estate. For my father hath not money to buy him clothes for us all, nor hath he any honor or estate saving only this ruined castle wherein we dwell. Wherefore it is not meet for me to lift mine eyes to one of your high estate and exalted quality."

Then Sir Geraint regarded her very earnestly, and he found her to be still more beautiful than he had at first thought her to be; and he said, "Enid, it may be that thy present estate and quality is not very great, yet thy face is more beautiful than that of any woman whom I ever yet beheld, wherefore I would fain have thee to consign thyself for my true and only lady. If thou wilt do this, it may be that I shall be able to be of great help and assistance both to thee and to thy father."

She said to him, "Lord, I will accept thee for my true and faithful knight."

Then Sir Geraint said, "Now I have no favor of thine to wear. I pray *Enid gives Sir* thee give me that belt thou wearest about thy waist, for I *Geraint her belt.* myself will wear it twisted about mine arm to-morrow." So Enid gave him her belt of leather and he buckled it about his arm.

Then he gave her his hand and she gave her hand to him. So, hand in hand, they departed from that place and entered the castle.

Sir Geraint and the Knight of the Sparrow-hawk

Chapter Second

How Sir Geraint fought with the Knight of the Sparrow-Hawk; how he set right the wrongs of the earldom and how he returned to the Court of the King.

NOW tell we of that notable battle betwixt Sir Geraint and the Knight of the Sparrow-Hawk.

In the level field below the town there was a fine field of green grass, such as was well fitted for knights to tilt upon. Here there was a high seat arranged for the earl of that town, and for his *Of the place of* court, and that seat was hung and draped with crimson cloth *battle.* embroidered with silver gryphons (which same was the emblazonment of the earl). Below the place of tilting and hard by that place was the silver sparrow-hawk under guard of six esquires clad all in crimson embroidered with silver gryphons. The sparrow-hawk was of pure silver, shining very brightly in the glorious sunlight. And it was set upon a cross-bar of pure silver, and the cross-bar of silver was supported by a rod of silver thrust into the earth.

Already the Knight of the Sparrow-Hawk had fought with several opponents that morning and had overthrown them all, the one after the other. So now, as none came against him, he waited in his pavilion till noon, against which time the silver sparrow-hawk should be assigned to him; and as to the people who were gathered to view the sport, they were grown restless and moved about and conversed together, for it seemed to them that no one would come to contest again with Sir Gaudeamus.

But of a sudden, a little group of four figures suddenly appeared coming across the meadowland beyond. The first of these was the old Earl of that town. Beside him rode a knight, tall and strong of *How Sir Geraint* figure, and behind these two came the lady of the Earl and *and his com-* his daughter. These presented a very dull and motley ap- *panions arrive* pearance, for the Earl was clad in frayed and weather-worn *at the place of* black, and Sir Geraint was clad in the ancient and battered armor of the *battle.*

Earl that had been given to him.   In this he presented a very singular appearance, as though he had stepped from an olden painting.

When those who were there perceived how poor and ancient was the armor that Sir Geraint wore, there began a ripple of laughter that spread and grew in magnitude until it was like a torrent of high sounding mirth. But ever the Earl of the town did not join in this mirth, otherwise he sat with great dignity in his seat, and neither laughed nor smiled, although all of his court made great mirth and applauded at Sir Geraint as though he were some jester clad in armor for their sport.

But Sir Geraint paid no heed to all this merriment; otherwise he rode forward through the field.   And after he had found place for the old Lord who was with him, and for the lady of that Earl and for Enid, he rode up to the high seat of the Earl and bespoke him thus:

"Lord, here stand I, a knight of the Court of King Arthur, and of his Round Table, to do battle upon behalf of the Lady Enid of this place for yonder silver sparrow-hawk.   Now I pray thee tell me, have I thy permission to engage in that battle?"

But now no longer was there any sound of laughter or of jeering from the lords and the ladies of that court; otherwise, all stood up to look upon him, although they could see naught of his face by reason that the visor of his helmet was lowered.

"Sir Knight," said the Earl, "this contest is open to all, wherefore it is also free to thee."

Then Sir Geraint saluted the Earl and his court, and riding across the *Sir Geraint* meadow of battle to the pavilion of Gaudeamus, the Knight of *challenges the* the Sparrow-Hawk, he smote with his spear upon the shield of *Knight of the* that knight with all his might and main so that it rang again *Sparrow-Hawk.* like a bell.   Then the Knight of the Sparrow-Hawk appeared at the door of his pavilion, and he said, "Who art thou in that ancient, outland armor who smites my shield with thy lance?   Art thou a jester?   If so, I think thy jest will cost thee very dear."

Quoth Sir Geraint, "I am not a jester, but am one who hath come to do battle with thee.   Therefore, prepare thyself to meet me, for I have great reason to be offended with thee.   If fortune betide me, this day shalt thou do penance to a great lady for thy dwarf and for his discourtesy to her."

"Hah!" quoth the Knight of the Sparrow-Hawk, "this is a very strange thing, that thou shouldst have taken up such a quarrel as this against a strange and misshapen dwarf.   As for thy challenge, it shall be answered immediately."   Therewith he of the Sparrow-Hawk went back into his pavilion again to put on his helmet and to make him ready for combat.

Meantime Sir Geraint rode to his stand, which he assumed in due order, preparing himself in all wise for this encounter that was about to befall.

Anon came the Knight of the Sparrow-Hawk, armed cap-a-pie in shining and very splendid armor. Upon his shield he had emblazoned a silver sparrow-hawk, and the crest upon his helmet was also a silver sparrow-hawk wreathed with a thin silver scarf. And all who beheld those two figures could not but applaud the splendor of his appearance, as they could not but laugh at the quaint appearance of Sir Geraint.

So when these two knights were in all wise ready, each in his place, the trumpets of the marshals of the list sounded the assault, and they rushed together like thunder and so that the earth trembled and shook beneath the trampling of their horses' hoofs. *Sir Geraint engages the Knight of the Sparrow-Hawk.*

So they crashed together in the midst of the course with a roar and a crackle of splintered lance.

For in that assault the lance of the Knight of the Sparrow-Hawk was broken into as many as twenty pieces, but the lance of Sir Geraint held, so that it pierced through the shield of the other knight, lifting him completely out of the saddle and casting him with great violence to the earth so that he rolled three times over ere he ceased to fall. *Sir Geraint overthrows the Knight of the Sparrow-Hawk.*

But when the people of the town beheld their champion thus cast to the earth by that strange knight in ancient armor they were very greatly displeased and murmured together saying, the one to the other, "What knight is this? Who is this clad in outland armor who overthroweth our champion? Is he a hero? Is he Sir Launcelot of the Lake; or who is he?"

But even whilst they thus spoke the Knight of the Sparrow-Hawk recovered from the terrible violence of his fall. His wits returned to him like a flock of scattered birds, and with them a knowledge of the shame of his overthrow. Then he leaped to his feet and drew his sword, crying out, "Sir Knight! Come down and do me battle afoot! For though thou hast overthrown me with thy lance, yet thou hast not yet conquered me."

And with that, others of those who were there assembled began to cry out, "Come down, Sir Knight! Come down, and fight him afoot!"

So Sir Geraint leaped down from his horse and drew his sword. And he set his shield before him and so approached his enemy, and meantime Sir Gaudeamus had made ready for that assault. Then suddenly they sprang together like two wild bulls in battle; lashing and lashing again and again. The dust arose up around them and for a time no onlooker could tell which had the *Sir Geraint does battle with the Knight of the Sparrow-Hawk.*

better of that fight.   But at last Sir Geraint waxed very angry at being so
withstood, wherefore he rained blow upon blow like the continual crash-
ing of thunder.   Then the Knight of the Sparrow-Hawk grew weak in his
assault.   He bore back and held his shield full low.   Upon that Sir Geraint
uplifted his strength and smote his enemy with so furious a might that Sir
Gaudeamus let fall his shield from his defence.   Then again Sir Geraint
smote him with all his might upon the crown of his undefended helmet, so
woful a blow that the blade bit through the iron of the headpiece and deep
into the bone of the brain pan.

With that blow the brains of the Knight of the Sparrow-Hawk swam
like water; the strength left his limbs; his thighs trembled and he fell down
He overcomes   upon his knees and sought to catch hold of the thighs of Sir
that knight.   Geraint.   But Sir Geraint avoided him, and reaching forward,
he catched him by the helmet and snatched it from off his head.   Then he
catched the Knight of the Sparrow-Hawk by the hair of the head and he
drew his neck forward as though to smite off his head upon the ground.
But the Knight of the Sparrow-Hawk, beholding death hovering above
him, cried out in a muffled voice, "Spare me, Sir Knight, spare my life!"

Then Sir Geraint cried out, "I will not spare thy life, Sir Knight, unless
thou wilt thus, upon thy knees, tell me thy name."
The knight pro-   "My name," said the Knight of the Sparrow-Hawk, "is Sir
claims his name. Gaudeamus of the Moors."

"Still will I not spare thee," said Sir Geraint, "unless thou wilt bind
thyself with a pledge to go to the Court of King Arthur and there tell
to Queen Guinevere thy name and thy degree of arms."

"All this," said the other, "I promise in full."

"Still I will not spare thee," said Sir Geraint, "unless thou wilt engage
that thy dwarf shall go with thee to earn forgiveness for his discourtesy to
the damsel of the queen whom he hath offended."

"This also," said the knight, "I will engage for him to do."

Then Sir Geraint said, "Arise, Sir Gaudeamus, for I spare thee."   And
Sir Geraint   therewith Sir Gaudeamus arose and stood upon his feet, still
spares the   trembling with the weakness of his battle, and the blood
knight his life.   running in torrents from the great wound upon his head.
Then came several esquires and Sir Geraint said to them, "Take him away
and look to his hurts," and they did so.

Now, after this, there came an herald upon the field of battle, and he
approached Sir Geraint and said to him, "Sir Knight, the earl of this town
hath sent me to beseech you to come to him."   Sir Geraint said, "Take
me to him."

So the herald led the way and Sir Geraint followed after him until he stood face to face with the Earl. The Earl said to him, "Sir Knight, I make my vow thou art a strong and terrible knight. I pray thee, tell me thy name that I may know to whom I am to give the prize of battle."

"Sir," said Sir Geraint, "I am called Geraint, and am the son of the King of Erbin, and I am a Knight of King Arthur's Court and of his Round Table." "Hah!" said the Earl, "then it is small wonder that thou didst win thy battle so easily, for thy deeds are famous in all the courts of chivalry. Now I pray thee, Sir, that thou wilt come to my castle and will feast with me to-night, so that I may do honor to so famous a knight, for all the world knoweth of thee and of thy deeds."

Then Sir Geraint looked at him very sternly and he said, "Messire, I will not sit down with thee at table unless I know by what right thou assumest thy state as earl, and by what right thou hast dispossessed the former earl of his state and his property."

At this the Earl's face fell, but he presently said, "Well, I will tell all these and several other things to thee if thou wilt come with me to my castle. And my brother the old Earl and his wife and his daughter shall also come. And when we sit at feast, I will lay all things before thee and thou shalt judge betwixt the old Earl and me, and I will abide by what thou decidest as to the rights of this case."

"Then," said Sir Geraint, "we will come to thy castle with thee."

So that night there was a great feast prepared in honor of Sir Geraint, and Sir Geraint and the old Earl and his countess and their daughter Enid sat with the Earl and his court at the castle of *Sir Geraint* the Earl. Sir Geraint sat upon the right hand of the Earl, *feasts with the young Earl.* and upon his left hand sat the old Earl.

So after they had eaten and whilst they sat with their wine before them, quoth Sir Geraint, "I pray thee now, my Lord Earl, for to tell me what thou promised to do; to wit, how it stands with thee and the old Earl of this city."

"Sir Knight," said the young Earl, "I will do so. Thus it was: When our father died he left this town to my brother, whilst to me he left that ruined castle yonderway across the valley.

"Now my brother was a very passive man and would do little to benefit this place either by regulating its laws or by punishing its criminals; or by establishing in it a court of chivalry.

"All the affairs of state were left to my command, whilst my brother contented himself with his domestic life and did very little to regulate the affairs of the state. Hence it befell that the people of this town looked

to me to help them and to advise with them. Thus, at last, I became
the real ruler of all our affairs. This continued for several years; then
The young Earl at last the people said, 'Why should we support our Earl
tells his story. who does nothing for us, whilst this lord whom we do not
support giveth us all that he hath in him to give?' So the people arose
one night, and drove their earl and his wife and his daughter out of the
castle and out of the town, and since that time he hath been dwelling in
that old ruined castle that one time belonged to me, where thou didst find
him; and I have been dwelling here. This, Sir Geraint, is the true story
of our affairs."

Then Sir Geraint turned to the old Earl and he said, "Sir, I pray you
tell me, is this true?" The old Earl said, "Methinks it is true." "Then,"
said Sir Geraint, "this is the doom that I pronounce: That the present
Earl shall rule this town as he hath ruled it heretofore, but that he shall
give to the old Earl the one-half of all the money receipts of the town,
so that he may support the style of living befitting his rank. And I
furthermore ordain that this Earl who rules this city shall transmit the rule
thereof to whatsoever heirs or assigns he may elect to succeed him."

Sir Geraint pro- So Sir Geraint decided his doom, and that which he said was
claims the doom satisfactory to all. And he abided several days at that place,
of the two Earls. and during that time he saw much of Enid and the more he
saw of her the more he loved her.

So one day, they two walking in the garden of the old castle alone together, he said to her, "Lady, I have seen many fair dames in my day,
but never did I behold one who was so dear to my heart as thou art. Now I
pray thee tell me, have I found favor in thy sight?" She said, "Yea, Lord,
thou hast found great favor." Said Sir Geraint, "Have I found such favor
that thou wilt depart hence with me as my wife?" Enid said, "Lord, if it is
thy desire to have me do so I will gladly become thy wife, and will depart
with thee whithersoever thou dost command; for, in truth, I have now no
other thought in all the world but of thee."

Then Sir Geraint kissed her and thus was their troth plighted.

So they were wedded, and before they were wedded the young Earl
said, "Sir Geraint, suffer that I purvey thy lady with a robe of cloth of
Sir Geraint is gold meet for such an one to wear upon the occasion of her
betrothed to marriage." But Sir Geraint said to him, "Not so, Messire,
Enid. for I won her whilst she was clad in this robe of plain blue
cloth. Thus will I take her to the Court of King Arthur and thus will I
present her to Queen Guinevere, and I will have it that Queen Guinevere
will provide her with fresh raiment meet for her to wear."

Then the young Earl bowed his head and said, "As thou sayst, so let it be."

Thus it befell that Sir Geraint was married, and the morning after his marriage he and his lady departed from that town. And he seated his lady before him upon the saddle and turned his horse's head toward the Court of King Arthur and so rode away.

Now return we to Queen Guinevere and to the Court of the King.

Three days after the departure of Sir Geraint the Queen was riding abroad, and several of her court attendants were with her, and amongst them was the young damsel who had inquired of the dwarf concerning the name of the knight whom he followed. As *Sir Gaudeamus* they rode talking and laughing together—chattering in clear *arrives at the* voices, like a bevy of bright and gloriously tinted birds—they *court of Queen Guinevere.* perceived coming toward them a procession. First they beheld a litter borne by several bearers and on the litter was a wounded knight. Behind the litter came the horse of the knight, and the horse was laden with his bright and shining armor, and led by an esquire. Behind the horse there came a fair young lady clad in scarlet riding upon a white palfrey, and behind her a small misshapen dwarf.

Now when this party had come a little nigher, Queen Guinevere perceived the face of the dwarf more clearly and she knew him for that dwarf who had rebuffed her damsel as aforetold. And she said to that one of her attendants who had aforetime met the dwarf, "Is not that the dwarf who rebuffed thee a few days ago?" The damsel said, "Yea, Lady." "Then," said the Queen, "meseems the knight his master hath met Sir Geraint and hath suffered in his encounter and is coming here to bespeak me. Let us go forward to meet them."

So the Queen and her court hurried forward until they had come beside the litter. Then the Queen said, "Sir Knight, I pray you tell me, what is it that ails you?" "Lady," said he, "I am a knight who hath suffered in battle. Now I pray you tell me, where may I find Queen Guinevere?"

The Queen said, "Messire, I am she." Quoth the knight, "Lady, is it truth you are telling me or are you making sport of me?" The Queen said, "Sir, it is the truth."

Then Sir Gaudeamus raised himself upon his elbow in the litter, and he said, "Lady, I come to thee upon command of Sir Geraint, who hath overthrown me in battle; and upon his command I am to tell thee that my name is Sir Gaudeamus of the Moors, and upon his command I am to seek for the damsel to whom my dwarf was rude."

Said Queen Guinevere, "This is she."

Then Sir Gaudeamus said to the maiden, "Fair damsel, of thee I am to ask pardon for the rudeness of my dwarf, and to crave of thee that thou from thy grace and kindness wilt forgive his offence."

Then the heart of Queen Guinevere was moved with pity for the knight, and she said to him, "Messire Sir Gaudeamus of the Moors, thou and thy dwarf are fully forgiven by her and by me. Now I pray you to come straightway to the castle where your hurts may be examined and cured."

So the Queen led the way to the castle of the King, and all they went thitherward. And after they had come to the castle she had the wounded knight laid upon a couch in a bright and cheerful room, and she had the king's physician to come and to look at his hurts and to dress them. And so Sir Gaudeamus was made in all ways as comfortable as might be.

So passed three or four days.

One morning the Queen looked out from her bower window and she be-
Sir Geraint and Enid arrive at the castle of King Arthur. held a knight riding toward the castle. And there sat before him upon his saddle a fair lady with golden hair, and the lady was clad in blue. The Queen called to her bower women and said, "Who is that knight coming yonder?" Said one of the women, "That, methinks, is Sir Geraint." The Queen said, "Yea, that is true. Methought it was he; let us hasten to meet him."

So she and her ladies made haste and they met Sir Geraint and Enid at the gateway of the castle. The Queen said, "Sir Geraint, who is it that thou hast with thee?" He said, "Lady, this is my wife, to whom I am but newly married. I have brought her here clad in blue cloth as I first beheld her. And I have hope that thou wilt clothe her as beseemeth her estate as the daughter of an earl, the lady of a knight-royal, and as my wife."

Then the Queen said, "Welcome! welcome, Lady! I give thee welcome!" And after that she assisted Enid to dismount from the horse. Thereafter she took her to her bower, and there she clad her in the richest robes that could be furnished for her. And the face of Enid shone from out of that raiment of silver and gold as the face of the moon upon a summer night shines from the thin and golden clouds that surround but do not obscure it.

Thus was the Fair Enid brought to the Court of King Arthur.

ir Geraint lies asleep

Chapter Third

How Sir Geraint lived with the Lady Enid at Camelot. How he sus-
pected her truth; how his suspicions were confirmed, and how he departed
with her in search of adventure. Also how they met with three unusual
adventures in the forest.

IT is not always well for a man to be married to a woman of half his age; for that which he thinks and loves she may neither think nor love, and that which she thinks and loves, he maybe does not think and does not love.

Now Sir Geraint was serious, as became his years, and Enid was gay and debonaire as became her youth, so that there were many sports and pastimes that she engaged in that he looked upon remotely and from afar, and not always without displeasure.

Amongst the lords of the Court of King Arthur was a young knight and lord, hight Sir Peregrans, who was son to King Ludd of Cornwall. This noble young knight-royal was very full of joy and gladness. He was ruddy-cheeked and gay, with broad black eyebrows and curly black hair, and he was ever ready for any sport or pastime that fell his way.

It befell that he and Enid were much together in company and sports of several kinds, and though Sir Geraint was too proud to appear to observe this, yet he did observe it and was much affected by it. For he would sometimes say to himself, "What pity it is that this dear lady of mine should be bound to my age and sobriety instead of to one like this Sir Peregrans who is in all ways suited to her!" Yet Sir Geraint would say nothing to Enid concerning his thoughts, but only kept those thoughts locked in his own heart, and so withdrew himself from her afar off.

This and several other things the Lady Enid observed, and it sometimes seemed to her either that her lord was in trouble or that he was offended, yet she wist not what offence she could have given to him in any way. For it did not seem to her that it could be any offence for her to play in the same sports with Sir Peregrans, but only that it was natural and seemly upon her part to do so.

Now one day Sir Geraint sat meditating concerning these things, and as he sat he gazed out of the window at the King's Castle. What time his eyes beheld a wide and fruitful stretch of meadow-land and fields, of glebe and of a river that wound through all this fair level fruitful *Sir Geraint sits* campagne like to a ribbon of pure and shining silver. The *in thought.* sun at that hour shot his slanting rays across the earth, so that all this fair prospect appeared, as it were, to be bathed in a pure golden brightness. From the level stretch of horizon, great clouds climbed up into the blue and radiant sky, peeping, as it were, over one another's shoulders down upon the peaceful earth.

All this the eyes of Sir Geraint beheld, yet he saw nothing of it. For the sight of his soul was turned away from such things, and was directed inward upon himself, and there he beheld naught but gloom and darkness.

To that place where he sat came the Lady Enid, and she beheld him where he was, but he did not turn his eyes upon her, nor seem to know that she was there.

Then she came to him and seated herself upon his knee. She put her *Enid comes to* thin fair arms about his neck, and interwove her fingers into *Sir Geraint.* one another. Then she said, "Dear my Lord, I pray thee tell me in what way I have offended thee. Thou art no longer toward me as thou wert when first I came hitherward to this court."

He said to her, speaking very gently, "Enid, thou hast in no wise offended me."

Then she said, "What is it that troubles thee, my husband?"

He said, "I have no trouble." Then, as in a second thought, he said, "Enid, I will tell thee somewhat." Therewith he unlocked her two hands and sat, holding one of them in his. "Sometimes," quoth he, "a man loveth the home that is his very own. So love I the home of my childhood and of my youth. There my father dwelleth in honor, and my mother also. It hath been many years since I have seen it and I long to see it now."

She said, "Dear Lord! Let us go thither."

He said, "Wouldst thou like to go, Enid? Well, then, we shall do so, and that as soon as my Lord the King shall grant us leave to depart."

So that very day Sir Geraint asked leave of King Arthur to leave the court for awhile, and King Arthur gave him permission to withdraw.

They two So the day after that day Sir Geraint and Enid departed *depart for the* from the Court of King Arthur, and travelling with a small *castle of Sir* party of noble attendants betook their way to Amadora (which *Geraint.* was the name of the castle of Sir Geraint's father), which place they reached within three days of easy journeying.

There they abided for several months, in which time there was hunting and hawking and jousting, so that the days were as full of joy and pleasure as it was possible to be.

But in all that while Sir Geraint did nothing of knightly daring or adventure, so that by and by the people of Amadora began to talk to one another concerning the matter, saying, "How is this? Our *Sir Geraint* Prince, the Lord Geraint, is surely besotted concerning his *takes sport at* wife, for he is with her all the while. The time was when he *his castle.* took his joys, but when the time of those joys was past then he performed many works of knightly daring, so that all we of this place were very proud of him. When now doth he enter into any such undertaking? Never. He is always the first in the chase or with the hawk or in the joust, yet his youthful glory is now departed from him, so that he lieth forever, as it were, with his head upon the knees of his wife."

Thus the people talked amongst themselves, and at last such words, or words like these, came to the ears of the Lady Enid and troubled her very sorely.

One day in the summer weather she awoke very early in the morning and the Lord Geraint lay upon his bed beside her. He had thrown aside the coverlets and he now lay with his great breast and his arms and shoulders bare to the softness of the air. These she beheld, how *Enid regards Sir* huge and mighty they were and how comely in their strength *Geraint whilst* and power. Then she looked at her own arm, how slender *he sleeps.* and white it was, how lacking of strength, how feeble and childish in its weakness, and she thought to herself, "Is it then true what they say— that my white and tender limbs may hold my husband away from those great adventures to which he belongs? Is it then true that mine arms confine him in a little and narrow circumference? Alas! Is it true that the love of a woman can sap a man of all purpose and ambition in his life of activity? Nay; it is not true, for many knights who are wedded to other ladies are still noble knights in the field of adventure. Alas and alas! The weakness of my lord must indeed reside in me." Here she sighed very deeply and with the deepness of that sigh Sir Geraint awoke from his slumbers and lay with his eyes still closed. Then she said, whispering as though to herself, "I am at fault and am no true, right wife for this noble hero."

Now Sir Geraint, lying with his eyes closed, overheard these last words that she thus whispered to herself. He heard her say that she was no true, right wife to him, and it seemed to him that she thus *Sir Geraint* confessed that she was unfaithful to him. This thought *hears her* was, as it were, a dagger thrust into his life, sudden, shining *words.* and very deep. And though he still lay with his eyes closed, he said to his heart, "Is she then false, and was I too late in bringing her away from the Court of King Arthur? Woe is me!"

Thereupon he opened his eyes, and looked her full in the face, and she, seeing that he was awake, smiled into his eyes. But he did not smile upon her in return, otherwise he said, "Lady, art thou there?" Then the smile slowly faded from her eyes, for she saw that he was in an angry mood. And so they regarded one another.

Then suddenly he arose and began dressing himself, and he said to her, "Arise, Lady, and clothe yourself." And she did as he commanded. He upon his own part accoutred himself in his full armor, that hung erstwhile shining against the stone wall of the room.

When they were thus apparelled he said to her, "Follow me." She said, "Whither, Lord?" but he made no reply to her. So they went forth together out of that apartment. And she followed him down the stairway to the courtyard, and she followed him from the courtyard to the stable, and still in all that while he spoke no further word to her.

Now this time was still very early in the morning, for the sun had only just arisen, round and red and full of the glory of daylight. The birds were chaunting with might and main, but all of the castle folk were yet asleep. All was cool and balmy and exceedingly pleasant, and the silence of the early daytime was full of the remote sound of the river below the castle, where it rushed down, roaring, through its deep and mossy gorges of green and slimy rocks and stones.

Sir Geraint entered the stables and Enid awaited him what he would do; and that while she stood not far off from the stable. After awhile he came forth from the stable again and by one hand he led the horse of Enid by the bridle, and by the other hand he led his own horse by the bridle.

He said to Enid, "Mount thy horse, Lady," and giving her his hand he lifted her very lightly to her saddle. Then he in his turn mounted his own horse.

Then when he was seated in his saddle, he said to the Lady Enid his wife, "Lady, for this day and haply for several days I will endeavor to prove to thee that strength and life have not yet left me, but that I am still a *They depart* strong and able knight and as well worth the love of any *from the castle.* woman as I was in the full heyday of my youth. Ride you forth and lead the way, and I will follow after you. But make yourself well acquainted with this: that under no circumstances are you to speak a word to me unless I give you leave to speak to me. Only ride straight forward, anywhither you may be inclined."

She said to him, "Lord, I will fulfil your commands."

So they rode away from the castle without any one knowing that they were gone, for there stood no guard at the gateway at that hour and the porter drowsed in his lodge.

So, according to the command of Sir Geraint, the Lady Enid rode ahead of him and he himself followed after her some considerable distance behind.

Thus they went forward for several leagues, and meantime the sun rose very full and round and shone down hotly upon the earth. So by and by they approached the purlieus of a thick dark forest, and as they drew near to it the Lady Enid was aware of the sudden shining of armor through the leaves, wherefore she wist that some threatening of danger must lie before them. As they drew still nearer to that place, she perceived that there were three armed men hidden in the thickets, and anon she heard them speaking the one to the other. And she heard the voice of him who was the chief of the three say to the other two, "Hitherward cometh good fortune to us this morning. For here is one man, well appointed in all ways, but sunk very deep in brooding thought, and with him is a fair lady. Now if we engage him as three against one, it is not likely that he can withstand our assault, and so he and his horse and his armor and his lady shall be ours by right of battle."

These words, or words like these, the Lady Enid overheard the chief of the robbers speak to the other two who were with him; *Enid overhears* and she said to herself, "Here is great danger threatening my *the words of the* dear Lord. Well, if I warn him he may be very angry with me *robber chief.* and may even chastise me for disobeying his command. But even if this is so, what will it matter?" So therewith she turned her horse and rode back toward Sir Geraint.

He, when he beheld her coming, appeared to be very angry, and he said, "Lady, what is it disturbs you?" She said, "Dear Lord, have *She tells Sir* I your permission to speak?" Quoth he, "It seems that you *Geraint of the* have taken that permission yourself. Well, say on." She *ambush.* said, "Lord, at the edge of yonder wood I perceived three men of ill intent hidden in the thicket. I overheard them to say that they purposed presently to assail you. Wherefore I deemed it expedient that I should warn you of their presence."

Then Sir Geraint frowned so that his eyes shone with a bright green light. "Lady," said he, "it may perhaps be that you would not be displeased to see me fall before the attack of those three men. Nevertheless, I have hopes that I shall not fail in this encounter. Meantime, continue here and consider you of your disobedience in breaking my command laid

upon you not to speak to me without my permission." Having thus spoken
Sir Geraint closed and latched the visor of his helmet, and then with spear
in hand he rode forward toward the edge of the woods.

Now when Sir Geraint had come pretty close to the woodland, all three
of those armed men suddenly burst forth from their covert and bore down
upon him in full charge, whilst he, upon his part, drave spurs into his war-
horse and charged against them. So they met in the midst of the course
with such violence that a clap of thunder could not have been so great.
All three of their spears struck Sir Geraint upon the shield, but he turned
them so that all three were broken into a very great many pieces. But
the spear of Sir Geraint held against him toward whom it was directed, so
that it penetrated his shield and it penetrated his armor and it penetrated
his body, so that he was lifted out of his saddle and cast dead the length of
a spear and an arm's length behind his horse.

Then Sir Geraint threw aside his spear and drew his bright shining sword.
Sir Geraint And he whirled his horse and with his sword in hand he bare
slays the down upon those other two villains. Then he arose in his
robbers. saddle, crying out, "Hah, villain!" and therewith he smote
down one. Then whirling about, he cried out again, "Hah, villain!" and
so crying he smote down the other. Each man fell with a single blow of
his sword. Thus in a little space of time, he slew all three of those villains
who had for a long time infested those parts.

When Sir Geraint had thus ended this work, he wiped his sword and returned it to its scabbard. Then he removed the armor from each of the
fallen men, and he lashed the armor to the saddle-bow of the horse to which
it belonged. Then he tied all three bridle reins together and returned
to where Enid sat watching him with terror and admiration commingled.
And Sir Geraint said to her, "Lady, take thou the bridle reins of these
three horses. Then ride forward as before, and this time bear well in
mind that thou turn not to speak to me under any condition whatsoever.
Once I have forgiven thee; twice I may not do so."

To this speech Enid made no reply, but taking the bridle reins of the
three horses into her fair white hand, she rode forward into the forest,
leading those three horses, Sir Geraint following after her as aforetime.

Thus they proceeded onward for a very considerable length of time
and until high noontide, beholding nothing but the forest before them or
behind them or on either side of them.

Thus they came almost to the centre of that wood where was a sudden
turn in the high-road, which here entered into a defile between two high and
very precipitous banks. At this place Enid perceived, not far away,

four armed and mounted men of a very evil appearance, and she overheard these men talking among themselves. The one who was chief of them was saying to his companions, "Look! yonder cometh a good prize for us to take. For there is a very beautiful damsel and three sets of fine armor and three horses. And all this is guarded only by one armed man. Let us slay him and all these will be ours to do with as we choose." *Enid overhears the words of the four men.*

Then Enid said to herself, "Well, I can die but once, and even though my lord shall slay me for breaking his command, yet it would be by his beloved hands that I should die. So I will turn back and tell him of this."

Therewith she turned her horse about and rode backward to Sir Geraint, and he, when he saw her coming, frowned very darkly. But she said, speaking very steadily, "Lord, have I your leave to speak?"

He said with great bitterness, "Lady, it appears that it does not need my leave for you to speak whensoever you choose to speak. Say on."

She said, "Lord, I have to tell you that there are four very powerful and fully armed men yonder. And I overheard the chief of them to say to his fellows that their intent is to slay you so that they may have your horse and your armor and me and these three horses and this armor to dispose of as they see fit." *She tells Sir Geraint.*

"Is that all," quoth he, "that thou hast to tell me? It seems that thy delight in talking is so great that thou canst not be checked. Bide thou here and I will go forward and deal with these men, and so will clear thy path for thee."

Thereupon he closed the visor of his helmet and latched it. Then he set spurs to his horse, and being thus in all ways prepared, he drave forward to meet his enemies.

Suddenly they appeared bearing down upon him and riding two together (because of the narrowness of the way that prevented them from riding all four abreast).

Then Sir Geraint drave his war-horse to the charge and so they came together with a great crash and uproar, their spears striking him in the centre of the shield.

But in that encounter both their spears brake into several pieces, but Sir Geraint's spear did not break. Otherwise it held and burst through the shield against which it was directed, and it burst through the armor and pierced through the body of the man within the armor so that he was cast dead upon the ground.

Then Sir Geraint threw aside his spear and drew his sword, and rising in his stirrups he smote the other man so fierce and direful a blow that he split asunder his shield and his helmet and pierced through the brain-pan of the head and into the brains themselves, so that he who was thus smitten cried out most dolorously, "I die! I die!" and thereupon fell grovelling to the earth.

Then Sir Geraint whirled his horse and setting spurs to its flanks he thundered down upon the other two, who sat beholding aghast how easily and quickly he had overthrown their comrades. Nor hardly had they recovered themselves than he was upon them, smiting to the right hand and to the left. Then observing an opening in the defence of one of them, he whirled upon him and smote with might and main, and the blade of the sword clave that man through from the shoulder to the midriff.

Then the fourth villain, seeing his companions fall thus terribly into *Sir Geraint* death, would have escaped away, but death was upon him. *slays the four* For he beheld Sir Geraint rise in his stirrups with sword lifted. *men.* Then the sword descended like a thunderbolt, and he too fell with his brain dissolving into death.

Then Sir Geraint dismounted from his steed and wiped his terrible blade, and thrust it back into its scabbard. And he stripped the armor off the dead bodies, and tied each suit of armor upon the horse to whom it appertained. After that he tied the reins of the four horses the one with the other, and gave them all to Enid, and he said to her, "I call upon thee to observe that I yet possess my knightly manhood, and that I am not yet altogether devoid of strength and even of youth. Take thou now these four horses together with the three horses which thou hast and ride on before me as heretofore, leading all seven horses. And see to it that this time thou dost not turn to me to say a word of any sort. For I find that the anger of battle is upon me, and in my rage I may smite thee with my sword in haste and ere I am able to control myself."

She said, "Lord, I will do as thou dost command."

So she rode on before Sir Geraint, and though she rode in silence yet her heart sank within her, for she said to herself, "Did ever any lady before me possess such a high-exalted and noble lord as this lord of mine?"

Now as Enid rode forward thus exulting she heard of a sudden the sound of voices talking together in the thickets near at hand. The one voice *Enid overhears* said to the other voices, "Look! hither cometh a beautiful *the words of the* damsel, leading seven good horses laden each with a noble *five outlaws.* suit of armor, and here is only one man in guard of all this train. Let us five make here an ambushment, and let us fall upon him from behind and from before. So we shall easily overcome him and obtain all those things for ourselves."

Then Enid said to herself, "It may be that my lord will do as he said, and will strike me with his sword in his haste if I disobey him for the third time by speaking to him. But what matters that? Rather would I die by his hands than suffer his anger without his love."

So she turned her horse and rode back to him and when she had come to him she said, "Lord, suffer me to speak to thee?"

He said, "Did I not tell thee to speak to me no more?"

She said, "Lord, this time I must speak to thee, for I cannot do otherwise."

He said, "So it appeareth. Well, then, say on!"

She said, "Lord, this is what I have to say, that ahead of *She tells Sir* thee are five men lying in ambushment against thee with *Geraint what* *they say.* intent to destroy thee."

Sir Geraint said, "Is this all that thou hast to say?" To which she replied, "Yea, Lord." He said, "Abide here with thy horses for a little and suffer me to go forward alone, to clear thy path for thee."

So Enid abided at that place, and Sir Geraint rode forward into the ambushment that was prepared for him.

So he reached that ambushment, and of a sudden there leaped all those five men out against him and about him.

Then there followed a great and bitter fight betwixt Sir Geraint and those who thus assailed him. And sometimes he might be seen and at other times he might not be seen for the press that gathered about him. His sword flashed like lightning and at every blow he uttered a great and terrible cry of war, for the fury of battle was now fully upon him. At first there were five against him and then there were but four, then three, then two and at last only one who cried out in terror, "Spare me, Lord! For I yield myself to thee."

Sir Geraint said, "I will not spare thee," and therewith he struck him so dreadfully that he clave his head asunder and he fell down *Sir Geraint slays* dead upon the ground. After he had thus overthrown all *the five men.* five of his enemies, he wiped his sword, panting, and put it away into its sheath. Then he stripped the armor from off the dead bodies of the five, and bound a suit of armor upon each horse. Then tying all *Enid leads the* five bridle reins together, he attached them to the bridle reins *twelve horses.* of the other horses and gave all twelve into Enid's hands, saying to her, "Lead them forward and speak to me no more, I charge thee."

So they travelled upon their way through the wood, and anon the day began to draw to a close, and the grey of twilight to descend. And Enid led the twelve horses with difficulty. This Sir Geraint observed, and was sorry for her, but still they rode onward. Then the darkness fell and the moon arose, very bright and clear and round, silvering the tops of the trees and laying patches of silver upon the earth between the shadows of the leaves.

Then Sir Geraint called to Enid and he said to her, "Lady, I do not think we shall get out of this woods to-night. Let us rest here until to-morrow."

She said to him, "Lord, may I speak?" He said, "Say on." She said, "What will we do to eat?" Quoth he, "Lady, it oftentimes happens when a knight travelleth errant, as I have travelled to-day, that he goeth without food to eat for the entire day—and sometimes for even longer than that. Let that suffice."

Therewith she fell silent and sighed, for she was very hungry.

Meantime Sir Geraint gathered the leaves together into a sort of bed and he spread a cloak upon them. Then seeing that Enid was very weary and in pity of her weariness, he said, "Lie thou here, Lady, and I will keep watch for the night."

So Enid laid herself down upon the bed of leaves and she was very sick for weariness. And for awhile she watched her lord, Sir Geraint, as he stood a little distance away, and she beheld how the moonlight *They abide that* flashed and sparkled upon his polished armor whensoever the *night in the* soft night wind of summer stirred the leaves; and she heard *forest.* the rustling and the stamp of the horses as they moved at their stations; and she heard a distant nightingale, singing from afar, now and then heard in the darkness, and the murmurous silence, and now and then silent again. Then all these things blended together, the darkness disappeared and she slept.

This was the first day of that journeying. Now if you would read of the second day thereof, I pray you to peruse that which hereinafter followeth, and which I have writ for your pleasure.

Chapter Fourth

How Sir Geraint and Enid came forth out of the forest into the land of an earl. How they abided at an inn, and of what befell them thereafter.

WHEN the next morning had come Sir Geraint, very early, awoke Enid from her slumbers. The pangs of hunger were great upon her but she made no complaint thereof. Otherwise, she mounted her horse and took the reins of the twelve horses into her hands and rode away, followed by Sir Geraint as upon the former day.

Anon and after awhile the trees of the woodland grew thinner and the sunlight came more freely through their branches. Anon again and the trees of the forest ceased altogether, and so *Geraint and Enid come into* Enid and Geraint came forth out of the woodland and into *the open* the open plains once more. *country again.*

Here were hedgerows upon either side of the way, and there were fields and open country beyond the hedgerows; and there were meadow-lands, and the mowers were mowing in the meadows.

Before them lay a river and toward that they took their way. And there was a ford to the river and they entered the river, and all the *They cross the* horses bowed their heads and drank of the water. Afterward *river.* they crossed the ford and ascended a steep high bank upon the other side of the river.

At the top of this bank there stood a slender youth with yellow hair. And the youth had a satchel of leather slung over his shoulder, and in his hands he carried an earthenware crock of milk.

Sir Geraint spoke to the youth, saying to him, "Whence cometh thou, fair youth?" Quoth the youth, "I come from the town which *Sir Geraint* you cannot behold from here, but which you may behold from *bespeaks the* the crest of yonder hill when you have reached it. And now, *youth.* Lord, if it be not too venturesome for me to ask, I pray you to tell me whence you have come?"

Said Sir Geraint, "Fair youth, we came from the forest yonder. All day yesterday we travelled through the forest and all night we slept there beneath the trees."

"Well," said the youth, "I daresay you had but small entertainment at that place, and I daresay also you are very hungry to-day."

"I would," said Sir Geraint, "find food for this lady if it be possible to do so." Said the youth, "we are then well met, for in this satchel I have bread and cheese, which I am taking to the mowers for their breakfast; and in this crock I have milk, which also I am taking to them for their breakfast. If you will partake of these things, I will gladly give you to eat and to drink." "I give thee thanks, fair friend," said Sir Geraint, "and gladly will I accept the offer of thy hospitality."

So the youth assisted the Lady Enid to dismount from her saddle, and *The youth gives* she and Sir Geraint took their station at the roadside beneath *them to eat.* the shade of a crab-apple tree. And the youth gave them to eat of the white bread and cheese from his satchel and he gave them to drink of the milk from the crock, and they were both greatly refreshed.

After the two had thus satisfied their hunger the youth said, "Now, Sir Knight, by thy leave I will depart for more food for the mowers."

Sir Geraint said, "Fair youth, I pray you to return to the town whence you came and to procure for us the best lodgings that are to be found at *Sir Geraint* that place. And I also pray you that you will, in return for *gives the youth* these courtesies of yours, choose whichsoever horse and suit of *a horse and the* armor that best pleases you out of all those that the lady is *armor thereof.* conducting, and I pray you that you will keep that horse and armor for yourself." "Lord," said the youth, "what have I done for such a great reward? That is too much to accept for so small a service." "Nevertheless," said Sir Geraint, "I pray you to do as I bid you."

So the youth joyfully chose a horse and a suit of armor that pleased him the best, and leading these he departed for the town to fulfil Sir Geraint's behest as to securing him lodgings.

Now as the youth entered the town a servant of the Earl of that town met him and the servant of the Earl said to the youth, "Where got ye that horse and that armor?" The youth said, "A noble and knightly lord, who hath eleven other such horses and armor, gave this one to me."

The servant said, "This is a strange saying. Come with me to the Earl and tell him concerning these things."

The youth tells So the servant of the Earl took the youth to that lord, and *the Earl of Sir* the youth told his story to the Earl of how he had met the *Geraint.* lordly knight and the lady, and of how the lady had led twelve horses loaded with armor, and of how the lord had given him one of those horses and the suit of armor that best pleased him. To all this the Earl hearkened, and then he said to the youth, "Go you and fetch that lord hitherward, for I would fain see him and his lady and entertain them at my castle. He shall lodge here with me."

So the youth hastened back to Sir Geraint where he sat with Enid resting beneath the crab-apple tree, and he said to him, "Lord, the Earl of yonder town hath sent me here to bid you come and lodge with him."

Then Geraint was displeased and he said to the youth, "How is this? I bade thee secure us lodgings, not with an earl but at some good inn. I will not lodge with the Earl, but will go to such an inn."

Then the youth was abashed, and he said, "I will take you to an inn."

So the youth conducted Geraint and Enid into the town, and he conducted him to the best inn in the town. Here the landlord came forth to meet him and Geraint said, "Show us to the best room of this place," and the landlord did so. Geraint said to Enid, "Keep thou yonder to that side of the chamber, and I will keep to this side, for I am weary and fain would sleep." And Enid said, "I will do so." And Geraint said to the youth, "When I awake, be thou here to serve me." *The youth conducts them to an inn.*

The youth said, "I will be here; but meantime I would fain go and see the Earl and tell him where you are lodged." Sir Geraint said, "Go, but return again."

So whilst Sir Geraint slept, the youth hastened to the castle of the Earl, and he said to the Earl, "Sir, certes this man is a prince or a knight-royal, for he commandeth all things as he wills." Then the Earl said, "Where is he lodged?" And the youth told him, and the youth said, "I go presently to serve him when he awakes, for now he sleepeth." "Commend me to him when he awakeneth," said the Earl, and the youth replied, "I will do so."

That afternoon when Geraint awoke, it was time for them to take their food. So Sir Geraint summoned the landlord and bade him prepare him a feast, and the landlord said he would do so. Then Sir Geraint inquired of the landlord whether he had not some companions whom he would like to entertain, and the landlord said, yea, that there were several. Upon this Sir Geraint commanded the landlord to summon those companions and to prepare for them *Sir Geraint bids the landlord to summon his friends to a feast.*
the best that there was in the town both to eat and to drink. "For," quoth he, "though I be unhappy myself, yet do I love to behold those about me as happy and as gay as may be." So the landlord went forth and bade many to come and feast with him, all these feasted at Sir Geraint's expense, so that the entire inn was full of light and laughter and noise and merrymaking.

That evening the Earl came to visit Sir Geraint, and with him he brought
The Earl visits twelve of the worthiest knights of his court.   Then Sir Geraint
Sir Geraint. arose and welcomed him, and the Earl greeted Sir Geraint and
sat down and conversed with him.   And he asked Geraint the object of his
journey, to which Geraint replied, "I have no object, saving to seek adventure such as may become the life of a knight-errant."

Then the Earl cast his eyes upon Enid, and he looked at her very steadily,
and he thought that he had never beheld a lady so fair and so beautiful as
she.   And as he gazed upon her his heart went out to her and he found that
he loved her very extremely.   Then he said to Geraint, "Have I thy
permission to converse with yonder lady?   For I see that she is not with
thee."   "Thou hast it gladly," said Geraint.

So the Earl went to where Enid sat, and he said to her, "Lady, thy hands
The Earl are soft and white and thy body is fragile and delicate; it
bespeaks Enid cannot be pleasant for thee to travel through the rough and
the Fair. cruel world with this man."   She said, "It is not unpleasant
for me to journey with him whithersoever he goeth."

The Earl said, "Lady, thou shouldst have youths and maidens to wait
upon thee and to attend thee and to serve thee."   She said, "It is pleas-
anter to me to travel alone with yonder man than to live in state with youths
and maidens to wait upon me."

"Listen," said the Earl, "I will give thee good advice.   Give up that
man and come with me.   All my earldom will be at thy disposal if
thou wilt do so, and thou shalt be the mistress of it and of me and of
my life."

Then Enid was very angry, and she said, "Lord, I will not go with thee!
Know thou that yonder man is dearer to me than all the earth and its
kingdoms and principalities, its dukedoms and its earldoms.   He was
the first man to whom I plighted my faith, and never hath it been withdrawn from his keeping.   Shall I then leave him now for the sake of this
little patch of ground, to live with thee in dishonor and suffer him to go
forth into the world alone?"

Then the Earl said, "Lady, thou art in the wrong in this, for if I slay
that man, then can I take thee by force.   And if I take thee by force, then,
when I tire of thee, I shall cast thee off into the world.   But if thou comest
to me willingly, then I will never cast thee off, but will keep thee as my
most precious treasure so long as I am permitted to breathe the breath of
life.   Come thou with me, and yonder man may be suffered to depart in
peace, hale and strong in limb and body, but come thou not with me and
he shall die."

Then Enid was greatly troubled at that which the Earl had said to her, for she saw that he had the strength and the will and the power to do with Sir Geraint whatsoever he chose. So at last she said to him, "Listen, O great Lord and Earl. All this that I have said to thee I have said for the sake of mine honor. But if thou art of the mind that thou sayst, I would rather abide with thee. Come hither to-morrow morning with twelve armed knights and bear me away as though by force. For thus it shall appear that I have not yielded up to thee, except by force." "I will do so," said the Earl. "This and all things shall be as thou sayst." After that, in a little while he arose and departed from that place.

But of all that had passed Enid said nothing to Geraint, lest he should be blinded by his rage against the Earl. Otherwise, she kept it secretly in her heart for that time.

That night they both lay in the same chamber. In a little while Sir Geraint fell asleep, but Enid did not sleep. When she heard *Enid prepares* his deep breathing she arose very softly and she gathered his *the armor of* armor together piece by piece. And she piled all the armor *Sir Geraint.* where he could easily lay hand upon it. Then she lay down and slept.

Before the day broke she arose and went softly to where Sir Geraint slept, and touched her finger upon his breast and with that he awoke and started up. "Lord," said she, "knowest thou what the Earl *Enid telleth Sir* of this town said to me last night?" Geraint said, "Tell me." *Geraint of the* So Enid told him all that the Earl had proposed to her. Then *Earl.* Geraint was very angry, and he said, "Thy beauty bringeth evil whithersoever thou bringest it. Now I will slay this Earl ere I leave this place, for he hath proposed dishonor to me."

"Not so," said Enid, "let be the Earl, for there are many scores against thee, and thou art only one. Rather put thou on thy armor and let us go hence with all the speed that we may, for there is yet time to escape, and thus only may we escape in peace."

Then Geraint perceived that what she said was very true, and that he was at that place in a parlous state. So he arose and put on his armor and he summoned the landlord and the landlord came to him.

Quoth Sir Geraint, "What do I owe thee, good fellow, for the entertainment that I have had at this house?" Said the landlord, "Not a great deal, Messire." "Well," said Sir Geraint, "take thou all those *Sir Geraint* eleven horses and the armor appertaining to them for thy *gives all the* reckoning. Will that pay our score?" "Heaven bless thee, *horses and all* Messire," cried the landlord, "but that is far more than thou *the landlord.* owest me; for thou hast not consumed in this house the value of a single horse." "Well," said Sir Geraint, "in that case thou wilt be all the richer. But put on thy cloak and thy hat and conduct me out of this place by some way that is another way than that by which we entered here, for I must hasten upon my quest." Quoth the landlord, "I will do so, Lord."

With that he hurried away. Anon he returned again, clad as for a journey. Then Sir Geraint mounted his horse and Enid mounted her horse, and they departed from that place after the landlord.

The landlord leads them from the town. So the landlord led them by another highway from the town, and when the sun arose Sir Geraint dismissed him from their service.

Now when the landlord returned to the inn he beheld that several men surrounded that place. Those men were the Earl of that town, and the twelve chief knights of his state, and all were clad in full armor. The Earl

The Earl follows Sir Geraint and Enid the Fair. was very wroth and when he beheld the landlord he cried out to him, "Fellow, where is the knight and where is that lady who were with thee last night?" "Lord," quoth the landlord, "they have departed and by now are many miles from this. For I myself conducted them far upon the way, and am only now returned from guiding them." Quoth the Earl, "What way went they?" and the landlord told him. Then the Earl and his court of knights departed thence. And they rode at a swift gallop upon the way that the landlord directed them. Anon they beheld the marks of horses' hoofs fresh upon the earth, wherefore they wist that they were upon the right way.

Now as Enid and Sir Geraint rode onward upon their course, Enid looked behind her many times. At last she beheld a cloud of dust that came rapidly nearer, and she was aware that in that cloud of dust were the Earl and his court of knights. Then she cried out to Sir Geraint, "Sir Knight, prepare for battle, for yonder come thine enemies."

Then Sir Geraint, who had been sunk in thought, became aware of the coming of those others. Thereupon he closed the visor of his helmet and prepared himself in all ways for the encounter. Thereafter he turned his horse in the middle of the highway and stood waiting for his enemies.

Anon they reached him and drew rein a little distance away. Then the Earl came forward and spake to Sir Geraint, saying, "Sir Knight, we mean no harm to thee, but only ask thee that thou wilt give up that lady whom thou hast with thee. For thou holdest her against her desire; her only desire being to go with us."

Then Sir Geraint turned to Enid and said, "Lady, is this true? If thou desirest to go with yonder Lord thou hast my leave to do so." "Nay," said she, "I do not desire to go with him. Rather would I go with thee to death than to go with him to joy."

So Sir Geraint said to the Earl, "Messire, the lady says thou art mistaken and she does not desire to go with thee."

The Earl said to Enid, "Lady, what didst thou tell me yesterday?" And Enid said, "Messire, I told thee many things to mislead thee, for the occasion called upon me to do so."

Then the Earl talked aside for a little while with his followers. Anon he called to Sir Geraint, "Sir Knight, I will not let thee go until thou hast tried a fall or two with these knights of mine for the sake of thy lady, her bright eyes and her slender body." "Well," said Sir Geraint, "I am willing to do battle with thy knights now or at any time." "And this shall be the result of this battle," said the Earl. "If thou winnest this battle, thou mayst go free, but if we win then thy lady must return with us." Quoth Sir Geraint, "That is certes a hard saying."

So the strongest and most powerful of all those knights made him ready for the assault, and when he was in all ways prepared, he and Geraint made a violent charge, the one against the other. Three times *Sir Geraint* they charged and at the third assault Sir Geraint overthrew *does battle with* him so violently that he lay like one dead in the middle of the *the followers of* high-road. Then one after the other all the others of those *the Earl.* twelve knights assaulted Sir Geraint, and each in turn was overthrown very violently upon the earth.

Then the Earl said to Sir Geraint, "Sir Knight, thou hast fought well and very valiantly for thy lady, and truly hast thou won her. Depart in peace." "Not so," cried Sir Geraint in great passion, "for I have one more to deal with, and that one is thou thyself. For I have yet to do with thee ere I depart from this place."

"Well," said the Earl, "be it as thou sayst. For I will fight with thee till either thee or I have overcome the other. And to that one who overthroweth the other thy lady shalt belong." "So be it," said Sir Geraint.

So each made him ready for the encounter, and when they were in all ways prepared they set spur to flank and drave the one against the other with such violence that they met with a crash as of thunder in the middle of the course. In that encounter Sir Geraint was upborn *Sir Geraint* by his passion so that he smote true and fairly against his *overthrows the* enemy's shield. But the spear of the Earl was shattered into *Earl.* a great many pieces. The spear of Sir Geraint held, so that it pierced the shield of the Earl, and Sir Geraint lifted the Earl out of his saddle and hurled him several ells behind the crupper of his horse, where he lay like one dead upon the earth.

Then Sir Geraint ran to where the Earl was. And he rushed off his helmet and he drew his sword and catching the Earl by the long hair of his head he drew forward his neck so as to sever his head from his body. Thereupon the Earl awoke from his swoon and perceiving that death loomed very near to him, he clutched Sir Geraint about the thighs, clinging to them and crying out, "Sir Knight, spare my life!" "Why should I spare thee?" cried out Sir Geraint very violently. "Hast thou not attempted my life and hast thou not attempted mine honor and the honor of my lady, and were we not guests in thy town? I will not spare thy life!" And he whirled his sword as though to strike.

Then Enid came to where Sir Geraint was and clutched him by the arm *Sir Geraint spares the life of the Earl.* and she said, "Worthy knight, Sir Geraint! I pray thee spare this man his life. For what canst thou gain by slaying him?" "Well," said Sir Geraint, "since this lady asks thy life at my hands I give it to her to dispose of as she pleases." Enid said, "I thank thee, Lord!" Then she said to the Earl, "Arise, and go thou hence in peace!"

So after that Sir Geraint remounted his horse and he and Enid departed from that place, riding as aforetime. That is, Enid rode a long distance ahead and Geraint rode behind, following after her.

But of the knights whom he overthrew in that encounter it is to be written that several were so sorely hurt that it was many weeks ere they were sufficiently recovered to be abroad again.

And now followeth the further adventures of Sir Geraint and of Enid at this time; so I pray you to read that which hereinafter appeareth.

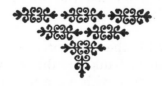

Enid and Geraint ride past
the Town bridge ❦ ❦ ❦

Chapter Fifth

Sir Geraint is wounded in his encounter with another knight. He is discovered by the Court of King Arthur and is healed of his wounds.

SO Sir Geraint and Enid travelled in that wise until at last they came through a thin, small woods and so out into another open place.

Here they beheld before them a valley of singular beauty, for through the centre of the valley there ran a wide, smoothly flowing river, and upon either side of the river there were meadow-lands and fields, and not far away from where they were there was a town, very large and considerable. All around the town was a wall of stone, very high and strong. And about the town was a fortress castle, tall and forbidding, that looked down upon the town and upon the high-road. The high-road upon which they travelled crossed a bridge over the river, and so entered the town, but ere it reached the bridge it branched and one branch ran down along one side of the river upon which they were. Upon either side of the bridge head were two tall towers that overlooked the bridge and guarded it.

So Sir Geraint and Enid sat for awhile looking down upon that fair prospect, and the more they looked upon it the more they delighted in it. As they so sat, anon they beheld a horseman come from the town and cross the bridge, and when he had crossed the bridge he turned *Sir Geraint* him in their direction. By and by he had approached closely *questions the* enough for Sir Geraint to speak to him, and thereupon Sir *horseman con-* *cerning the* Geraint rode forth and met him and they two saluted one *town.* another. Then Sir Geraint said to him, "Sir, I pray you tell me; what town is that yonder, and who is the lord of this fair and beautiful valley and of yonder town?" "Messire," said the other, "I will gladly tell thee that and anything else that I am able. The town itself is called the Town of Redlands. The lord of all this country is a very brave, renowned and valiant Earl called the Little King. He is so called because he rules this place away from all other lords as though he were king of it in his own right."

Sir Geraint said, "May I pass by yonder bridge head where are the two

towers without crossing over the bridge and into the town?" The other
replied, "Messire, I will tell thee truly. The Little King hath ordained
it that no one shall pass into his land without his permission, wherefore
he will not allow that any knight shall pass by yonder bridge and into the
lands beyond it." "Nevertheless," said Sir Geraint, "I am of a mind to
pass by that bridge and into the country beyond it maugre his will that
wise or otherwise." "If thou dost do so," said the other, "thou wilt in all
likelihood meet with shame and disgrace." "No matter for that," said
Sir Geraint, "I shall assume even such a risk as that." At that the other
laughed, and so they saluted each one the other again and then the knight
departed upon his way.

So Sir Geraint followed the Lady Enid and she preceded and he followed
after her. Thus together they went down to the river. Coming there,
Sir Geraint and he bade her not to cross the bridge, so in obedience to that
Enid pass by command they went past the bridge and past the two towers at
the bridge head. the bridge head, and so rode along beside the river. Thus
with Enid riding before him and he riding behind her, he had gone a considerable distance when he became suddenly aware that some one was galloping behind them. Then Sir Geraint turned him about and beheld that
an armed knight was following after them at a swift gallop.

So Sir Geraint drew rein and waited for the other to come up with them,
and when the other knight had come pretty close to where he stood, he
also drew rein. The Strange Knight said, "Sir Knight, is it through
ignorance or through presumption that you travel thus without leave
through my dominions?" Him Sir Geraint answered very proudly, saying,
"Messire, how should I know that this road was forbid to those who would
pass to travel along it?"

"Nay," said the other fiercely, "thou didst know that it is forbidden to
any one to pass into my land without my permission and so thou hast in-
fringed the rules of my earldom. Hence thou shalt come now with me to
my court and do me satisfaction." "I will not come with thee to thy
castle," said Sir Geraint, "and I will not do thee any satisfaction. For this
is an high-road and it is free for any one to travel upon it who chooses to
do so." "Well," said the other, "let that be as it may; but I tell thee that
thou shalt this day do satisfaction to me or else I will suffer defeat at thy
hands." "That," said Sir Geraint, "shall be as Heaven shall foreordain."
Sir Geraint does So upon that each knight made him ready for the combat,
battle with the and Enid stood to one side to observe what happened. Anon
knight. they were in all ways prepared, and each took post for a tilt.
When all this was prepared, each knight shouted to his horse, and each

drave spurs into the flanks of his steed and each launched the one against the other with wonderful speed and vehemence. So they met in the midst of the course with a crash like to thunder, and in that encounter the lance of each knight held so that the horse of each sank back upon his haunches quivering from the shock of that assault.

Then each knight threw aside his lance and sprang from his saddle, and each drew his sword and each rushed the one against the other like two fierce bulls raging for battle. Each lashed at the other many terrible and severe strokes, and for a time neither had any advantage over the other. Several times Geraint was wounded and several times more he wounded his adversary. Thus they fought for a long while, and Geraint suffered many wounds, until at last, because of the smart of those wounds, his anger flamed up like fire and added strength to his strength. Then he rained blows fast and furious upon his assailant, striking him with terrible violence again and again and yet again, so rapidly and so fiercely, violently and furiously that the Little King bore back before him, holding his shield full low because of his weariness and wounds. Then Geraint beheld the opening that the other gave him, and with that he rushed in upon him, and he smote him with might and main upon the crown of the helmet.

So terribly fierce was that blow that it split apart the helmet and the iron cap beneath and cut deep into the bone beneath the cap.

Then the wits of the Little King flew away from him like a flock of flies, his strength deserted him, his thighs trembled and he sank *Sir Geraint* down upon his knees. Thereupon Geraint rushed upon him *overthrows the* and plucked the helmet off of his head. Then he catched him *knight.* by the hair of the head and drew his head forward, whirling his sword aloft as though to strike the head off from the body.

At that the senses returned to the Little King, and he beheld that death was very near to him. So he clutched Sir Geraint about the knees, and cried out aloud, "Lord, spare me my life." "I will spare thee," said Sir Geraint, "upon one condition, and that is that thou wilt swear to be true fellow to me henceforth and shall be faithful to me as I shall be to thee. For certes thou art the noblest, worthiest knight that ever I have yet encountered." Then the other arose from his knees. "Sir Knight," said he, "I know not who thou art." "I am Sir Geraint," said Sir Geraint, "the son of King Erbin."

"Well do I know of thee," said the Little King. "Often have I heard of thee, and had I known who thou wert, I would not have assaulted thee." Then the Little King said to Sir Geraint, "Sir Knight, Sir Geraint, I perceive that thou art hurt in several places, and I am very sorry for that. For lo, the leg-pieces of thine armor are all red with blood, and blood is flowing from thy body armor from several wounds. Thou art not fit to travel in the hot sun, so I pray thee that thou and thy lady will return with me to my castle. There thou mayst refresh and recover thyself from thy hurts, and rest and reinvigorate thyself for thy continued journeyings.''

But Sir Geraint refused him. ''Nay,'' said he, ''I will not go with thee to thy castle, but instead of that I will go forward upon my way.''

Then the Little King looked at Enid, and when he beheld how fragile and how beautiful she was, and when he beheld how grieved she was that Geraint had suffered so many and such grievous wounds, he felt great pity for her. ''Messire,'' he said to Sir Geraint, ''thou dost wrong not to rest thyself and have thy wounds looked to and dressed, for if thou fallest in with another adventure such as this, it is not likely that thou wilt be able to defend thyself from assault. Who then would have care of thy lady if harm should befall thee?''

Then Sir Geraint cried out very fiercely, ''Sir, already have I answered thee that I will continue on my way, therefore do not try to dissuade me any further, for both I and my lady are going forward upon our way!'' So saying he went to his horse and he mounted upon his saddle and he took his spear in hand and rode away from that place, and he bade the Lady Enid to ride on before him as aforetime she had ridden and so they quitted that place.

Now the day was very hot so that the blood within the armor of Sir Geraint when he ceased to bleed, it dried upon him by reason of the heat of the sun. Then the wounds that Sir Geraint had suffered were glued with

Sir Geraint suffers because of his wounds.
blood to the armor, so that he suffered three times more pain from those wounds now than he suffered when he had received them. But of this he said naught, only he rode along very grimly. But at last he could endure his pain no more, wherefore he called upon the Lady Enid to halt for a little while at a certain place where the oak trees of a woodland came down to the road and shaded the high-road. Then the Lady Enid would have helped him to dismount, but he would not

Sir Geraint stands beneath a tree.
suffer her to do so but forbade her, saying to her, ''Go and stand aside under yonder tree, for my wounds ache me and I would be alone for a little while.'' So Enid went to the other tree and stood there weeping, and Sir Geraint dismounted from his horse and stood under his tree, suffering very bitter pain from his wounds.

As they thus stood, there came the sound of a sudden tumult of horses and of voices, and the cause of that tumult was that King Arthur and his court were come hunting into the neighboring woodland. So whilst Sir Geraint was considering which way he should go to escape from them, he was espied by a foot-page who was attendant upon Sir Kay the Seneschal.

This page went to Sir Kay, and he said to him, "Sir, yonder under that tree is a man in broken and defaced armor who appeareth to be wounded." Sir Kay said, "Where is he?" and then he too beheld Sir Geraint.

So Sir Kay came to where Sir Geraint was, and at his coming the Lady Enid slipped behind her tree, for she was ashamed for Sir Kay to behold her weeping in that place. So Sir Kay did not know Sir Geraint, but Sir Geraint knew Sir Kay. Sir Kay said to Sir Geraint, "Sir, *Sir Kay* how is this? I perceive you are wounded! What art thou *bespeaks Sir* doing here?" Sir Geraint replied, "I am standing under the *Geraint.* shade of this tree so as to avoid the heat. For in the sun my armor clings to my wounds so that they ache me." Said Sir Kay, "Whither dost thou journey, and who art thou?" Quoth Sir Geraint, "It matters not who I am. As for my journeying, wist thou that I am in search of adventure." Said Sir Kay, "I wit thou hast had adventures enough for one day. Come with me and I will take thee to King Arthur, who is near by." "I will not go with thee," said Sir Geraint, "for I am not fit to stand before the King." Said Sir Kay, "Thou must needs come with me." And so saying, he advanced and laid hold of the arm of Sir Geraint.

Now in all this time, as hath been said, Sir Geraint knew Sir Kay who he was, but Sir Kay knew not Sir Geraint because his shield was so defaced with battle and his armor so stained with blood. But when *Sir Geraint* Sir Kay laid hold of Sir Geraint, the anger broke hot within *strikes Sir Kay.* the wounded man, wherefore he lifted his spear, and he smote Sir Kay upon the head with the butt of the spear (for he scorned to strike him with the point thereof), and with the force of that blow Sir Kay fell down upon the ground, like an ox when the butcher smites it with a mallet.

After a little while Sir Kay stirred and then he sat up. Then he awoke and arose and went away, leaving Sir Geraint standing where he was.

Now it happened that the pavilion of Sir Percival was not far away. Thither went Sir Kay, and Sir Percival was in his pavilion. Sir Kay said to Sir Percival, "My page tells me that over yonder under that tree there stands a wounded man in armor. Hadst thou not better go and see who it is and bring him to King Arthur?" Sir Percival said, "Where is he?" Sir Kay said, "Over yonder. But beyond doubt he is hasty of temper, so be wary of thy approach to him."

Then Sir Percival went thither to that tree and he beheld where Sir Geraint was standing, and he knew him not because his armor was so defaced and wounded and stained.   But Sir Geraint knew Sir Percival who

Sir Percival bespeaks Sir Geraint. he was.   Sir Percival said to Sir Geraint, "Sir Knight, wilt thou not come to the tent of King Arthur and have thy wounds searched and dressed?"   "No," said Sir Geraint, "I will not do so."

Now the Lady Enid heard the voice of Sir Percival and knew it, so she

Sir Percival knoweth Enid the Fair. appeared from behind the tree and her face was all wet with weeping.   And she cried out to Sir Percival, "Sir Percival, I beseech thee to compel him to go to King Arthur."

Then Sir Percival knew the Lady Enid and he wist that the wounded man must be Sir Geraint.   So he cried out, "Sir Geraint, is it thou?"   Sir Geraint said, "Nay, I am not Sir Geraint."

But Sir Percival put these words aside and he said, "What condition is this that thou and thy lady are in, and whither wouldst thou go?   If thou goest forward, thou wilt die, and if thou stayest here thou wilt die."

Sir Geraint said, "I will go forward," and at those words Enid fell to weeping again.

Now there was a page standing a little aside and Sir Percival beckoned to him and the page came to Sir Percival.   Sir Percival whispered to the page, saying, "Go, find King Arthur and tell him that Sir Geraint is standing here wounded," and the page made haste and ran away.

Then Sir Percival spoke aside to the Lady Enid and he said to her, "How is it that thou and thy lord are in this outland place?"   Enid replied, "I know not how it is, but my lord commanded me to ride errant with him and I have done so."   Sir Percival said, "Certes, I think he is mad."

Anon King Arthur and several of his court and Queen Guinevere and several of her court came to that place.   Sir Percival said to King Arthur,

King Arthur comes to Sir Geraint and Enid the Fair. "Lord, this is Sir Geraint whom thou seest here in such a sad melancholy condition."   And Geraint said nothing, only he groaned very dolorously.   King Arthur said to the Lady Enid, "Enid, how came ye to this pass?"   "Lord," said Enid, "I know not how it is, only that whithersoever my lord goeth, thither also I am bound to go."   Then King Arthur said to Queen Guinevere, "Lady, I pray thee take the Lady Enid and care for her.   As for Sir Geraint, him shall I put beneath the care of my physicians."

"Lord," cried out Sir Geraint, "I beseech thee to let me go upon my way thither I was going."   "I will not do so," said King Arthur.   "Thou art mad, for that would let thee go to thy death.   Thou canst not live with such wounds as those that cover thee, fresh and undressed as they are." Then Sir Geraint said, "They are not so bad," but King Arthur would not listen to this.

So King Arthur had a tent pitched at that place, and he had a soft couch laid within the tent, and he had Sir Geraint laid upon the couch. And the King had his own physicians come to search the wounds of Sir Geraint and to anoint them and to bind them up, and so Sir Geraint was put in great comfort from their attention. *The physicians search the wounds of Sir Geraint.*

Meanwhile the Queen brought the Lady Enid to her pavilion and she had her change her riding robes for clothes of another sort. And she asked Enid many things and Enid told her many things of her adventures, and all marvelled at what the Lady Enid had to relate.

So Geraint and Enid remained at that woodland court of King Arthur for nearly a month, and Enid was very well entertained by the court of the King. And whilst it was so that she was not permitted to see Sir Geraint nor to speak to him, yet she heard very intimately from him from day to day, and wist that ever he was becoming healed of his wounds. For, after that month was passed, Sir Geraint's wounds were knit together and were scarred over with fair white flesh. And even at that time Sir Geraint grew restless, for as he grew stronger of body he remembered more and more strongly the words that he had over-heard the Lady Enid speak that morning when he awakened, and again he doubted her.

So one day he said to King Arthur, "Lord, I pray thee let me depart from this place, for I must be upon my journeying again." King Arthur said, "Messire, whither wouldst thou go?" Geraint said, "I know not, saving only that I would go errant in search of adventure."

King Arthur said, "Then let thy Lady abide at this place." Quoth Sir Geraint, "She cannot abide here, but she must travel abroad with me." King Arthur said, "Sir, this is not folly but madness, for thy lady's body is too soft and delicate for her to endure such hardships as thou wilt have to endure." "No matter," said Sir Geraint, "she must travel with me whithersoever I go."

Then King Arthur considered a little and after a little he said, "Sir, I will not let you go until my physicians declare you to be healed." Quoth Sir Geraint, "Call the physicians."

So King Arthur summoned the physicians and he asked them if Sir Geraint was healed of his wounds and the physicians declared that he was healed.

So King Arthur gave leave to Sir Geraint to depart and that day Sir Geraint took leave of King Arthur and his court and he and the Lady Enid departed as aforetime. That is to say, the Lady Enid rode some distance ahead of Sir Geraint, and Sir Geraint rode some distance behind the Lady Enid as it was before.

Sir Geraint and Enid depart from the Court of the King.

Here followeth the further adventures of these two which you may read if you will peruse that which is herein written.

The King's physicians attends Sir Geraint. ℐ ℐ ℐ ℐ

Chapter Sixth

How Sir Geraint destroyed three giants of the highway. How he was hurt, and how he and the Lady Enid were carried off by a knight of that country. Also how Geraint slew the knight.

NOW after they had travelled in that wise for some time they came to a wood, and the wood was very thick and dark and dismal, and some way in the wood they heard the sound of a voice lifted in lamentation. Thitherward they directed their steps and anon they came to an open glade of the forest. Here they beheld a lady *Sir Geraint finds* and two horses and the figure of a knight who lay dead, all *a lady in grief.* covered with blood, upon the ground. Sir Geraint said to that lady, "Lady what ails thee?" "Alas!" she said, "I have journeyed thitherward, but three gigantic oafs broke out of the woodland upon us. Him they slew as thou beholdest and so I sit mourning for him here."

"What way went these giants of whom thou speakest?" said Sir Geraint. "They went yonder way by that path," said she.

Geraint said to Enid, "Bide thou here for a little while with this lady, and I will ride forward and punish those three giants." Enid said, "Lord, remember thou art only now fresh from thy bed of pain."

But Sir Geraint paid no heed to what Enid said, otherwise he rode forward upon the path that the lady had pointed out. After awhile he beheld before him the three gigantic men, walking side by side along the way.

Each wore about his body a huge body-piece of armor, and each carried over his shoulder a huge club shod with iron.

Upon them Sir Geraint charged, and the first of the three he ran through his body with the lance. Then he withdrew the lance very quickly, and charged the second of the three, and him also he transfixed with his spear. But ere he could withdraw his lance again the third of the *The giant* three smote him a terrible buffet with his club so that his shield *strikes Sir* was split and his helmet was split and the armor was beaten *Geraint.* off from his shoulder. Under that blow Sir Geraint fell upon his knees,

59

and all his wounds burst out bleeding as though they were freshly given. But quickly he recovered himself. He drew his sword, and rushing at the giant he smote him with the sword so that his head and his neck and his shoulders were split asunder even to the pap of the breast, and that giant also fell dead to the ground.

Then leaving those three where they lay, Geraint mounted his horse *Sir Geraint* again and returned to where he had left Enid and the widowed *swoons a death-* lady. And when he came to her he tried to speak but he *swoon.* could not speak. He began by saying "Lady—" but then he stopped, and swaying from side to side, he fell lifeless from his horse to the ground.

Then Enid ran to him and lifted his head and laid it in her lap. And Enid thought that he was dead, for his face was the color of wax for whiteness. Then believing him to be dead she lifted up her voice and wept very loud and shrill.

Now it chanced that an earl known as the Earl of Limours was in that part of the forest, and several of his attendant knights were with him. These heard the loud piercing sound of Enid's grief, and the Earl of Limours said, "Hark! What is that sound?" And one of his attendant knights said, "It is the sound of somebody in grief." Quoth the Earl, "Let us go thitherward."

The Earl of So the Earl of Limours and his attendants galloped toward *Limours comes* that place, and anon they came out into the forest glade. *to that place.* There they beheld the four horses, and the two ladies and the two knights.

The Earl of Limours said to Enid, "Lady, what is the cause of thy grief?" "Alas, Sir," she cried, "the only man that I ever loved or ever shall love is slain." Then the Earl of Limours said to the other lady, "What is the cause of thy grief?" Quoth she, "They have slain my husband also." "Who was it slew them?" said the Earl of Limours. "My husband," said the Lady, "was slain by three giants. This other knight pursued the three giants, and when he returned he was as thou seest." "Whither went those giants?" said the Earl. She replied, "They went yonder ways." "I will go and see what has befallen them," said the Earl of Limours.

So that Earl took several of his knights and he went in that direction, *The Earl finds* and in a little while he found all three giants lying dead upon *the dead out-* the ground. "Pardee," quoth he, "yonder was a parlous *laws.* strong knight to slay all three of those giants."

After that he returned to the forest glade and he made examination of the knights that lay there. The one knight he found was dead, but it did not seem to him that Sir Geraint was altogether dead. So the one knight he buried, but Sir Geraint he laid in the hollow of a shield with his sword behind him. And he laid him upon a *The Earl carries* bier and so he bore him away toward his castle, the two *Sir Geraint to his castle.* ladies accompanying them.

By and by, after a very long journeying, they came to the castle of the Earl of Limours. And the castle was very large and comely and strong.

The Earl and those who were with him entered the castle and he had the shield with Sir Geraint stretched upon it borne into the hall of the castle. And he had his physician to come and examine Geraint and the leech came and made examination of him. Then after due examination the leech said that he was not yet dead, but that he was exceedingly near to death.

Then the Earl bade the two ladies to go and change their clothes and to assume garments that were more fitting to grace that hall, and the other lady went as he bade, but Enid would not go.

The Earl of Limours said to her, "Lady, thou art not wise in this, for I mean well by thee. Thou pleasest me very greatly by thy appearance. When thy lord is dead, then will I marry thee and will bestow upon thee myself and this castle and all these lands through which we passed to-day, and all other things thou shalt have that are mine." But Enid only wept, and she said, "Alas! I know not what to do, for I am very lonely. If my lord dieth, nevermore shall I have any more joy or happiness as long as I shall live."

The Earl of Limours said, "Take heart, my pretty one." But she said, "I cannot take any heart." Then the Earl gave orders that a feast should be made ready, and it was done according to his command. And when that feast was ready, he said to Enid, "Come and sit here beside me and eat." She said, "I will not eat and I will not sit at table unless my lord sits here also." Then the Earl laughed, and he said, "Lady, thou art very foolish in this, for thy knight will never sit at table again, for he is dead, or else he is dying." Then Enid wept again, very bitterly.

The Earl said, "Come sit beside me, and I will have thy knight at table also." So he had them bring the bier whereon Sir Geraint lay to the side of the table. Then he took Enid by the hand and led her *The Earl of* to the table and compelled her to sit beside him. But still *Limours strikes* she would not eat. Then the Earl offered her a goblet of wine *Enid the Fair.* and he said, "Drink this wine, for it will help thee to forget thy sorrows." "I will not drink," she said, "until my husband shall arise and drink with me." Then the Earl of Limours became angry. "A plague upon thee and thy knight!" he cried, and so crying he lifted his hand and delivered to her a box upon the ear.

Then Enid felt her loneliness as never before. For she knew that had Geraint been with her the Earl of Limours would not have dared to serve her thus. So when she felt that blow upon her face she lifted up her voice and shrieked aloud.

Now Geraint had been recovering from his swoon, but still he lay with his eyes closed listening to what was said and done about him. And he heard Enid how that she refused to eat or to drink, and he heard the blow that the Earl of that place delivered upon her face, and he heard her shriek with the pain thereof. At that the eyes of his soul were opened, and he beheld how mad and how blind he had been, and he knew how faithful to him Enid had been, maugre any words she might have uttered. Then rage and shame flamed up like fire within him, the last vapors of his swoon passed away, and he felt within him the strength of ten.

Thereupon he grasped the sword that lay beside him in the hollow of the shield and he arose from the shield all white and wan and smeared *Sir Geraint* with blood, and those who beheld him saw him arise as though *slays the Earl* from the dead. Then they shrieked and screamed and fell *of Limours.* aside before him. But Geraint leaped from the hollow of the shield and he ran to where the Earl of Limours sat, and crying out, "Wouldst thou dare to smite my wife?" he smote him with all his might upon the head. So terrible was that blow that it smote asunder the head and the neck and the breast of the Earl, and was only stopped by the oaken board of the table against which the sword blade smote in its descent.

Then all those who thus beheld the dead man arise from his death and strike that blow, shrieked and roared aloud, and they fled away from that place in terror and amazement, and no one was left but Geraint and Enid, and the dead man sitting dreadfully in his seat.

Then Enid said, "O my lord! Art thou dead or art thou alive?" And Geraint said, "Beloved, I am alive and well." And Enid said, "I thank God for that." But Geraint said, "Let us hasten to escape from this place whilst we may, for presently these people will return again." And he said to her, "Where are our horses?" She said, "I know not where is my horse, but thy horse is in the house yonder, for I saw them put him there."

So Geraint and Enid went to the house that was near at hand and there Geraint found his horse. And Geraint took his horse out of the stable and he mounted upon his horse and he reached his hand to Enid and lifted her up from the ground and placed her upon the horse behind him; and she clasped her arms around his body and felt his body with her arms with great joy and delight.

So they rode away from that place and no one dared to stop *Sir Geraint and* them, for all believed that it was the living riding with the *Enid depart from that place.* dead.

Then, when they were come out into the sunlight again, Sir Geraint turned his head and looked his lady, Enid, in the face, and he perceived how she had lost her color and was grown thin and fragile because of the hardships to which his anger and his injustice had subjected her. Then he turned his own face away and bowed his head.

By and by he lifted his head and said to her, "Lady, canst thou forgive me?" To that she smiled a little, but very faintly. "I do forgive thee," said she, "but never shall I forget." Therewith the tears ran from her eyes and fell like diamonds down her cheeks, and Sir Geraint turned away his face again and again bowed down his head.

So they rode in silence, each occupied with his or her own thoughts, until at last they came to a place where there were high hedges upon either side of the way. At this place they heard the sound of many horses coming toward them, and in a little while they perceived the points of a number of spears between them and the sky over the top of the hedge. So Geraint put Enid upon the other side of the hedge and made him ready to face those who were coming.

Anon there came a small host of horsemen in armor into that road, and the first of all those who came was the Little King. Then Geraint cried out with joy, "Is that thou, the Little King?" And the *The Little King* other said, "Yea, it is I, but who art thou?" For he did *finds Sir Ge-* not know Sir Geraint because of the blood that was upon *raint and Enid.* him and because of his changed appearance. Then Geraint said, "It is I, Geraint the son of Erbin."

Then the Little King came forward, and embraced him. And Enid came forth from her hiding, and the Little King paid his respects to her. Quoth the Little King, "I was in search of thee, Sir Geraint, for I heard thou wert in trouble. So I am here." And Sir Geraint said, "That is according to the conditions of our bond."

So Sir Geraint and Enid and the Little King returned along the way toward the castle of the Little King, and when they reached the castle the wounds of Sir Geraint were searched and dressed and he was made in all wise as comfortable as he could be.

Conclusion

THUS have I told you the story of Sir Geraint and of Lady Enid at this, its fitting time.

This story has been very often sung and told and so you have no doubt heard of it or read it before this. For it hath been told by a great poet, and it hath been told by the ancient bards of Wales, and both that great poet and I have obtained it from those ancient chronicles of the Welsh Mabinogi. *Of the story, how it hath been sung of old.*

But as this story concerns the story of King Arthur and his court, so it must be written when it cometh in its due place and so I have written it.

So I pray you read it and consider it as a very famous story of one of the chiefest knights of the Round Table of King Arthur.

And now I shall have to tell you of the coming of Sir Galahad and of the Quest of the Grail by certain of the Knights of King Arthur and his Round Table, and of how certain other knights failed in that quest. So if you will read that which followeth you shall be informed of all those very wonderful things which many people for many years believed to be sooth and real.

PART II

The Story of Sir Galahad

HERE beginneth the Story of Sir Galahad, which same includes the history of the recovery of the Grail and its deposit in the Minster of Sarras, also its exaltation into Paradise, as follows:—

ir Galahad cometh with the Hermit of the fforest:

Chapter First

How Sir Galahad was made a knight; how he came to the Court of King Arthur, and of the several miracles that happened at that time.

ONE day Sir Launcelot sat at court with many lords and ladies of high degree who were gathered there at that time. Suddenly there entered that place a maiden clad in a long, straight robe of white, girdled about the middle of the body with a crimson girdle of leather. And the girdle was embroidered with threads of gold. This *A damsel comes* maiden stood at the door of the hall and called out in a high *to the Court* and very clear voice, "Sir Launcelot of the Lake—which *of the King.* knight is he?"

To this Sir Launcelot made reply, "I am he; what seekest thou of me?" The maiden said, "Sir Launcelot, I bid thee arise and follow me." Quoth he, "To what purpose?" She said, "Thou shalt see."

So Sir Launcelot arose and, clad as he was and without armor of any sort, he followed her.

Outside of the hall were two horses standing; one of them was a white palfrey, the other was a black stallion. Sir Launcelot assisted the *Sir Launcelot* maiden to mount upon the white palfrey and he himself mounted *rides with her.* upon the black stallion, and so together they rode away from Camelot.

They travelled for some while until they came to the skirts of the forest. Then they rode into the forest, and all day they traversed the woodlands.

Toward eventide of that same day they came to an open place amidst the surrounding trees, where was a quiet and very fruitful valley, stretched out wide to the length and breadth of a league. In that valley Sir Launcelot beheld orchards and fields of wheat and barley, and meadow-lands where cattle were browsing in numbers. For it was a very beautiful and fertile spot.

In the midst of this valley there stood a nunnery, with white walls and green trees all about it. Above the nunnery was the clear and radiant sky, very blue and all full of floating clouds. A soft wind blew up the length of the valley, and upon the breeze there came the remote sound of a crowing cock and the voice of the ploughboy as he drave the plough horses along the smoking, upturned furrows, the ploughman following laboring behind them.

Quoth the maiden, "Thither is where I am taking thee." Said Sir Launcelot, "To what end?" "That thou shalt presently see," said the maiden.

So the maiden rode down into the valley and Sir Launcelot rode after *They come to* her. Thus, anon, they came to that pleasant and secluded *the nunnery.* convent. Here the gate was opened to them by a fair and youthful esquire, and they entered the portals of the place. Then several came and assisted them to dismount, and took the horses of Sir Launcelot and the maiden.

After that the maiden led Sir Launcelot across the quadrangle of the convent and so to the chapel, and they entered the chapel. Here Sir Launcelot beheld four ladies kneeling upon four cushions before the altar; and he beheld that beside these ladies there were two knights kneeling, each upon a cushion. Of the four ladies, one was the Lady Abbess of that convent; and of the two knights, one was Sir Bors de Ganis and the other was Sir Lionel.

Anon they who kneeled there ceased their orisons and arose, and Sir Launcelot beheld the faces of Sir Bors and Sir Lionel and knew them, and *Sir Launcelot* they knew him. Then Sir Launcelot said to them, "Messires, *finds two whom* what is it brings you hitherward?" To this Sir Bors replied, *he knows.* "Sir, we were in distant places and to each of us came a fair maiden who was the messenger who brought each of us to this place. Since our coming we have been waiting for thee, and now thou art here." Sir Launcelot said, "For what purpose have I been brought hither?" Sir Lionel said, "Thou shalt see." Then Sir Lionel said to the Abbess, "Bring him forth that Sir Launcelot may behold him."

Upon this the Lady Abbess turned to one of the nuns who stood beside her and she spake aside to her, and with that the nun left them and went away. For a little while she was gone, and then in a little while she returned, bringing with her a youth of eighteen years of age, *Sir Launcelot* very tall and fair, and clad from top to toe in clothes of white *finds his son.* silk. Said Sir Launcelot to the Abbess, "Lady, what youth is this?" The Abbess replied to him, "Sir, this is thine own son, hight Galahad, and his mother was the Lady Elaine the Fair."

Then Sir Launcelot cried out in a loud voice, "How is this? I knew not that I had a son. I beheld the Lady Elaine the Fair upon a certain black and terrible day, lying dead in a boat at Camelot, and I stood upon the quay and the boat floated beneath my feet. All this I beheld, and never shall I forget it; but I knew not that she left a son behind her." Said the Abbess, "Ne'ertheless she did so, and this is that son. Here hath he lived with us since the time of his birth when Sir Bors fetched him hither, and no one knew that he dwelt with us saving only Sir Bors de Ganis. But now hath the time come that he must quit us, for the period is imminent when the search for the Holy Grail shall be begun, and this is he who shall achieve the Grail. He is now to be knighted, and for that purpose thou hast been sent for that thou mightest make him a knight. This is the reason for thy being brought hither." Quoth Sir Launcelot, "Let me then make him a knight. For I know of no joy that would be greater than that, that I should make him a knight."

So that night Galahad watched his armor in the chapel, and Sir Bors and Sir Lionel sat near to him to support him in his watch. And when the morning was come, they two took him thence and bathed him, and Sir Bors marked the sign of the cross upon his right shoulder and *Sir Launcelot* Sir Lionel marked the sign of the cross upon his left shoulder, *makes Galahad* each with the water of the bath. Thereafter that, they clad *a knight.* him in a robe of white, pure and spotless, and they brought him to where Sir Launcelot was, and Sir Launcelot made a knight of him, according to the accepted custom.

So was Sir Galahad made a knight by the hand of his own father, Sir Launcelot of the Lake.

Now, after this ceremony was completed, Sir Launcelot besought Sir Galahad that he would accompany them to the Court of King Arthur, so that the King might behold him (for Sir Launcelot desired *Sir Launcelot* that Sir Galahad should be manifested to the entire world of *returns to the* chivalry). But to this Sir Galahad replied, "Sir, I cannot *court.* yet go to the Court of the King, for all is not yet accomplished to prepare me for that going. Anon, however, I shall come thither; meantime, do thou wait for me at King Arthur's Court." So, shortly after this, Sir Launcelot and Sir Lionel and Sir Bors de Ganis departed from that convent, and that same day they reached the Court of the King at Camelot.

But they said nothing to that court concerning the knighting of Galahad, for at that present it was not to be made known to the world that there was such an one as Galahad, and that he was Sir Launcelot's son and a knight of Sir Launcelot's making.

So it befell Pentecost Day, what time the Feast of the Round Table was held. Upon this day those miracles happened that are here written of, and that were afterward so much talked of and concerning which so much was written.

For it happened upon that day, early in the morning when the water-carriers went down to the river to draw water, they there beheld at that *Concerning the* place a very strange, and wonderful sight. For beside the river *miracle of the* they beheld where there stood a great block of red marble— *sword.* cubical in shape, and polished until it was smooth as glass. And into that cube of stone there was thrust a sword, half way down its blade into the marble. And the hilt of the sword and the haft, thereof, was studded all over with precious stones of divers sizes and colors, very rich and glorious to behold. And the blade of that sword (so much thereof as could be seen) shone like to lightning for brightness.

Then they who beheld the wonder that appeared before them made all haste to the castle of the King, and straightway told the news of what they had seen. Anon this reached the ears of the King and of several of those lords who were in attendance upon him. Then the King spoke to those lords, saying, "What is this I hear tell of? Let us straightway go and see."

So the King, and those lords of the court who were in his company, went *The King and* down to the river to look upon that wonder, and amongst those *his lords view* lords were Sir Launcelot of the Lake and Sir Percival of Gales *the sword.* and Sir Bors de Ganis and Sir Lionel and Sir Ector and Sir Gawaine, and several other high lords of chivalry.

When they had come to that place where the sword was they beheld that there were words written around about the blade thereof. So King Arthur commanded Sir Launcelot that he should read those words, and Sir Launcelot read as follows:

"This sword is for the greatest knight in the world and for him who shall win the Holy Grail."

Then he read:

" Whoso draweth forth this sword from the stone, to him shall that sword belong; but upon him who shall endeavor to draw it forth and shall not be able to do so, shall fall a wound from the blade thereof."

Then King Arthur said to Sir Launcelot of the Lake, "Messire, thou art the greatest knight in the world, and perhaps thou shalt win the Holy Grail. Let me see thee draw forth that blade."

Quoth Sir Launcelot, "Lord, I know not that I am the greatest knight in the world, and I fear me that I shall not be able to win the *Sir Launcelot* Grail, for I am a sinful man. Look you; it saith here that he *will not attempt* who shall endeavor to draw it forth from the marble and shall *the sword.* fail to do so, he shall be wounded by the blade thereof. So I would fain not endeavor to draw forth this sword."

Then King Arthur turned him to Sir Gawaine, and he said, "Sir, let me see thee attempt that sword, for mayhap thou mayst be able to draw it forth out of the marble." Sir Gawaine said, "Lord, if Sir Launcelot dare not attempt that sword, so, also, do I not dare to do so." King Arthur said to him, "Gawaine, I command thee upon thy fealty to attempt that sword." Quoth Sir Gawaine, "Dear my Lord, if thou dost command me upon my fealty, then I must attempt to obey thy command." King Arthur said, "I do command thee thus."

So Sir Gawaine came forth and he laid hand to the hilt of *Sir Gawaine* the sword and drew strongly upon it, but the sword did not *attempts the* move a hair's breadth in the marble stone in which it stood *sword.* emplanted.

Then Sir Launcelot spoke and said, "Alas, Sir Gawaine, that thou shouldst have made that attempt and failed therein. For if thou art wounded by that bright-shining blade it may be of more injury to thee than it would be if thou shouldst lose three several castles." Quoth Sir Gawaine, "That may well be, Sir Launcelot, but yet it was incumbent upon me to do that which the King's command called upon me to do."

Then up spake Sir Percival, "Lord," said he, "let me also attempt that sword, for if it should be turned against Sir Gawaine I would *Sir Percival* have it that it should be turned equally against me. Else I *attempts the* would endeavor to draw it forth from the stone for mine own." *sword.* The King said, "Try thou for the sword." So Sir Percival laid his hand to the sword and drew upon it very strongly, but neither could he move it so much as the breadth of a single hair.

After that no other lord of all those present chose to attempt the sword, but all avoided it from a distance, no one coming nigh enough to it to touch it.

So, thereafter, they all withdrew from that place and went away, marvelling at the miracle. And all that day many came to where was that sword and the block of marble, and these stood to look upon that sight and to marvel at it.

Such is the story of the sword so far as this, and so have I told it to you as I have read of it in an ancient book of olden days, wherein these adventures and several other adventures are spoken of.

Thus that day of marvels began, and by and by came the time of the Feast of the Round Table.

Now all they of the Round Table were gathered about that board and every man sat in his place, and behind every knight stood a young knight *Sir Galahad is* to serve him with meat and drink. Thus, as they all sat there, *brought to the* there came, of a sudden, a commotion at the doorway, and *Feast of the* after that commotion there appeared at the doorway an old *Round Table.* man clad all in white. That old man was the Hermit of the Forest, and with him he brought a tall, fair young knight and that knight was Sir Galahad. At that time Sir Galahad was clad in flame-colored armor from top to toe, but he bare no shield for his defence upon his shoulder, nor was there any sword within the sheath that hung empty and hollow at his side. From his shoulders there hung a long mantle of flame-colored cloth, and the mantle was lined with sable and trimmed and bordered with sable.

The old man lifted up his voice and spake aloud to all who were there, saying, "Lords, here by the grace of God come I amongst you with him who is to be the greatest knight that ever the world beheld. Also, he is to be the one who shall achieve the Holy Grail. So I have brought him hither to this place."

Him answered King Arthur, saying, "Holy Sir, if thou sayest sooth, then this is a very great and marvellous thing. But soon shall we put it to the test; yonder is the Seat Perilous wherein no one hath dared to seat himself for all this while of the Round Table. Let this youth take there his seat, for that seat is for him who is without sin of the flesh—then will we believe that which thou tellest us. Also, down beside the river there is a strange and marvellous sword in a cube of marble. Let him draw that sword and then shall we certes believe in him."

The old hermit said, "Sir King, it shall be done as thou desirest. Let him take that seat." So the old man took him by one hand and *Sir Galahad* King Arthur arose and took him by the other, and so together *assumes the* they led Sir Galahad to the Seat Perilous. Here he took his *Seat Perilous.* seat, and lo! no harm of any sort befell him. Then, anon, Sir Launcelot reached forward and drew aside the silken coverlet that hung at the back of the seat upon which Sir Galahad sat, and, behold! there was a word estamped upon the back of the seat in letters of gold; and that word was:

𝕾𝕴𝕽 𝕲𝕬𝕷𝕬𝕳𝕬𝕯

Then a great shout went up from all the Knights of the Round Table, for thus was the Seat Perilous achieved, and so was the Round Table completed.

Then King Arthur said, "Lo! this youth is he for whom we have been waiting for all this time. For so the miracle of the Round Table is fulfilled. Let us now take him to the sword thrust into the marble stone, for certes he shall draw forth that sword, and it shall be his. For, wit ye, that this is he who shall indeed achieve the Holy Grail."

So all they arose from their seats and went forth, and they conducted Sir Galahad down to the river. There he beheld the stone of marble and the sword thrust into the stone, and he said to those who stood *Sir Galahad* about that place, "This sword is assuredly mine, for I have no *draweth the* sword, and for that sword I have come hitherward." So Sir *sword.* Galahad went to where was the sword and he set hand to the sword and drew it forth from the stone very smoothly and easily, and where the sword came forth it left no mark upon the stone, for, lo! it was solid and whole and without any blemish whatsoever. Then Sir Galahad thrust the bright-shining blade into the scabbard that hung beside him, and it fitted to the scabbard, and so he was armed.

Thereafter King Arthur took him by the hand and kissed him upon either cheek, and the King said, "Hail, Sir Galahad! All hail to thee! For thou art to be the crowning glory of my entire reign. For many mysteries and miracles have befallen in that reign, but thy coming is the greatest miracle of all." And he said, "Come, let us go up to the castle that I may present thee to the Queen."

Then Sir Galahad said, "Not so, O Lord! I cannot go with *Sir Galahad* thee now. For one cometh and is nigh to here at this present, *will not stay* and with her I must go. For I go first to seek for the shield *at Camelot.* of Balan, who slew his brother Balin unwittingly at the time of Uther

Pendragon. Through him the Holy Grail was lost to the earth, so that I must recover first his shield and then the Holy Grail. After I have thus armed me with that shield, then must I go to search for the Holy Grail, for that same is my mission here in life. Likewise I have this news to tell thee, that two of those knights here present shall win the Grail along with me; but who those two shall be, I may not relate to you at this time.''

Thus said Sir Galahad, and even as he ceased speaking there appeared in the distance a damsel clad all in white raiment, and the maiden came thith-

A maiden cometh for Galahad.

erward, riding upon a white palfrey, and by her hand she led by its bridle-rein a coal-black charger of great size and girth. So as she drew near, Sir Galahad went forward to meet her, and to him the maiden said, speaking very high and clear, ''Art thou ready, Sir Galahad?'' Whereunto he said, ''Yea, I am ready.'' And she said, ''Come!'' So Sir Galahad mounted upon the black charger, and he saluted King Arthur and he saluted Sir Launcelot and he saluted Sir Bors and Sir Lionel, and after that he rode away from that place, leaving them all in great wonder and amazement, both at his coming and at his going, and at all that had befallen.

So, when he had gone, King Arthur turned to his court of lords, and he said, ''This is certes a very wonderful visitation, for this youth came to us like an angel from heaven, and, like an angel, he hath gone. Let us now go and hear the mass ere we return to the Hall of the Round Table.''

So all they who were there went to the mass, and as they were going Sir Gawaine said to Sir Launcelot, ''Messire, this is a sad day for thee, for now there is a greater knight than thou art in the world.'' Him answered Sir Launcelot, ''Not so, Messire, there is no sadness in this for me, for, wit you, that this is mine own and well-beloved son. Wherefore I, being his father, may well surrender unto him that glory which I cannot carry with me into paradise, but which I would not be willing to yield to any other man.''

So said Sir Launcelot, and thus all the world became acquainted with that fact that no one but Sir Bors and Sir Lionel knew until then; to wit, that Sir Galahad was the true son of Sir Launcelot of the Lake.

Now, after the mass in the minster was over, all they of the Knights of the Round Table retired to the Hall of the Round Table, and there they took

The knights vow to attempt the Grail.

their seats in due order. Then, when all were seated, King Arthur up and said, ''Messires and Lords of the Round Table, all ye have heard what Sir Galahad hath said but a little while since; to wit, that two of you who are here should achieve the Grail with him. Now it doth seem to me that several of you who are the chief of all the knights should go forth in search of that Holy Chalice, so as to be able to join him. For, by not going, those two may miss the chance of achieving that great glory."

So said King Arthur, and, in answer, all those who were there arose, each man in his place. And each man drew his sword and each held up the handle of his sword before his eyes as a crucifix. And each man swore upon that crucifix that he would presently depart from the Court of the King, and that he would search for the Holy Grail either until he discovered it or until he should perish, or until the Grail should have been achieved.

Then King Arthur was filled with sorrow, for he would not that all of his knights should go in that wise, for many of them he would have kept with him at his court. And most of all he was grieved that Sir *King Arthur* Gawaine should go, for he loved Sir Gawaine above all the *takes sorrow.* knights of his court, because Sir Gawaine was the son of the well-beloved sister of the King. So he said to Sir Gawaine, "Alas, Gawaine, you have slain the joy of my life! For with this oath that ye all have uttered there departeth from this court all that was of joy therein. Until now there hath been great joy and good content at this Court of Camelot, but now that joy hath taken wing and hath flown away. For, though many of you shall return to this place, yet I foresee that many shall die; and I foresee that from this time there shall follow great bitterness and rancor, and anon that death and devastation shall overtake us all. For this is the time foretold by Merlin, of which ye all have heard tell. For, according to that prophecy, this day the Round Table hath been filled to its completion, so that hereafter it shall soon fall apart into warring and contention until it be altogether destroyed."

Then Sir Launcelot said to the King, "Comfort you, my lord, for though the Round Table may indeed perish thus, yet, ere it be dissolved, there shall come great honor and a great glory unto you and unto us all. *Sir Launcelot* For what greater glory can there be to you than that the *comforts King* knights of your Round Table should achieve the Holy Grail? *Arthur.* And what greater honor can there be than that we should endanger our lives in that quest? For we all seek death hither and thither, and if it so befall that death cometh to us in this cause, how much better is it to die in that wise than to have death come to us in some vain quarrel or adventure."

Quoth King Arthur, "That which thou sayest, Launcelot, is very true, yet do I greatly grieve for this happening. For though we may look forward to a glorious sorrow, yet when that sorrow cometh to us it appeareth to be so much greater than the glory that it hides that glory from our eyes. So, Launcelot, is it with me; for though I may take glory that my knights shall achieve the Holy Grail, yet is the sorrow very great to me that this Round Table should be dissolved. Alas, and alas, that it should be so!"

Thus the Knights of the Round Table went forth in quest of the Grail—fifty of them in all. All of those who thus went had adventures, and many of them lost their lives and did never return again. But of those of whom this history telleth there is only Sir Launcelot, Sir Gawaine, Sir Percival, Sir Bors, and Sir Galahad, and one or two others. Of them and of their adventures it remains now to be told; wherefore, followeth the history of those things hereinafter written.

he Lady of the Lake and Sirs Galahad :

Chapter Second

How Sir Galahad was led by a strange lady to a monastery of White Friars. How he met there two other Knights of the Round Table. How King Bagdemagus wore the shield, and how it was taken from him and given unto Sir Galahad. Also the story of the shield.

SIR GALAHAD rode away from Camelot, where was the Court of King Arthur, following after the maiden clad all in white. Thus they wended onward until they reached the skirts of the forest. At this place the maiden said, "Sir Galahad, I must here leave you. But go you farther upon yonder path, and by and by you will be met and entertained."

So Sir Galahad rode forward upon that path as the maiden directed. And he rode a great distance into the forest until at last he reached the Forest of Arroy, otherwise called the Forest of Adventure. Here, after he had ridden for a considerable time, he came at last to a very *Sir Galahad* strange place. For he found the trees grew thin and thinner *comes to a* about him. Then, at last, the trees ceased around him, and he *strange country.* found himself upon the edge of a wide and open plain. And he beheld that all about him in this plain there were great quantities of lilies, and there were also daffodils, and all those flowers moved this way and that, very slowly in the gentle air, as though they saluted him in coming. And Sir Galahad beheld that this was a very wonderful place indeed, for the light that illumined it was not the light of the sun nor of the moon, but it was a radiant and golden glory that was not due to the light of either of those luminaries.

And in the midst of that flowery plain Sir Galahad beheld that there was a wide and very placid lake that was in no wise troubled by the soft breeze that blew across it, but that was otherwise like a smooth mirror of clear water.

So as Sir Galahad beheld all these things and marvelled at them, he was aware that this was not the land of common earth, but that it was fay.

Then anon he was aware that voices were calling aloud, saying, "Welcome, welcome, Sir Galahad!" as it were with great rejoicing. So he looked, and lo! he beheld to one side a fair and shining pavilion of green silk. And there were many people gathered in the field near the pavilion, and some of them were ladies and some were lords and others were pages, and all were clad in very gay and rainbow colors, so that it appeared as though it were a flock of gaudy birds of various plumage that was gathered in that place.

So Sir Galahad turned him toward that gay and jocund company, and as he drew near to them he beheld that they were weaving garlands and wreaths of fair flowers.

(For these, you are to know, were the attendants of the Lady of the Lake, and that was the lake in which was her habitation, and he had been led to that place for a certain purpose that they and others might see and know him.)

So this place pleased Sir Galahad very greatly, and he remained for *Sir Galahad abides there for four days.* three days, taking great joy in that jocund company. For somewhiles they feasted and somewhiles they sang; somewhiles they danced and somewhiles they related pleasant tales and contes of several kinds. So it was that these three days passed very pleasantly and very quickly with Sir Galahad.

Then, upon the morning of the fourth day, there appeared a lady in their *There cometh the Lady of the Lake.* midst to whom all who were there paid great deference and high respect; and this lady was of a very wonderful appearance. For she was clad in green samite from head to foot, and her hair was long and extraordinarily black, and very soft and glossy. And her face was pale, like to ivory, and her eyes were bright, like to jewels set in ivory. And upon her neck and around her arms were chains and bracelets of gold inset with emerald stones. Wherefore, from these things, and from the appearance of all about him, Sir Galahad was aware that that lady was not mortal, but that she was fay.

(For this was indeed the Lady of the Lake, although he knew it not then nor afterward.)

So Sir Galahad kneeled in the grass before the lady and he set his palms together. But she smiled upon him and she said to him, "Arise, Galahad, and kneel not to me, who am not of the spirit, but of the earth." And she said to him, "Where is thy shield?" He said to her, "Lady, I have no shield." She said to him, "Let us go and find thee a shield."

So straightway there came several attendants, and some of these brought Sir Galahad his black charger, and others brought for the lady a beautiful janet as white as milk. And upon the back of the janet was a saddle of scarlet Spanish leather, embossed with gold and jewels, so that it shone and glistered with great splendor.

Then Sir Galahad mounted his horse and the lady mounted herself upon the janet, and so together they rode away from that place.

Thus they rode for all that day, and against the sloping of the afternoon they had come to the edge of the forest opposite to that part of the forest where was the town of Camelot. At this place there was a monastery of White Friars, and to this the lady pointed and said to Sir Galahad, "Thither thou wilt find a shield." *The Lady of the Lake leadeth Sir Galahad to a shield.*

Then Sir Galahad would have thanked her for bringing him thither, but lo! she was gone from his sight and he was alone. Then the monastery bell began ringing, and Sir Galahad rode down to that holy house.

So he came to the monastery and smote with the butt of his lance upon the gate. Then the porters came and opened the gate to him, and when they beheld him they gave him welcome to that place. So he entered the courtyard of the monastery, and several came and gathered about him. Some of these took his horse and led it away to the stable; others conducted him into the house and afterward brought him to the chamber wherein he was to be lodged. Here they removed his armor and brought him to a bath of tepid water. After that they clad him in raiment that was soft and warm so that he had great ease and comfort. *Sir Galahad enters the monastery.*

Then, when he was thus clad, they conducted him to the hall of that monastery, and there he beheld that there were two other knights then present. The one of these was Sir Ewaine, and the other was Sir Bagdemagus, erstwhile called King Bagdemagus. These were both Knights of the Round Table, wherefore they greeted him and gave him great welcome. *Sir Galahad findeth Sir Bagdemagus and Sir Ewaine.*

Sir Ewaine said to him, "I pray you, sir, tell us how you came hither." Sir Galahad said, "I will tell you." So he told them how he had abided in the midst of the forest near to that magic lake for the space of three days. And he told them how that lady, who was fay, had conducted him to that place, and had told him that there was here a shield with which he might provide himself. To all this Sir Ewaine and King Bagdemagus listened, and then Sir Ewaine said to Sir Galahad, "Messire, no doubt that lady who accompanied thee hitherward was the Lady of the Lake, for so hath she appeared to several of King Arthur's Court as she hath appeared to thee."

Just then came the Abbot of that place, and King Bagdemagus said to him, "Sir, I pray you tell us, is there at this place a shield of such and such *The Abbot tells* a sort?" The Abbot replied to him, "Aye, sir, there is here a *of the shield.* strange and miraculous shield, and it hangeth behind the altar, and it hath hung there for God knoweth how long." King Bagdemagus said, "I would fain see that shield." The Abbot replied, "I will show it to you to-morrow morning, but not to-night. For I am come to conduct you to supper, and not to show you a shield."

So, when they were seated at supper, Sir Galahad said to the two knights, "I pray you tell me how you came hitherward to this place." "That I will do," quoth Sir Ewaine. And he said, "Sir Bagdemagus and I set forth from Camelot in search of the Grail. After we had journeyed for a long distance, we came to that part of the forest that is called the Forest of Arroy, or otherwise the Forest of Adventure. Here we wandered for some while without being freed from it, for the Forest of Adventure is not very difficult to find, but is often very difficult to escape from. After a while, however, we found a way to escape from that forest, and so came out upon the further side of it. There we beheld, below us, this place and so we came to it. Such, sir, is the way in which we came hither."

Thus these three knights and the high officers of that monastery ate and drank together, discoursing very pleasantly the while. And when they had ceased eating and drinking and talking together, they were weary, and each withdrew to his couch and to sleep.

Now, when the next morning had come and when they had broken *The Abbot* their fast, King Bagdemagus said to the Abbot, "I pray you *takes the three* now to show us that shield concerning which we spoke last *knights to the* night." The Abbot said, "I will do so. Come with me." *shield.* So he led them to the chapel and he led them behind the altar, and there they beheld the shield where it hung. And the shield was exceedingly white and shining, as it were of brightly polished silver. And upon the shield was marked a red cross, very strong and bold in its marking.

But when King Bagdemagus beheld the shield, he coveted it exceedingly, and he said, "That is a very beautiful shield. I pray you let me *King Bagde-* have that shield for mine own, and I will give my shield to *magus covets* Sir Galahad." To him the Abbot replied, "Messire, I would *the shield.* gladly give you that shield, but there is said of it that whoever taketh it except the one man for whom it is destined, harm shall come to him, and great suffering." King Bagdemagus said, "That may be so, but, haply, I am he for whom it is destined. At any rate, I am a tried and well-approved knight, wherefore if I take it I will essay to keep it, as a knight of standing may hope to keep his shield." The Abbot said to him, "Then take it, sir, in God's name."

So King Bagdemagus took the shield and hung it about his neck. And he said to those other two knights, "Messires, I know not whether there is any malaventure appertaining to this shield, but, at any rate, I shall essay to keep and to hold it. Nevertheless, I pray you to await me here for this day. And if anything happeneth to me, I will return and give you report as to that happening."

To this Sir Galahad and Sir Ewaine replied that they would remain at that place until the following morning.

After that Sir Bagdemagus mounted horse and rode away. And he directed his horse into the forest, and rode there a considerable distance away from the monastery. So, by and by, he came to a place where two highways parted, and where there was a cross of stone, and at *Sir Bagdemagus* that place he beheld a knight in white armor, seated upon a *rides errant into* white horse. This White Knight stood across the way upon *the forest.* which Sir Bagdemagus was travelling, and he appeared to be very threatening and austere. So, when Sir Bagdemagus came pretty close to that White Knight, the White Knight said to him, "Messire, I prithee tell me, where got you that shield that I behold hanging upon your neck?" Sir Bagdemagus said to him, "I got this shield at a monastery of White Friars, at some distance from this." The White Knight said to him, "I bid you take back that shield, and return it whence you got it, for it belongeth not to you." Quoth Sir Bagdemagus, "That will I not do until I am compelled. For now that I have this shield I propose to keep it for mine own, unless it is taken away from me in battle." To this the White Knight replied, "Very well, then, thou shalt do battle for it, and that anon. Now prepare thyself straightway for battle with me."

Upon this each knight made himself ready, and when they were in all ways prepared, they dashed together with great violence. *Sir Bagde-* In that encounter the spear of Sir Bagdemagus passed very *magus is over-* smoothly from the shield of the White Knight, but the spear *thrown by the* of the White Knight pierced the shoulder of Sir Bagdemagus, *White Knight.* over above the shield which protected not that part of his body. And the point of the spear of the White Knight passed through the shoulder of Sir Bagdemagus, so that he was flung with great violence to the earth.

Then anon the White Knight came to where Sir Bagdemagus lay, and he said to him, "Sir, how fares it with you?" Quoth Sir Bagdemagus, "Alas, Messire, I am very grievously hurt, for thou hast pierced through my shoulder with thy lance, and I suffer very greatly."

Therewith the White Knight dismounted from his horse and he lifted and raised Sir Bagdemagus. And after that he had beheld the wound, he laid Sir Bagdemagus upon his horse. Then he took the bridle-rein of Sir Bagdemagus' horse, and he led the horse and the wounded man back to the monastery whence he had that morning come.

So, by and by, they two arrived there, and several came and took the horse of Sir Bagdemagus. And they lifted him from his horse and carried him into the house, and laid him upon a bed, and searched his wound. But when they came to look for the White Knight, he was gone, nor wist they whither he went. And the wound of Sir Bagdemagus was very deep, so that for a long while he hung, as it were, balanced betwixt life and death.

The White Knight bringeth Sir Bagdemagus to the monastery.

But Sir Bagdemagus did not die; otherwise, the next day, he summoned Sir Galahad to him. And when Sir Galahad had come to him, Sir Bagdemagus said to him, "Messire, I had no right to that shield and I suffered for taking it. I believe that it belongeth, indeed, to you; wherefore I pray you for to take it and to wear it, henceforth, for your own. But who that White Knight was who met me, or whence he came, or how he knew that I had that shield, I know not, nor perhaps ever shall know."

To this Sir Galahad answered, "Sir, I will assume that shield and all the dangers that appertain to it, trusting that it belongs to me, and doing battle to retain it if need be."

So Sir Galahad took the shield and hung it about his neck. Then he called for his horse, and mounting upon it he rode away from that place.

Sir Galahad takes the shield.

But King Bagdemagus lay there at the monastery for many days and for several weeks ere he was fit to travel again.

After that Sir Galahad travelled for all that day, and anon, toward the sloping of the afternoon, he was an hungered, and he wist not where he should come at refreshment for to eat. At that time he passed through a little woodland, and when he had traversed it he came out of it upon a small, open place upon the other side of it, where there was a fair meadow of short green grass.

Here he beheld a pavilion of particolored silks, and he beheld that before the pavilion there stood a tall and noble-appearing knight, clad in white armor. This knight, beholding Sir Galahad, said to him, "Sir, whence come you?"

To this Sir Galahad made answer, "Sir, I came from a monastery over yonderways, where I got me this shield." Quoth the White Knight, "Art thou Sir Galahad?" and Sir Galahad replied, "Yea, I am he."

Then the White Knight said to him, "I pray you, sir, to dismount from your horse and to come in and refresh yourself, for I have been awaiting you this long while." And Sir Galahad replied, "Sir, I give you grammercy for your kindness." *Sir Galahad meets the White Knight.*

So the White Knight assisted Sir Galahad to dismount from his horse. And he brought him into the pavilion, and Sir Galahad beheld that there was there set a feast spread ready for his coming. So they seated themselves at table, and three esquires clad in green samite waited upon them, and they both ate and drank of the food and drink that was set before them, and which was very excellent.

Then the White Knight said, "Sir, to-morrow we shall ride together for a little way, meanwhile let us rest here to-night." And Sir Galahad said, "So let it be."

So, by and by, there came two other esquires who took Sir Galahad and brought him to where was a soft and luxurious couch of down, and there he rested and slept for the night.

And when the morrow had come, Sir Galahad arose and the White Knight arose and the esquires came and armed them. Then they each mounted his horse, and so they rode away together.

Now when these two, to wit, Sir Galahad and the White Knight, were thus upon their way, the White Knight said to Sir Galahad, "Sir, wit you what is the story of the Grail, and what is the history of that shield that you wear at your neck?" Sir Galahad said, "Nay, but I pray you to tell me that story." Quoth the White Knight, "I will do so. It is as follows: *The White Knight tells Sir Galahad of the shield.*

"In the old days of Uther Pendragon there were two knights who were twin brothers. One of these knights was hight Balan and the other was hight Balin.

"Now at that time there was in the enchanted city of Sarras two very great marvels; one of these was the spear with which the blessed side was wounded at the time of the crucifixion, and the other was the chalice into which the blood was drained from that deep and pitiful wound. But how they came to the city of Sarras is too long a story to tell.

"Now Sir Balan was in the city of Sarras, and he was entertained at the castle of the king of that country, whose name was King Pischer. This King was at enmity with Sir Balan, whom he very greatly hated. So that night when Sir Balan lay upon his bed, King Pischer, at the head of several men, attacked Sir Balan where he lay unarmed. He, starting up from his sleep, beheld them coming, and so he fled away from those who would assail him, and so he escaped into the chapel of the castle, where those two holy relics—to wit, *How Sir Balan came to Sarras.*

the spear and the chalice—were kept. Hither his enemies followed him and would have slain him, even upon the steps of the altar, only that, beholding the spear, Sir Balan seized upon it and ran with it against them. In that assault he smote King Pischer with the spear, a very great and bitter stroke. For the point of the spear penetrated the corselet of King Pischer, and inflicted a deep wound in the shoulder. And after that Sir Balan attacked the others who were with King Pischer, and drave them all before him. So Sir Balan used that holy spear for his own preservation.

"But as Sir Balan stood holding the spear and beholding his enemies retreat from that place, there came to him a voice as from heaven, saying to him, 'Balan! Balan! what hast thou done?'

"And as the voice ceased its words there came, as from beneath, a deep and hollow rumbling. And the rumbling grew louder and louder, until it *How there came* became a great earthquake, so that the earth rocked beneath *an earthquake.* the feet. Then the chapel and the castle and all that place reeled, and the castle fell, one stone upon another, so that all who were within it were buried beneath the ruins. At the same time the spear and the chalice disappeared from that place, and neither have they ever been seen from that time—saving only that in visions they have been seen. For Sir Percival beheld both the spear and the chalice, and others have beheld them from time to time.

"Sir Balan was not killed by the fall of that castle, nor was King Pischer *How Sir Balan* killed, but all others in the castle perished in its fall. But *escapes.* rather had King Pischer been killed, for that wound in his shoulder remained unhealed, and King Pischer could not die for a long while, though he suffered very greatly from that wound every day that he lived. Such, O Galahad! is the story of the Grail.

"Now touching this shield; wit you it is the shield of Sir Balan, and the way in which it came to the monastery of the White Friars is as followeth:

"One day Sir Balan came to a certain part of the country where was a monastery of White Friars, and where he had news of a knight who guarded the ford of a river at that place. So Sir Balan went to that river and he *How Sir Balan* beheld there the knight guarding the ford. Then Sir Balan *fought with the* attempted to pass the ford, but the knight would not allow *Knight of the* him to do so, wherefore they came to battle with one another. *Ford.* They fought for an entire morning, and for longer than that, and each gave the other many grievous wounds, and what with loss of blood and with continuous fighting they grew ever weaker and weaker, so that neither of them could stand without great ado. But at last Sir Balan gave to his enemy a deadly blow that brought him to the earth.

Then he rushed off his helmet to make an end of him, but when the face beneath was free from its helmet he beheld it, and saw that it was the face of his twin brother, Sir Balin, whom he was about to slay.

"Then he cried out in horror, 'Alas, and woe is me! Is it thou, Balin, whom I am about to slay? Lo! I am thy brother Balan!'

"Then Balin, feeling that he was near to death, wept a great deal. And he forgave his brother Balan, and he bade Balan, when he *How Sir Balan* was dead, to bury him at that place beneath a thorn tree that *slew his brother* grew there and that was covered all over with spikes, as it *Balin.* were a chevaux de frise. Then he died, and Balan performed that task— to wit, to bury him there.

"Anon came several White Friars from a monastery that was near by, and these took Balan to the monastery and there he died, for he was very sorely wounded, and his heart was broken.

"But ere he died he took his shield to him and he drew upon it a great cross in his own blood. And he told the friars of that place to keep that shield until he should come who was to achieve the Holy *How Sir Balan* Grail and to return it unto Sarras again. And Sir Balan *marked the* predicted of that shield that it should always remain bright *shield.* as silver until that time, and that the cross of blood should ever remain as red as it was that day; and he predicted of it that no one should be able to wear that shield saving only that one for whom it was intended; and he predicted of that shield that it should never be pierced by the point of any weapon forged by the hand of man. So it was and such is that shield which thou carriest, Sir Galahad."

All this Sir Galahad listened to and heard, and when the White Knight had ended his words, he said, "Sir, I would that I knew who thou art. I pray thee to tell me that." But to this the White Knight only smiled and made reply, "I may not tell thee who I am, only this I may say, that I am he who hath had that shield under continual surveillance until now, and now I find that it hath fallen into hands that are even better able to care for it and to cherish it than were the hands of Sir Balan of old."

Thus these two knights travelled forward together until night to the setting of the sun. Then at last they came to a place where the roadway divided, and at that place the White Knight said to Sir Galahad, "Messire, here I must leave thee. Continue upon that way and *Sir Galahad* anon thou wilt come to a chapel where thou mayst be re- *parts from the* freshed, and where thou mayst lodge for the night." So *White Knight.* saying, the White Knight saluted Sir Galahad, and he saluted the White Knight again. Then the White Knight rode down one path into the woods, and Sir Galahad entered upon the other path as he had been directed to do.   But Sir Galahad turned his head to look after the White Knight ere he should reach the forest, but lo! he was not there, nor was anything to be seen, saving only the trees of the woodland and the red light of the sunset that lay upon the ground, falling through the leaves of the trees like to liquid gold spread there upon the earth in small, round, and brightly shining discs.

After that Sir Galahad continued upon his way until, anon, he heard the ringing of a bell, and with that he wist where he was, and that he was not far distant from the chapel of the Hermit of the Forest.   So Sir Galahad spurred forward and in a little while he beheld the chapel, and he beheld the Hermit of the Forest, ringing the bell for vespers.

So he came to that place that was very quiet and innocent, for he be-
Sir Galahad lodges with the Hermit of the Forest. held that many birds sat perched upon the branches of the trees coadjacent to that place, and that several of the wild creatures of the woods, together with a wild doe and its fawn, were also there.   For these things loved the Hermit of the Forest, and followed him whithersoever he went about that place.

Then the Hermit of the Forest beheld Sir Galahad and gave him welcome, and he brought him to eat and drink and prepared a lodging for him for the night.

Thus, then, was Sir Galahad armed with his shield, and therewith was he armed completely, for he needed no other thing to arm him for his defence.

So I have told you the history of these doings that you might know of them how they were.   Now, having thus armed him entirely, ·so shall we turn to the further history of the adventures relating to these things.

ir Galahad meets Sir Melyas :·

Chapter Third

How Sir Galahad met with Sir Melyas. How Sir Melyas was overthrown, and how Sir Galahad overthrew his enemies. Also how Sir Galahad did at the Castle of Maidens.

NOW Sir Galahad departed next morning betimes, after he had broken his fast. And he wended his way through the forest, he knew not whitherward. After a considerable while he came to where two roads crossed one another, and where there was a cross of stone. Here was a clear, limpid fountain of cold water, and at the fountain Sir Galahad beheld that there sat a young knight.

This young knight had been refreshing himself with draughts of the water, and now sat with his helmet beside him, whilst the soft and gentle wind blew upon his forehead and his hair.

Anon, when Sir Galahad had come nigh to him he said to the youthful knight, "Sir, I pray you tell me who you are." "I will do so," replied the young knight. "But you must also tell me your name and degree." "That I will do," said Sir Galahad. "Wit you that I am *Sir Galahad* called Galahad, and that I am lately made a knight of King *meets Sir* Arthur's Round Table." "And I," said the other, "am *Melyas.* hight Melyas, and I am the son of the King of Denmark." Quoth Sir Galahad, "I give you grammercy for your information." And he said, "I pray you tell me, what do you here in the forest alone?"

"Last night," said Sir Melyas, "I came hitherward, and since then I have been travelling through the forest. I slept in the woodland then and I have not broken my fast since the prime of yesterday." "Hah!" said Sir Galahad. "Now I will give you advice. Journey whence I came and by this road, and you will, by and by, come to the chapel of the Hermit of the Forest, which is not very far distant. He will give you to eat and to drink."

Quoth Sir Melyas, "I give you thanks, Messire." Thereupon he arose, and assuming his helmet he mounted his horse; and, having saluted Sir

Galahad and Sir Galahad having saluted him, they parted company, each going upon his way.

Now Sir Melyas had not gone half a mile from that place when he met *Sir Melyas meets two strange knights.* two knights, and as Sir Melyas approached them, one of the knights set his horse athwart the way and he said, "Sir, I pray you tell me who you are and whither you go." Him answered Sir Melyas very mildly, "Messire, my name is Melyas, and I travel toward the chapel of the Hermit of the Forest."

Quoth the knight, "Well, sir, since you come hitherward, I will have it that you try a pass with me. So prepare yourself to encounter me forthwith."

Him answered Sir Melyas, "Messire, I have naught against you, but if it is your will that I do battle with you, then I must do so."

So Sir Melyas prepared himself in all ways for that encounter, and the other knight likewise prepared himself, and when both were in all ways ready they launched themselves the one against the other with the utmost *The strange knight overthrows Sir Melyas.* violence. So they met in the midst of the course and the spear of Sir Melyas was broken into a great many pieces in that encounter, but the spear of the other knight held, so that it pierced through the shield of Sir Melyas, wounding him in the side, and casting him with such violence to the earth that he lay there without motion, like one who is dead. Then the other knight leaped from his horse and he ran to Sir Melyas and rushed the helmet from his head and he set his misericordia to his throat, saying, "Yield thee, Sir Knight, or I shall presently slay thee." And Sir Melyas reviving from his swoon said, "Sir, slay me not, for I am sorely hurt."

Now turn we to Sir Galahad:

As he rode onward upon his way, a voice suddenly spoke within him, as it were in his very ears. And the voice said, "Return, Sir Galahad, for Sir Melyas is in peril of his life." And again it said, "Return in haste, for Sir Melyas is in peril of his life."

Thereupon Sir Galahad turned his horse about and set it to the gallop, for he thought that were he mistaken in the voice, then was there no great *Sir Galahad rides to rescue Sir Melyas.* harm done in returning. So he rode back whence he had come. And anon he reached that place where Sir Melyas had fallen, and he beheld the knight kneeling upon Sir Melyas with the misericordia at his throat, and he heard the words that the knight uttered and that Sir Melyas uttered. Then Sir Galahad cried out in a loud voice, "Sir Knight, withhold thy hand. Turn thou to me, for I am here to defend that knight."

Then the knight withheld his hand, and he cried out, "Who art thou, Sir Knight, who cometh hither?" Sir Galahad replied, "It matters not who I am, saving only that I am here to defend that fallen knight." "Well," quoth the other, "let it be that way if such is your will. Make you ready." So the knight arose and ran to his horse and mounted thereon; and he took his spear in hand, and when he was in all ways prepared, each knight took stand for the assault.

Then they rushed together like a thunderbolt and each knight smote the other in the midst of the shield. But the spear of the knight could not penetrate the shield of Sir Galahad; otherwise, it slid away from it as though it had been made of adamant, and in sliding away *Sir Galahad* the spear was broken into several pieces. But the spear of *overthrows the* Sir Galahad held, so that with it he pierced through the shield *strange knight.* of the other, and pierced through his body until the spear's point stood a hand's breadth out behind his back. With that the knight was flung to the earth with such violence that his neck was broken and he lay dead.

When the other knight beheld him fall, he cried out, "Hah, Messire, what have you done? You have slain my brother." Therewith he drew his sword and rushed at Sir Galahad, and Sir Galahad threw aside his spear and drew his sword in defence. Then the knight launched a blow at Sir Galahad, which he turned with his sword and his shield. Then rising in his stirrups he launched a blow at the knight that was like a stroke of lightning for speed and force.

The other knight tried to turn that blow, and he did turn it from his head, but the blow fell upon his left shoulder with great and *Sir Galahad* terrible force, so that the edge of the sword cut through the *overcometh the* epulier of the shoulder and it cut through the flesh and the *other knight.* bone of the arm so that the arm was severed from the trunk.

Then the knight emitted a great loud and bitter cry, and casting aside his sword he set spurs to his horse and sped away through the forest, crying aloud as he spurred, "Oh, God! Alas, and woe is me!"

Then Sir Galahad wiped his sword and thrust it back into its scabbard. And he turned to Sir Melyas, and he said, "Sir, how fares it with you?" Quoth Sir Melyas, "Messire, I am sorely wounded, but you have saved me; for never did I behold so fierce and terrible a blow as that *Sir Galahad* which you struck just now, nor did I think it possible that *bringeth Sir* anyone could strike with such dreadful force as that." Quoth *Melyas to the* Sir Galahad, "Nor could I have struck such a blow were it *Hermit of the* not that meseemed that those two knights represented two great sins; the *Forest.* one of the sin of pride, the other the sin of cruelty. So that thought gave

me, as it were, the strength of ten, wherefore when I struck I struck with
the strength as of ten." After that he turned to the knight lying upon
the ground and found him dead. And he raised Sir Melyas and set him
upon his horse. And he upheld him in that wise and returned with
him to the chapel of the Hermit of the Forest. There the Hermit received Sir Melyas, and laid him upon a couch. And he searched his
wound and dressed it, and Sir Melyas was put to all possible ease
with him.

This was Sir Galahad's first adventure, and so I have told it to you as it
happened, for so have I read it in the ancient history of these things.

Now, after Sir Galahad had quitted that forest he came out the next day
upon a fair and fertile plain. Anon he met an old man and a young lad.
These he saluted, and he said to the old man, "Reverend Sir, I pray you

Sir Galahad heareth of the Castle of the Maidens.

tell me, is there any adventure hereabouts that a young knight
such as I am might undertake to his honor?" Quoth the old
man, "Aye, I know of such an adventure." And he said,
"Know you that there is not far from this a castle called the
Castle of Maidens. At that castle there are ten knights dwelling, who
exact tribute from every passer-by. Moreover, these knights are very
cruel and unruly, for they now govern all this land as with a rod of iron,
exacting taxes from the people thereof where no taxes are due, so that all
in this country groan beneath the burden laid upon them. Pass you by
that castle, fair sir, and you will have adventure enough and to spare
from those ten knights."

Then Sir Galahad inquired, "Whither is that castle whereof thou speakest?" And the old man pointed in a certain direction with his hand,
saying, "Yonderway you will find it." So Sir Galahad gave the old man
grammercy for that which he had told him, and he rode away whitherward
the other pointed.

Anon he came to the crest of a high, steep hill of no very great extent,
and from that hilltop he beheld beneath him a large and noble castle.
And the castle had tall, red roofs of tile, and great quantities of rooks
and daws flew about those roofs like bees about a beehive. And a river
ran down past the castle and beyond it, and where it ran past the castle
the pollard willows were pressed close against the castle walls, because of the
narrowness of the space between the castle wall and the waters of the river.
Beside the walls of the castle there was a town, and the town was very
populous, for Sir Galahad, from the hilltop where he sat, could behold
many people coming and going along the stony streets thereof. Then

Sir Galahad surmised that this must be the Castle of Maidens (though why it was so called he did not know then nor till afterward).

So Sir Galahad gathered up his reins and he rode down that hill and toward the castle, and he was not aware that anyone knew of his coming. But as he rode past the castle beneath the walls thereof, he was of a sudden called to from above. And when he looked up he beheld *Sir Galahad* there a small turret, and he beheld that upon that turret there *cometh to that* stood ten fair maidens, and these were they who called to him. *castle.* Beholding these ten fair young ladies at that place, he bespoke them, saying, "Ladies, heaven keep and defend you. Now, I pray you tell me, what is the name of this castle, and what is it you do here?" They say to him, "Fair Sir, this castle is called the Castle of Maidens. We are prisoners here, and are kept in this duress by ten wicked and discourteous knights, from whom heaven keep you. For if you travel on the road upon which you are journeying, you will pass by the bridge-head of this castle, and they will maybe come down to assail you." To them Sir Galahad said, "Ladies, I know not whether I could do battle with success as one against ten—yet if I considered these knights as being the ten deadly sins, me-thinks I would have strength given to me to do combat with them. Now I pray you tell me, how may I assure myself to meet these knights?"

Quoth one of the ladies upon the turret, "Sir, assuredly thou hast a great heart within thee. Now if thou wilt pursue the way thou art going, thou wilt by and by come by the bridge-head. Thereby thou wilt find an iron horn hanging from a stone pillar. If those knights do not appear, set thou that horn to thy lips and blow upon it, and anon thou wilt behold those ten warriors of whom we have been speaking."

So Sir Galahad saluted them and rode away, and anon he came to where the bridge crossed the stream, and there he beheld the post of *Sir Galahad* stone and from it, hanging by a chain, he beheld the horn of *bloweth the* iron. This horn he set to his lips and blew very loud and shrilly *castle horn.* upon it, so that the walls of the castle echoed back the bleat of that horn.

Soon after that the gates of the castle were opened and the portcullis let fall, and there came thundering forth from that place ten knights, armed cap-a-pie in shining armor.

The foremost of those knights rode up to Sir Galahad and said to him, "Sir, art thou shriven?" "Why ask you that?" said Sir Galahad. "Because," said that knight, "thou art presently to die, therefore thou shouldst be shriven." "So far as that is concerned," said Sir Galahad, "I am not unready to die." "Then," said the other, "thou shalt presently awaken in paradise, since thou art ready for it."

So each knight assumed such stand as appeared to him to be fitting, and each set his spear in rest, and then each dashed at the other with might and main. So they met in the middle of the course with such violence and uproar as was wonderful to see and to hear.

In that encounter the spear of the knight of the castle slipped from the *Sir Galahad overcometh the first knight.* shield of Sir Galahad, and was broken into many pieces, but the spear of Sir Galahad held, wherefore he overthrew that knight with such terrible violence that his neck was broken in his fall, and he lay dead upon the earth.

Then when the other knights beheld the fall of that knight, they cried *Sir Galahad doeth battle with nine.* out, "Hah! A rescue! a rescue!" Therewith they all nine made at Sir Galahad to overwhelm him with numbers. All nine of them struck him upon the shield at one time, but their spears glanced from the shield of Sir Galahad and could not penetrate it, nor was he overthrown by their assault, nor did he lose even a foot from his stirrup.

Then Sir Galahad cast aside his spear and drew his bright, shining sword, and he rode at those nine knights and he rode in amongst them, striking with his blade to the right hand and to the left. Nor could their blows harm him, for in that short time he struck down to the ground three of those knights, so that there were but six of them left.

Then the hearts of those six knights began to fail them, and they bore back across the bridge with intent to enter the castle once more. But meantime the people of the castle, seeing how affairs went with them, had raised the *Sir Galahad overcometh the knights.* bridge and had closed the castle gates against them. Nor would they lower the bridge nor open the gates again, wherefore those knights wist not what to do in their hour of need. Then Sir Galahad was upon them and smote down two more of them and with that the four who were left fled with great speed and he pursued them back across the bridge. And Sir Galahad still pursued them, and he struck once and again, now to the right and now to the left, so that ere they could escape from him and in those two blows Sir Galahad had struck down two more of them. Then the two who were left made their escape and they fled from that place with might and main. And Sir Galahad pursued them also with might and main, but their horses were fresher than his, and so they escaped away from him.

So Sir Galahad rode back again slowly to the castle, and at his coming the gates were opened with great sound of rejoicing. For the streets were full of people of all sorts and conditions, and these lifted up their voices with loud and prolonged applause. And of those eight whom he had overthrown, all of them were dead. For those who had not died by their fall, the people had put to death upon their own account.

Then Sir Galahad said to the chief magistrate of that town, "Where are those ten maidens who bespoke me ere I came to this place?" And the chief magistrate answered him, "Sir, we will bring them to you." So anon came those ladies, and when they had come to Sir Galahad they kneeled before him and kissed his hand and gave him great praise and loud acclaim. Sir Galahad said to them, "Why do you kneel to me, and why do you kiss my hand?" They say to him, "Because of your strength and your prowess." He said, "Nay, that strength and that prowess I gave not to myself; therefore, if I have shown strength and prowess, give praise therefor unto the God who gave them to me, and not to me who am their continent." And he said, "Where is the chief lord of this town?"

The ten maidens said, "Sir, he is our father, and he is a prisoner now in the dungeon of this place. For those ten knights overthrew him and made him prisoner, wherefore he now lieth in duress." Sir Galahad said, "Bring him forth that I may behold him." So several ran to where *Sir Galahad* he was, and anon they returned with him, and the chains *liberates the* that bound him were still upon his hands and feet. Sir *captive lord.* Galahad said, "Let these chains be removed," And when they were taken off of that knight, he said to him, "Take back that which is thine own and oppress not thy people. For so have they been oppressed of late by their ten masters, who were the ten knights whom I have overthrown. But now thine enemies are either slain or put to flight, so that thou art free. Nor shall you ever be put to such pain again."

Then, again, was there great applause.

Then the eldest of those ten maidens said to him, "Sir, will you not rest here awhile with us?" Sir Galahad said, "I may not rest with you, for my time is short and there is much to do in that time; wherefore I must be again upon my way."

So he bade them farewell, and after that he departed from that place, taking with him the thanks and the blessings of all the people dwelling therein. Yet for many long years afterward, the memory of Sir Galahad was held at that place, and parents told to their children, and those children to their children for several generations, how that Sir Galahad of the Grail had come thither and had done those great and redoubtable actions at arms that are herein told of and recounted. For it was not until afterward that he became known as the greatest knight that the world had ever beheld until that time.

Such is the story of Sir Galahad and of the Castle of the Maidens; so he, one knight, overcame the ten knights of that castle, and thus he departed thereafter.

Now turn we from Sir Galahad and take we up the adventures of Sir Launcelot at this time. Wherefore I pray you to read that which followeth.

he Grail is manifested, and Sir *s*
Launcelot sleepeth:

Chapter Fourth

*How Sir Launcelot and Sir Percival met Sir Galahad, and what befell them.
Also how Sir Launcelot beheld the Grail in a dream.*

AFTER Sir Launcelot left the Court of the King of Camelot, he
wended his way from place to place, meeting no adventure anywhere. So, upon a certain day, he came to a farmhouse, close to
the borders of the forest, and there sought shelter for the night.

She who met him was the farmer's wife, and she was both brown and
buxom. Beside her stood two children, holding by the skirts of her garments. She gave Sir Launcelot welcome, and said to him, "Here, to-day,
hath come another knight who hath sought shelter as you now beseech
it." Sir Launcelot said, "Who is he?" She said, "I know not, only that
he is gentle and kind."

So Sir Launcelot entered the house, and he whom he beheld there was
Sir Percival, and at that he was very glad. And Sir Percival *Sir Launcelot*
was also very glad to behold Sir Launcelot. So the next *meets Sir*
morning early, and after they had broken their fast, they *Percival at the*
took horse and rode away very lovingly together. *farmhouse.*

So they journeyed for the great part of that morning, and about high
noontide they had come to a very pleasant part of the country where were
hills covered with green fields rising up against the sky; where were many
pleasant streams and watercourses; and where were flocks and herds
browsing in the long, damp grass of the pasture lands.

Here in a dale where there was a small wooden bridge crossing a glassy
and smooth-flowing river, they beheld a knight coming from the other
direction, and Sir Launcelot and Sir Percival were upon one side of the
bridge, and that knight was upon the other side. And that other knight
was Sir Galahad, though neither of those two knew who he was.

Then Sir Launcelot held up his hand, and he cried out, "Messire, I pray
you for to wait until we have crossed the bridge, for three of us cannot
cross it at the same time."

"Nay, sir," quoth Sir Galahad, "my business does not allow me to wait, so I pray you to let me pass."

"Not so," quoth Sir Launcelot, "I cannot let you pass until you have *Sir Launcelot* proven your right to pass. You must run a tilt with me, *challenges Sir* and if I overthrow you, then will you wait to let us pass; *Galahad at the* but if you overthrow me, then will we wait to let you pass." *bridge.* So said Sir Launcelot, for it did not seem to him to be possible that the strange knight could overthrow him.

So each knight set his spear in rest, and anon each charged with great violence at each other. Thus they swept together like a hurricane, *Sir Launcelot* and so met in the centre of the bridge. In that encounter *is overthrown.* the spear of Sir Launcelot struck the shield of Sir Galahad, directly in the centre thereof; but the blow that he gave glanced aside as if the shield had been a polished mirror. But the spear of Sir Galahad struck Sir Launcelot in the middle of the shield and it held, and so violent was the blow of Sir Galahad that both Sir Launcelot and his steed were overthrown upon the planking of the bridge.

Sir Percival looked with great amazement at the overthrow of Sir Launcelot. Then, crying out in a great voice, "Sir, what have you done? Defend yourself from me!" he drew his sword and rushed forward upon *Sir Percival is* the bridge. And Sir Galahad, when he beheld Sir Percival *wounded.* approach in that manner, cast aside his spear and drew his sword likewise. So, when they met in the middle of the bridge, Sir Percival smote Sir Galahad a great buffet with his sword, which stroke Sir Galahad turned with his shield. Then Sir Galahad rose up in his stirrups and he launched a blow like a thunderbolt against Sir Percival. Sir Percival endeavored to turn that blow with his shield, but he could not turn it, for it smote through his shield and it smote through his helmet and it smote through the iron cap beneath the helmet, and, had the blade not turned in the hand of Sir Galahad, it would have slain Sir Percival. As it was, Sir Percival's head swam beneath that blow and he swooned away, swaying from side to side in his saddle until he fell from his saddle and lay upon the bridge without life or motion, like one who was dead.

But Sir Galahad did not stop to inquire who were those two knights whom he had overthrown, nor did he pause to inquire how badly he had hurt them; but regaining his spear and setting spurs to his horse he rode away from that place, leaving them lying upon the bridge.

Anon Sir Launcelot aroused himself, and he beheld Sir Percival where he lay. Then Sir Launcelot arose and went to Sir Percival, and removed his helmet. And he cast water into the face of Sir Percival so that, in a little while, Sir Percival was aroused from his swoon. Then Sir Launcelot said, "I would God I knew who that knight was, for never have I felt such a blow as I just now received, nor have I ever been so shamed as I was shamed this day." Said Sir Percival, "Wit ye not who that knight was?" and he said, "Meseems it was none other than your son, Sir Galahad." Quoth Sir Launcelot, "At that I would take comfort were he my son, but not at anything else."

Then each knight mounted his horse, and so together they presently rode away from that place. But Sir Launcelot's head hung down upon his breast, for the memory of that blow which had overthrown him, and for the shame thereof; for never had he been overthrown from his horse before this day in all of his life. And, somewhiles, he thought that he who had overthrown him was, maybe, Sir Galahad, and at that he took comfort, because Sir Galahad was his son. But otherwhiles he thought that it was not Sir Galahad, and then he was filled with shame because of his overthrow.

So riding in that wise they, by and by, came to where the road divided into two ways, and here Sir Launcelot said, "Sir, let us part *Sir Launcelot* company, for you shall take one road and I will take the *and Sir Per-* other." Quoth Sir Percival, "Are you then weary of riding *cival part* with me?" "Nay," said Sir Launcelot, "but I have been *company.* overthrown and I am ashamed." Said Sir Percival, "What shame do you take in that, seeing it was your own son that overthrew you?" But to this Sir Launcelot made no reply.

Then, seeing that Sir Launcelot was determined to quit him, Sir Percival took the left-hand road, and Sir Launcelot took the right-hand road, and so they parted.

Now follow we Sir Launcelot after they had thus separated.

Sir Launcelot rode for the rest of that day without meeting further adventure, until about evening time, when he came to a bare and naked knoll covered with furze bushes. Here, in the midst of that wild, he beheld an ancient ruined chapel, and he said to himself, "Here *Sir Launcelot* will I rest me for the night." So he rode around that chapel, *findeth a* seeking for the door thereof, but he could find no door upon *deserted chapel.* any side of the chapel, but only windows, very high raised from the ground. And he could not enter that chapel by any of its windows, because they were built in the wall so far beyond his reach that he could not attain to them. Then Sir Launcelot said, "This is a very strange chapel that it should have no doors, but only windows so high that I cannot enter by them. Now I will rest here and see what is the meaning of this place."

So saying, he dismounted from his horse, and lay down beneath a thorn-bush that was not far distant from the chapel.

Now, as Sir Launcelot lay there, a drowsiness began to descend upon him, and though he could not sleep yet it was as though he did sleep, for he could move nor hand nor foot. Yet was he conscious of all that passed about him as though he had been wide awake. For he was conscious of the dark and silent vaults of sky, sprinkled all over with an incredible number of stars, and he was conscious of his horse cropping the herbage beside him in the darkness, and he was conscious of the wind that blew across his face, and that moved the corner of his cloak in the silence of the night time. Of all these things was he conscious, and yet he could not move of his own will so much as a single hair.

Anon, whilst he lay in that wise he was presently aware that some *There cometh* people were approaching the chapel in the darkness, for he *a wounded* heard the sound of voices and of the feet of horses moving *knight.* upon the road. So, in a little while, there came to that place a knight and an esquire. And the knight was very sorely wounded, for his armor was broken and shattered by battle, and the esquire sustained him in the saddle so that, except for the upholding of the esquire's arm and hand, he would have fallen prostrate down upon the ground.

Then Sir Launcelot, as he lay in that waking sleep, heard the knight say to the esquire, "Floradaine, is the chapel near at hand, for mine eyes are failing and I cannot see." And the esquire wept and he said, "Yea, Lord, it is here. Sustain yourself but for a little and you will be there."

To this the knight made answer, "Floradaine, I cannot sustain myself for long." And the esquire said, "It is here." The knight said, "Give thanks to God for that, for had it been a little farther I would have fallen from my horse. Now, Floradaine, lift me to earth."

Therewith the esquire drew rein and he dismounted from his horse and he lifted the knight down from his charger, and the knight groaned very dolorously as the esquire lifted him down. Then, breathing very heavily and with great labor, the knight said, "Floradaine, is there a light?" And the esquire said, "Not yet, Messire." Again, after a little, the knight said, "Is there yet a light?" And again the esquire answered, "Not yet, Messire." And again, after awhile, the knight said for the third time, "Floradaine, is there yet a light?" And this time the knight breathed the words as in a whisper of death. Then of a sudden the esquire called out in a loud and joyful voice, "Yea, Lord, now I behold a light!"

All this Sir Launcelot beheld in that waking dream, and though it was in the darkness of night, yet he beheld it very clearly, as though it were by the sun of noonday. For he beheld the face of the knight that it was white as of pure wax, and that the sweat of death stood in beads upon his forehead. And he beheld that the esquire was young and fair, and *There cometh* that he had long ringlets of yellow hair that curled down *a light.* upon his shoulder. Then when the esquire said that he beheld a light, Sir Launcelot beheld the windows of the chapel that they were illuminated from within with a pale blue lustre, as though the dawn were shining in that chapel. And he heard the sound of chaunting voices, at first very faint and far away, but anon ever growing stronger and stronger as the light from the chapel grew stronger. And those voices chaunted a melody that was so sweet and ravishing that it caused the heart to melt as with an agony.

Then the walls of that chapel opened like a door and a light shone forth with a remarkable lustre so that it illuminated the face of that dying knight, and of the page who upheld him. And at the same time the song burst forth in great volume, as it were a thunder of chaunting.

Then forthwith there came out of the chapel a bright shining spear, and two fair hands held the spear by the butt, yet Sir Launcelot could not behold the body to whom those two hands belonged. And after the spear there came forth a chalice, and two fair, white hands held that chalice, but neither could Sir Launcelot behold any body to which those hands belonged. And the chalice seemed to send forth a light of such dazzling radiance that it was as though one looked at the bright and shining sun in his glory.

Then Sir Launcelot was aware that this was the Holy Grail of which he was in search, and he strove with all his might to arouse *Sir Launcelot* himself, but he could not do so. Then the tears burst out *beholdeth the* from his eyes and traced down his cheeks in streams, but *Grail in a* still he could not arouse himself, but lay chained in that *dream.* waking sleep.

So the chalice advanced toward that knight, but the knight had not strength to reach forth and touch it. Then the esquire took the arm of the knight and raised it, and he raised the hand of the knight so that the hand touched the chalice.

Then it was as though Sir Launcelot beheld the virtue of the Grail go forth from it, and that it passed through the hand of the *The Grail* wounded knight, and that it passed through his arm and *healeth the* penetrated into his body. For he beheld that the blood *wounded* ceased to flow from that wounded knight, and that the color *knight.* flooded back into his cheeks and that the light came back into his eyes and that the strength returned to his body.

Then the knight arose and he kneeled down before the Grail, and he set his palms together and he prayed before the Grail.

Then, slowly, the light that had been so bright from the Grail began to wane. First the spear disappeared, and then the hands that held it disappeared. Then, for awhile, the Grail glowed with a faint, pallid light, and then it, too, vanished, and all was dark as it had been before.

So Sir Launcelot beheld the vision of the Grail, but as in the vision of a dream as I have told it here to you. And still the tears rained from his eyes, for he could not rouse himself to behold it with his waking eyes.

After this the knight and the esquire approached to the place where Sir Launcelot lay asleep, and the esquire said to the knight, "Messire, who is this man, and why sleepeth he here whilst all these wonders pass him by?" And the knight said, "This knight is a very sinful man, and his name is Sir Launcelot of the Lake." Quoth the esquire, "How hath he sinned?" To which the knight replied, "He hath sinned in this way. He had a beautiful and gentle lady, and he deserted that wife for the sake of Queen Guinevere. So his lady went away and left him, and anon she gave birth to Galahad, and in that birth she also gave her life. So Sir Launcelot betrayed his wife, and because of that betrayal he now lieth sleeping, and he cannot waken until after we are gone away from this place."

The knight taketh Sir Launcelot's horse. Then the esquire said to the knight, "Messire, behold; here this knight hath a good, strong horse. Take thou this horse and leave thine own in its stead. For this horse is fresh and full of life, and thine is spent and weary with battle." And the knight said, "I will take that horse."

So the knight took the horse of Sir Launcelot instead of his own. And he left his own horse behind him. Then he mounted the horse of Sir Launcelot and the esquire mounted his horse, and after that the knight and the esquire rode away from that place.

Then, after they had gone, Sir Launcelot bestirred himself and awoke. And he would have thought that all that he had beheld was a dream, but he beheld the worn and weary horse of the knight was there, and that his horse was gone. Then he cried aloud in great agony of soul, "Lord, my sin hath found me out!" And therewith he rushed about like a madman, seeking to find a way into that chapel, and finding no way.

Sir Launcelot is absolved by the Hermit of the Forest. So when the day broke he mounted the worn and weary horse that the knight had left, and he rode away from that place and back into the forest; and his head hung low upon his breast. When he had come into the forest and to the cell of the hermit thereof, he laid aside his armor and he kneeled down before the Hermit of the Forest, and confessed all his sins to him. And the Hermit of the Forest gave him absolution for these sins, and he said, "Take peace, my son. For although thou shalt not behold the Grail in thy flesh, yet shall God forgive thee these sins of thine that lie so heavily upon thy soul."

Then Sir Launcelot arose chastened from his confession. And he left his armor where it lay and assumed the garb of an anchorite. And he went away from that place, into the remoter recesses of the forest. There he dwelt in the caves and in the wilds, living upon berries and the fruits of the forest. And he dwelt there a long time until he felt assured that God had forgiven him. Then he returned to his kind again; but never after that day was he seen to smile.

So hath this been told to you that you may see how it is that the sins that one hath committed follow one through one's life and in the end bring the soul such distress and failure as that which Sir Launcelot here suffered and endured. For it hath already been told in another volume than this book (which same is called "The Story of Sir Launcelot and His Companions") how that Sir Launcelot of the Lake remained at the Court of King Arthur whilst his Lady, Elaine the Fair, quitted the court, and how that he remained at that court, being held there by the wiles and the charms of Queen Guinevere. Then it was told how that the Lady Elaine died for loneliness and grief in giving birth to Galahad, and it was told how that Sir Launcelot repented him for that death with deep and bitter remorse.

So it was because of that sin that he was not now permitted to behold the Grail with his waking eyes nor to touch it with his living hands. For a sin doth not quit a man because he hath remorse for it nor is it wiped from his soul because he repents him of it, but always it remaineth by him and by and by the time cometh when he must pay to the full the account of that sin which he hath one time committed.

For so it is with all of those who commit a sin, be it great or be it less. For they cannot correct that sin by remorse or by repentance, but only by so living a life of righteousness that that sin shall be removed away from them, so that it becometh as though it were not.

So it was with Launcelot, for he was to pay in full for that sin which he had committed. For never did he behold the Grail other than it was at that time and never did he touch it with his hand; nay; never did he touch it even with so much as a single finger; but otherwise he remained as a recluse in a cell coadjacent to the cell of the Hermit of the Forest, as aforesaid.

There leave we him to follow the other parts of this story, for here followeth the story of Sir Percival, which you are now to read if you would enter further into the history of these things herein told of.

Sir Percival rideth the black horse:

Chapter Fifth

Sir Percival findeth a horse that nearly bringeth him to destruction. Also he meeteth a fair damsel and feasts with her. Finally he enters a boat and there finds rest and comfort.

NOW, after Sir Percival had left Sir Launcelot as aforetold of, he rode upon his way alone. And his way led him, by and by, through a waste of land where was nothing growing, but where there were great quantities of stones scattered all over the earth. Here he rode for some time, looking forward before him for something that grew.

So while the mind of Sir Percival was elsewhere, the horse which he rode slipped his foot upon a round, loose stone, and the stone turned under the horse's foot so that it strained its shoulder. At first *Sir Percival's* Sir Percival knew naught of this mishap, but presently, anon, *horse falleth* the horse began to limp as it walked. And every minute the *lame.* horse of Sir Percival limped worse than it had limped the minute before. So Sir Percival wist not what to do, for here was he with a horse that could not fare farther with him, and there was no house within sight, and there was no person within sight upon all that barren waste.

So Sir Percival dismounted from his horse, and he took the bridle of the horse over his arm, and so he walked with the bridle over his arm and the horse limped behind him.

Thus he travelled for a great way, and anon he left that stony waste behind him, and came to a country where green things grew. And anon after that he came to a place that was spread all over with fertile fields of grass interspersed with plantations of trees, both oak trees and elm trees.

Here, passing by a small fountain of water, he beheld a fair damsel sitting beside the margin of that fountain, and the damsel was *Sir Percival* clad all in red, from top to toe. This damsel had with her *meeteth a* a palfrey and a great black horse beside that palfrey, and *damsel in red.* the black horse was very remarkable for breadth and sinew, for his shoulders were deep and his legs were corded with muscles, and his fetlocks were adorned with long and curling hairs, and his eyes were very bright and shining as with fire beneath them, and his ears were sharp and pointed, as though they had been cut with a fine knife, and his mane and tail were thick and black, like the clouds of night, and there was not a white hair upon him, from the tip of his nose to the end of his tail.

Quoth Sir Percival, "Hah, maiden, that is a fine horse that thou hast there." Said she, "Yea, Messire; he is a very fine horse." Said Sir Percival, "I would that thou wouldst sell me that horse; for *The damsel giveth a horse to Sir Percival.* mine own, as thou seest, is gone lame." The maiden said, "Sir, are you not Sir Percival of Gales?" Then Sir Percival was greatly astonished that the damsel should know him, and he said, "Yea, damsel, that is my name." "Then," quoth she, "I cannot accept money from you for this horse. But if you will take him for your own, then you may have him. So leave you your lame horse here, and take this horse instead of it. For wit you I have been sent with this horse that you might have it to ride upon."

Then was Sir Percival still more astonished at what the damsel said, and he knew not what to think that the damsel should be there at that place with a fresh, sound horse for his use when his own horse had fallen lame. So he thanked the damsel in great measure, and he handed her the reins of his horse, and took the reins of the black horse. Then he put his foot in the stirrup and mounted the black horse at one leap.

So the horse stood quite still until Sir Percival had his seat and his feet in the stirrups. After that it bowed its head and took the bit in *The horse rideth away with Sir Percival.* its teeth. Then immediately it rushed away to the southward with great speed like the wind, and its mane and tail stood out straight behind it because of its speed. Nor could Sir Percival control or guide it, for the horse held the bit between its teeth and it was as though blinded, rushing forward like the wind. And ever it ran toward the southward, without let or stay. And Sir Percival said to himself, "What sort of a beast is this upon which I am sitting, is it a horse or is it a lion or is it a dæmon?"

So the horse rushing onward began, by and by, to draw nigh to the sea, for now and then Sir Percival could catch glimpses of the sea across the *The horse bringeth him to the sea.* uplands like a thread of bright silver against the distant horizon; for by this time night had fallen. And anon he could hear the roaring of the sea beating upon a place where there were a great many rocks, and where the water spouted and churned amongst the rocks as white as milk. Then, reaching this spot, the horse stopped all of a sudden, panting and trembling and all a lather with sweating foam.

Then Sir Percival dismounted from the horse, and as soon as his foot touched the earth the black horse vanished and Sir Percival stood there alone. And he wist not what to do, but stood there doubting and wondering.

Anon as he so stood he beheld something coming a great way off, and ever it came nearer and nearer, and by and by he perceived that it was a boat, and that it was approaching very rapidly the place where he stood, and that without either sails or oars to urge it upon its course. *Sir Percival* So Sir Percival stood there and watched the boat as it drew *meeteth a* rapidly nearer to him, and by and by he perceived that there *beautiful lady.* was someone in the boat, and then he perceived that it was a beautiful lady, and that there were seven beautiful damsels attendant upon her. And he beheld that this lady was clad all in red, and that her hair was red, the color of gold, and that it was emmeshed in a net of gold. And around her dress and her neck he beheld that there were chains and ornaments of gold, so that the lady sparkled and gleamed as though she had been an image of jewels and of gold. And the attendants of the lady were also clad in red and also wore ornaments of gold about their necks, wherefore the whole boat gleamed and shone as with a shine of golden light.

Thus that boat came to the beach where Sir Percival stood, and the lady stepped from the boat upon the sand, and Sir Percival came forward and assisted her to disembark. And the lady said, "Hail, Sir Percival, and give thee peace." And all the attendants of that lady also said, "Give thee peace."

Quoth Sir Percival, "Who are ye who know me and I know not you?" To the which the lady made reply, "We are fay and not of this earth, therefore we know many things that you wit not of."

Then that lady bade her attendants to set up a pavilion and they did so, and the pavilion was of red samite, and above it was a great *Sir Percival* banner of white samite embroidered with the figure of a *sits at feast* leopard in threads of gold. And in the pavilion they set a *with the lady.* table of gold, and they covered the table with a napkin of finest linen, and the lady of the boat took Sir Percival by the hand and led him into the pavilion.

Then Sir Percival and the lady seated themselves at the table, and the damsels attendant upon the lady served them with food. And certain of these attendant maidens took harps into their hands, and they played upon the harps, and sang in unison to those two, and so sweet was the music they made that it melted the heart to listen to them.

And those who waited upon Sir Percival and the lady brought to them all manner of dishes, dressed with spices and condiments of all sorts, and Sir Percival and the damsel ate together. Then others brought wines of all sorts, both white wines and red, and this wine was very powerful and sweet, and Sir Percival and the lady drank together. And the wine flowed very strongly through the veins of Sir Percival so that his head swam with the strength of that wine and with the potency thereof.

Then, by and by, the lady grew very fond toward Sir Percival, and she put her arms about his shoulders and held him very close to her. With this the wine swam still more powerfully in Sir Percival's head, and he knew not very well what he said or did. And he said, "Lady, tell me— what is this, and why am I here?" To this she answered, "Percival, thou glorious knight! this is the pavilion of Love, and I am the spirit of Venus who inhabits it. So yield thou to that spirit and take thou the joy of thy life whiles thou mayst."

Therewith she reached her arms again to Sir Percival and he reached *Sir Percival* his arms toward her and he took her into his arms. And *kisses the lady.* Sir Percival kissed her upon the lips and the fire from her lips passed into his heart and set his soul aflame.

Then, in that moment, he knew not why, he suddenly bethought him of that fair lady whom he had met in the tent when first he went forth as a knight, clad in his armor of wicker-work. And he thought of how he had kissed her that time; and he thought of how he had beheld her in that cold and windy room of the castle, lying dead and white before him; and he thought of how he had beheld the Spear and the Grail that time in the castle. Then it was as though a wind of ice struck across the flame of his passion, and he cried out thrice in a loud voice, "God! God! God! What is this I would do, and why should I sin in this wise?" And therewith he drew upon his forehead the sign of the cross.

Then in an instant the lady who sat beside him shrieked very loud and *The lady* shrill, and all about him was confusion and turbulence. And *disappears.* Sir Percival looked, and behold! it was not a strange and beautiful lady who sat beside him like a wonderful goddess, but it was the Enchantress Vivien, clad in red and bedecked with her jewels. For it was she who had thus planned the undoing of Sir Percival by causing him to sin.

Then Sir Percival cried, "Hah! Is it thou who wouldst betray me?" And therewith he reached for his sword which he had laid aside. Then, seeing what he intended, the Enchantress Vivien shrieked again, and she smote her hands together, and in that instant she disappeared, and all her attendants disappeared, and the pavilion and the table and all of the feast and wine disappeared, and the boat in which she had come disappeared, and Sir Percival found himself sitting alone upon the seaside.

Then Sir Percival kneeled down and he set his hands together and he prayed. And he said, "O God! how hast thou saved thy servant by means of a floating thought? For the thought of that which was sacred and holy hath purged my sin that was very close to me." And he said, "How shall I thank thee for this; for lo! I trod upon a crust so thin that, had I borne even a part of my weight upon it, I would have fallen through that crust as into a lake of fire."

So he prayed for a long time and by and by he was comforted. Then he arose and stood up, and he girded his sword tight about him. And he cast his eyes all around and he beheld that he was alone and in a very desolate place. And, at that time, the full moon was shining very brightly.

Anon he beheld in the gloom of the distance an object that approached very rapidly. And this object also was a boat, but there was no one in it.

And when the boat approached nigh enough he beheld that there was a couch within it, and that the couch was covered with white linen. But no other thing was in the boat but that.

Then Sir Percival said, "What is this? Is there a sin also in this, or is it without sin?" And he said, "If this be sin, then let it declare itself," and therewith he marked the sign of the cross upon his forehead.

But there followed not any malignant sign after that, but the boat remained there where it was.

Then Sir Percival perceived that it was intended for him to enter that boat, and he did enter it. And at that time the moon had *Sir Percival* arisen very full and round. And the moon shone down upon *entereth a* the earth with a wonderful radiance. So that what with the *boat.* light in the sky from the moonlight, it was as though a strange and magical radiance embalmed the entire earth.

Then the boat moved away from the shore very rapidly and smoothly. And it ran past the sharp and treacherous rocks, and it went *The boat sails* past all obstructions and so out into the broad and heaving *away with* surface of the sea beyond. *him.*

Here all was stillness and peace, for all about was the hush and silence of night time, and there was no sound whatsoever to mar that stillness, but only the moon and the stars shining above in the sky.

So Sir Percival laid him down upon the couch and anon he slept a very deep and dreamless sleep.

Now leave we Sir Percival lying in that boat, and turn we to the story of Sir Bors de Ganis and how it befell with him at this time.

ir Bors rides with the white knight:

Chapter Sixth

*How Sir Bors confessed himself to the Hermit of the Forest. How he over-
threw a knight, and how he came to the seashore and of what befell him
there.*

UPON a certain day Sir Bors rode into the forest, and by and by he
came to the chapel of the Hermit of the Forest. And the Hermit
welcomed Sir Bors, saying, "God save thee," and Sir Bors greeted
the Hermit, saying, "God save thee and keep thee, Sir Hermit." So Sir
Bors abided that night with the Hermit of the Forest, and when the
next morning had come he besought the Hermit to confess
him. And the Hermit of the Forest shrived Sir Bors, and he *Sir Bors con-*
beheld that the soul of Sir Bors was very white and clean and *Hermit of the*
that he was extraordinarily free from sin. And the Hermit *Forest.*
said to him, "Sir, if valor and if purity of life may so recommend a man
that he may win the Grail, then will you certainly behold it with the eyes
of your body and touch it with the hand of your flesh. For you are both
very brave and very pure of life."

To this Sir Bors said, "Sir, that which you tell me is exceedingly comfort-
ing to me, for so would I rather achieve a sight of the Grail and touch that
sacred vessel than anything else in all the world. Now, I pray you, tell me
if there is anything else that I may do that may better fit me to find that
holy chalice."

Quoth the Hermit, "There is but one thing, and that thing is that you
finally purify yourself by refraining from eating any manner of meat, and
that you fast upon bread and water until you have beheld and *Sir Bors vows*
have touched the Grail." Said Sir Bors, "Holy Father, so will *a fast.*
I fast from meat and wine." And the Hermit said, "And this also shall
you do. You shall lay aside your armor and shall ride forth in leathern

doublet and hose and shall wrap yourself in your red cloak against the inclemencies of the weather." Said Sir Bors, "That also will I do."

So Sir Bors laid aside his armor of defence, and he wrapped himself in his red cloak, and thus he rode forth into the world.

After that Sir Bors travelled for an entire day, and whensoever he came to a roadside cross, he kneeled down before it and recited a prayer. So against early eventide he came to a part of the country that was altogether strange and new to him, for here were bogs and marshes, and many pools and ponds of water where were heron and other water-fowl. So Sir Bors wist not where he should lodge that night. But anon he beheld in the distance before him a single tower standing upright upon that flat expanse, and the tower was like a finger of stone pointing up into the sky. So Sir Bors made his way toward the castle, and by and by he came to where the castle was.

Coming to that place Sir Bors smote upon the doorway of the castle, *Sir Bors cometh* and he smote again and again. By and by one came and *to a castle.* opened the door, and that one was a very aged porter clad all in buckram, and the buckram was stained and blotched, as with the stain of many years.

The porter said to Sir Bors, "Sir, who are you, and whence come you?" And to this Sir Bors made reply, "I am one seeking lodging and shelter for the night." The porter said, "Sir, I pray you enter, for you are exceedingly welcome, and the lady of this castle, though just now in very great sorrow, is about to sit at supper."

So Sir Bors entered the courtyard, and he tied his horse to an iron ring that was in the side wall of the castle in the courtyard. Then the aged porter led Sir Bors to his room and there left him to wash and to refresh himself, whilst he returned to the horse to put it into the stable and to feed it.

After Sir Bors had washed and refreshed himself he descended from his room again, and there he found the aged porter awaiting him. The porter said, "Sir, come with me," and Sir Bors followed him. And the porter led the way from that place into a hall, where there was a table set out for refreshment.

Here Sir Bors beheld a young and very beautiful lady, and she was the chatelaine of the castle. The face of this lady was very white and exceedingly sorrowful, and her eyelids were red as with continual weeping. And she was clad in a long, straight black robe, without ornament or adornment of any sort. She received Sir Bors with great civility, albeit she did not smile at all; and anon they sat down at table together.

So the supper was brought in and set before them, and it was the old porter who served them with their meal. But Sir Bors ate no meat, neither did he drink any wine; otherwise, he ate of the bread and drank of the water that was set before them. Anon the chatelaine of *Sir Bors sups* the castle said to him, "Sir, you do not eat of the food of the *with a beauti-* castle that is set before you. How doth that happen?" *ful lady.* Quoth he, "Lady, I do not eat the food because I have assumed a vow to eat no meat of any sort until I have accomplished a certain purpose, and I drink the water because I have made the same vow concerning wine." And the lady said, "To what purpose is that, Messire?" Quoth he, "I am in quest of the Grail, and to that end I travel, fasting and mortifying myself."

Then, after a little while, he said to her, "Lady, you are sad, will you not tell me the cause of your sorrow?" To the which she said, "Sir, that will I gladly do. It is thus: my father was the king of all this land as far as you can see to the westward of this. For this castle standeth *The lady tells* upon the marches of my father's country, and is very near to *her story.* the lands of another king who is neighbor to this place. My mother died, and my father married another lady who was both wicked and cruel. So when my father died this lady seized upon my inheritance, and cast me out into the world upon mine own dependence. After that she drove me from castle to castle until this is my last refuge and defence. For now I dwell herein with only this ancient porter and his wife in attendance upon me. Nor is she satisfied to leave even this poor house in my possession, for to-morrow she cometh with several knights to drive me forth from this my last refuge."

So said the Lady Chatelaine of that place, and when she had ceased speaking she wept with a passion of tears. Then the heart of Sir Bors was greatly moved with sympathy, and he said to her, "Lady, I am greatly grieved at thy sorrow and at its cause." And he said, "What *Sir Bors offer-* is thy name?" She said, "It is Leisette." Then said Sir *eth himself for* Bors, "Lady Leisette, let me tell thee that had I but a suit of *her defence.* armor to wear, I would stand as thy defender upon this occasion, and that to-morrow I would stand between thy father's wife and thee, even though the knights that follow her be several and I be but one." "Sir," said the lady, "It may hardly be that one knight could withstand the assault of several; but I may tell you that in this castle there is a suit of armor (though of a bygone date), that might serve your purpose. But to what end would you use it? For the knights attendant upon this lady are all well-tried knights of battle, and you are maybe not accustomed to wearing armor, seeing that you travel through the world without armor of any sort upon your body." Then Sir Bors smiled, and he said, "Let that be as it may; nevertheless, I have worn armor more than once in my life; so I pray you to send that suit of armor to my room to-night, that I may look at it, and perhaps try it on." And the lady said, "It shall be done as you ask."

So that night the old porter brought the armor to the room of Sir Bors, and he assisted Sir Bors to clothe himself in the armor, and Sir Bors found that the armor fitted him very exactly, and he was glad.

Now when the next day was come Sir Bors walked with the Lady Leisette in the gardens of the castle. And Sir Bors beheld that she was exceedingly beautiful and his heart went out to her, and he said to her, "Lady, meseems your trouble lyeth in this, that you have no knight for your husband who may defend your rights and claims. Were you wedded to such a knight, then, you would not suffer these wrongs." Quoth she, "What knight would take me for his wife, who am a dowerless lady, with only one castle left of all her inheritance?"

He said to her, "I say naught concerning myself and mine own strength and valor. But this I will say, that if I have such fortune as may lead me to overcome your enemies to-day, I would offer myself to you as your hus- *Sir Bors talketh at length with the lady.* band." She said, "Sir, thou doest me great courtesy. Were I owner of those three considerable towns that were once my father's then I would take thee for my suitor. But as I am now the puppet of so sad a fate, what shall I say to thee?" Quoth he, "Say aye." And she said, "Who art thou, sir?" Quoth he, "I am called Sir Bors de Ganis." Then she said, "Aye," speaking with downcast eyes, and so low a voice that he could hardly hear her. For the name of Sir Bors was very well known throughout the entire world, both because of his strength and his valor. Wherefore she was very much pleased to have him with her.

Just then there came to them the old porter of the castle and he said to them, "Prepare yourselves, for hither cometh the Queen of this country, together with a court of lords and ladies, and with several knights champion for her escort." Then Sir Bors said, "Now I will go and arm myself for battle." And she said, "Go!"

So Sir Bors withdrew to his room and the porter of the castle went with him, and the porter put upon him the pieces of armor and buckled them very tightly together so that they joined and fitted. And they buckled a great sword upon one side of him and a misericordia upon the other. Then when he was in all wise prepared, he took a mighty lance into his hand and went down into the courtyard and mounted upon his horse. Then came the Lady Leisette to him and saluted him and he said to her, "Give me, I pray you, some favor for to wear." And she said, "I will do so," and therewith gave him the scarf from about her throat. And she tied the scarf about his arm. Then the porter of the castle opened the gate, and Sir Bors rode forth from the castle and took his stand in the high-road in front of the castle, and awaited the coming of those others who were now drawing near to that place.

Anon the Queen of that country perceived Sir Bors where he stood and she cried out to him, "Sir, who are you who stand there, and why do you confront us so?" To the which Sir Bors made reply, "Lady, I am the champion of the lady of this castle, and as her knight I stand here to await your coming." *Sir Bors offereth himself as champion.*

She said to him, "Know you to whom you speak?" and he said, "Yea, I know very well; therefore I am here."

Then the Queen was very angry, and she cried out to one of her knights, of whom there were seven in all, "Remove this man from our path so that we may enter the castle and turn out of it that lady who now holdest it."

Thereupon, with that saying, the knight to whom she spoke rode forth from the others, and he said to Sir Bors, "Sir, will you do battle with me?" Quoth Sir Bors, "Very gladly, and for that purpose am I here."

So each knight prepared himself in all wise for battle, and when each had assumed his proper place, the word of command was given and they rushed together, thundering and with great violence. So they met in the midst of the course, and in that encounter the spear of the knight who assaulted Sir Bors was broken into as many as twenty or thirty pieces, but the spear of Sir Bors held, so that the knight was hurled out of his saddle and down to the earth with such violence that his neck was broken, and he died. *Sir Bors overthroweth the knight.*

Then the Queen was astonished that her chiefest knight should be so overthrown, and therewith she cried out to her other six knights, "Hey, Messires! Assault him all at once so that he may be overthrown, and so that we may enter this castle!" So, upon that word of command, all six of those knights drew their swords and rushed upon Sir Bors. He, beholding them coming thus, threw aside his spear and drew his brightly shining sword, and so they all met together, Sir Bors in the midst of them.

In that battle he well proved his right to be a knight of the Round Table, for he wheeled his horse to this side and to that, and ever as he wheeled it about he smote from right to left and from left to right. Two knights fell before those strokes, and then another fell, so that there were but three left standing against him.

These, seeing how he dealt with them, presently bore back before his fierce assaults, and so he sat for awhile, panting for breath, and with the crimson flowing from several wounds he had received.

Then the Queen chided the three knights, crying out upon them, "How now! How now! Are you, three knights, afraid of that one knight who is already wounded in several places? Go ye against him and overthrow him!"

But ere these three could bring themselves to assail him again, he, not waiting for their assault, rushed upon them shouting and in that sudden assault he smote down another of them with his sword. Then the two who were left, beholding their comrade fall, were filled with terror and dismay. Their hearts melted like wax within them, and they drew rein and turned and immediately fled from that place.

So Sir Bors pursued them thence shouting, and the two fled straight through the midst of the court of the Queen, and the court dissolved away to right and left from before them, shrieking with terror. Just beyond *Sir Bors chases the fleeing knights.* the purlieus of that court Sir Bors overtook the first of those two who fled, and he smote him so that he fell like a sack from his horse, and rolled over and over upon the ground. Then anon he reached the last of those knights, and coming to him he rose up in his stirrups and smote him with all his might and main. And the blade of that sword shore through the helmet of that knight and it shore through the iron cap beneath the helmet, and it shore through his skull to the throat. Then that knight emitted a dreadful groan, and fell dead to the earth, and his horse galloped on without him.

Then Sir Bors rode back again to that court, and he rode up to the Queen with a threatening countenance, and at his coming she was struck as white as an ash of wood. And Sir Bors said to her, "Lady, what do you here at this place?" Then the Queen trembled before him, and anon she said, "Sir, I come hither seeking my rights." He said, "Those rights you seek are not yours, they are another's. Come with me."

So saying, he suddenly catched her horse by the bridle and drew her thence, and no one of all that court dared to prevent him. And Sir Bors *Sir Bors takes the Queen into the castle.* led the horse of the Queen toward that solitary tower of stone, and when he reached the gate he cried out aloud, "Open to me!" Then the porter of that castle opened the gate thereof, and Sir Bors led the Queen into the castle. Then the porter shut the gate of the castle again, and the Queen was within the walls of the castle and her court of lords and ladies was without the walls thereof.

All this the lady of the castle had beheld from the battlements, and her heart was filled with joy and triumph thereat. So anon when Sir Bors appeared upon the roof of the turret where she was, she ran to him and catched him and embraced him with great passion, wounded as he was.

But Sir Bors put her aside, and he went to the edge of the wall, and he spake to the court of the Queen, saying, "Why wait ye there? Your Queen is here with us, and here she shall remain our prisoner until justice is done to the lady of this castle. So return ye to your towns and tell them this word of mine to you: that justice must be done to this lady, or else she who called herself Queen cannot go free."

After that he withdrew himself from their sight, and he went to his room where he might bathe himself and dress his hurts. Meantime the court of the Queen went away from that place, and they were left alone.

That same day in the afternoon there came three knights thitherward, and with them came three esquires, and each esquire led a horse, and upon each horse was a chest.

Of these three knights, one each was from one of the towns of that kingdom.

Then the knight from the chiefest of those three towns blew upon a bugle-horn, and anon Sir Bors appeared upon the battlement of the tower where there was a small turret. Then the knight from without greeted him, saying, "Sir, hail to you. We three come hither to tell you that we repent us that we have done wrong to the lady of this tower, wherefore we will accept her for our *Of the three knights of the towns, their mission.* queen. Only this: that she shall marry some good, worthy knight such as yourself, and that he shall be our King as she is our Queen. For that which we need at this place is not a woman to rule us, but a man."

Then Sir Bors laughed and he said, "Sir, I will take you at your word, and in a little while this lady shall marry some gentleman who shall rule over you." For Sir Bors thought to himself, "Haply I shall be that man."

So the gates of that castle were opened, and the three knights entered the courtyard thereof. Then they opened the three chests that their esquires had brought into the castle courtyard, and in those chests were all manner of raiment of silks and velvets, together with jewels, and golden ornaments of divers sorts and designs such as were fit for a queen to adorn herself withal.

These were conveyed to the rooms of the lady of the castle, and she arrayed herself in them, and when she was thus arrayed she shone with a wonderful beauty and splendor, even as the sun shines when the mists of heaven dissolve before his face.

After that the lady of the castle and Sir Bors and the three knights and
Sir Bors and their esquires all mounted upon their horses and rode away
the lady ride from that castle, leaving behind them the lady who had been
away from the the Queen of that land. For there she should abide for
castle. awhile under guard of the old porter of that place.

So, at last, they reached the chief city of that kingdom where were great
concourses of people assembled to welcome them. These shouted aloud
with a tumult of applause as their new Queen rode up the stony street
amongst them. And everywhere were banners and streamers of many
colored silks, fluttering in the sunlight from the pinnacles of the houses.
So that all the sunlight was gay with radiant tints of red and blue and
yellow and green, and divers gaudy colors, and all the air was merry
with the shouting of multitudinous voices.

Thus they reached the castle, and so the rightful queen became queen
again.

Now one night Sir Bors had a dream. He saw before him a tall and splen-
Sir Bors hath did knight, clad all in pure and shining white, and the knight
a dream. said to him, "Sir Bors! Sir Bors! What is it you do?" And
Sir Bors dreamed that he said to him in reply, "I would abide here and
rule this kingdom justly." The knight said, "Hast thou so soon forgot the
quest of the Grail that in such a short time thou shouldst think only of this
and not of that?"

Then it seemed to Sir Bors that he was stricken to the heart with
remorse and he cried out aloud, "I will not forget! I will not forget!"
And with that cry he awoke from his dream and found that it was a dream
and that he was trembling as with an ague.

And all that day the thought of the dream haunted him, so that in the
afternoon, whilst he and the Queen were walking in the garden of the
castle, he spoke to her of it. And after he had told her what he
had dreamed, he said to her, "Lady, ere I wed thee and settle in this place,
there is a duty I must yet perform. For wit you I am in quest of
the Grail and the Grail hath not yet been found. So bid me now to go
forth and to continue my search of it, and when I have found it, then I
shall return to thee and wed thee." To this the Queen made reply,
"Sir Bors, you have only been with me now for four days, and your wooing
is not yet grown warm. Would you then leave me before that wooing
groweth warm so that it may cool the quicker?" Quoth Sir Bors, "My
wooing shall not grow cold, for I will hold it close to my heart in thy remem-
brance, and there I will keep it warm, so that when I return again it will be

sprung into life." The lady said, "Do not leave me, Sir Bors, for now that my rights are won, thou must remain near to me to help me to protect those rights. Else it may be that my enemies shall rise against me once more and overthrow me. It is well for thee to search for the Grail, but what peculiar virtue will there be in it, or in thee when thou hast found it?"

Sir Bors said, "Lady, I do not think that thine enemies can arise against thee. For thine enemy is thy father's wife, and she is yet confined in that solitary castle in which I found thee. But come what may, I must now quit this place and go forth again upon my quest. For when a knight hath vowed to undertake a certain thing, that thing he must continue to pursue until he hath completed it—even though that thing may appear to be small unto others. Yet the recovery of this Grail is not a small thing; otherwise it is a very great and a very considerable thing for any knight to undertake."

Then the Queen of that town began weeping, and she said, "Sir Bors, if thou quittest me now, I know that it must be that thou quittest me for aye. For in the recovery of the Grail thou wilt forget me, and wilt never again return to this place. What, then, shall I do without thee?" Then Sir Bors bowed his face full low and he said, "Lady, that is a hard saying that thou utterest. Yet even were it so, still should I be compelled to search for the Grail. For that is the crowning work of the Round Table, and if so be I shall be instrumental in its recovery, then shall I, indeed, have done a great work in the world and shall not have lived in it in vain."

After that Sir Bors withdrew from that place. And he went to his rooms and summoned three esquires. These assisted him to his armor, and when he was armed he descended to the stables and there *Sir Bors quit-* he gave orders that his horse should be brought forth to him. *teth the lady.* And he mounted upon his horse, and so he rode forth upon his way once more. And he did not again speak to that Lady Queen; for he said to himself, "Of what avail can it be to bid her adieu? It will but cause pain to her and pain to me. So I will go without bidding her adieu."

For thus it was whenever a knight of old made a vow, then that knight set behind him all that was of pleasure or of profit, and drave straight forward to fulfil that vow which he had made. Hence it was that those great knights of King Arthur's Round Table achieved all their vows that it was possible for them to achieve. For thus is it better to do one's duty at all hazards and no matter what may befall one in the doing thereof. For duty lyeth before all the pleasures and all the glories of the world, wherefore he who doeth his duty under all circumstances, that man cannot go astray in his performances.

So Sir Bors rode forward for all that day and for part of the next day, and toward evening of the second day he found himself in a strange, wild place. For he knew not where he was or what place it was to which he had come. For there was a wide stretch of dark and dismal land upon all sides of him. And very little grass grew upon that land, but many thorn bushes, most of them without leaves or foliage of any kind. And anon a carrion crow would spring from the earth and fly heavily away against the grey and dismal sky, but beyond such things there was no eye of any sort at that place, but only darkness without any soul alive within it.

Here he came to a cross-road and as he approached that cross-road he *Sir Bors meets* was aware of a solitary knight who was there and waiting. *a White Knight.* And this knight was clad all in white armor, and he sat upon a white horse, and he was the knight whom Sir Bors had seen in his dream; and when Sir Bors drew nigh he saluted him, saying, "Greeting, Sir Bors, whither goest thou?"

Then Sir Bors said, "Messire, who art thou who knowest me and I know not thee? For I beheld thee last night, but in a dream." The White Knight said, "It matters not who I am, but wit you this, that I know you very well, and I know that you seek the Holy Grail. Sir Galahad shall achieve that Grail, and you and Sir Percival, who am the next purest knight to him, shall find it with him. Here have I been waiting for you for some while, and at last you have come. So come now with me." And Sir Bors said, "I will do so."

So after that they two rode together side by side. And anon the sun sank and the moon arose, very still and bright, and ever they two rode on in that way side by side together.

And Sir Bors spoke no word to the White Knight and the White Knight spoke no word to Sir Bors, but ever they rode in silence all bathed by the white moonlight; their shadows, black and obscure, following them.

So at last they came to where there was a wide and stony waste without a blade of grass or a tree growing upon it, but only a great stretch of round hard stones of various sizes spread thick all over the earth before them. Then the White Knight said to Sir Bors, "Yonder is our road; let us go thither."

So they two rode straight forward as that knight had directed they should do, and all about them lay the white and silent moonlight, like to a bath of pure and limpid silver. So anon and after a considerable while Sir Bors heard a great roaring, though far away from where they were. Then the White Knight drew rein and said, "Hearken, Sir Bors, hear ye that sound, and wit ye what it is?" Sir Bors said, "What is that sound?"

The White Knight said, "That is the sea breaking upon the beach. Thither it is we go."

So by and by they came to where there was a little cove of the sea, and beyond the cove the great waves burst upon the beach. So *They come to* the White Knight rode down to the shores of that cove, and *the sea.* Sir Bors followed, and at that place there was a hard and level beach of pure white sand, and some rocks were beyond that sand.

Here Sir Bors beheld that there was a boat beside the rocks, and the boat rested against the shore, and it was hung within with pure white linen. And within the middle of the boat was a couch, and on the couch there was a knight lying asleep. And Sir Bors perceived that that knight was Sir Percival.

Then the White Knight said to Sir Bors, "Sir Bors, enter yonder boat, for so only shalt thou find the Grail."

So Sir Bors dismounted from his horse and he entered the boat, and with that Sir Percival awoke and sat up. And when Sir Percival *Sir Bors enters* perceived Sir Bors there in the boat he gave him greeting, *the boat.* and Sir Bors greeted Sir Percival.

Then the White Knight gave the boat a thrust from the shore, and the boat immediately sped away very swiftly into the night-time. And as Sir Bors and Sir Percival gazed back behind them they could yet see the figure of the White Knight seated upon his horse as still and motionless as though he were carved in marble stone. And though neither of them knew it, yet that knight was the spirit of Sir Balan who had returned to lead those knights champion to find the Grail.

Then anon that white figure faded into the dimness of the moonlight and was gone, and all about them lay the sea, very strange and mysterious and yet full of motion. And the bright whiteness of the moonlight lay moving upon the crests of the waves, and ever it wavered this way and that as though it were liquid silver poured upon the waves.

Such were the adventures of Sir Bors at this time.

Nor shall you think ill of him because he left that beautiful lady who was his betrothed wife to seek the Grail. For wit you that the Grail was thought by all the world to be the greatest and the most important thing in that world; and its recovery was adjudged to be the most splendid and the noblest deed that any knight could undertake. Wherefore it was that Sir Bors would surrender all his hope of love and of riches and of worldly honor to seek for that Grail.

This he did not for his own glory but for the glory of heaven, and not for his own honor, but for the honor of Paradise, where that Grail really belonged.

Wherefore he would turn aside from all that the world had to offer him and would direct his face and all his endeavor to the recovery of that sacred chalice, content, if he should recover it or aid in its recovery, to sacrifice all the world for the sake of that recovery.

For be it said at this place that the Lady Leisette did not wait the return of Sir Bors, but, finding him gone, she took for her husband a certain noble knight of that kingdom, and he ruled that land in her behalf with great benignity of judgment and with high honor of knightly wisdom.

Now pass we from the story of Sir Bors and turn we to the further adventures of Sir Galahad at that time, as followeth.

ir Galahad rides with the Lady :·

Chapter Seventh

*How Sir Galahad smote down Sir Gawaine, and how he accompanied
a Fair Lady to the seashore. And of what happened thereafter.*

NOW, after Sir Galahad had smitten down Sir Launcelot, as aforetold
of, he rode for a long while in a wild forest and had many adventures of divers sorts, of which no account hath been given, though
mention is made of them in the ancient histories of those things which I
have read. That while he dwelt in the forest and slept in the forest, and
was fed, when he was an hungered, by the people of the forest.

So it befell that one morning he rode out from the forest and found himself in an open country that sloped down very deep to a valley, as though
it were a deep bowl of the earth.

And Sir Galahad sat upon his horse on the edge of that bowl and gazed
down into it. And he beheld a great way off a castle; and *Sir Galahad*
he beheld that there was a concourse of many knights gathered *beholds several*
about that castle. For the early sunlight shone down upon *knights in the*
the armor of those knights, so that the armor caught the light *valley.*
and flung it back again as it were in brilliant points of pure and blazing
flame.

Then Sir Galahad said to himself, "What is that concourse of knights,
and why gather they around about that castle in such a wise?" And he
said to himself, "I will ride down thither into the valley, and will see for
myself what is the meaning of that assembly."

So therewith he drew rein and descended down into the valley as he
proposed to himself to do. And so he approached ever nearer to that
distant castle. So by and by he was near enough to them *Sir Galahad*
to bespeak them, and when he had come still a little nearer *bespeaketh*
he said to them, "Messires, what is this that you do at this *those knights.*
place?" They say to him, "Sir, at this place there was not long since

133

held a tournament of eight knights. In that tournament a certain young knight was slain. We be his relatives and his friends who have come hither to avenge him. So we wait here outside the castle, and those seven knights hide them away from us within the walls of the castle."

"For shame!" said Sir Galahad. "For shame, that ye who are several should thus besiege seven men who cannot stand against ye. Get you gone and let them come forth."

They say to him, "We will not get us gone from this place until we have taken those seven men with us. Because it is for that purpose we have come hither and for that purpose shall we stay until it be achieved."

"Well, then," said Sir Galahad, "I will assail ye upon this side, and then they will come forth and assail ye upon the other side, and so will we raise this siege."

At this they all laughed, saying, "Is it possible that one knight can lift the siege of so many against seven? Well, then, let us see if he can do so."

So they began to prepare themselves for battle, and Sir Galahad began *Sir Galahad* to prepare himself also for battle. So, when he had cast *doeth battle* aside his lance and had drawn his sword he lifted up his shield *with those* on high, and, shouting, he drave against them. And he drave *knights.* into the midst of the press, lashing upon this side and upon that. And so terrible were the strokes which he gave that many fell down before them, and all bare away from him, so that anon he had carved a small open space about him.

Now in that party who were thus besieging the castle were Sir Gawaine and Sir Ewaine his cousin. But Sir Galahad knew not these two knights, and they knew not him. For his armor was much defaced in battle and in the adventures through which he had passed, and at that time he wore a leather covering to his shield. So they knew him not.

So they stood about and looked upon Sir Galahad and he looked upon them, and meantime the knights of the castle made them ready to come forth.

Then Sir Gawaine said, "For shame that we should thus be driven back by one man! Now I will have to do with him myself." So he came *Sir Galahad* forward against Sir Galahad, and Sir Galahad awaited him. *overcometh* Then when Sir Gawaine had come close enough, Sir Galahad *Sir Gawaine.* arose in his stirrups, and he launched a blow at Sir Gawaine that nor leather nor iron could stay. For that blow clove asunder the shield of Sir Gawaine, and it clove asunder his helmet, and it clove asunder the iron coif beneath the helmet, and it bit deep into the bone of the brain-pan itself.

Then the brains of Sir Gawaine swam like shallow water, and he reeled this way and that in his saddle, and would have fallen had it not been for Sir Ewaine, who catched him ere he fell beneath the feet of his horse, and so held him up in the saddle.

Then Sir Gawaine said, "Ah, Ewaine! That was none other than Galahad who smote me that blow. For none other than he could give such a stroke as that. So have I suffered for attempting to draw forth that sword out of the marble stone. Ah! woe is me." So saying, his dissolving wits left him, and he swooned away as though he were dying.

Meantime the knights within the castle had given command that the gates should be opened. So they were flung open according to that command, and the seven knights within the castle issued out to conduct the assault from that side. But Sir Ewaine cried out, "Messires, give over, and we will withdraw from this place. For here is most sorely wounded a very excellent knight, who is the nephew of King Arthur." "Alas!" cried Sir Galahad. *Sir Galahad bringeth Sir Gawaine into the castle.* "Woe is me! For so have I carried out the provisions of that prophecy relating to the sword. For it was predicted of this sword that it should bite deep into the life of Sir Gawaine, and lo! it hath done so." And he said to Sir Ewaine, "Convey him into this castle, for here shall his wound be searched, and he shall be cared for." And he said to those of the castle, "See to it that all care is given to this gentleman." And they say to him, "We will do so."

So Sir Gawaine was conveyed within the castle, and was laid upon a couch. And his wound was searched, and balm was laid upon it. Thus was he put at ease at that place, and so was the prophecy concerning that sword fulfilled.

Then they all beseeched Sir Galahad that he would stay at that castle for a little while, but he would not stay at that place. Otherwise he said, "I must go upon my way, I know not whither. For I have a mission to fulfil, and in fulfilling it I know not whither I go." So he drew rein and rode away, leaving them behind him.

Now wit ye how the knights of those days fared when they rode errant? I will tell you.

About the middle of that day Sir Galahad came to the house of a farm yeoman, and the wife of the yeoman and the daughter of the yeoman stood in the doorway of the house. The woman who was the wife was large and buxom, but the daughter was very slender and brown.

Of these Sir Galahad besought food to eat, and they brought to him a loaf of bread, a piece of cheese, and a crock of cider, and Sir Galahad ate

How Sir Gala-
had refreshes
himself.
and drank, sitting under the shade of a wide-spreading tree. Meanwhile, those people watched him from afar with great interest and curiosity, for never had they beheld a knight so tall and so noble as Sir Galahad.

Thus did these bright-armed knights who wandered errant through the world in those days refresh themselves, and so were they received and entertained by the people whom they met. Thus have I told you of that so that you might know thereof.

That evening, after the sun had set, and the soft and starry night had descended upon the earth like a sparkling coverlet of darkness, very damp and warm, Sir Galahad found himself in a wide moorland, and he wist not where he should sleep.

So at last the moon arose, shining very brightly and tranquilly, and by the light thereof Sir Galahad perceived before him a small chapel. And he said to himself, "Here will I lodge me for the night."

So Sir Galahad rode up to the door of the chapel and he smote very loudly upon the boards of the door with the handle of his misericordia. Anon

Sir Galahad
lodges at a
chapel.
there came the recluse to whom that chapel belonged, and when he beheld Sir Galahad standing there he bade him to enter. So Sir Galahad entered the chapel, and after the recluse had put the horse of Sir Galahad into the stable nigh to the chapel, he came to where the knight was, and set before him some broth and some pulse, together with some freshly gathered fruit, and Sir Galahad ate thereof with great heartiness.

Now, whilst Sir Galahad sat there eating, there came another knock upon the door, and when the recluse went to open it, he beheld standing there a very beautiful lady clad all in white, and with her dark hair bound

There cometh a
lady to the
chapel.
around with a ribbon of silver. And the lady was mounted upon a cream-white jennet, and the saddle of the jennet was of crimson Spanish leather, embossed and studded with plates and buttons of silver.

When the door was opened, the lady said to the recluse, "Sir, I pray you tell me, is there here within a knight hight Galahad?"

This heard Sir Galahad, and hearing it he arose and came forward, and he said, "Lady, I am Galahad. What would you have of me?"

She said, "Sir, I pray you to come and ride with me and I will lead you to such an adventure as you have never had in all of your life before." Quoth he, "Where is that adventure?" She said to him, "It is not very far distant from here. But I cannot tell you more than that." Sir Galahad said, "Whither would you lead me?" She said, "Come and I will show you."

So Sir Galahad went back into the chapel and armed himself, and the recluse brought forth his horse out of the stable. And anon Sir Galahad, being in all ways armed, came forth out of the hermitage and mounted his horse.

Immediately he was mounted the lady drew rein and turned, and rode away from that place, and Sir Galahad followed her.

So they rode away across the moorland together. All around them was the stillness of the night-time, and overhead and about *The lady and* them lay the silent whiteness of the effulgent moon. And the *Sir Galahad* shadows of each and the shadows of the horse of each followed *ride together.* them across the moorland, very black and mysterious.

So they travelled a considerable while in silence, for the lady did not speak to Sir Galahad, nor did Sir Galahad speak to her. But each rode in silence, and each was occupied with his or her own thoughts.

Thus, by and by, they reached a high part of the moorland, and of a sudden Sir Galahad beheld the sea, over above the downs. *Sir Galahad* And the moon shone down upon the sea so that it looked like *beholds the sea.* a shining stretch of pure and radiant silver against the night sky that lay behind it. Then Sir Galahad said, "Lady, yonder is the sea." "Aye," quoth the other, "and it is thither that I am bringing thee."

So after awhile they came to where the sea lay below them, and they beheld the waves illuminated by the light of the moonshine lapping against the shore. Then they rode down to the sea, and there was at that place a rocky promontory that stretched out into the water. And they rode across that promontory, and there Sir Galahad beheld a boat lying in the moonlight moored, as it were, to the shore, although no rope attached it to the shore. And as they two approached the boat, Sir Galahad perceived that the boat was all draped and hanged with white linen, and he perceived that there were two men within the boat.

The faces of these two were cut out very clear and sharp and white from the darkness behind because of the moonlight that shone upon *He perceives* them, and Sir Galahad perceived that the one of those faces *Sir Percival* was the face of Sir Percival, and that the other face was the face *and Sir Bors* of Sir Bors de Ganis. These two, beholding Sir Galahad there *in a boat.* upon the shore, gave him loud and joyous greeting, crying out, "Greeting, Sir Galahad! And welcome to thee!"

Then Sir Galahad sprang down from off his horse, and he ran down to the shore, leaping from rock to rock. And he sprang into the boat and kissed each of those two upon the cheek, and they kissed him upon the cheek in return. And Sir Galahad said to them, "What do ye here?" To the which they replied, "We wait for thee." And they say, "What lady is that with whom thou hast come hither?" He replied, "I know her not, but she hath brought me to this place."

And then they beheld that the lady had also dismounted from her horse and was approaching to them. And she came to them down the rocks and she stood close to the boat, and when she did so Sir Percival saw her

Sir Percival beholdeth his sister. more clearly and he knew her. Then he cried out, "I know thee! Thou art my sister!" She said, "Yea, that is true." He said to her, "Sister, what doest thou here?" She replied, "I come to give you information, and it is this: You shall sail away from this place, and by and by you shall find another boat of a very magnificent sort. For that boat is the *Ship of Solomon*, and it is waiting for you. In it you will find the Grail established, and the ship itself will take you whither the Grail belongeth. So enter the *Ship of Solomon* freely, for no harm shall befall you in it, and it shall convey you to the city of Sarras where the Grail belongeth." Then turned she to Sir Galahad, and she said, "And to thee, Galahad, am I permitted to say this thing: That it is given to thee that when thou willest thy soul shall depart from thy body. And it shall leave thy body behind, and shall ascend with the glory of angels into Paradise at thy command. All this I have to tell you, and now fare you well."

Thereafter the lady turned away from them and mounted her horse and rode away. And as she departed she wept, for she was aware that she would never behold Sir Percival again.

Then that boat in which they were moved away from the shore, and anon it moved very swiftly. And it sailed past the headland and out into the sea, and, in a little while, the land disappeared from sight, melting, as it were, into the soft glory of the moonlight that illuminated all the darkness of the earth. And so they sailed swiftly across the sea and the great waves of the sea, and ever the moonlight lay all about them, and they were cradled in the arms of the sea.

So they sailed for all that night, and anon the day dawned, and then they perceived before them another and a larger ship than the boat in which they sailed. And the boat in which they were moved very swiftly toward the ship and at last came close beside it.

Then they beheld that that ship was of a very wonderful sort, for it was

They come to the "Ship of Solomon." built all of santal wood, and was tinted with vermilion and ultramarine, and was glorified with gold. And the sails of that ship were of variegated silk, very wonderful to behold. And the decks were spread with rich carpets, and there was no human being of any sort to be perceived about that ship.

Then Sir Percival said, "This wonderful ship must be the *Ship of Solomon*, and into it we are destined to enter and to discover the Grail. So let us enter it forthwith and without loss of time."

So they departed from their own boat and entered the *Ship of Solomon*, and as soon as they had done so the boat in which they had sailed disappeared and was gone, and they saw it no more. And at that time they were hushed as with a great awe.

Then Sir Percival said, "Come, let us behold the Grail, which is here." So with that saying they all descended below the deck of that boat, and coming there they beheld a table of carved silver, and against *They find* the table there leaned the spear and upon the table was a *the Grail.* purple velvet cloth, spread over something that stood upon the table, and the cloth was embroidered very richly with gold and ornamented with many precious stones of divers colors. And from beneath it there shone a clear and brilliant light, and that light was emitted by the Grail.

Sir Galahad went to the table and took the cloth by the corners and lifted it up; and lo! beneath it was the Holy Chalice itself. And it blazed with a light that was like that of the sun—very splendid and effulgent—so that they could scarcely look upon the splendor thereof.

Then they all three kneeled down before the Grail, and set their palms together, and gave all honor and glory to its splendors. And Sir Percival said, "I have seen this before, but never so near at hand as this." And again they all gave praise to it.

So the *Ship of Solomon* sailed very swiftly away with those three knights in it, and it sailed for all that day, and near eventide it approached a great city that stood upon a high and rocky hill.

And that city was the city of Sarras, and it appeared to the eyes of the three knights to be very great and beautiful. For they be- *They come to* held that there were very many high pinnacles and towers *the city of* to that city, and they saw that these were illuminated by the *Sarras.* setting sun, so that they appeared as though they were built of pure and shining gold.

So the boat in which they sat sailed very swiftly toward the city, and anon it ceased its voyage beside a wharf that was there.

Then Sir Galahad said, "Let us convey this Holy Chalice to the minster, for, certes, this is where it belongeth." And Sir Bors and Sir Percival said, "Let us do so."

So they three took up the silver table by three of its corners, and they bare it toward the gate of the town.

Now the history of these things telleth that at the town gate there sat a cripple begging, and the cripple had not walked for thirty years. They *How the cripple was healed.* say to him, "Come, help us bear the fourth corner of this table." He said, "How can I help bear the table? Lo, I have been a cripple for thirty years, and in that time I have not walked a step without my crutches." Sir Galahad said, "Nevertheless, arise and come hither." Then the man arose, supported by his crutches, and they brought the table of the Grail to him, and he laid hands upon the silver table.

Then, no sooner had he touched that table, than the strength flowed into him; his joints became strongly knit and supple, and he was, as it were, no longer a cripple. Then he cried out, "Lo! I am healed!" And with that he skipped and leaped in his strength.

So the Grail was achieved, and now followeth the account of how those three worthy knights brought it in return to the city of Sarras where it belonged, and of what befell them there; so I pray you to read the conclusion of this passage hereinafter written.

Conclusion

NOW the news of the healing of this cripple became known; it went all through the town, so that when they entered the town, great crowds presently gathered and followed them, and the noise of the tumult of that following was like to the noise of the roaring of many waters. For ever the crowd gathered more and more to it, until all that part of the town was filled full of a slow-moving concourse of people.

Thus they came to the minster, what time the Bishop of that minster was there, and seeing them enter with the silver table he said, *They bring the* "What have you there?" Sir Galahad replied, "Sir, this is *Grail to the* the Holy Grail upon this table, and we who have achieved the *minster.* quest of it have brought it hither where it belongeth." The Bishop said, "Let me see that Grail."

So Sir Galahad took the velvet covering of the Grail by the corners and lifted it, and lo! the glory of the Grail blazed forth before the eyes of all. And so great was that glory that it illuminated the entire interior of the minster, so that it was like the illumination of sunlight that was burst into that place. And all they who beheld the Grail and that sudden illumination bowed down before it and uttered their prayers of thanksgiving that it was returned to where it belonged.

So the Grail and the spear were placed before the high altar, and there they remained unveiled; and the glory of them illuminated all the coadjacent spaces with brightness.

So the Grail remained exposed in that city for three days, and at the end of that time it was elevated from earth to heaven, as shall now be told of.

The three knights were there in the great minster, kneeling and praying before the high altar where stood the Grail, when of a sudden they heard a voice from on high, saying, "Hail, ye heroes, and all praise to ye! For ye have recovered that Grail which here and now is to be translated from earth to heaven."

With that voice there came two hands, very white and shining, and they took the Grail, and there was no body to be seen with those hands, but *How the Grail* only the hands themselves. And there came two other hands *ascends to* and took the spear, and neither was there any body to those *heaven.* hands. So those four hands lifted the Grail and they lifted the spear, and they bore those two holy relics aloft and away from that place. And they ascended, as it were, through the roof of the minster and were gone in a burst of glory that lingered for some little while and then faded away into darkness.

So it happened with the Grail that it was elevated into heaven, and that this was so was avouched for by many who were in the minster at that time; and several of these beheld those four hands, and saw the Grail elevated from earth to heaven. So this is to be believed in as here narrated.

Then there sounded from on high to the ears that were unstopped to hear that sound, a great anthem as of thanksgiving, as it were the tones of a mighty organ, or as it were the tones of a wonderful and melodious thunder, and they three heard that melody of music, but no other who was there heard it. And they were aware that it was the rejoicing of heaven over the return of those sacred relics to that place, wherefore they were filled with an ecstasy that was not of this world, but of heaven, and that was of great joy, yet was of awfulness and of a sort of terror.

Then was the spirit of Galahad exalted, and he lifted up his voice and cried aloud, "There is nothing remaining for me to live for. So now let me depart in peace."

Thereat with those words the soul was drawn out of his body and the *Of the passing* eyes of those two knights who kneeled beside him were opened *of Galahad.* and they beheld his spirit ascend into glory, and they beheld that the illumination of heaven shone round about it, and at the same time they heard, with a louder and more momentous tone, the thunder peal of heavenly triumph as the spirit of Galahad was received into its glory, together with the Grail which he had achieved.

Then the brightness closed from their eyes and they beheld themselves to be kneeling in the dark and empty minster. And they looked at the body of Sir Galahad, and behold! it was dead.

So passed Sir Galahad, and at that time he was yet not twenty years of age.

Sir Bors went to the Bishop of that minster, and he said to him, "Sir, this man was altogether a good, virtuous, and perfect knight. It is our desire that his dead body should lie here in this minster at that spot whence the Grail ascended into heaven but now. Wherefore, we beseech you to suffer it to lie at that place." To these the Bishop said, "Let, then, that be fulfilled as you ask. For I believe that that knight was indeed a very good, excellent, holy man withal."

So they buried the body of Sir Galahad there in the minster, beside the spot whence the Holy Grail ascended into heaven, and there the tomb of Sir Galahad remained to be seen for many years after his body was so buried.

After this was over and done, it being then the fourth day after they had come thither, Sir Bors said to Sir Percival, "Sir, whither now *Sir Percival* shall we go?" And Sir Percival said to him, "I shall not go *taketh holy* anywhere; for here shall I remain, and here I shall take upon *orders.* myself holy orders and shall live and die as a monk in those orders. But return you, Sir Bors, to the Court of King Arthur, and tell them of the court concerning all those things that have befallen; to wit, tell them how the Grail was achieved by us three, and how that it was taken up into heaven before our eyes, and how we beheld it enter the gates of heaven. So go you to Camelot, and tell them concerning all these things."

Thus said Sir Percival, and Sir Bors said, "I will do as you bid me." So the next day Sir Bors kissed Sir Percival upon the cheeks and either wept salt tears over the other. Then they parted *Sir Bors* company and Sir Percival remained at that place and became *returneth* a monk, and Sir Bors departed thence, returning back again to *to the* Camelot. *Court of the King.*

There he arrived at the ending of a year and a day, and all they who were there made great joy over his return. For all those knights who had gone forth in search of the Grail and had not died in that quest had now returned, saving only Sir Launcelot of the Lake. For it had become known throughout the world that the Grail had been found, and that it had been elevated into heaven, so that all those who were seeking for it were returned back home again.

Then Sir Bors told them all the circumstances of the finding of the Grail, and how it had been elevated in the minster at Sarras, and of how Sir Galahad had died, and of how he had beheld the soul of Sir Galahad exalted to heaven.

And King Arthur had that history written down in three great books, and one of those books was established at Salisbury, and another at Camelot (which same is Winchester), and the third at Carleon upon the Usk; and from these three volumes the story of the Grail has descended to us of the present day, and so I have written a part of that for your delectation.

It remaineth now only to be said that Sir Bors, after all these events, returned to that lady whom he had quitted to search for the Grail. But the happiness of earth was not to be his, for he found that she had wearied of waiting for his return, and had married elsewhere. So Sir Bors returned to Camelot, and there he abided until the time of that quarrel that preceded the ending of the reign of King Arthur.

For wit ye that he who aims high will often miss the small joys of this life, and so it was with Sir Bors de Ganis. For though he was one of those who achieved the Grail, yet he missed the lesser joys of wedded life, and of that kingdom which belonged to them.

Thus hath been told to you the famous history of the recovery of the Grail and of its translation into Paradise. And this was the crowning glory of the reign of King Arthur. For after these circumstances had happened, as herein told of, there came dissensions and battles amongst those knights—knight against knight—until the famous Round Table of King Arthur was severed and shattered, never to be reunited again.

But of that more anon, for it is hereinafter to be told of. So now I pray you for to read that which followeth if you would learn the ending of all these things.

PART III

The Passing of Arthur

*H*ERE *beginneth the history of the passing of Arthur, of his Round Table, and of many of the splendid and glorious knights thereof. With it comes the conclusion of this history, for no more shall then remain to be written thereof.*

The Queen's pages clothe Sir Launcelot:

Chapter First

How Queen Guinevere visited Sir Launcelot in the forest; how Sir Launcelot returned to Court as aforetime, and how he fled once more from the Court.

NOW it hath been told how that after the quest of the Grail all those knights who had not died in that quest, or who were able to return did return to the Court of King Arthur.

But Sir Launcelot of the Lake did not return with the other knights, for he abided in the forest not very far distant from the habitation of the Hermit of the Forest. There he lived a recluse in pious meditation, considering of his sins and repenting of them.

Sir Launcelot dwelleth in the forest.

Several knights had seen him at that place where he was dwelling and they knew him, and they brought away from that place news of him and of the life he led. That news became known at the Court of King Arthur, and there was much talked of, and King Arthur said, "What a pity it is that so great and so noble a knight as Sir Launcelot should thus deny himself to the world. For in the world he is the greatest knight of the world, but out of the world he is as any other man."

All these things Queen Guinevere heard and she meditated upon them as she sat thoughtfully in her bower. So one day she called to her a page, and she said to him that he should ride to such and such a part of the forest,

*Queen Guine-
vere sendeth for
Sir Launcelot.* and that there he would find Sir Launcelot. And the Queen said to the page that he was then to tell Sir Launcelot to return to the Court of the King. And she said to the page to tell Sir Launcelot that all the court spake of him continually, and that all desired that he should return to them.

So the page went to that part of the forest as the Queen had commanded, and there he found Sir Launcelot in his cell; and the cheeks of Sir Launcelot were hollow and his limbs and body were thin and shrunken from continual fasting and meditation. Then the page kneeled down before him and said, "Sir, the Queen bids you for to return to the Court of King Arthur; for all the ladies and the lords of the court desire you to return there and be the ornament of that court as you were aforetime."

Sir Launcelot said to the page, "Return thou to the Queen and say to her that I will not return back into the world as she desires me to do. For here I dwell in peace and quietness and I repent me of all my manifold sins as it becometh me to do. For those same sins have stood as a shadow betwixt me and the Grail, so that when the Grail was present I slept, and when it was gone I awoke and found that it was gone. Wherefore I repent me of those sins. And so I will abide here and meditate upon them for all the rest of my life."

So the page returned to Queen Guinevere and delivered these words of Sir Launcelot to her, and the Queen said, "How is this? He will not come? Then will I go myself and bring him."

So she procured a great white horse, and she procured rich and gaudy

*Queen Guine-
vere goeth to
Sir Launcelot.* raiment, such as a knight at court might wear, and with these things and with a court of knights and ladies and several pages she betook her way into the forest.

Then all that part of the forest into which she penetrated became gay and jocund with her coming. For it was as though the sunlight had suddenly burst through the leaves of the forest. All the silent woodland was made noisy with the clear sounds of talk and laughter, and of musical and merry chattering.

So the Queen came to that part of the forest where Sir Launcelot was, and Sir Launcelot came forth from his hut to meet her. And he stood afar off from her and said, "Lady, what wouldst thou here?" She said, "Launcelot, I come to thee to bring thee away from this lonely place, for the Court of the king is the fittest place for thee to be in. For thou art the greatest knight in Christendom, wherefore it ill becometh thee to hide thyself away in this desolate place."

Then Sir Launcelot lifted up his voice and cried aloud, "Get you gone, Lady, and trouble me no more, for I know you not. Yet it was because of you that I cast aside my wife so that she died because of my neglect. Because of that sin and because of other sins that thou wottest of I slept while the Grail passed before me, and could not awake until after it was gone. So lie I here thinking of that and of other misfortunes that have visited me because of my many sins. Thus it is that here in the woodlands I endeavor to purify my soul of those sins."

Then the Queen drew nearer to him and she said to him, "Launcelot, thinkest thou that thus thy sins may be remitted unto thee? *The Queen* Wit thou that thy sins are like an enemy, and that the only *speaketh to* way in which thou canst conquer those sins is to battle man- *Sir Launcelot.* fully with them and not to fly from them. Arise! shake off this sluggishness and come forth into the world again, for it awaits thee. There and there only may thy sins be remitted unto thee."

Then Sir Launcelot groaned and he hid his face in his arms and anon he said, "Lady, tempt me not." Then after another while he said, "I cannot go with thee, for I have no horse to ride."

Then Queen Guinevere smiled and she said, "Launcelot, I have purveyed thee with a horse, and it is here." Then Sir Launcelot cried out again as in a sort of despair, "Still I cannot go with thee for I have no clothes fit to wear at court."

And again Queen Guinevere smiled and she said, "Also I have provided thee with clothes; they, too, are here." Then she commanded two of her pages to convey the chest of clothes into Sir Launcelot's cell and they did so. Then they opened the chest and Sir Launcelot gazed into it, and beheld all that noble apparel of silks and velvets, of gold and jewels, of silver and of lace.

So Sir Launcelot suffered those two pages to clothe him in that raiment, and presently he came forth from the cell, shining as with great glory. And he mounted upon the great white horse which the Queen had brought him, and so they rode away together from that place.

Now there were at court several who were unfriends to Sir Launcelot; some of these were unfriends because they were malicious, others because they were jealous of his fame; others for this reason, and *Sir Launcelot* others for that reason. Two of these were Sir Mordred and *returneth to* Sir Agravaine, who were brothers to Sir Gawaine. Then *the court.* there was Sir Kay the Seneschal and Sir Florence and Sir Lovel, who were sons to Sir Gawaine, and who were jealous of Sir Launcelot upon Sir Gawaine's account.

These and several others were unfriends to Sir Launcelot, and they talked much amongst themselves concerning the return of Sir Launcelot, saying, "Lo! this knight hath come forth out of the forest and hath assumed his knighthood again over us all, yet at first he would not come, but when the Queen went thither then he beheld her and followed her forth."

These words and words like them came to the ears of Sir Launcelot, and because of them he withdrew himself from the presence of the Queen, *Sir Launcelot heareth un-friendly talk.* and consorted with other lords and ladies of the court. This the Queen observed, and was grieved at it, for she wished for Sir Launcelot to be with her, and she desired to have him near to her. So one day she sent for Sir Launcelot to come to her and she gazed at him for some time without speaking. Anon she said to him, "Launcelot, why dost thou keep thyself afar off from me?" He replied, "Lady, I avoid thee for thine own sake and not for my sake." To the which she said, "How is that?"

He said, "I will tell thee. There is much talk about this court concerning thee and concerning me, and that talk links our names together. I fear not this talk upon mine own account. For it cannot hurt me, but it may do great injury to thee; therefore do I hold myself away from thee."

Then Queen Guinevere began weeping, and she said, "Ah, Launcelot, Launcelot! Thou art not to me as thou one time wert. For one time thou wert ever ready to come to me, but now thou keepest thyself afar off from me. That which thou sayst is thy excuse for not being with me, and is not the cause of that absence." Then she said of a sudden to him, "Go! Get thee away from this court, for thou bringest nothing but disturbance to my soul."

Then Sir Launcelot said very bitterly, "Lady, it would have been well for both of us if thou hadst permitted me to remain where I was in the forest, and not have tempted me to quit my sanctuary."

Then the Queen cried out upon him, "How now! What is this thou sayst? I went to thee to save thee and not to tempt thee. If thou longest for thy husks again, return to them. At any rate, get thee gone from me, and never come near to me again. For thou bringest naught but sorrow and great tribulation to me."

So Sir Launcelot bowed and withdrew from where he was, and his heart *Sir Launcelot departeth again from the court.* was filled with a great despair. So he came to where Sir Bors and Sir Lionel were and he told them all that had passed. And he cried out to them, "What now shall I do who have sacrificed my sanctuary and have got naught by that sacrifice?"

Then quoth Sir Bors, "It would have been well for thee, if thou hadst never quitted that safe sanctuary within the forest. But as thou now hast quitted it, so mayst thou not return to it again. For so wouldst thou strive to walk backward into that which hath passed. No man may do that in the life which he leads.

"As for the anger of the Queen, soon will she forget that anger, and as soon as she forgets it, then will she desire to see thee again. For so hath she done several times before, and so will she do again."

Said Sir Launcelot, "I will go to my castle of Joyous Gard and there will I abide until her anger against me hath grown cold again."

"Not so," said Sir Bors, "the Queen spake truly in this; that thy place is in the field, and neither in the hermit's cell, nor enclosed *He departeth* in the walls of that castle. But get thee to the castle of Sir *to the castle* Brasius the Good Knight, and there abide for a little while, *of Sir Brasius.* seeking such adventures as may be found around about. For when the Queen's mind changes toward thee, then wilt thou easily be found at that place, and either I or Sir Ector will come to seek thee."

"Thou sayst well," said Sir Launcelot. "Thither will I go and there will I stay until thou or Sir Lionel sendest for me."

So Sir Launcelot took horse and rode away to the castle of Sir Brasius, and there took up his inn.

But never, at any time, did anyone ever behold him to smile. For though in the earlier days of his knighthood he had a happy and jocund spirit and frequently smiled, yet now that happiness had departed from him and he never smiled. For many sad things had happened to him in his life, and those things had destroyed that happiness as a hailstorm destroys those flowers that to-day are and to-morrow are not, but are withered and dead like the grass in the fields.

Thus I have told you all those circumstances that led to Sir Launcelot's returning to Court, and as to his withdrawing himself thence again. For so it is that though a man may think to return again into that life from which he has passed, yet he cannot do so. For the life that is lived in once and which hath been laid aside for another life, that first life is dead and cannot be revivified again by the man's entering into it again, but remaineth dead for aye.

So it was with Sir Launcelot, for, when he had committed the sin of leaving the Lady Elaine the Fair, he had committed it, and all that befell him thereafter became colored by that evil happening. For, because of that sin he failed to behold the Holy Grail with the eyes of his body, and now, because of that sin, and of what was said concerning him and his doings, he was compelled to exile himself again from that court in which, by grace of his chivalry and force of arms, he truly belonged.

So let us take warning by this example and let us not try to return to the life which we may have left, but let us endeavor to live that other life that now presents itself to us after such a happening, whether of good or of evil.

Now followeth that which treats of the poisoning of Sir Patrice of Ireland at the feast given by Queen Guinevere; so if you would hear how Sir Launcelot saved the life of the Queen at that time, I pray you to read what followeth.

ir Mador de la Porte

Chapter Second

How Queen Guinevere held a feast, and how Sir Patrice of Ireland was poisoned at that feast.

NOW after Sir Launcelot had quitted the Court of King Arthur as aforetold of, the Queen pretended to great joyousness of heart, although there was no joyousness within her. "I was hasty," she said to herself, "and Sir Launcelot was hasty and hath left me again. But this was my fault and I must show no repining, but must appear to be cheerful to all. So I will give a feast, that my seeming joyousness may be made manifest to the world, and no one shall have cause to say that I repine at the loss of Sir Launcelot." So said the Queen to herself upon that occasion.

So she proclaimed a feast, and she had at that feast the following knights of the Round Table: there were Sir Gawaine and his brothers, to wit, Sir Agravaine, Sir Geharis, Sir Gareth, and Sir Mordred. Also *Queen Guine-* there were Sir Bors de Ganis, and Sir Bleoberis de Ganis, and *vere proclaim-* Sir Blamor de Ganis, and there were Sir Galahad and Sir *eth a feast.* Galyhadin and Sir Ector and Sir Lionel and Sir Palamydes and Sir Safyr; and there were Sir Persavant and Sir Ironside and Sir Brandiles; and there were Sir Kay the Seneschal and Sir Mador de la Porte and Sir Patrice of Ireland, and Sir Alyduke and Sir Artamore.

Now at that time Sir Lamorack of Gales had been slain, and report placed his death at the hands of Sir Gawaine (although this report was not true), and of two of Sir Gawaine's brothers, to wit, Sir Agravaine and Sir Geharis.

There was at the Court of King Arthur a certain knight hight Sir Pinal the Savage, who was cousin to Sir Lamorack, and Sir Pinal was very bitter against Sir Gawaine, and was anxious to be revenged upon him, yet he wit not how to take that revenge.

Now Sir Gawaine had a custom of eating an apple immediately after he had dined, and this Sir Pinal was aware of. So Sir Pinal took the fairest apple he could find, and he introduced into it a very subtle and very

*Sir Pinal,
surnamed the
Savage, poison-
eth an apple.*
malignant poison, and this apple he placed in the centre of the table, and in the midst of all the fruit.   For he said to himself, "There will Sir Gawaine find this apple, and he will take it and eat it and will die."   And he said, "Queen Guine-vere will be blamed for that death, for all the world knoweth that she and Sir Gawaine are unfriends."   So said Sir Pinal, for he thought thus to be revenged for the death of Sir Lamorack upon Sir Gawaine, and he knew not how else to achieve that vengeance.   For next to Sir Launcelot, Sir Ga-waine was the strongest knight of the court, and he was besides nephew to King Arthur and of great importance in the King's household.   Where-fore it was that Sir Pinal sought to slay Sir Gawaine by that poisoned apple.

But at the end of that feast Sir Gawaine did not take the apple, but

*Sir Patrice of
Ireland eateth
the apple, and
dieth.*
instead of Sir Gawaine, Sir Patrice of Ireland took it.   And Sir Patrice bit a great bite into that apple, and he ate that piece.   Then anon he cried out in a very loud and piercing voice, "Hah!   What is this that ails me?"   And then he cried out in a very terrible voice, "Alas!   I am poisoned and I die from eat-ing this apple!"   And he cried out again, "Friends, see that my death is avenged!"

Therewith he fell down to the ground in great agony, lashing with his hands and feet and frothing at the mouth, and so in a little while he died.

Then Sir Gawaine rose up, and he turned his face toward the Queen, and his face was very white, and he said, "Lady, how is this?   This apple was poisoned!   For whom was it intended?"

The Queen hid her face in her hands for horror of what she had beheld, and she cried out in a very shrill voice, "I knew not that it was poisoned,

*Sir Gawaine
accuseth the
Queen.*
and I know not how it was poisoned!"   Sir Gawaine said, "That apple was poisoned, and thou knewest that it was pois-oned.   Methinks it was intended for me.   Thou hast always borne enmity toward me, wherefore thou didst place that apple upon the table that I might eat of it.   One time thou wert innocent, but now thou art innocent no longer, but art full of malice and guile, wherefore thou hadst the will to poison me."

Then the Queen cried out with a great passion, saying, "Gawaine, thou and I were never friends, but rather would I cut off my right hand than to do so evil a thing as this, to seek to poison thee."

Then Sir Mador de la Porte stood up before them all, and he said, "Lady, that which thou sayst may deceive some who are here, but it shall not deceive me. For I know of thy comings and of thy goings, and I know how thou didst of malice hold Sir Launcelot here at court when he would fain have followed the Lady Elaine away from this place, and because that Sir Launcelot remained here the Lady Elaine died. From this I know that thy heart is full of guile and wickedness, wherefore it is but a step from that sin to the sin of poisoning." *Sir Mador de la Porte also accuseth the Queen.*

So saying, Sir Mador went out from that place, and all the other knights followed after him; for Sir Mador was a king's son, and of great importance at the court. Then the Queen was left there alone, weeping with great passion, for she wist not how that poison had been administered to Sir Patrice. After that came several men who were in the suite of Sir Mador, and they took up the body of Sir Patrice and they bore it away from that room. *The Queen weepeth.*

As soon as might be, Sir Mador de la Porte appeared before the King as he sat in council, and he appealed the Queen of treason in that she was a murderess; and this he proclaimed before the King and all his council. *Sir Mader appeareth before the High Court of the King.*

Then King Arthur turned very white and he bowed his head and anon he said, "Sir Mador, what wouldst thou have me do in this case? For lo! thou dost attaint the Queen of murder, and I do not believe it possible that she could do so wicked and so evil a thing as this. Wherefore thou must tell me what thou wouldst have me do in this instance."

Quoth Sir Mador, "Lord, I do accuse her of having administered poison at her feast, whereof my cousin Sir Patrice died. In that she certes hath committed treason against thee and against us all, for this feast of hers was held here, in this castle, and we were her guests. So accusing her, I am ready to defend that accusation with my body." So saying, he flung his glove down upon the ground, and he cried out, "Here lieth my glove in gage of battle, and I will defend my accusation with my own person, my accusation being that the Queen is a murderess." Quoth the King, "Hast thou no pity and no mercy for this lady who is thy Queen? Hast thou no honor and no regard for me, thy King?" And Sir Mador made reply, "Not in this case! For in this case I have no regard for anything but to punish the guilty." *Sir Mador challengeth the Queen of treason.*

Then the King arose, and he said, "Send for the Queen to come hither, so that she may face her accuser."

So anon the Queen came, and two ladies supported her, one upon one side and the other upon the other. And the Queen wore her veil over her face for she had been weeping *The Queen appeareth at the High Court.*

continually and with great passion ever since the ending of that feast. Now there were many knights gathered there and many lords and ladies of several sorts, and some of these were the Queen's friends and felt sorrow for her, but some of them felt satisfaction that she was accused.

The King said, "Arise, Lady, and stand." And thereupon the Queen stood up before the King and Sir Mador de la Porte and the entire council. Then the King said to her, "Lady, this knight, Sir Mador de la Porte, accuses thee of having used poison at thy feast. What hast thou to say to that?"

Then the Queen put back her veil and she had ceased to weep. and her eyes were very hard and proud, albeit her face was extraordinarily white. "Sir," she said, "thou knowest me well—no one better—and thou knowest that with all my shortcomings (and they be many), I could never do such a thing as that, to poison an enemy at mine own table. For I have many enemies at this court, and amongst them is thine own nephew, Sir Ga-waine; for he is my bitterest enemy, and hath always been so. It was he who first accused me at that feast of having used poison, and because he is thy nephew and because he is so powerful at court, there be few knights here who will defend mine innocence against mine accusers, when he stands at the head of those accusers, holding that I attempted to poison him. Had I Sir Launcelot here at court, then would I have had a good worthy defender of mine honor, but I have driven Sir Launcelot away from me by my pride and anger, and he is not now here to defend mine innocence. Yet I believe that someone will arise to defend it, wherefore I will accept this knight's gage of battle and will abide by it, come life, come death."

Then the King groaned, and he bowed his head, and at last he said, "Lady and Queen; thou art the wife of my youth, and I would fain defend thee myself. But this cannot be, for I am the King, and the head of all the laws. Nevertheless, I believe that some champion will arise for thee; for it is not possible that in this court there is no knight who will arise to defend thine innocence. Wherefore, let it be as thou sayst. Here shall the glove of Sir Mador de la Porte lie upon the ground, until some defender arises to take it up, and if no other defender arises, then will I take it up mine own self. Let us now depart."

So with that they all arose and left that place, and left Sir Mador de la Porte's glove still lying upon the floor of the council chamber.

The Queen asketh Sir Bors to defend her

That night a messenger came to Sir Bors asking him to come to the Queen, and Sir Bors went with the messenger, who took him to the bower of the Queen where she was. When Sir Bors entered that place he found that the King was with the Queen. Then the Queen arose and stood before him. And she set her hands together, the palm of one against the palm of the other, and she said, "Sir Bors, will you not serve as my champion in this quarrel?"

Then Sir Bors bowed his head, and anon he said, "Lady, I would you had asked someone else to act as your champion."

The Queen looked at him very proudly, and she said, "Why do you say that? Had I known that your feelings were such, then I would not have troubled you by asking that service of you. But you are the nephew of Sir Launcelot, and you are a good worthy knight and one of those three who have achieved the Grail. Wherefore I ask you why you are not willing to serve as my champion. Do you then also believe that I would poison a guest at the feast which I prepared for the entertainment of such noble and worthy champions?"

"Nay," said Sir Bors, "I think no such thing as that of you, Lady. But in this quarrel there be many upon either side who are my friends, and if I fight upon one side then my friends upon the other side would fall away from me because I did so."

"Alas!" said the Queen. "The time was when I had many knights upon my side. For did not Sir Pelles in the days of my youth take a foolish quarrel upon him for my sake? And did not Sir Launcelot stand ever ready to defend me? Oh, Launcelot, Launcelot! If thou wert but here to stand my champion in this quarrel! But thou art not here, for I, in my haste, have driven thee away from me, I know not whither." So said Queen Guinevere, and with that she began weeping as though her heart would break.

Then Sir Bors was very much moved and he said, "Weep not, Lady, for thou hast yet no cause for weeping. Thou yet hast many good true knights who would defend thee. Yea; I will serve as thy champion unless a better champion arise to defend thee. So take thou heart of grace in this, that thou art innocent of this crime; wherefore, may God defend the right." *Sir Bors will serve as the Queen's champion.*

At this the Queen took comfort and wiped her eyes and smiled, and she said, "Sir Bors, for thy satisfaction I hereby make thee my solemn vow that I did not do this thing of which I am accused. And methinks I know who it was who laid that poisoned apple upon the table, for there was an attendant at that table who stood behind a screen, and this attendant beheld a knight come into that room ere others came thither. But I cannot accuse that knight now, for I myself am accused, wherefore if I accuse him, all will say that it is to shelter myself that I make that accusation." *The Queen declareth her innocence.*

Sir Bors said, "Lady, if this be true, it shall be as you wish, and I will certes do all that I am able to defend you."

Then King Arthur spoke and said, "Sir Bors, there is not any knight in all the court who is so well fitted to defend my Queen as thou. For as thou art one of the most virtuous knights who ever lived, so will thy virtue shine upon any undertaking to which thou settest thy hand. And besides this high virtue of thine, there is no knight at this court, unless it be Sir Gawaine, who is so strong and so excellent a knight as thou."

So spake they at that time, and after those speeches Sir Bors went to the council chamber where lay the glove of Sir Mador de la Porte, and he took up that glove and he thrust it into his belt. With that glove he paraded the court, and many beheld the glove of Sir Mador in his belt. Some came to him and proclaimed that they were secretly pleased that he had assumed the championship of the Queen; but others came and were very angry that he had assumed it.

Amongst these last was Sir Gawaine who said to him, "Sir, what is this you do? Are you not aware that the poison served to us at dinner was *Sir Gawaine is* meant by the Queen for me and not for Sir Patrice who was *angry with Sir* poisoned by it?" To him replied Sir Bors, "Friend, in this *Bors.* you are mistook. For though the poison might have been intended for you and not for Sir Patrice, yet it was not the Queen who placed it there. For I think I know who placed it there, and by and by it will be made manifest to all after that the Queen is freed from this accusation under which she lieth."

Then Sir Gawaine smiled very bitterly and he said, "Thou art easily satisfied, Sir." "If I am," said Sir Bors very calmly, "there is this virtue in my belief; that I cannot believe that my Queen and the wife of my King should do this thing. Nor do I envy those who so easily believe evil of their Queen."

Now when the next day was come, Sir Bors took horse and rode to the castle of Sir Blasius, which place he reached before the sun set. There *Sir Bors* he found Sir Launcelot, and he told Sir Launcelot all that had *rideth to Sir* befallen, and when Sir Launcelot heard it he was very angry. *Launcelot.* "How is this?" he cried. "Do they dare accuse the Queen of this offence? They do it because they know I am absent and cannot defend her." And Sir Bors said, "Yet even so it is. For there is a large party at court that is willing to ascribe that wickedness to her. And that party is headed by several of those who are of most influence at court."

"Well," said Sir Launcelot, "I ask not who they are who believe this evil of her. But I will be there to defend the Queen when her trial cometh.

Meantime, do thou take her championship upon thee till I come; for if it be necessary to prove the innocence of that noble lady, then *Sir Launcelot* thou, who art one of the three knights of the Grail, can best sus- *and Sir Bors* tain it. Besides this, Sir Mador is a very hot and heady knight, *talk together.* wherefore, if thou wilt keep up this quarrel against him till I come, he will be the more ready to do battle according to his beliefs. And it is necessary that the Queen should be defended by arms."

Then Sir Bors told Sir Launcelot that it was the Queen's belief that it was Sir Pinal the Savage who had placed the poisoned apple upon the table; and he also told how the Queen did not dare to bring this accusation against Sir Pinal until she herself was cleared of that accusation.

All this while Sir Launcelot sat frowning as he listened, but at the end of Sir Bors's speech he only said, "I will be there as the Queen's defender, but tell nobody that thou hast spoken to me." And Sir Bors said, "I will not tell of this."

So Sir Bors bid adieu to Sir Launcelot, and Sir Launcelot *Sir Bors* bid adieu to Sir Bors, and Sir Bors returned that night to *returneth to* Camelot again, reaching his inn at that place before the dawn *court.* of the day.

ir Mador begs for his Life :.

Chapter Third

How Sir Bors was relieved of the defence of the Queen, and of how Sir Mador de la Porte was overthrown.

SO came the eve of the day of that conflict when the innocence of the Queen was to be approved by conflict. That evening the Queen sent for Sir Bors de Ganis, and she said to him, "Sir, what is your mind in this battle which you are to fight to-morrow?" Quoth Sir Bors, "Lady, it is even as it was aforetime. For ever I do believe in your innocence and deem it be impossible that you could administer poison to one of your guests. So I will do battle for you to the best of my ability as I promised you I would do. But should another knight, better fitted by skill at arms than I, appear to assume that honor, then would I surrender the honor to that knight; yea, even at the last minute."

So after Sir Bors had departed from her, the Queen went to the King and told him what Sir Bors had said to her. Quoth the King, "Lady, thou hast one of the best champions that can be found in the *The King* entire world to defend this case in thy behalf. For I know of *praiseth Sir* no knight who could be better chosen to defend thine honor *Bors.* than Sir Bors, unless it were his kinsman, Sir Launcelot of the Lake. For even Sir Gawaine is not stronger nor better, nor was Sir Percival stronger nor better than is Sir Bors de Ganis."

So said the King, and at his words the Queen took great comfort and cheerfulness.

So came the next day of trial. For at about the eleventh hour of the morning there came to the open square within the walls of the town the King and the Queen and the Court of the King. At that place the Lord Constable was already come, and to one side was a great pile of dried *The Queen* fagots laid cross wise, the one upon the other, and in the midst *cometh with* of that pile of fagots was an iron stake with fetterlocks at- *the King to* tached to it about as high as one could reach, standing before *the lists.* that stake. Those high lords and ladies who were there looked very closely at the Queen, and they beheld that she smiled as she looked about her, but that her face was white like to purified wax for whiteness. And the Queen was clad entirely in white; for her robe was long and spotless of color, and she wore a belt of white leather, studded with silver, bound about her waist, and her hair hung down upon either side and was wound about with ribbons of white and silver. And some of those who looked upon her were grieved and sorrow-struck at her trouble, but others were pleased and triumphant to see her thus brought low, even to the trial of her life and her good fame.

Then King Arthur called the constable to him and he said to him, "Lord Constable, here do I commit to thee the tender body of this my Queen, who stands here wrongfully accused of the crime of murder. Take her; she is thine until after this trial of battle." So saying, the King took the Queen by the right hand and led her to the constable, and he gave the right hand of the Queen into the hand of the constable. And the constable took the Queen by the hand, and he said, "Lord King; here take I the body of this lady who is my Queen. But I take that body only to return it unto thy ward; so hold thou this lady in thy keeping, and may God keep ye both, amen."

Therewith the constable replaced the hand of the Queen into the hand of *The King sitteth beside the Queen* the King, and thereupon withdrew to one side. Thereafter the King conducted the Queen by the hand up the flight of steps to a high seat that had been prepared for her beside his own seat. Then the King said, "Let the accusers of this lady be summoned."

Then came Sir Mador de la Porte, clad all in very brilliantly shining *Sir Mador de la Porte appeareth.* armor, and riding a red-roan horse, whose coat glistened like red silk. So he drew rein in front of the King's pew in the list. And the King looked at Sir Mador, frowning till his eyes disappeared beneath his brows; yea, till the veins at his forehead became expanded and knotted, and until his entire visage became empurpled with blood.

Anon he found his voice, and he said, "Sir, what brings you here? For you claim to be a gentleman of my court and of my Round Table, and yet you bring accusation against your Queen, and the lady of all others whom you should be most called upon by honor to defend."

Then Sir Mador spoke up in a very bold voice, both high and loud. *Sir Mador challengeth the Queen.* "Sovereign and awful lord," said he, "here stand I for justice and for right; without awe and without fear of anyone or of anything. Wit ye then, that some days ago I and several others sat at feast with the Queen. What time my near kinsman, Sir Patrice of Ireland, ate an apple at that feast, and the apple was poisoned and he died of eating thereof. Now that was the Queen's feast and we were the Queen's guests; how, then, was the poisoning done, saving by the Queen's orders? So here stand I now to accuse that Queen of the treason of poisoning; nor will I rest satisfied from that accusation, saving only as someone shall overthrow me in this, my coming battle."

Then spake the King, "Sir, did you make research concerning this accusation, or did you question anyone concerning this affair? *The King* For certes it is very criminal and very wicked to administer *challengeth* poison to another; but it is none the less criminal and none *Sir Mador.* the less wicked to utter such treason as you do by accusing the Queen unjustly and without cause. Wherefore, Sir, you should be very certain of your accusation."

Quoth Sir Mador, "Sir, I believe the testimony of mine eyes; for they beheld that which my lips have spoken, and so my hand shall uphold in this, my just encounter against the Queen's strong champion."

Then the King spoke very haughtily. "Sir," quoth he, "you have entrusted the verity of your case to the testimony of your eyes, and that testimony has deceived and misled you. Nevertheless, I shall not answer you here, for anon you shall be answered to your pain." Then the King spake to an esquire who stood below in the tilt yard. "Hasten," said he, "and bid Sir Bors de Ganis to come hither."

So the esquire departed and anon he returned, leading the white horse of Sir Bors by the bridle. And Sir Bors was clad all in armor *Sir Bors* of pure and virgin white, and all his trappings and the trap- *appeareth.* pings of his horse were white, so that he shone glistening, like to a figure of pure silver.

"Sir," said Sir Mador to Sir Bors, "Knowest thou why I am here, and upon what accusation?" Sir Bors said, "Aye, I know it well." Then said Sir Mador, "Dost thou stand for the other side?" Sir Bors said, "Yea, I stand heart and soul for the other side. But I will tell thee truly. I said that I would undertake this quarrel upon the Queen's behalf unless some better knight than I should take that battle upon him. *Sir Bors* I know you, Sir Mador, for a noble and valiant knight, and *appealeth for* you know me for what you have beheld of me, wherefore you *delay.* know that I fear not to meet you or any knight in all of the world, and that I would do battle with anyone with all of my might in a lesser quarrel than this. Wherefore I ask you now to postpone this battle until the hour of noon, for by that time there may come more worthy than I to defend this honorable and much abused lady."

*Sir Mador
denieth him
any delay.*
"Is that all you have to say?" said Sir Mador. "Well, then, Messire, either come you to battle with me without loss of time, or else withdraw you from the field for someone else to take your place."

"Take your horse and your arms," said Sir Bors, "and as I suppose you will not tarry long, so also will I not tarry long, but will be with you anon." So each knight withdrew from the field, and each busied himself in preparing for the conflict. In this Sir Mador was the quicker, and so rode out of his pavilion and around the course, and whilst none applauded him in that procession, yet there were some who frowned not upon him.

So Sir Bors, when he was made ready, came forth from his pavilion, and
*A new cham-
pion appeareth
upon the
Queen's behalf.*
he cast his eyes toward the forest and immediately he was aware that a knight was coming thence, riding easily yet swiftly. And this knight was clad in strange armor, and he bore a shield without any escutcheon, nor was there any emblazonment about him whatsoever to tell what knight he was. But Sir Bors knew very well that that knight was none other than Sir Launcelot of the Lake.

Anon this knight came quickly to where Sir Bors was, and he said to him, "Messire, I give you grammercy for assuming this quarrel upon behalf of the Queen. But now I come to assume that quarrel myself and so you are freed from it." Sir Bors said, "Come you to King Arthur." And the knight said, "Conduct me to him."

So Sir Bors conducted the knight to where King Arthur sat, and when
*The new
knight appear-
eth before the
King.*
he was come there King Arthur said to him, "Sir, what knight are you? For that I should know ere I consent to establish you instead of Sir Bors in this quarrel." To which Sir Bors made reply, "Lord, I know this knight, and I know that he is a better knight than I am, so I yield my rights in this quarrel unto him."

Then King Arthur said to Sir Mador de la Porte, "Sir, will you accept this new knight in your quarrel?" To which Sir Mador replied, "Sir, I will accept him or any."

So each knight withdrew to his end of the lists and there they made
*Sir Mador is
overthrown.*
themselves ready. And when they were all prepared, then each launched against the other with all the speed and vehemence that he possessed. So they met in the midst of the course and in that encounter the spear of Sir Mador was broken all to pieces, but the spear of the other knight held so that Sir Mador and his horse were both overturned into the dust.

But Sir Mador recovered from his fall very suddenly, and drawing his sword and setting his shield in front of him he came forward to the assault of his enemy as though this were the very beginning of the battle. Upon this the other knight leaped very nimbly and quickly down from his horse, and setting his shield before him, he drew his sword and came forward as with great eagerness for battle.

Each struck at the other with great fierceness, for Sir Mador was a very strong and powerful knight, and was further upheld by his indignation. So they fought for above an hour, and in that time Sir Launce- *Sir Mador is* lot held his strength, but the strength of Sir Mador began to *beaten in battle.* wane so that he could hardly sustain his arm. Then Sir Launcelot redoubled his strokes until Sir Mador held his shield full low. At that Sir Launcelot lifted up his sword and he smote Sir Mador so terribly upon the helm that he fell grovelling to the earth. Then Sir Launcelot drew near to Sir Mador to smite him again, but Sir Mador raised himself a little and lifting his sword he smote Sir Launcelot through the thick of the thigh.

But when Sir Launcelot felt himself to be thus wounded and when he beheld how that the blood flowed forth in a red stream from the wound in his thigh, he drew away and waited for Sir Mador to rise again. And when Sir Mador had arisen he rushed upon him and smote him again, so terrible a blow that the blade bit through the iron helmet, and the leather coif and into the bone beneath the coif.

Then Sir Mador fell down and lay upon the ground like one who was dead, and Sir Launcelot ran in to where he lay and seizing the helmet that covered the head, he cut the thongs with his misericordia *Sir Launcelot* and rushed it off from his head. With that the light shone *spareth Sir* in upon the face of Sir Mador and aroused him from his *Mador.* swoon; and beholding Sir Launcelot standing terribly above him, he cried out, in a loud piercing voice, "Spare me my life, Sir Knight! Spare me my life!" Quoth Sir Launcelot, "I will not spare thee thy life, unless thou dost confess that thou wert mistaken concerning the guilt of the Queen, and that she is innocent of evil." Said Sir Mador, "I do confess it."

Then Sir Launcelot called the Lord Constable of the lists to him and he said to Sir Mador, "Confess what thou hast confessed to me to this gentleman." And Sir Mador said, "Sir, to this constable I do confess and acknowledge that I was mistook as to the guilt of the Queen, and that she is indeed guiltless of that of which I have accused her, and of all other crimes whatsoever."

Then Sir Launcelot said, "Bear this knight hence away from this spot."

Upon that there came several attendants to that place and they lifted Sir Mador and carried him away from that place.

Then Sir Launcelot and the constable went from that place of conflict to the presence of King Arthur, and the King and the Queen descended from their high seats to welcome him. Quoth the King, "Sir, well have you fought this day, and well may we guess who you are who have done this battle. We do both give you thanks—I for that you have saved to me my Queen; she that you have saved to her her life and her honor."

"Lord," said Sir Launcelot, "here have I brought with me this constable to avouch for it that Sir Mador hath confessed that he hath wrong-

Sir Mador confesseth a wrong accusation.

fully accused the Queen of this crime, and that she is as guiltless of it as she is of any other crime at this present." And the constable said, "I do avouch for the truth of that." Then the King said to Sir Launcelot, "Sir, I perceive that thou art wounded. Wilt thou not refresh thyself with a glass of wine?" And Sir Launcelot said, "Yea, Lord, for wine would be exceedingly grateful to me at this present."

So a little page ran and presently returned, bringing a flagon of sparkling yellow wine, and Sir Launcelot unlaced his helmet and removed it from his head, so that all beheld his face and knew him for Sir Launcelot.

And then King Arthur said, "Sir, methought that you were Sir Launcelot of the Lake when I beheld how you did battle a little while ago. Moreover, when Sir Bors spoke of a better knight than he rising for the Queen's

Sir Launcelot pledgeth the Queen.

defence, I wist he must mean you, for you are the only one who is better than he. But now we have you, we will not let you go again." "Lord," quoth Sir Launcelot, "I will not leave this court again unless I am bidden to go. For here may I defend both your honor and the honor of your Queen. For first of all do I owe my duty to you who made me a knight; and then do I owe my duty to her who is my revered and honored lady." Then, taking the flagon of wine into his hands he turned him about and lifting that flagon on high, he cried in a loud, clear voice so that all might hear him, "Here do I drink this flagon of golden wine to the truth and innocence of my Queen. Health to her friends, confusion to her enemies, and may harm fall upon those who contemplate harm to her!"

Then he put the brim of the flagon to his lips and drank off the entire draught of wine ere he removed it again.

Then King Arthur said, "Let us go visit that wounded knight, for I have something that I would say to him." So Sir Launcelot and the constable and King Arthur went across the meadow of battle to the pavilion of Sir

Mador. And they entered the pavilion and Sir Mador was lying upon a couch and the surgeon was searching his wounds.

King Arthur said to him, "Sir, who besides yourself were the accusers of the Queen?" Sir Mador said, "Lord, I was her only accuser." The King said, "Thou liest, for there was a conspiracy against her to undo her, and thou wert but the instrument of that conspiracy. I will ask thee no further to betray those who were with thee in this affair. Only I have this to say to thee, that if by to-morrow morning thou art within the purlieus of this court, *King Arthur dismisseth Sir Mador from the court.* or if at any future time thou comest into my power again, or if ever I meet thee in battle or out of battle, that time spells for thee thy death. Bear my words well in mind; for though I spare thee this time upon behest of the Queen, yet will I not spare thee again upon the beseeching of anyone in all of the world."

Sir Mador said very bitterly to the King, "My Lord, thou speakest as a sound man to one who is very grievously wounded and who may not defend himself." "Not so," said the King very calmly, "I speak, first of all, as a king to his knight, and next I speak as one knight to another knight who hath wrought him a greivous injury. For thou canst not undo what thou hast done; for thy quarrel hath sowed dissension and evil thought among my entire court, so that I, who was one time loved by my entire court, know not now who are my friends and who mine enemies." Then the King turned to the constable, and he said, "Lord Constable, thou hearest what I have said. If this man is found hereabouts to-morrow day, cast him immediately into prison and report the same to me. For if after this day he falleth into my power, then he shall himself suffer destruction by the flames, as he would have consigned his own Queen to the flames."

Thereupon the King turned upon his heel and left Sir Mador de la Porte gnawing his finger nails.

That day the King held a council of his chief lords and subordinate kings. And before this council came that servant who had hidden behind the screen as aforetold of. And this servant told of how he had beheld Sir Pinal place the apple upon the table whereon the feast was to be held. This evidence they *The servant telleth how Sir Pinal placed the apple.* all heard and listened to, and when it was ended the King said, "Send for this Sir Pinal and let us hear what he hath to say to this."

So they sent for Sir Pinal, but he was nowhere to be found, for the Queen's enemies had told him that that evidence was to be admitted and he had fled away from the court into the wilderness, never to return again.

So was the innocence of the Queen proven. But still there were some who disbelieved that evidence, for they said, "See ye not how it is? For *Yet is the* first they overthrow Sir Mador and then they drive him away *Queen accused* from this court. Then they bring in this evidence to clear *by many.* the Queen from guilt and they lay that guilt upon poor Sir Pinal, who is not of the Round Table. Thus there is no one to contradict the evidence of this poor knave, and so the Queen is to be cleared of the suspicion of guilt."

So spake several, and the news of this was brought to the ears of Sir Gawaine. But Sir Gawaine would say no word upon the matter, for whilst he felt bitter enmity toward the Queen, and whilst he suspected the worst things of her, yet he would not give voice to that which he suspected. Neither would he give accusation against her, but went his own way thinking his own thoughts and keeping those thoughts within his own bosom.

Thus have I told you the history of these things as I myself have read *Of the* of them in the ancient books that treat of them. For this *dissensions* was the first beginning of the end. For now that the Grail *at the court.* had been lifted from the earth, there was naught to hold together the Court of King Arthur as it had been held together before. But each knight began now to think of his own glory and of himself, and not of the glory of the King and the Good of the world.

So now begin we with the history of those dissensions that presently broke forth in the Court of the King.

ir Launcelot defends the door:·

Chapter Fourth

How there came quarrels at the court, and how Sir Launcelot of the Lake was assaulted by the brothers of Sir Gawaine.

NOW there was at court at that time much dissension and many angry recriminations back and forth between the one party and the other party. For the one party maintained that the Queen had been ill-used and had suffered much, and would have suffered death, saving only for the defence of Sir Launcelot of the Lake; and the other party maintained that the Queen possessed an evil soul, and that Sir Launcelot was her dishonorable lover and that it was for this reason that he had fought for her.

Of this latter party were some of the brothers of Sir Gawaine, who were at the head of that party; to wit, there was Sir Mordred and Sir Agravaine. These knights spoke very boldly and openly, saying *Sir Mordred* that Sir Launcelot practised treachery with the Queen against *and Sir* the King's high honor. Sir Agravaine said, "Well is it that Sir *Agravaine accuse* Launcelot is the greatest knight now living on the earth (for *Sir Launcelot* this is true now that Sir Galahad had departed in glory), yet *of treason.* it is not to be forgotten that he is not greater in his strength than several knights who might come against him at once. So when Sir Launcelot next visits the Queen, if a number of us shall fall upon him, it can scarcely be but that those knights should overcome him, and that so the King's honor should be revenged."

Whilst he so spoke, Sir Gawaine sat at one side gnawing his mustache. Then he up and spake, saying, "What is this you would do? Would you practise treachery against Sir Launcelot and against the Queen? God knows I have no love for the Queen, and never have had love *Sir Gawaine* for her, but neither would I practise treachery against her, *will not join* but would assail her openly and against the entire world. *with them.* As for Sir Launcelot of the Lake; long hath he been my dearest friend and companion at arms; am I then to practise treason against him?" Then

turning to Sir Geharis and Sir Gareth, he said, "What say you, my brothers? Speak!" Then Sir Geharis and Sir Gareth said, "What thou sayst,
Gawaine, we also say." And Sir Gareth said upon his part, "I cannot
now forget and I can never fail to remember that it was Sir Launcelot of
the Lake who made me a knight. Shall I then sit in judgment upon my
godfather in knighthood, and undertake to practise evil against him?"

Quoth Sir Mordred, "I say with my brother Agravaine that the Queen
is altogether evil and that Sir Launcelot is her lover, and that saying I am
ready to maintain to the peril of my life."

Said Sir Gawaine, "I pray you tell me; what is it you seek to do?" Him
answered Sir Mordred, "We seek to spy upon Sir Launcelot and, when next
he visits the Queen in her apartments, we would make assault upon him. When we have thus espied upon him, then
we and several others will fall upon him and seize him and
hale him before the King for trial." Said Sir Gawaine,
"That is no such easy matter for to do. And when you have done it, it
will be but of little avail; for the King will not condemn Sir Launcelot
upon such uncertain accusation. For what accusation shall you bring
against Sir Launcelot and the Queen that you dare mention to the King?"

Sir Mordred declares that he will arrest Sir Launcelot.

Then Sir Mordred made no immediate answer, but when he was come
to a place apart from those three, he said to Sir Agravaine, "Sir Launcelot is guilty of thou knowest what treason against the King. Now I told
Gawaine that we would arrest him and bring him to the King. What I
really purpose is this: that we assault Sir Launcelot in the Queen's apartments, and that we slay him. For once he is dead the King will quickly
forgive us and will believe the Queen to have been guilty, but if Sir Launcelot is alive he will never forgive us. Hah, brother, a dead lion is a less
dangerous enemy to a man than a living fox. So it were best that Sir
Launcelot died." In this Sir Agravaine agreed with him; so after that
they set watch upon Sir Launcelot to take him when next he should visit
the Queen. But Sir Launcelot was warned by one who overheard them,
and for that while he did not visit the Queen in her apartments.

So one night Sir Mordred called to him a page of the Queen's court when
the page was passing, and he said to him, "Lanadel" (for such was the
page's name)—"Lanadel, go you to Sir Launcelot of the Lake
and tell him that the Queen would fain speak with him in
her bower." Thereupon the page, suspecting no evil, went
to Sir Launcelot, and delivered that message to him, and Sir Launcelot,
suspecting no evil, fulfilled the terms of that message, and went secretly
thither to the Queen's apartments.

Sir Mordred betrayeth Sir Launcelot.

Finding the Queen there, Sir Launcelot said to her, "Lady, what is it thou wouldst say to me?" She looked upon him in astonishment and said, "Sir, I did not send for you to say anything to you." *Sir Launcelot* Sir Launcelot said, "How is this? Your page, Lanadel, came *goeth to the* to me and brought it to me as a message that you would speak *Queen's bower.* to me at this place." She said, "Launcelot, I sent no such message as that to thee. Yet, in very truth, it hath been long since thou hast been hither to speak to me. Art thou affronted with me, Launcelot?"

He said to her, "Lady, thou knowest that I am not affronted with thee. But there is this: I must consider thine honor and reputation as I do mine own. But, Lady, touching this message of late delivered to me, here is treachery of some sort, for certes that message came to me as from thee, wherefore I know that some treachery is brewing against us, though I know not what that treachery is."

Now turn we to those enemies of Sir Launcelot to see what they did upon this occasion. For Sir Mordred watched at the entrance of the Queen's apartments until that he beheld Sir Launcelot enter them. Upon that he ran to Sir Agravaine, and said to him, "Brother, wit ye that Sir Launcelot is at this time in the Queen's chamber. Let us now make haste to take him." So those two called about them certain knights who were at enmity with Sir Launcelot, and they said to them, "Gentlemen, let us hasten and take that traitor knight who is even now in the Queen's bower."

Now those knights whom they called upon to accompany them were as follows: There were Sir Colgrance and Sir Gingaline, and Sir Melyot of Logris, and Sir Galleron of Galway; there were Sir Melion of the Mountain, and Sir Petypas of Winchelsea; there were Sir Gromer Somerjour and Sir Astamore, Sir Cuselaine, Sir Florence, and Sir Lovel. And these last two were sons to Sir Gawaine.

These eleven knights, together with Sir Agravaine and Sir Mordred, making thirteen in all, went together in a party to the apart- *The Queen is* ments of the Queen. And the ladies of the Queen beheld them *warned.* coming, and wist that they came for no good purpose. Wherefore these ladies ran screaming and in haste and bolted and barred the door. Then they ran to the Queen's apartment and they found that Sir Launcelot was there and they cried out, "Lady, arouse you, for your enemies are upon you!"

By this those knights were at the door, and Sir Agravaine *The thirteen* knocked and cried aloud in a very loud and thunderous *knights chal-* *lenge Sir* voice, "Thou traitor knight! What doest thou here? Why *Launcelot to* liest thou behind locked doors in the Queen's apartments? *appear.*

Come forth to us who are thy fellows of the court and of the Round Table, and render an account to us.   For we are here to receive thine account!"

These words were uttered so loudly and so powerfully that they echoed and re-echoed throughout that entire part of the castle, and when they struck upon the Queen's ears, she fell as white as an ash of wood and sank back upon a couch, placing her hand above her heart.

Then Sir Launcelot stood up from where he sat and he cast his eyes around him from side to side, but he could see no armor for defence, and no way of escape.   And ever those knights without smote upon the door, and ever Sir Agravaine cried out, "Sir Launcelot of the Lake; what doest thou there in the Queen's chamber?   Come forth and deliver thyself to us."

Then Sir Launcelot said, "Lady, I prithee tell me, is there ere a suit of armor in this place as I could clothe myself withal?"   She said, "Nay, Launcelot, there is no armor in this room."   Then Sir Launcelot said to her, "Then must I defend myself without armor; for I know that these knights have no purpose for to take me prisoner to the King.   Otherwise, that which they purpose is to take my life."   Then the Queen sank down terrified upon her knees before him, and said, "Launcelot, go not forth to them, for assuredly they mean thy death."   He said to her, "Lady, I must go; but this I beseech of thee, that thou wilt pray for me. And this also I beseech of thee, that, should I fall in this encounter, thou wilt go with my relatives, Sir Ector and Sir Bors and Sir Lionel and Sir Ure, and bid them that they shall take thee to an asylum of refuge at my castle of Joyous Gard.   For there is now no safety for thee at this place, and only great and continual dangers.   For ever there is growing at this court against thee a rooted jealousy of all that thou sayest or doest, and if so be I lose my life, then these, mine enemies, will overwhelm thee."   Then the Queen wept, and she cried out, "Launcelot! Launcelot! Go not forth to them!"

As thus they spake, those knights without continually beat upon the door, crying ever in louder and more violent tones, "Traitor! Open to

The thirteen knights threaten to burst in the door. us!"   And the door was not opened, but remained closed. Then they cast their eyes about and they beheld a great form that stood there in the hall.   And Sir Agravaine said to certain of the others, "Bring hither yonder form, and let us beat down the door with it.   For thus alone may we hope to come at this traitor!" So they brought that form and they beat with it upon the door, and the door cracked and bent beneath their blows.

Then Sir Launcelot wrapped his cloak about his arm, and he took his sword in his hand, and he said to those who were beating upon the door, "Messire, cease your uproar and I will come forth to you." Then he turned the key in the lock of the door, and he opened the door a little, but not very far, setting his foot against it lest they should burst it open from without and so rush in, many at once, upon him.

Sir Launcelot defendeth himself with a cloak.

But when the door was opened and they beheld Sir Launcelot standing there without any armor of defence whatsoever saving only the cloak that was wrapped about his arm, they took heart of grace that they should easily overcome him. Then there came forward a tall and very powerful knight, hight Sir Colgrance of Gore, and he struck a terrible strong and powerful blow at Sir Launcelot with intent to hew him down. This blow Sir Launcelot put aside with his sword and immediately delivered a blow in return.

In that blow he smote Sir Colgrance upon the head, and the blow bit through the bascinet upon his head and it smote deep into the bone of the brain so that Sir Colgrance fell down grovelling to the earth, and immediately he died.

He slayeth Sir Colgrance.

Then Sir Launcelot seized Sir Colgrance's body by the shoulders and dragged it into the room ere the others had recovered, and immediately he bolted and barred the door as it was before. And Sir Launcelot said to the Queen, "Lady, here hath Providence delivered armor into my hands. I prithee aid me to arm myself."

So the Queen and her affrighted ladies hastened to Sir Launcelot and together they stripped the armor off the body of Sir Colgrance. And they assisted Sir Launcelot to clothe himself very quickly and nimbly in that armor. Then, having thus armed himself in the armor of Sir Colgrance, Sir Launcelot came to the door of the room and he spoke to those without, and he said to them, "Messires, what is it you would have with me?" They say, "We would have you come forth and surrender yourself to us so that we may take you to King Arthur." Sir Launcelot said, "I cannot surrender myself to you, but this I will promise to do: if you will go hence and leave me in peace, I will surrender myself to King Arthur to-morrow morning, and will then abide by his justice." Sir Agravaine said, "We will not do this. We will not trust thee. Deliver thyself to us immediately, or we will slay thee."

Sir Launcelot armeth himself in Sir Colgrance's armor.

Then Sir Launcelot said, "I come!" and therewith he flung wide open the door. And Sir Launcelot strode out amongst them like to a lion into the midst of a pack of dogs. And they beheld that Sir Launcelot was clad all in the armor of Sir Col-

Sir Launcelot assaileth his enemies.

grance. And Sir Launcelot fronted Sir Agravaine and the eyes of Sir Launcelot flashed forth pure fire from under the vizor of his bascinet. And Sir
Launcelot strode to Sir Agravaine, crying out, "Thou first!" And therewith he smote Sir Agravaine with might and main.

Sir Agravaine warded the blow, but so wonderfully powerful was it
that it smote down that ward; and it smote Sir Agravaine upon the bascinet; and it cut through the iron of the bascinet and through the bone
of the brain pan and into the brain itself.

Then Sir Agravaine cried out very terribly and fell down dying to the
earth; and Sir Launcelot put his foot upon the neck of Sir Agravaine,
He slayeth Sir and wrenched forth the sword out of the cut that he had made.
Agravaine and Then Sir Launcelot smote to the right hand and to the left; and
several others. of those eleven knights who were with Sir Agravaine and Sir
Mordred he slew nine in that little room. And he smote Sir Mordred upon
the shoulder so that he sheared the flesh of the arm, a great slice from the
bone, and the other two knights were more or less wounded, so that anon
they fled in tumult from that place.

And Sir Launcelot was also wounded in many places in that conflict,
so that he was, as it were, all bathed in crimson from head to foot. Then,
having put his enemies to flight, he turned him and re-entered the Queen's
chamber.

But when the Queen beheld him thus all bathed in red, she shrieked
aloud, for she thought him to be mortally wounded. But Sir Launcelot
said to her, "Fear not, Lady, thine enemies are put to flight and I am not
Sir Launcelot sorely hurt." And he said to her, "Lady, my love for thee
is wounded. hath ever been my curse, and now it hath brought us to this
end. For in thy defence and in my defence I have slain the nephew
of the King and two of the sons of Sir Gawaine. So now the King
will be my foe, and so I must quit this place for aye. But I cannot
leave thee, Lady, for without me thou wilt be defenceless. So I prithee
prepare thyself for a journey. I will go forth and gather about me a
number of knights of mine own kindred and friends, and we will take
thee hence away from this place. For to-morrow they will bring thee
forth to trial, and when they bring thee forth, then will we seize thee
and carry thee away."

Then the Queen fell to weeping very bitterly, and she said, "Ah, Launcelot! Alas and alas! Is this then the end?" And he said, "Aye, Lady."
Therewith he went forth from that place and left her.

So Sir Launcelot came to Sir Bors's inn, and when Sir Bors beheld him,
all covered and ensanguined with blood, he cried out, "God save us!

What is this? What aileth thee?" Then Sir Launcelot told Sir Bors all that had befallen, and when he had told it Sir Bors sent for *Sir Launcelot adviseth with Sir Bors.* Sir Ector and for Sir Lionel and for Sir Ure, and fourteen other knights, relatives and friends of Sir Launcelot, and Sir Launcelot told unto them what he had told to Sir Bors.

Then Sir Bors said to those who were there gathered, "Messires his is a very sad and bitter quarrel. For I do avouch that my relative, Sir Launcelot, is in all ways perfectly innocent toward the Queen. For we know that he was deceived into her presence by a false message delivered unto him by someone who was an enemy to him and who meant to undo him. So this lady hath also been misused in such a way that it is contrary to his honor as a knight that we should suffer such harm to approach her. Now it is my advice that we await to see what shall presently befall. For if this quarrel is condoned by the King, then is all very well; but if the King seek to punish Sir Launcelot by bringing the Queen to a trial, then shall he save her from that trial and shall convey her away to Joyous Gard where she may remain safe from harm."

Then all those other knights to whom Sir Bors spake held up their swords with their handles before them, and they said, "Here- *Other knights swear fealty to Sir Launcelot.* with and upon this holy sign of the crucifix do we swear that we will ride with and aid Sir Launcelot of the Lake in this undertaking. And, if it be demanded of us, we will assist him to bring this lady to Joyous Gard, and we will there aid and defend him and her with our bodies until the last extremity and until death."

Meantime, Sir Mordred had had his wound bound up and had taken horse and had ridden to the inn of King Arthur, and he appeared before King Arthur in the room when the King was then with several of his court. And when the King beheld him thus wounded, *Sir Mordred accuseth Sir Launcelot to the King.* he started up and cried out, "Hah, Sir Mordred! What bringeth thee before me in this plight? Where gottest thou that wound?" Then Sir Mordred kneeled down before the King, and he said, "Sovereign Lord and Master, I got this wound in thy service. For Sir Launcelot visited the Queen recently in her bower, and I and twelve other knights sought to arrest him there and to bring him before thee. But he resisted that arrest, and of the thirteen who assaulted him nine are dead and one is like to die."

Then the King drew his breath very hard between his teeth, at that news, and anon he said, "Who are dead? Are they any of my friends?" Sir Mordred said, "All are thy friends, and three are of thy kin." Quoth

King Arthur, "Who are those of my kin?"   And Sir Mordred said, "One of them is Sir Agravaine, thy nephew, and the others are Sir Florence and Sir Lovel, the young sons of Sir Gawaine."

Then the King groaned and Sir Gawaine who was with him covered his head and also groaned in sorrow.   Quoth the King, "To-morrow day *Sir Gawaine* this shall be inquired into, and the Queen shall be brought *sorroweth.* to trial for this treason."   And with those words he arose and withdrew from that place, accompanied only by Sir Gawaine, Sir Geharis and Sir Gareth and Sir Mordred; and leaving the other knights who were attendant upon him sunk in silence, not knowing which way to look or what to say.

So when the King was come to a private place, he seated himself and buried his face in his hands.   And he groaned aloud, and he said, "Alas is me!   This is certes the beginning of the end that was foretold by Merlin!"   And anon he said to Sir Gawaine, "To thee, Gawaine, will I entrust the pushing of that inquiry which must follow.   For thou and Geharis and Gareth shall go with a company of an hundred knights, and ye shall arrest the Queen, and shall bring her for trial for this offence."

Then Sir Gawaine kneeled down before King Arthur, and he said, "Sovereign and lawful Lord and Master, I pray you to spare me from this."   King Arthur said, "Why should I spare thee?"   Sir Gawaine said, "For these two causes: firstly, I am sworn brother in arms to Sir Launcelot; secondly, I am not friendly with my lady the Queen and so am not fit to serve her as her escort."

Then King Arthur said, "I do not understand your refusal, Messire. Was not Sir Agravaine your brother?   And was not he a strong and noble knight?   And were not Sir Florence and Sir Lovel your sons?"

"Yea, Lord," said Sir Gawaine.   "All this is true; but I suspected evil in this affair, and I strongly advised them to refrain therefrom.   This they have refused to hearken to and so they have perished, armed and in fair conflict with Sir Launcelot—he one against many."

Then King Arthur's face flushed very red with anger, and he turned to Sir Geharis and Sir Gareth.   "And you, Messires," said he, "do you also refuse me this duty?"   "Sir," said Sir Gareth, "if you bid us upon our duty to undertake this commission, we will do so.   Yet wit you that Sir Launcelot was he who made me a knight; wherefore I will not go in arms to escort the Queen.   But if thou commandest me to go, then will I go without armor or defence of any sort to protect me.   For I will not stand in arms before the avowed lady of him who made me a knight."

King Arthur said, "I do command you both to go, so let there be an end to this argument. But see to it that the Queen shall be brought to her trial in a plain white robe without a girdle and that she come in her bare feet like to any criminal. For I shall not believe her to be innocent until she be proved so."

Now when the next day was come, it being then about the tenth hour of the morning, Sir Geharis and Sir Gareth took those five *Sir Gareth and* score knights and they rode to the lodgings of the Queen. *Sir Geharis go* Meantime, word had been sent to the Queen that she was *unarmed to* to clothe her in such a guise as the King had said; to wit, *Launcelot.* ungirdled and in white, and in her bare feet. And it was said to her that she was to come to her trial like to a criminal—barefoot in that wise, and without a girdle about her waist.

Then the Queen wept very many bitter tears, and said, "Alas, my lord, the King, hath already condemned me in his heart, so that my trial will mean my death." And the ladies of the Queen wept *The Queen* with her and they said, "Lady, alas for thy happiness! For *weepeth.* this is certes the end." Then the Queen dried her tears and she said to them, "Comfort ye! For I have done many evil deeds in my life, but ye know that I am innocent of this deed." They say, "Yea, we know it and will avouch for it."

Now word of all these things had also been brought to Sir Launcelot, and when he heard of them he aroused himself and called his esquires about him. Then he went forth in his full armor and he found Sir Bors and Sir Lionel together. And Sir Launcelot said to them, "Messires, do you remember that you and several others promised to aid me in the rescue of the Queen? Well, then, the time is come, for she is about to be brought forth to her trial, for they have sent for her. She shall not come to the disgrace of trial, for I will bear her hence. Go you and summon all those who will support me and bring them in haste to the Queen's inn, for I go there immediately." Sir Bors said, "Go not thither from this place until we summon aid." Sir Launcelot said, "Then make haste."

So Sir Bors and Sir Lionel hastened away from that place, leaving Sir Launcelot walking in great strides up and down the length of the room.

Anon came one running to where Sir Launcelot was, and said to him, "Sir, the Queen biddeth thee to come to her in haste, for they are taking her barefoot to her trial."

Then Sir Launcelot waited for no further word, but hastened with all speed to where the Queen was, and when he had come there he found many of his knights already there, and several came immediately there-

after.   And as Sir Launcelot approached he beheld the Queen seated
upon her horse in her bare feet and surrounded by that
armed escort which the King had sent.   Then the Queen
beheld Sir Launcelot and she called to him, saying, "Sir
Launcelot, make haste!"   And she reached out her arms toward him.

*Sir Launcelot
hasteneth to
aid the Queen.*

Then Sir Launcelot emitted a great loud and bitter cry.   And therewith he drew his sword like lightning and his friends drew their swords
and they rushed into the throng smiting from right to left and
from left to right again.   And those who were thus assaulted
smote back again at those knights and bore them hither and
thither by weight of numbers because they who fought for the Queen
were so few.   But the knights of Sir Launcelot were prepared for this
assault and the knights of King Arthur were not prepared for it, wherefore those latter were quickly separated and driven back.   Now in the
fury of that small battle Sir Gareth was pushed near to Sir Launcelot
and he was unarmed as hath been told of, and Sir Launcelot saw him but
knew him not.   So Sir Launcelot smote Sir Gareth upon the head with
his sword and he clave asunder the head of Sir Gareth to the throat and
Sir Gareth fell dead beneath the horses' feet.

*Sir Launcelot
slayeth Sir
Gareth.*

And Sir Launcelot thought nothing of what he had done by that blow;
for in his fury and raging he beheld the Lady Queen Guinevere before
him.   With that he spurred forward without looking down upon the earth
to see who it was whom he had smitten down, and he catched the Queen
up from her saddle and seated her on his saddle before him.   Then he
shouted, "Let us away and escape while there is yet time!"

So with that Sir Geharis put himself forward to stay Sir Launcelot, and
Sir Launcelot, beholding him there in the way and not witting
who he was, smote him also with his sword and slew him.

*He slayeth
Sir Geharis.*

So with that they all ceased fighting and spurred away from that place,
cleaving their way before them and taking Queen Guinevere with them.
And they rode away from that place and from that city, and
they ceased not to ride until they had come to the confines of
Joyous Gard, where there was an asylum of peace and safety.

*Sir Launcelot
escapeth with
the Queen.*

And in that battle there were lost twenty-seven knights of the King, and
of these there were eleven knights of the Round Table.   And there were
lost sixteen knights of Sir Launcelot's party and of them there were nine
knights of the Round Table.   And in that battle Sir Kay the Seneschal
and Sir Gareth and Sir Geharis and Sir Griflet lost their lives.

he Bishop of Rochester and the King:-

Chapter Fifth

How King Arthur attacked Sir Launcelot at Joyous Gard; how Sir Lionel was slain and how Sir Bors was wounded.

NOW come we to the beginning of the end of this great and glorious reign of King Arthur of Britain. For so Sir Launcelot stepped between the Queen and the law as hath afore been told of, and having done so there was no recession for him from that act. For so was he bound to protect the Queen and to cherish her if he could do so; and King Arthur was bound to recover his Queen to bring her back to her duty again if he could do so.

Yet in all this the Queen had not sinned against King Arthur, saving only that she had escaped from her enemies and from justice at Camelot, and also because King Arthur supposed that her affections had wandered from him and toward Sir Launcelot. For in all other respects *Concerning* the Queen was ever as honorable and as pure as she had been *Queen Guine-* when first she came to King Arthur that long while before at *vere and Sir* Camilard (which same hath been told in full in the Book of *Launcelot.* King Arthur). Yet there was this, that the coming of Sir Launcelot from the Lake and the greatness of Sir Launcelot as a knight, and the beauty of the person of Sir Launcelot, so fascinated her that she could not let him go his way without meddling with his fortunes. Wherefore she demanded him for her knight, and she was angry at any interference that prevented him from serving her as her knight both singly and in all things.

But now had come to her the end of all this. For now was she escaped from her lord the King, and from justice, and she was hiding under the protection of Sir Launcelot of the Lake and of those knights of his blood and kindred at Joyous Gard. So had the end come to her of all the joy of her life, for King Arthur could now never condone or forgive her offence.

For when the news of that battle came to the ears of King *King Arthur* Arthur, he was filled with anger and with grief. "Alas!" *grieveth.*

cried he, "that this quarrel should have begun, for in it I behold the end of my reign. For already the joy of the Round Table is past and gone, and never shall it return again."

For wit ye that that joy which is gone can never return, but only its memory shall live in the heart to lend a dim and distant lustre upon the sorrows of the present, and of that King Arthur was very well aware. So also he knew that the glory of the Round Table had departed, and he knew that ere the end of that Round Table should come many knights should die in that quarrel that was now toward.

Then the King said, "Doth Sir Gawaine, the high prince, know that his two brothers have been slain?" They say to him, "No, Lord." (For they did not then know that Sir Gawaine had already been informed thereof.) The King said, "Then let him not be told of it, for if he is told of it now he will, in his haste, vow vengeance against Sir Launcelot who was his sworn comrade in arms and his very dear friend, and so there will be added war to this war." They say to the King, "He shall not be told, but it shall be kept secret from him."

The news cometh to Sir Gawaine. But meantime there had come a messenger hastening to Sir Gawaine, and said to him, "Lord, the Queen hath escaped and is now upon her way to Joyous Gard with Sir Launcelot of the Lake."

At this Sir Gawaine gazed at the messenger and for a little while he said nothing, though he thought many things. And the face of Sir Gawaine grew white like to wax for whiteness, for he feared what further news should come to him. Anon he said, "What news is this? Were not my brethren set as a guard upon her? How then did they suffer her to escape from them?"

The messenger said, "Sir, Sir Launcelot, and others of his blood, assaulted that guard and they seized upon the Queen and took her away. And in the mêlée at that time Sir Gareth was slain unwittingly. And then Sir Geharis was also slain whilst attempting to stay Sir Launcelot."

Then Sir Gawaine covered his head with his cloak, and he sat there for a long time with his head covered. And ever he wept beneath the cloak, but his face was hidden, and no one could behold his tears. And anon he *Sir Gawaine grieveth.* said in a muffled voice, "Five of them are gone! Five of them are gone!" meaning by that that his two sons and his three brothers had already died in that war. And after a little while he said, "There was comfort for me in that those three of them who died aforetime were armed for battle. For so I advised them that they should not enter this dispute; and yet they did enter it, and lost their lives therein. But

these latter two were naked and unarmed, and of one of them Sir Launcelot was godfather when he was knighted.   And he loved Sir Launcelot
more than he loved his own blood and his own brethren.   Ah, Gareth!
Gareth!   All things could I forgive in Sir Launcelot saving only thy death.
For I loved Sir Launcelot above all others in the world, and to him could
much be forgiven; but this I can never forgive.   For those two were his
friends and not his enemies, and they meant him good and not harm; yet
he slew them, all naked and unarmed as they were."

And Sir Gawaine said, "Where is the King?"   They say, "The King
is at such and such a place."   So by and by Sir Gawaine arose and went
to where King Arthur was.   And Sir Gawaine said to King Arthur, "Lord,
what now will you do?"   King Arthur said, "I know not *Sir Gawaine*
what I shall do."   Sir Gawaine said, "Sir, know you that my *cometh to the*
two brothers are slain?"   And King Arthur bowed his head *King.*
and said, "Yea, I know it."   Sir Gawaine said, "I will tell you what you
shall do.   You shall wage war to the extremity of life against this false
and traitorous knight, Sir Launcelot of the Lake.   What?   Hath he not
taken your Queen from you and carried her away to his own castle?   Hath
he not slain your blood and kindred?   Hath he not bathed his hands in
the blood of your knights of the Round Table?   Hath he not slain Sir
Kay, your foster brother, in this last assault?   Hath he not slain Sir
Griflet and my kinsman Sir Aglaval and my two sons and my two other
brethren who were all unarmed and defenceless against his attack?   Sir,
arouse yourself.   Call for your kings and princes, your earls and barons
and knights, and let us set forth as an army and utterly destroy this nest
of traitors and murderers.   I myself will call my dependants around me
and will accompany you to that war, for now it shall either be Sir Launcelot's life or my life.   For never will I forgive him so long as I have breath
in my body."

Quoth the King, "Nephew, if these knights will return the Queen to
me, then I will forgive them, and if I forgive them cannot you *The King*
also forgive?   For these are Knights of the Round Table, and *offers*
I must not destroy the Round Table so utterly as you advise *forgiveness.*
me to do."

Sir Gawaine said, "I cannot forgive Sir Launcelot, nor shall I ever forgive the deaths of my innocent brothers.   For they were naked and
unarmed, and they loved Sir Launcelot, and yet Sir Launcelot slew
them.   Naught can wipe this from my memory saving only the blood of
him who slew those two gentlemen.   Wherefore, prepare for war and I
will join you."

So King Arthur armed himself and he summoned those knights and princes, earls and barons who were dependent upon him to his assistance. And he summoned all of those knights who were still allied to him. All this he did, but he did it very reluctantly, for he wished not to wage war with Sir Launcelot and his knights.

The King summoneth his vassals.

And news of this call to arms that King Arthur had made came to Sir Launcelot, and he upon his part gave call to all of those lords and knights who were allied to him to come to him and to aid him to defend Joyous Gard. And they or many of them went to him as he bade them.

Then King Arthur led his army to Joyous Gard and it was so vast and multitudinous that it covered all the hills and valleys as it advanced. And red clouds of dust hung over it as it passed forward so that the bright and tranquil light of the sun was obscured by those clouds. And great flocks of carrion crows accompanied the army, for they smelt the blood of many carcasses as from afar, wherefore they flew accompanying that army. So this army came and settled down and about Joyous Gard, and it was like an army of locusts that had settled at that place.

How the King cometh to Joyous Gard.

And Sir Launcelot and his brother Sir Ector stood upon the parapet of the castle of Joyous Gard, and they looked out upon the hills and upon the multitude of the hosts that were there foregathered and that encompassed them. And when Sir Ector beheld the vast and limitless extent of that army, his heart failed within him and he said to Sir Launcelot, "Behold, oh brother! the vast and limitless host that surrounds us. However shall we withstand such a host as that? Would it not be better to compromise with the King and to surrender the Queen to him?" Quoth Sir Launcelot, "How talk you of compromise, Messire, and how talk you of surrendering the Queen? Wit you that to surrender the Queen at this time would be to dishonor ourselves in surrendering her to dishonor? For unless we fight for her, what terms can we now make that would insure her safety? No, brother, let us abide their coming, and defend ourselves with all our mights."

That night the Queen also spoke to Sir Launcelot, and she said, "Launcelot, why do you suffer for me? Surrender me unto King Arthur and with that this war will cease. Else will there many worthy knights perish in this war. For there are a great many knights here foregathered of the Round Table, and there be many other famous and worthy knights and nobles and kings here foregathered. Is my one life then worth more than all their lives?"

The Queen adviseth Sir Launcelot.

Then Sir Launcelot groaned, but he said, "Lady, I will not surrender

you until I am sure that your safety is insured. Let first the King assure
your safety and then we shall consider whether or not you shall return
to him."

Then the Queen burst out weeping and she cried out, "Oh, woe is me
that I should have brought so much trouble and sorrow upon this world!"

Now the army of King Arthur made assault upon Joyous Gard and
they made assault upon assault. And somewhiles they made breaches
in the walls; but ever those breaches were rebuilded at night *The King*
so that they could not enter the castle. And the army of *assaults*
King Arthur lost many hundreds of men, both of knights and *Joyous Gard.*
yeomen; but the defence of the castle lost many scores, and those scores
were of greater loss to them than the hundreds that King Arthur lost.
For those hundreds could be replaced by other hundreds, but the scores
could not be replaced by other scores.

So the knights who kept the castle held a council of defence, and there
were at that council Sir Bors and Sir Lionel and Sir Ector and Sir Bleoberis and Sir Blamor de Ganis, and there were other knights and worthies
of the blood of Sir Launcelot. Sir Lionel said, "Why remain
we here within this castle? Ever we grow weaker and weaker, *The friends of*
and by and by our enemies will break within the castle and *Sir Launcelot*
then we shall all be put to the edge of the sword. Let us sally *advise with*
him.
forth against those who thus surround us, for so haply we may cut our
way through them and thus escape to the sea-shore and to France. There
we shall be safe from those who could work for us our undoing." Sir
Launcelot said, "Sir, even if we could do this thing, what blood would
be spilt in doing it, and what friends would we slay in that attempt!"
Quoth Sir Ector, "What matters that? Are they not seeking our lives
and our blood, and are we not defending ourselves? These men are no
longer our friends; they are our enemies, and are seeking our lives. Let
us then go forth and assail them." All this Queen Guinevere heard, and
she wept many and very bitter tears as she listened to that council. As
for Sir Launcelot, he groaned very deeply but anon he said, "Let it then
be so as you say, only first I must bespeak King Arthur."

So that afternoon he appeared upon the battlements of the castle. And
he leaned out over the battlements and called out to those who were below, saying to them, "Where is King Arthur? I would speak with him."

Those who heard him ran to King Arthur, and they said to the King,
"Lord, Sir Launcelot asks to speak to thee. Haply he meaneth to surrender to thee."

So King Arthur hurried to that place where Sir Launcelot was: and Sir

*The King
speaketh to
Sir Launcelot.* Gawaine and the King of North Wales were with him.   King
Arthur said to Sir Launcelot, "What wouldst thou have of me,
Messires? Dost thou surrender this castle?" "Not so,"
quoth Sir Launcelot, "I do not surrender it, but I would speak to you of
other things."

"Sir," said King Arthur, "concerning what other things have you to
speak to me withal?"

"Lord," said Sir Launcelot, "this is what I would say to you. What
seek you here in thus assaulting this castle?   Here within are many lordly
knights and many knights of the Round Table who were a short time
ago your friends and dependants. Some of them you yourself made
knights as you made me a knight, and all of those would gladly surrender
their lives for your sake. What benefit or what honor can it then be to
you to slay them, who were your support and your defence, and who
would be so again if you would live in peace with them? Would
it be to your honor that you should slay these good, worthy honorable
knights?"

"Sir," said King Arthur, "you forget that you have seized upon my
Queen and that you hold her from me in this castle. First surrender to
me my Queen, and then I will consider all these things that you have to
say and will reply to them as I deem to be fitting."

"Lord," said Sir Launcelot, "thy Queen is held here in high and honorable regard. With us she is safe from harm or injury of any sort. Would
she be thus free from danger of harm and dishonor if she were with you?
Pledge me first that you would do her no harm or injury, and then it will
beseem us as true and honorable knights to consider the surrender of her
to you."

"Am I then," said the King, "to make treaty with you for the return
to me of that wife with whom I have lived in amity for all these years?
Sir, you do not consider how unfit such a treaty would be upon my part."

Then up spake Sir Gawaine. "Also, Messire, you have forgot another
thing, and that is that you have slain my two young brothers who stood

*Sir Gawaine
accuseth Sir
Launcelot.* before you defenceless and unarmed.   I reckon naught of those
whom you slew, armed and in battle.   For I loved you well
and truly for many years, and I advised them not to hazard
battle with you; but they would hazard battle and so they were slain by
you. But of those two others, they did not hazard battle; for they were
unarmed and naked, and they would have stood your friends; yet you
slew them as though they had been enemies. This I will never forgive

you, but either you will answer for it with your blood, or I will answer for it with mine."

Then Sir Launcelot groaned, and he said, "God pity us all for our sins, and God pity you, Sir Gawaine, for your unchristian hatred." And with that he turned away.

So when the next day had come, they of the castle prepared themselves for battle and for escape. They placed the Queen in their midst and they surrounded her upon all sides. Then, of a sudden, all the gates *The defenders* upon one side of the castle were flung wide open and they *of the castle* issued out in full armor. And at that time the sun shone out *sally forth.* very brightly, and it gleamed and sparkled like flames of fire upon the brightly polished steel of those knights. Then they, the defenders of the castle, shouted very loud, and they charged against their enemies, bearing the Queen with them in their midst.

And for awhile they carried all before them and no one could withstand them; and so they might have escaped, had it not been that the Queen was with them and retarded them in their charge and their advance. For, in a little while, owing to that delay, those of King Arthur's army armed themselves, and in another little while the friends of Sir Launcelot were almost entirely surrounded by that vast multitude.

Then Sir Launcelot beheld that in a short time they would be shut off from return to the castle, but that as yet the way was still open to them. Wherefore he lifted up his voice and shouted, "Retreat! Retreat!"

Then, through the roar and thunder of battle and of blows and of sword blade upon steel armor, all those who were there heard these words, "Retreat! Retreat!" And they beheld that that retreat was *They of the* nearly cut off, but not quite. So they turned their horses and *castle retreat* made their way slowly backward toward the castle again, with *into it again.* the Queen still in their midst. Those before turned their horses toward the castle, and those behind fought with their faces toward their foes. And many who assaulted that band tried to come to the Queen, but none could do it because of the close array of horsemen that surrounded her. Many lost their lives in that attempt, for if they penetrated the first line of horsemen they were slain by the second line of defence.

In that mêlée Sir Gawaine sought ever to come at Sir Launcelot, but he could not do so because that Sir Launcelot remained ever near to the person of the Queen. But Sir Gawaine charged against Sir Bors and pierced him with his lance through the shoulder; and then he *Sir Gawaine* charged with great violence against Sir Lionel, and in that *overthroweth* charge he pierced through the body armor of Sir Lionel so *Sir Lionel.*

that the point of the spear stood a hand's breadth out behind his back. Then Sir Lionel would have fallen from his horse only that the press that surrounded him held him up and kept him from falling. And with that blow against Sir Lionel, the end of Sir Gawaine's spear broke off, and it remained penetrated into the body of Sir Lionel, a part of it showing in front and a part of it showing behind.

Then Sir Lionel felt that he had received his death-wound, and he groaned very dolorously. And Sir Gawaine heard him groan and perceived how badly he was hurt. And he redoubled his attack, endeavoring to obtain the body of Sir Lionel. But he could not obtain that body for it was still held upright upon the horse, supported by several, and others gathered about to defend it.

Then Sir Gawaine was furious with rage and he fought as though he had gone wode. For his sword flashed like flashes of lightning, and ever *Sir Lionel* as he struck he cried out in a loud and terrible voice, "That *dieth.* for Sir Launcelot!" and "That for Sir Launcelot!" and ever again "That and that for Sir Launcelot!" And so fierce and terrible were the blows that he gave that many fell down before them and never moved again. But in spite of his striving, they bore away Sir Lionel from his endeavor and so brought him into the castle, where that night he died in a great agony of thirst and of torment.

In that battle, King Arthur and those who were with him made many charges against the centre of Sir Launcelot's array, and anon they had come so close to where was the Queen that the King could almost have *King Arthur* touched her with his lance. So King Arthur came at last face *is overthrown.* to face with Sir Launcelot, and Sir Ector was beside Sir Launcelot. And ever the King strove to come at Sir Launcelot, but was unable to do so. For somewhiles Sir Launcelot warded the blows from himself, and otherwhiles those who were with him took those blows from him. Then Sir Ector perceived how the King neglected his guard in assaulting Sir Launcelot, and he arose in his stirrups and smote the King a terrible buffet upon the helmet. At that blow the King's brains swam, and he reeled and fell off from his horse upon the earth. Then Sir Ector leaped from his horse and he said, "Here will I put a stop to this war at its fountain-head." Whereupon he rushed off the King's helmet and whirled his sword, and prepared to smite the head off from the King.

But Queen Guinevere perceived the King's danger and she shrieked *They spare the* out very dolorously, "Spare the King his life, Sir Ector!" *King his life.* And Sir Launcelot said to Sir Ector, "Sir, how is this? Would you slay your King? Remember it was he who made you a knight and who made me a knight. Haply he may forget that he made us knights, but let us not forget it."

So with that Sir Ector put up his sword again, and he and Sir Launcelot lifted the King and set him upon his horse once more. And the King wept bitter tears to see how noble and knightly was Sir Launcelot, and he said, "Ah, Launcelot, Launcelot, that this should be!"

So after that Sir Launcelot withdrew into the castle with the Queen and the gates were closed behind him. But ever King Arthur sat still weeping and saying, "Ah, Launcelot, Launcelot, that this should be!"

Then the friends of Sir Launcelot wist not what they should do in this extremity, for there were they within the castle again, and could not come out thence because of those who besieged them in that place. And ever they were growing weaker with each assault, but the armies of King Arthur were not growing weaker.

At this extremity there came the Bishop of Rochester to the camp of King Arthur, and the purpose of the Bishop was to make peace betwixt these parties. So the Bishop came to where King Arthur *The Bishop of* was, and he found King Arthur sunk in grief. For already *Rochester com-* three-and-twenty Knights of the Round Table had lost their *eth to the King.* lives in these wars and contentions, and King Arthur grieved for them very sorely. For there were no more knights like those first knights fore-gathered about the Round Table, nor have there ever been such knights as they were from that day to this.

Then the Bishop stood before the King, and the King looked at him remotely as though he were a great distance away, for his eyes were dimmed with weeping. And the Bishop said to the King, "Lord, let this quarrel cease between you and Sir Launcelot, and let there be peace in the land. For now is the entire land distracted with this quarrel. For friend fight-eth against friend, neighbor against neighbor;—yea, even brother against brother. As for you, my lord, these knights are of your Round Table and of your making; what pleasure or what honor then can it be to you to destroy them?"

The King said to him, "Sir, this war was not of my forming or my seeking, but of Sir Launcelot's. For first Sir Launcelot resisted arrest in a just cause, and then he resisted the arrest of the Queen. So he and his fellows took the Queen away from me, and they have her in this castle. Let them then deliver the Queen to me and there shall be peace betwixt the friends of Sir Launcelot and my friends."

The Bishop said, "They will not deliver the Queen to thee, Lord, ex-cepting thou wilt declare upon thine honor that no harm shall befall her.

For it is said of all that the life of the Queen is in danger from thee.
Yet she is an honorable lady and as pure to thee as the day upon
The Bishop   which she came to thee.   For she is free from sin or from
intercedes for   guilt of any sort.   Wherefore, unless thou wilt declare that no
the Queen.   harm shall befall the life of the Queen and wilt declare that
same in writing, she will not be returned, but otherwise they will lay
down their lives to guard her safety."

Then the King sat with his fist upon his forehead, and he considered
for a long time what the Bishop had said, and at last he said, as in a
smothered voice, "Well, then, let the Queen be delivered to me at Camelot,
and I upon my part shall promise that no harm shall be done to her life,
either to threaten it or to deprive her of it."   The Bishop said, "Let me
have that in writing."   And the King said, "I will do so."

So the King called to him his scribe and he had him write those words;
to wit, that if the Queen would return to him, no harm should befall or
threaten her life in any way.   And the King signed and sealed that document and the Bishop took it with him and entered the Castle of Joyous
Gard.

Thus the Bishop came before Sir Launcelot and his kindred, and Queen
Guinevere was with them at that time.   And the Bishop looked at the
face of the Queen and he beheld that it was all white and wan with sorrow
The Bishop   and that her eyelids were red with continual weeping.   And
grieveth for the   the Bishop was very sorry for the Queen and for her sadness.
Queen.   So the Bishop came to her and took her by the hand and he
said to her, "Lady, stint thy sorrow, for the time of sorrow is passed.
For here am I with this document that saith that no harm or injury of
any kind shall be meditated against thy life, but if thou wilt return to
the King all shall be forgiven thee.   For wit you well that the King is
determined that you shall return to him, even if it cometh to the tearing
down of this castle stone from stone."

Then the Queen took the document that the Bishop had and she read
it very carefully, and when she had ended she said, "Lord Bishop, how
is this?   I see here that mine own safety is provided for, but that the
safety of no one else is mentioned.   How of those good worthy knights
and gentlemen who have endangered their safety in my behalf; where
is their safety provided for in this parchment?"

Quoth the Bishop, "I will bespeak the King that point.   Meantime,
do you remain here without endeavoring either to attack or to escape."

She said, "I will remain here in peace until this time to-morrow."

So the Bishop returned to the King and he brought that word to him;

that a pledge must also be given for the safety to the life of those knights who thus guarded and sheltered the Queen. Then the King frowned, and he said, "What other conditions will they impose upon me; why should I give this pledge to those who have acted treasonably against me?"

Then Sir Gawaine plucked the King by the sleeve and the King turned aside with him. And Sir Gawaine whispered for awhile with the King and by and by the King turned again to the Bishop and he said to the Bishop, "Very well, then; take thou this my word to those knights that I will in no wise do harm to them whilst they are within this Kingdom of Britain. Take thou that word unto them." *The King promises to spare the knights of the castle.*

So the Bishop took that word to them within the castle and they were very glad of it. And Sir Launcelot said to the Bishop, "Let the King return to Camelot, and I will bring the Queen to him in three days' time surrounded by all the pomp and circumstance that appertain to her lordly grace."

So the King withdrew his army from that place and he returned to Camelot. And Sir Launcelot made ready to bring the Queen to him at Camelot.

Thus came to an ending that sad and cruel war in the which many good knights and warriors lost their lives and in which fourteen worthy knights of the Round Table lost their lives.

For though all those knights were commanders of armies and of battalions, yet death came to them as to other men of lesser note, so that many of them, even to the highest, laid down their lives in this dolorous war.

For so the hand of Fate lay heavy on that great and glorious company, for though all grieved and made great sorrow over the war, and over those who had died therein, and though comrade grieved over comrade who died therein—even over those who were upon the other side and who were enemies—yet the hand of Fate thrust them forward to do what they were compelled to do, and to slay and to be slain in that sorrowful battle.

And so it was to the end, for ere that end was reached others who were the foremost and the greatest of them all laid their bodies down to an eternal sleep upon the bosom of that earth that gave them shape and foothold. For yet were there other wars to come until all but a very few of those who were left had given all that they had of the earth to give in those wars.

But of this anon; for that which followeth has to treat of those things.

So now followeth the history of those things that remain to be hereinafter related in that which followeth, as shall now appear.

ir Gawaine challenges Sir *J J*
Launcelot:

Chapter Sixth

Sir Launcelot brings the Queen to King Arthur at Camelot. He quitteth England, and King Arthur and Sir Gawaine pursue him.

SO the King went to Camelot, and upon the third day the Queen was brought to him at that place.

Thus saith the history of these things when the Queen was brought to the Court of the King, to wit:

First there came an hundred knights clad cap-a-pie all in armor and with fittings and trimmings of green velvet. And these knights wore olive wreaths upon their heads, indicative of peace. Followed these, four and twenty esquires clad all in green velvet, and these were *How Sir* also crowned with olive wreaths. After these came four and *Launcelot* twenty ladies in waiting upon the Queen, and these, like all *brings the Queen to* the others, were clad in green velvet and were embroidered *Camelot.* with pearls and precious stones even to the heels of their horses, and the bridles of their horses were bound with wreaths of olive. Then came the Queen and Sir Launcelot clad all in white samite, and the Queen carried an olive branch in her hand and Sir Launcelot was crowned with an olive wreath. And the raiment of these two was all aglitter with the jewels and pearls with which their clothes were embroidered until they were stiff with that embroidery.

At that time King Arthur received them seated upon his throne with great dignity in the hall of the Castle at Camelot. And the throne upon which he sat was of wrought gold and was cushioned and trimmed with crimson velvet, embroidered in gold with the figures of leopards. *How the King* And over above the throne was a great canopy of crimson *sat at Camelot.* velvet ornamented with the figures of leopards, embroidered with threads of gold. The King was clothed all in white, and he wore a gold chain studded with jewels about his neck and he wore his royal crown upon his head. Upon the left hand of the King stood seven bishops in full canonical robes, and upon his right hand was a throne like to his, and on that throne the Queen should have been seated. But she was not seated there, for otherwise it was empty.

Upon the left hand of the King, but upon the second step below the throne, sat Sir Gawaine, the beloved nephew of the King. And all about the hall were several hundred knights in full armor and armed cap-a-pie with sword and lance, so that that hall glittered and gleamed with the shine of that armor.

So King Arthur sat in state to receive the return of the Queen, and anon she came to that place where the King awaited her. First came the knights and esquires of Sir Launcelot, and these drew up in two parties extending the length of the hall, leaving a line between them. Then came Sir Launcelot and the Queen walking hand in hand up the length of that lane, and the faces of Sir Launcelot and of that lady were both of them exceedingly pale—hers with fear and his with fear for her. Behind these two came the four and twenty ladies in waiting upon the Queen, and these stopped in the midst of that lane and waited, whilst she and Sir Launcelot approached King Arthur.

So Sir Launcelot and the Queen came to the foot of the throne where sat the King, and when they had come to that spot Sir Launcelot kneeled and the Queen stood before King Arthur.

Quoth Sir Launcelot, "Dread Lord and King, here I bring to you your Queen as I have promised to do, and if I took her away in sorrow and in haste, then do I return her to you with ten thousand times the joy as *Sir Launcelot* compared to what was that sorrow, and in ten thousand *speaketh.* times the peace and amity to what was that haste. Lord, for thirteen weeks has she dwelt at Joyous Gard with all the state and circumstance due to her royalty, and she cometh to you now as pure and as virginal as she came to you at Camilard when first you loved her at that place and she loved you. Lord, I pray you that you will take the Queen to your heart, and will cherish her there as you one time cherished her, for, excepting that you pledged me your word that no harm should befall her, she otherwise would not have been thus brought to you as she is brought to-day."

Then King Arthur frowned until his eyes disappeared beneath his eyebrows. For a little he answered nothing, then in a little he said, "Messire, one time you were my friend and the best-beloved of all my knights, but *The King* that time is past and gone, never to return again, for now it *rebukes Sir* is altogether otherwise with me and with you. Messire, I ad-*Launcelot.* mire at your coolness and phlegm. For you took my Queen away from me by force and by force have you held her for all these several months.   Many knights have died by your hand and through your instrumentality, and several of those knights were knights of my Round Table that one time held you to it in bonds of love and amity.   Yet now you stand before me and recommend to me that I shall take back my Queen into my heart again.   Messire, wit you not that that which hath been done can never be undone, but is and must remain altogether finished and completed?   So it is with this thing that you have done; for it also is and must remain altogether finished and completed.   Look you, Messire, here beside me is this throne, which is empty.   So it shall remain forever empty for me, for never again shall Queen Guinevere or any other queen occupy it, for I hereby and herewith renounce her utterly and entirely.   She hath withdrawn herself from my court and my bed and so she shall forever remain withdrawn from them, for never again will I take her to my heart, or place her in that estate which she once occupied.

"I have pledged myself that no harm shall come to her through me; but herewith I give her over to the Church. *The King sendeth the Queen to a convent.* There she shall remain a recluse until the day of her death."

So said King Arthur, and at a motion of his hand the Lord Bishop of Rochester came forth and took the Lady by the hand and led her away; and as he led her away, she was weeping very bitterly.

So the Bishop of Rochester took the Queen to the Convent of Saint Bridget at Rochester, and there she remained the lady abbess of that convent even to the day of her death, as shall hereinafter be related.

Now all this while Sir Launcelot still kneeled before King Arthur, and anon the King said to him again, "Messire, your own doom I will not announce to you; but I will relegate the annunciation of that doom to this lord, my well-beloved nephew, Sir Gawaine.   For the injury which you did to him is a thousand times greater than the injury which you did to me.   For though you took my Queen away from me, yet you did her no harm.   But with him, you slew five of his blood; to wit, three of his brethren and two of his sons.   And whilst three of them were in arms against you so that you slew them wittingly and in self-defence, yet two of those stood unarmed and naked before you, and those two loved you better than anyone in all the world.   One of those two your own hand made a knight and the other was knit to you with many acts and deeds of friendship and of love.   Accordingly, I commit your doom to Sir Gawaine to announce to you."

Then Sir Gawaine smiled very bitterly upon Sir Launcelot, and he said,
"Messire, this is the doom that I pronounce. The King hath, in his great clemency, promised you that no harm shall befall you in life or in limb. So no harm shall come to you in that way if you are reasonable and obey the commands of the King. This is his command—that in fifteen days from this you must quit this kingdom, and that you shall never again return to it whilst I live or while the King liveth.

"Also I pronounce the doom of banishment against those who have been associated with you in these late affairs, to wit, against Sir Ector
de Maris, Sir Bors de Ganis and Sir Ure, and Sir Blamor and Sir Bleoberis de Ganis, against Sir Galahautin, and Sir Galahud, and Sir Menaduke, and Sir Galahadin, and Sir Hebes, and Sir Lavaine, and Sir Melias de Lisle, and Sir Palamydes, and Sir Safyr, and Sir Clegis. Upon all of these I pronounce the doom of banishment upon behalf of this King, and if any of you be found within this isle of Britain fifteen days from now, you will be arrested and hanged as traitors. Meantime all your castles, earldoms, and baronies shall be forfeited to the King."

Said Sir Launcelot, "Sir, that is a bitter sentence; for here in this island have I lived all my life, and of it I love every stock and stone that mine eyes behold. But if I be outlawed and cast forth from this kingdom, then will I go to my Castle of Chillion in the land of France, and there I believe I shall be right well welcome and protected. So come, my lords, and let us be gone to that country whiles there yet remains time for us to depart."

So Sir Launcelot and all those lords who were condemned with him departed from the coast of England and entered into France, where they took up their lodging with much sorrow and repining.

And King Arthur seized upon all their earldoms, baronies, and estates, and some of these he bestowed elsewhere and some of them he held for the crown.

Now after those knights had departed for France, Sir Gawaine urged upon King Arthur that he should follow them to that kingdom and attack them there at the Castle of Chillion. King Arthur said, "Sir, why should I do this thing? Did not Sir Launcelot bring back my Queen to me and did I not forgive him for what he had done? Is he not now banished from the land, and is he not then punished for all those things that he has done? Let him now live and die in peace."

But to this Sir Gawaine ever answered, "Sir, I cannot reconcile it to myself thus to surrender my rights in this case. For Sir Launcelot slew my brothers and my sons, and never will I forgive him for that offence. Either his blood or my blood shall answer for this; wherefore, if thou wilt not follow him to France, then I myself will go thither and will seek him out and punish him. As for thee, thou mayst forgive him as a man, but yet thou mayst not forgive him as a king. For as a king thou art the head of the law, wherefore thou mayst not forgive one who hath broken the law. So with Sir Launcelot of the Lake, for he broke the laws and he brought these Knights of the Round Table against thee and to follow him; wherefore it is thy duty under the law to assail him and to punish him for his treason, and also to punish those who follow him likewise for their treason."

Now by this time King Arthur was growing toward being an old man, and he was much broken by sorrow and by cares, wherefore *The King* these words of Sir Gawaine so moved him that at last he *moveth against* agreed to sail with an army into France and to attack Sir *Sir Launcelot.* Launcelot and his friends at Chillion. So King Arthur entrusted the government of Britain to his nephew, Sir Mordred (who was brother to Sir Gawaine), and he and Sir Gawaine departed with a great army for France.

So this army appeared before the Castle of Chillion, and they shut Sir Launcelot and his friends up within the castle and besieged them at that place.

Then said Sir Launcelot, "How is this; hath not King Arthur any mercy upon us, or doth he seek our lives and our blood? Well, if he seeks those lives and that blood, then will there be many cruel and bitter battles betwixt us, and many knights shall fall, and so will come the entire end of the Round Table. Ah, well, if God willeth that it be so, so it must be."

So there were many battles around about Chillion and many lost their lives. And though the knights of King Arthur lost more *Of the battles* lives than did the knights of Sir Launcelot, yet they could *about Chillion.* better afford to lose those lives because new knights were constantly coming from Britain to replenish the army of King Arthur, but no new knights were coming to the army of Sir Launcelot, wherefore his losses were not replenished to him.

Now at that time there was a very wise and learned physician in the camp of King Arthur, and one day Sir Gawaine sent for this learned man to come to him. When that wise man stood before Sir Gawaine, Sir

Gawaine said to him this, "Sir, can you not produce for me a lotion that shall render me free from all wounds of any sort?"

Quoth the wise man, "Sir, this is impossible. But I can give to you a medicine of this sort, that if you take it, you will, from the ninth hour of morning until the prime of noon, have the strength in your limbs and in your arms as of ten men." Sir Gawaine laughed, and said, "Provide me then with that medicine."

The wise man provides medicine for Sir Gawaine.

So the wise man prepared that medicine and gave it to Sir Gawaine, and so it was for him as that physician had promised. For from the ninth hour of the morning until the prime of noon, Sir Gawaine was uplifted in arm and body to the strength of ten men.

So the next day after this medicine had been delivered to him, Sir Gawaine went to the walls of the castle and he paraded under the walls of the castle, and he called out, "Sir Launcelot, come forth and do me battle. For this satisfaction thou owest to me for slaying my kindred." But Sir Launcelot would not come forth to do him battle. For Sir Launcelot still loved Sir Gawaine and he loved King Arthur; both for the sake of those times that were past and gone, when they had joy and pleasure together. So because that the one was Sir Gawaine and the other was King Arthur, he would not come forth to do battle. Nay, because of his love for those two, Sir Launcelot would not fight in that part of the battle where Sir Gawaine or King Arthur was, but would do battle at other parts.

Sir Gawaine giveth challenge against Sir Launcelot.

But when the next day had come, Sir Gawaine came again and the strength of ten men was in his arms and his body. And he paraded back and forth under the walls of the castle, and ever as he paraded he cried out aloud, "Sir Launcelot, thou caitiff knight! Come forth and do me battle! For thy doom is upon thee, and thou shalt die in this war; wherefore, come and do me battle, or else announce that thou art afraid of me."

But still Sir Launcelot would not go forth against him, but he sat in the castle and groaned for sorrow and bitterness of spirit. Then Sir Ector came to Sir Launcelot, and he said, "Kinsman, suffer me that I go forth and do battle in thy behalf; for this man shameth us by this challenge."

Then Sir Launcelot wept, and he said, "Thou shalt not go, for wit you that I loved this man better than mine own blood. And if he should be slain, then will my heart be filled with grief such as can never vacate it again. And if thou art killed, then will I be without my brother, and must take it upon me to fight Sir Gawaine upon the behalf of thy death. Wherefore, I pray thee go not forth to meet him."

But ever Sir Ector besought Sir Launcelot saying, "Brother, suffer me to go!" And at last Sir Launcelot said, "Well go, and may God be with thee!"

So Sir Ector armed himself and departed out of the castle to meet Sir Gawaine.

Then Sir Gawaine rode up to Sir Ector and he said to him, "Sir, what knight are you?" Quoth Sir Ector, "I am Sir Ector de Maris, the brother of Sir Launcelot of the Lake." Said Sir Gawaine, "Why come you here?" And Sir Ector replied, "I come to do battle with you upon my brother's behalf." Then Sir Gawaine laughed and he said, "Sir, you are welcome. Rather would I have it that you were Sir Launcelot, but failing him I will accept you as his proxy. So make yourself ready to encounter me."

So each of those two knights rode to a certain distance and prepared himself for that encounter. And when they were in all ways *Sir Gawaine* prepared they charged very furiously against one another. *overthroweth* In that meeting the spear of Sir Ector broke into many pieces, *Sir Ector.* but the spear of Sir Gawaine held. And because he had the strength of ten men behind his spear, it penetrated the shield of Sir Ector and it penetrated his body, so that it stood a handsbreadth out behind his back.

Then Sir Ector fell from his horse and, in passing, the spear of Sir Gawaine was broken so that the baton of the spear of Sir Gawaine remained sticking in the body of Sir Ector; a part of it sticking out before, and a part of it sticking out behind.

Then Sir Gawaine rode back to where Sir Ector lay, and he said to him, "Sir, how fares it with you?" Quoth Sir Ector, "Alas, Messire! I have received my death-wound." Then Sir Gawaine laughed very bitterly, and he said, "So shall it always be with traitors, such as thou."

Then with that Sir Gawaine turned his horse and rode away from that place, leaving Sir Ector lying where he was.

Anon there came forth those from within the castle and they lifted up Sir Ector where he lay. And they laid him in the hollow of the shield and bare him into the castle. And all who saw Sir Ector in that condition wept to behold him so.

So they bore him to a chamber and laid him upon a soft couch and Sir Ector groaned very dolorously with the agony of his wound, and Sir Launcelot and several others stood before him, and ever as Sir Launcelot considered him, the tears welled out of his eyes and rolled like shining jewels down his cheeks.

So about the eleventh hour of the night Sir Ector said to Sir Launcelot, "Sir, this wound is my death-wound. I pray you to draw out the baton of that spear and let me pass." Sir Launcelot said, "I cannot draw it forth." Sir Ector said, "Is there no friend here who will draw forth this baton, and suffer me to die?"

Then said Sir Bors, "I will draw it forth," and with that he came to the bedside of Sir Ector and he laid hold of the baton of the spear. And he drew very strongly upon that baton and it came forth out of that wound and with it came a great effusion of blood.

Then Sir Ector groaned very deeply and he said, "I pass," and with *Sir Ector dieth.* that he closed his eyes and in a little while he was dead. Then they who were there wept a great passion of tears, for Sir Ector was well-beloved of all of them.

Now when the next morning was come, Sir Gawaine came again before the castle and rode there as aforetime. And ever as he rode he cried out, "Sir Launcelot, thou craven knight, come forth and do me battle." But still Sir Launcelot would not come forth against him. Then Sir Bors de Ganis came to Sir Launcelot and he said to him, "Sir, suffer me to go forth against this knight, for he bringeth shame upon us all."

Quoth Sir Launcelot, "I crave you not to go, Sir; for this knight, Sir Gawaine, is a very strong and powerful knight. Already hath he slain Sir Ector, and should you also lose your life, what great loss that would be to us all." "Nevertheless," said Sir Bors, "I would fain go forth against him. For God may give me the victory, in which it will be a great benefit to us all in that he will no more come to trouble us."

Then Sir Launcelot turned away his head, and anon he said, "Go, in God's name, and may good fortune attend you. As for me, I cannot go against Sir Gawaine because of the love I held for him. For should he slay me, that would be a great misfortune for us all, but should I slay him, never would I cease to sorrow and to repine for his death. Wherefore, I cannot now go against him, but you may go against him."

So Sir Bors armed himself and went forth out of the castle, and when Sir Gawaine beheld him coming he was rejoiced, for he thought that this was Sir Launcelot.

So Sir Gawaine rode up to him as he approached, and he said to him, "Messire, what knight are you?" Him Sir Bors made answer, "Sir I am Sir Bors de Ganis, and I have come forth here against you upon behalf of Sir Launcelot of the Lake."

"Sir," said Sir Gawaine, "you are very welcome; though rather would I have to do with Sir Launcelot of the Lake than with any other man in all of the world. For I have no quarrel against you, but against him I have a quarrel."

"Nevertheless," said Sir Bors, "I stand here now upon his behalf to do battle for him."

Quoth Sir Gawaine, "Prepare yourself then for battle!" So Sir Bors took his assigned place and when they were in all wise prepared they rushed together with great violence and fury.

In that encounter the spear of each knight was broken into many pieces, even to the very fist that held the spear, and the horse of each recoiled so that it sunk back upon its haunches and would, perhaps, have fallen, had not the address of the knight rider recovered it. Then each knight cast aside the truncheon of his spear and voided his horse, and each drew his sword with great readiness and rushed to the battle very furiously, violently and impetuously. Each smote the other many sore buffets and strokes so that each knight was wounded in several places.

But Sir Gawaine was possessed of the strength of ten, and Sir Bors was possessed but of the strength of one, so that by and by Sir Bors was obliged to hold his shield low because of weariness from the redoubled fury of Sir Gawaine's attack.

So Sir Gawaine perceived that opening which he made in his defence, and, grinding his teeth together, he whirled up his sword and *Sir Gawaine* smote Sir Bors upon the shoulder of that arm that held his *woundeth Sir* sword. So violent and savage was the blow that it sheared *Bors* through the iron of the epulier and it sheared through the flesh and bone of the shoulder so that the arm of Sir Bors fell and hung down from the shoulder and his hand dropped the sword that he held.

Then Sir Gawaine laughed and ran forward and he set his foot upon the sword of Sir Bors. And Sir Bors sank down upon his knees *Sir Bors asks* and he said in a weak and faltering voice, "Sir Gawaine, I am *his life.* sorely wounded. If it please thee to do so, I pray thee to spare my life."

Quoth Sir Gawaine, "Why should I spare thee thy life? Thou art a traitor knave, and it is not fit that I should spare thee, but rather I should slay thee as thou kneelest before me. But I cannot forget our long and many associations; and I cannot forget that thou wert one of those three knights who achieved the Grail, and brought the Grail back again to Sarras. So I will forgive thee, and will spare thee thy life, if so be that God will also spare it."

Then Sir Gawaine turned and sheathed his sword, and he mounted his horse and rode away. And anon there came the friends of Sir Bors from the

Castle of Chillion, and they lifted him up and laid him upon a litter, and so they bore him away into the castle.

And they took Sir Bors to a room of the castle and stripped off his armor and beheld the wound that it was very ghastly and dismal. And so much blood was emitted from that wound that Sir Bors fainted and for awhile he hung hovering upon the edge of death.

But he did not die then or afterward, but he revived and his wound *Sir Bors doth* was healed so that he, by and by, became well and strong *not die.* again.

Then Sir Launcelot came to where Sir Bors was, and he said to him, "Sir Bors, how fared it with thee?" And Sir Bors said in a fainting voice, "Sir, I know not how it was with Sir Gawaine. For I found him to be so passing strong that never have I found a stronger. For he smote down my defences and he smote me this blow that I have received, and from which I shall maybe die. For mine arm is nearly severed from its shoulder, and I wit not whether I shall ever be strong and hale again."

Then Sir Launcelot wept and he said, "Alas, that this is so! For now I cannot forego this battle with Sir Gawaine any longer. For yesterday he slew my brother, Sir Ector, and to-day he hath nearly slain thee. So to-morrow I shall have to have ado with him, or else, by and by, all shall perish at this place."

Then Sir Bors said, "Sir, beware of him, for he hath strength more than human, wherefore I fear that he may prove to thee thy undoing."

To that Sir Launcelot answereth, "I should be sorry to find it so. But whether it is thus or not, still must I have ado with him upon the chance that I may thus save the lives of others within this place."

So it came that Sir Launcelot was prepared to do battle with Sir Gawaine.

Now if you would hear more of this famous fight betwixt Sir Launcelot and Sir Gawaine, I pray you to read that which followeth. For there it shall be fully and distinctly set forth as it hath been told of in several ancient histories dealing with these things.

he Paſsing of Sir Gawaine:

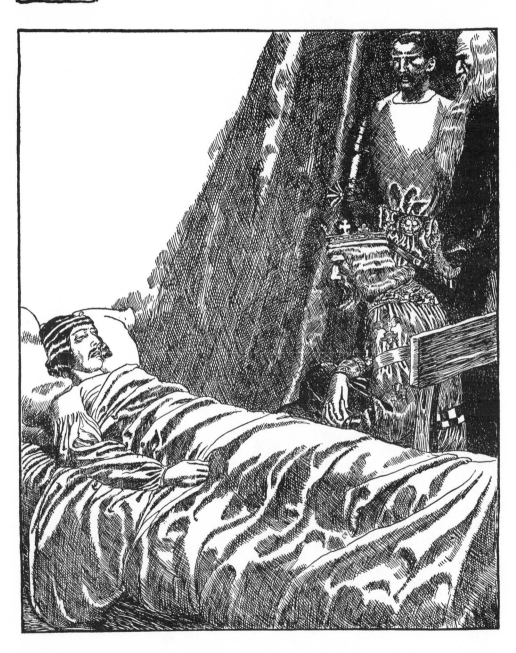

Chapter Seventh

*Of the battle betwixt Sir Launcelot and Sir Gawaine. Also how King
Arthur returned to Little Britain.*

SO came the next day and Sir Gawaine had his esquires to enclose his
body in full armor of proof, and he mounted his horse and took a
good stout lance of ashwood in his hand, and he set forth once more
to seek Sir Launcelot as aforetime he had done. So Sir Gawaine came
beneath the wall of the castle, and he paraded before the wall, and ever
as he thus paraded he cried aloud and on high, "Come forth, Sir Launcelot
of the Lake! Come forth, thou caitiff knight, and do me battle!"

Then Sir Launcelot wist that now the time was come for him to do that
battle.

So Sir Launcelot mounted upon his horse and took into his hand a
good stout lance of ashwood for his defence, and thus armed *Sir Launcelot*
he gave orders and the portcullis of the castle was raised and *goeth against*
the drawbridge was let fall and Sir Launcelot rode forth all *Sir Gawaine.*
clad in that armor of proof to meet Sir Gawaine.

Then Sir Gawaine rode up to Sir Launcelot and gave him greeting and
he said to Sir Launcelot of the Lake, "Sir, I pray you tell me, are you Sir
Launcelot of the Lake, or are you another knight than he? For by your
figure and by your conduct and by that device which is upon your shield,
I wit you to be Sir Launcelot, and yet I know not whether you are he or
not he. For this is the third time I have challenged, and heretofore he
would not come out against me."

Quoth Sir Launcelot of the Lake, "Sir, I am Sir Launcelot indeed, and
wit you, Sir Gawaine, I have well tried to avoid this battle, *Sir Launcelot*
for I fear me in this battle or in some other battle of its kind, *bespeaks Sir*
either you or I shall be slain. And I would not slay you for *Gawaine.*
the love that was of old betwixt us; for still I remember me of that love,
and I hold it very dear to my heart. Wherefore I would not do battle
with you if that battle could be avoided."

Quoth Sir Gawaine, "What prate you of love, Sir? This battle cannot be avoided, for wit you that even if ever I loved you, yet all that love is now passed away, or rather it is transformed into hate. For you have wounded me so deeply in my heart that no man can wound me so deeply and yet live while I live also upon the earth. Wherefore either you or I shall die by the hand of the other, if not at this time, then at some other time."

Quoth Sir Launcelot, "How have I wounded thee, Gawaine, or in what way have I done thee such hurt as this? Tell me that I may make that wrong right again."

Said Sir Gawaine, "Wit you not that I have often told you how that first *Sir Gawaine* you slew two of my sons, and my brother, and how that after-*accuses Sir* ward you slew two more of my brothers? Is not that injury *Launcelot.* enough for any man to bear within his heart and yet to live under that injury?"

Then Sir Launcelot sighed and he said, "Sir, wit you that those two sons and that brother I slew in battle and they were armed, and assaulting me, and I knew them not. As for those two of your brothers whom I afterward slew, them I slew in the press and fury of fighting. For I saw not their faces in that fury and knew them not. For if I had known them, wit you that I would have held my hand and spared them? Sir, for that I am grieved to the heart, for I loved them both very well; more especially Sir Gareth whom I made a knight in the field."

Then Sir Gawaine laughed very bitterly, and he said, "Sir, you make a very good excuse, still you did that which you did, and having done it you must pay for it. For so every man must pay for that which he hath done; let it be good or let it be ill. Come, Sir, prepare yourself for battle, for I am hungry to have battle with you."

Then again Sir Launcelot sighed, this time so deeply that his heart had been lifted from its strings within his bosom by that sigh. And with that sigh he closed his helmet, and reined in his horse and withdrew to that part of the field which was to be his assigned place of battle.

Then many of the defenders of the castle came down to the walls of the *Many view* castle and stood there, and looked down from those walls *the battle.* upon the two who stood so in array of battle. And King Arthur and many others came from the camp of the besiegers, and also stood them afar off to behold the battle, so that with those and with these who were there it was as good an assembly as any knights could have chosen in which to do battle.

And the sun shone very clear and strong—yet not too strong. And the breeze blew very freely so that all the poplar trees around about the castle were turned white with its blowing, and the river that ran down past the castle was dusked and rippled by that wind, and all the reeds of the river bowed and dipped into the water thereof.

So those two knights prepared themselves for the assault, making their armor in all ways tight and secure. Then when they were in all ways ready, they shouted to their horses and so sprang to the charge, galloping against one another with a noise like to the noise of thunder.

So they met in the midst of the course and smote one another, in the centre of the other's shield. And before that shock the spear of each was split into a great many very small pieces, even to the hand that held it. And each horse sank quivering back upon its haunches at the recoil of that blow, and would have fallen, were it not that the extraordinary address of the knight rider recovered his horse with spur and rein and voice. Then each knight cast aside the truncheon of his spear and drew his sword, and each rushed at the other very furiously and valiantly. Then each smote the other with great power and strength.

But though Sir Launcelot smote with all of his strength, yet Sir Gawaine smote with the strength of ten. So that Sir Launcelot *Sir Launcelot* was driven backward, and around and around in small circles, *faileth.* and in that assault he was altogether astonished at the fury and the strength of Sir Gawaine. For he wist not that Sir Gawaine had that strength of ten men, and he knew not that Sir Gawaine had taken that medicine to lend him that strength.

And Sir Launcelot had much ado to defend himself so that he made no attack, but only a defence with sword and shield against the attack of Sir Gawaine. And Sir Launcelot thought that never in all of his life had he fought with so strong and so powerful a knight as Sir Gawaine—nay, not even when he fought with Sir Turquine that day at the ford before the castle of Sir Turquine. For anon the blood began to flow forth from him in spite of all his defence, so that in a little while the ground on which he fought was all sprinkled red with that blood, and his armor was all ensanguined with the crimson streams that bathed it. And in all that while Sir Gawaine had hardly any wounds at all, but he fought with all his strength and might, and with the purpose to beat down his assailant.

But though Sir Gawaine fought in that wise, yet, by and by, it reached the prime of noon, and still he had not struck down Sir Launcelot. Then that strength of ten that he had with the medicine that he had taken began to fade and wane away as the flame of a candle flickers and wanes away when the wax is consumed. So anon Sir Launcelot felt that the attack of Sir Gawaine was no longer so furious and so violent as it had been, but that it was weaker. Therewith he redoubled his own battle with tenfold violence. And now he no longer made defence, but instead of defence he made attack. And he drave Sir Gawaine backward before him, for Sir Gawaine could not stand before the fierceness of that attack now that his strength was waning.

So Sir Gawaine bore back from before those blows, and by and by he *Sir Gawaine* began to hold his shield full low for weariness. Then Sir *faileth and is* Launcelot perceived his opening, so he rushed the attack with *overthrown.* double fury, and anon he swung his sword and smote Sir Gawaine with it full upon the head. And so violent was that blow that it clave asunder the helmet and the coif, and it wounded the head beneath the coif.

Then Sir Gawaine sank down upon his knees, his hand relaxed and the sword that was in his hand fell out from it upon the ground. Then Sir Launcelot ran to Sir Gawaine and he set his foot upon the sword and he rushed off the helmet of Sir Gawaine and he cried out very fiercely, "Sir, yield yourself to me or I will slay you!" But Sir Gawaine said, "I will not yield me to thee, so thou mayst slay me at thy pleasure!" Then Sir Launcelot gazed at Sir Gawaine, and as he gazed at him the fury of battle passed away from his soul like a mist from before the face of the sun; and Sir Launcelot felt such great love for Sir Gawaine and such great pity for him that his eyes ran all with tears.

Then Sir Launcelot said, "Sir Gawaine, even if you do not ask me for *Sir Launcelot* your life, yet will I grant it to you. Arise and depart!" *spareth him* To this Sir Gawaine said, "Messire, in this you are foolish. *his life.* For if you do not slay me now, then when I am well and healed again, I will come back against you, and will assail you again as I have assailed you to-day. For wit you that in this quarrel either you shall die or I shall die."

Sir Launcelot said, "Sir, this matters not to me! I cannot slay you now and I will not slay you."

So Sir Launcelot turned away from that place. And he mounted his horse and departed thence. And as he rode back to the castle Sir Launcelot wept so that hardly could he see the way before him because of the tears that rained down from his eyes.

Then came those from King Arthur's side who had looked upon the battle, and they raised Sir Gawaine up and led him away to his tent. And when he had come to his couch they unarmed Sir Gawaine and searched his wounds and found that they were very deep and sore. So they dressed the wounds of Sir Gawaine and put salves and unguents upon them, and so he was made in all ways as comfortable as could be.

And Sir Gawaine sent for that cunning and learned physician who had given him the medicine of strength, and he said to him, "Cannot you give me a stronger medicine than that, and one that will make in me the strength of twenty?" The physician said, "Sir, I cannot do that, for I have no such power." Sir Gawaine said, "Then can you not give me a medicine that will make me stronger for a longer time than till the prime of noon?" But the physician said, "Sir, I cannot do that either." Then Sir Gawaine sighed and he said, "Woe is me! I fear me I shall never be able to overcome Sir Launcelot."

Meanwhile the wounds of Sir Launcelot were being searched at the castle and also were found to be very sore and very deep. So it was several weeks before Sir Gawaine or Sir Launcelot recovered from those wounds. But after those several weeks were over, then each knight was as strong and as hale as he had ever been.

So, after Sir Gawaine was in all ways healed again, he clad himself in armor and took in his hand a very strong and powerful lance and mounted upon his horse once more. And Sir Gawaine rode out to the castle and he rode up and down before the walls of the castle, and ever as he rode he called out on high, "Sir Launcelot, come forth, thou caitiff knight, and do me battle!"

Sir Gawaine is healed.

He challengeth Sir Launcelot.

Then they who heard those words went to Sir Launcelot, and they said to him, "Sir, here Sir Gawaine is riding beneath the walls of the castle, and he uttereth his challenge against you." Sir Launcelot sighed and anon he said, "Send mine armor here to me"; and he said, "Send Galliard hither" (Galliard being the name of the esquire of Sir Launcelot).

So the esquire came and he aided Sir Launcelot to put his armor upon his body and his limbs, and so Sir Launcelot was in all wise armed cap-a-pie in that armor. Then Sir Launcelot took a good stout strong spear in his hand, and he mounted his horse. And the gates of the castle were opened to him as they had been aforetime; and Sir Launcelot rode forth into the sunlight to meet Sir Gawaine as he had aforetime done.

So Sir Launcelot rode up to where Sir Gawaine was and he said to Sir Gawaine, "Sir, I am here to meet thee." Sir Gawaine said, "I see that thou art, and I give thee welcome." Sir Launcelot said, "Sir, it is with greater grief than ever that I come forth to meet you to-day. For this is the fourth challenge that you have given to me, and I cannot receive any more challenges from you. So it is this day either you or I shall have to die. For I cannot suffer it that you shall come to me for day after day as you do, to utter your challenge against me." Said Sir Gawaine, "Messire, it is to my mind also that either you or I lay down our life to-day. If it be I who must die, then am I glad to lay down my life for my sons and my brothers whom you have slain; if it be you who are to die, then am I still more glad to sacrifice you to their spirits. Yet as you slew them unarmed, so it will be a greater pleasure to me to slay you for their sakes."

Quoth Sir Launcelot, "Are you ready?" and Sir Gawaine said, "Yea, I am in all wise ready."

So once more as it was before so it was now, for many of those of the castle came and stood upon the walls of the castle to behold that battle; and also there came many from the camp of King Arthur, and these stood upon the surrounding hills so that all those hills were covered with a multitude of men watching that combat.

So each knight having assumed his place of battle, and each being in all wise prepared, each set his spear in rest and each shouted to his horse to advance. Then the one charged against the other with great speed and violence, and so each met the other in the middle of the course with a crash like to a clap of thunder.

They two do battle together. As it was before, so now each lance was shivered to splinters, even to the very truncheon of the spear, and each horse reeled back from that assault. Then again each knight recovered his horse with spur and voice so that he did not fall in that recoil.

Then each knight cast aside the stump of his spear, and each leaped from his horse, drawing his sword from its scabbard for the assault. So they rushed together as aforetime, striking and lashing with might and main.

But again Sir Launcelot found Sir Gawaine possessed of such strength as astonished him, for he felt that he was fighting with his own strength against the strength of ten men.

In that battle he received many wounds that were worse than they had been before; for this time Sir Gawaine fought with great desperation to end that battle before high noontide. But ever Sir Launcelot made very strong and powerful defence, striking but few blows of assault, but putting himself ever in the posture of defence. Yet in spite of that defence, both the armor upon his body and the earth upon which he stood were all ensanguined with the blood that flowed from the many wounds that he received in that battle.

But at last it came high noontide, and with the coming and passing of noon the strength of Sir Gawaine reached its height and limit, and then it began its decline. So Sir Launcelot felt the waning of Sir Gawaine's strength and therewith ceased from his defence and began to frame his attack against the other. Then Sir Gawaine retreated backward, and he assumed such defence as he was able. But Sir Launcelot rushed upon him and beat him again and again and yet again with his sword. And Sir Gawaine was wounded in many places, for the blood gushed in streams out of many deep cuts through his armor plate.

Then from weariness the shield of Sir Gawaine began to fall full low, and Sir Launcelot perceived this and ran in upon him. And Sir Launcelot whirled his sword and smote Sir Gawaine with all his might upon the neck upon the left-hand side. And the blade of Sir Launcelot's sword sheared through the armor *Sir Launcelot wounds Sir Gawaine mortally.* at that place, and it sheared through the neck and the breast, and so deep was that wound that Sir Gawaine suffered from that blow his death-wound.

Yet Sir Gawaine would have stood to fight if he could have done so; but he could not stand. Otherwise, he sank slowly down upon his knees and there rested, with his hand upon the earth. And the blood poured down his arm and wet the earth beneath him.

Then Sir Launcelot ran in upon him and he rushed the helmet off Sir Gawaine's head, and he cried out, "Sir Gawaine, yield thee or I will slay thee!"

Quoth Sir Gawaine, "Messire, already thou hast slain me. For this wound which thou hast given to me is my death-wound. So I feel it to be, for the life is already passing out of me through that wound."

Then Sir Launcelot wept and he said, "Sir, say not so. Now I pray thee that thou wilt forgive me for this wound and for all else that I have done against thee!"

But Sir Gawaine looked at the blood that ran in streams down his arm, and he said, "I will not forgive thee, Launcelot, for otherwise, I will die in my hatred of thee. For thou hast slain me as thou hast *Sir Gawaine* slain my brothers, and upon thee I voice my curse and their *will not forgive* curse as well. For my curse and their curse is this: that *Sir Launcelot.* never after this day shalt thou prosper in anything that thou shalt undertake. Never shalt thou join in any battle from this time forth; and the dearest wish of thy heart shall disappear from thy hands when thou closest them upon that wish. Thou shalt live in sorrow and shall die shut away from all sounds and sights of knightly battle. This is my curse and my sons' curse and my brothers' curse upon thee, so wit you that though I die yet you shall be in a worse estate than I who am dead."

Then Sir Launcelot knelt weeping before Sir Gawaine, and Sir Gawaine said, "Get you hence, Sir knight, for my friends are coming."

Then Sir Launcelot raised his head and looked and he beheld that the Knights of King Arthur were coming in that direction. So he turned and mounted his horse and rode away at a hard gallop toward the castle, and he entered the castle and the gates thereof were closed behind him.

Then many of those knights who were dearest to Sir Launcelot came *Sir Launcelot* about him to give him praise for overthrowing Sir Gawaine. *grieveth.* But Sir Launcelot would not look at them. Otherwise, he turned away his head from them and withdrew to his own inn. For wit you that Sir Launcelot loved Sir Gawaine better than any man in all of the world; yea, better than his own blood and kindred. And now he knew that he had slain that one whom he loved the best of all; wherefore he lay with his face turned to the wall and melancholy enclosed him all over, like to a cloak of black.

But meanwhile Sir Gawaine had swooned so that when those knights and gentlemen, his friends, came to him, he lay on the ground like one who was dead. Those gathered him up and laid him upon a litter, and they bore him away in that litter to his tent. There they unlaced the armor and removed it, and anon the chirurgeon came to him to search his wounds. But when the chirurgeon beheld that great wound in his neck, he wit that Sir Gawaine could not live. So the chirurgeon sent for King Arthur to come hither, and he said to the King, "This man cannot live, but must die." King Arthur wept, and he said to the chirurgeon, "How know ye that he must die?" To which the chirurgeon replied, "Lord, when I looked in at that wound in the lower part of his neck, methought I could see his heart beating beneath it. Wherefore, I know that if the heart groweth cold through his wound, then he must die."

Then King Arthur hid his face and for awhile he said nothing. Then he went to the bedside of Sir Gawaine, and he said to him, "Messire, how is it with you?"

Sir Gawaine smiled at him and said to him, "Sir, wit you that I must die of this hurt." King Arthur said, "I trow not." Sir Gawaine said, "In that you are mistook, for here have I my death-wound, and in a little *Sir Gawaine* while I must die." King Arthur said, "Sir, keep up your *advises the* heart." To this Sir Gawaine made answer, "My heart *King.* faileth not, but my life hangeth fluttering upon my lips, and soon it must pass away from me." And Sir Gawaine said, "Sir, wit ye of this, your own case is as bad as mine. Return you again to Britain as fast as you are able, for I trust not more than need be to Sir Mordred's truth, albeit he is my brother. For he hath ever had a dark and gloomy spirit. And he hath ambition for the throne, and now that he hath the power behind that ambition, and now that you have lost so many good and worthy knights at this castle, he will certes seize upon your throne unless you are by to wrest it out of his hands. Wherefore I pray you to return to Britain as soon as may be."

King Arthur said, "Sir, these are imaginings upon your part. For Sir Mordred is a Knight of the Round Table, and is bound to me in fealty. Why, therefore, think you he would be treacherous to me?"

Sir Gawaine said, "Lord, I lie now very close to the edge of death and all things appear extraordinarily clear and distinct to mine eyes. Sir Mordred hath no love for any soul save only for himself. Wherefore, I fear me he will sacrifice you to his desires, and will seize upon your throne. Lord, I shall not live until to-morrow morning, wherefore, I charge you that when I am dead, you shall bury me here in haste, and depart straightway for England, for I fear me for your kingdom in Britain."

So that night in the second hour after midnight, Sir Gawaine drew his last breath and died. And King Arthur was there at that *Sir Gawaine* passing, and several knights companions of the Round Table *dieth.* were there, so that Sir Gawaine did not die in loneliness. And after he had passed, King Arthur wept and he said as follows:

THE LAMENT OF KING ARTHUR

"So passeth this dear and faithful friend. There is not of all those who are left anyone whom I love so well as I loved him. For *King Arthur's* though he was passionate in his angers and his indignations, *lament.* yet to me he was always loving and full of dutifulness and kindliness. He was the right hand and support of my throne and its chiefest prop in all of its weaknesses, and I had hoped that he would have occupied that throne after I had departed from this earth.

"But now this is past and gone and he is taken who was, next to Sir Launcelot of the Lake, the brightest and most glorious figure of all my Round Table.

"He was the companion of my youth. For when I had fought my battles and come to my throne, he was among the first who came and laid his hands between my palms. Also he was one of the first of all those knights-elect of the Round Table to take his seat at that table.

"But now he is gone and I am left alone, like the tree in the forest that hath been struck by lightning. Yea, like that tree my foliage is withered and now I stand stark and bare against the sky. For my Queen, who was the lover of my youth, is estranged from me, and I shall never behold her more. My Round Table, that was otherwise the chiefest glory of my reign, is broken and scattered and many of those who were one time dearest to me in love are now my foes. Where are now the defenders of my throne? They are gone; and that throne itself totters to its fall.

"All these are sad and woful happenings, but the saddest and most woful of all is that this good worthy knight hath died. Would that I had died in his stead and that he had not died, but that I had died for him. What worse hath Fate in store for me than this that he is dead?"

So in words such as these or in words like to them, King Arthur mourned for Sir Gawaine; for it seemed that no worse blow could befall him than this; to wit, the death of Sir Gawaine.

That morning King Arthur was aroused very early from his couch of *News cometh* grief by a messenger that came to him with a message from *to the King of* Britain, and that message was this: that Sir Mordred had *Sir Mordred.* seized upon the throne and the crown of Britain, and was holding them for his own.

This message came from Sir Constantine of Cornwall, who was the cousin of Sir Gawaine and who was yet living in England. And Sir Constantine said, "Hasten! Hasten your return, O Lord King, and let nothing delay that return!"

Then King Arthur gave command that the siege of Chillion should be raised, and that after Sir Gawaine was buried they should all return again to Britain.

So that day the funeral of Sir Gawaine was held with great pomp and *Sir Gawaine* circumstance. Four bishops conducted the mass for the rest *is buried.* of his soul, and the whole army knelt to pray for him. And those people within the Castle of Chillion also kneeled upon the battlements of the castle wall and prayed for the rest of his soul. For next to Sir Launcelot, he was the greatest knight in the world.

So they laid him at rest at that place—a good worthy knight and one well established in all courts of chivalry both then and thereafter. For if he was violent of temper and if he sought revenge upon Sir Launcelot for the death of his sons and his brethren, yet he gave his life for that anger and that revenge, and that the manes of his kindred might be satisfied.

So endeth the history of Sir Gawaine.

ir Mordred the traitor :·

Chapter Eighth

How King Arthur returned to England. How he fought his last battle with Sir Mordred.

SO the news came to Britain that King Arthur was returning to that realm, and that news was conveyed to Sir Mordred where he was. And when Sir Mordred heard thereof he sat sunk in melancholy, his head bowed upon his breast, and his food and wine standing untasted beside him. *Sir Mordred despaireth.*

And several of the friends of Sir Mordred were with him at that time, and with them was Sir Mador de la Porte, who had, since his battle with Sir Launcelot, been an enemy to King Arthur. These say to Sir Mordred, "Sir, why are you so cast down? Wit you that King Arthur is not yet returned, and that when he doth return he must do battle with you to regain his kingdom."

Quoth Sir Mordred, "Yes, that is very true, but wit you that I have given out word to the world that King Arthur was slain in battle before the Castle of Chillion, and in that word lay my strength. Wherefore now, when King Arthur returneth to Britain, and when the people find that he is yet alive, they will turn to him and will cast me out."

Quoth Sir Mador de la Porte, "Then it behooves you, Sir, to make stir and to proclaim to the people that with King Arthur there will be continued wars, but that with you there will be peace and tranquillity. For wit you that King Arthur for this year past *His friends advise him.* hath been continually at war against Sir Launcelot, and during that time you have not had one single war in all of Britain. Wherefore, as people love peace, so they will cling to you. Beside this, you should summon the Archbishop of Canterbury to your presence and have him crown you as king. For if you be a king in your own right, then will you have that much more strength to do battle for your own rights. Now here at hand is the Archbishop of Canterbury, and he shall be summoned and shall crown you at your demand."

Sir Mordred beseeches the Archbishop to crown him. So they sent for the Archbishop of Canterbury, and he came to where Sir Mordred was. Sir Mordred said to him, "Sir, wit you why I have sent for you? It is that you shall crown me King of Britain."

Quoth the Archbishop, "I cannot do this thing that you ask of me, for *The Archbishop refuses.* the news is that King Arthur is returning to Britain. How then can you be crowned King of Britain when the rightful King of Britain is still alive?"

To this Sir Mordred made reply, "I have not set for you to reason with me, but to crown me as the King of this realm. For if you crown me, then do I believe that I shall be well able to defend my crown and my kingship, but if you do not crown me, then will I do battle with King Arthur as a usurper to make myself a king instead of him."

Then said the Archbishop, "Sir, you shall not do this thing. For I, as the head of the Church in this realm, bid you to surrender your rights and claims unto the just and lawful king who now returneth. For he surrendered his kingship to you for a little while whilst he was away from Britain, and not for a permanency. Yet you would make that surrender permanent, for you would make yourself king instead of him. Wherefore, if you do not surrender yourself to King Arthur's mercy upon the day of his landing, then will the Church curse you with bell, book and candle as the usurper of those rights that belong to another." Then Sir Mordred was filled with rage against the Archbishop and he cried out, "Sir, get you gone, or I shall forget myself and draw my sword and slay you perhaps."

So the Archbishop withdrew from the presence of Sir Mordred, and he *The Archbishop withdraweth.* called his court about him, and he recounted to that court all that had passed between him and Sir Mordred. And he said, "Let us fly from this place. For we are in danger here." So the Archbishop took him a strong horse and he mounted upon it and his court also mounted upon horses, and then he and his court rode with great haste away from that place and to Dover, where King Arthur was expected to be about to land.

After the Archbishop had gone and when Sir Mordred found that he had gone, Sir Mordred collected such of his army together as were there at hand; and he also descended to Dover, taking that army with him; his intent being to prevent the King from landing if he could do so.

So came King Arthur to Dover, and as one stood upon the cliffs one beheld that his ships and galleys covered the entire sea as far as the eye could behold. And as the King approached the shore, he beheld that there was a considerable army drawn up in array upon the beach where he was to land, and he knew not whether that array were to welcome him or to do battle with him. But at length he perceived Sir Mordred in the fore-front of that array, and he wist that that army was there to do battle with him. Then he groaned aloud and he said, "Is there yet more blood to be shed? Well, then, it must be shed, for never will I give up my throne unless I give it up with my life. For eight and twenty years have I held that throne, and shall I now surrender it to this man, my nephew Mor-dred? No; never!"

So as the boats drew near to the shore, those who were in them leaped into the water and waded to the shore. And the army of Sir Mordred came down to the water and did battle with those who sought *Of the battle* to land. And so a great battle was fought there at the edge *of Dover.* of the water, so that the water was all discolored red with the blood of those who were wounded or slain and who fell into the flood. Wherefore it was that with each recurring wave this red water ran upward upon the white sands, and then receded, leaving the sands all stained red where it had flowed upon it.

But yet Sir Mordred did not prevent that army from landing, for ever more knights and yeomen and still more leaped from the boats and into that shallow water, and so at last the army of Sir Mordred was forced back from the water and King Arthur's army landed upon the shore.

Then Sir Mordred withdrew his army from that place and King Arthur took possession of that part of Britain.

After that the Archbishop of Canterbury came to where King Arthur was, and he gave him greeting, saying, "Greeting, King Arthur, and give thee joy of landing upon this soil. For here am I who am the head of the Church and I give thee welcome to thy realm. For wit you that Sir Mor-dred would fain have had me crown him king, but I would not crown him, having heard that thou wert still alive."

Then King Arthur embraced the Bishop and kissed him upon either cheek, and said to him, "Sir, I thank you for your welcome. And I thank you that you have guarded and protected my rights."

Now, after having been thus driven away from Dover, Sir Mordred withdrew to Baremdown, and at that place he gathered about him all those of his followers who had hitherto been tardy in coming to him. And he assembled with him all those who had been friends to Sir Launcelot (for these were now at enmity with King Arthur). So at that place Sir Mor-dred had a very considerable army to confront King Arthur withal.

Then Sir Mordred stationed that army upon a rise of land where were three steep hills. For so he could charge down those hills against his enemies, whilst they must charge up those hills against him.

So came King Arthur, and when he perceived the dispersion of Sir Mordred's army, he also arranged his army into three divisions. The centre division he took himself; the right division he entrusted to the King of North Wales, and the left division he placed under the leadership of Sir Ewaine, who had not quitted Britain for all this time.

Then King Arthur charged his army up those hills against his enemy, *Of the battle of* but he could not climb those hills because of the steepness *Baremdown.* thereof, and because of the defence of the enemy at the top of the steeps. And afterward he charged again and again, but still he could not gain the crest of those hills.

Then Sir Ewaine's division overlapped the army of Sir Mordred, and he charged up that hill both before and behind. And he doubled Sir Mordred's party up upon itself and threw it into great confusion.

But that wing of Sir Mordred's army could not retreat to the rear by reason that Sir Ewaine's knights were there; wherefore, it fled back upon the centre of the army and threw that centre also into confusion. Then King Arthur charged for the fourth time, and this time he took the centre hill of the three, and with that the army of Sir Mordred broke and fled. And the army of Sir Mordred fled toward Salisbury, and a great many knights were slain in that flight. And the army of Sir Mordred took up its station not far from Salisbury, and not far distant from the sea.

So King Arthur won the battle of Baremdown, but with sad and bitter loss. For many knights fell in that assault and amongst them was Sir Ewaine, who was mortally hurt.

Now when King Arthur heard that Sir Ewaine was hurt, he went to where the wounded knight lay in his pavilion. And Sir Ewaine's face *Sir Ewaine* was very wan and hollow and pale, and the dew of death stood *is wounded.* upon his forehead. Then King Arthur went to the couch of Sir Ewaine and he kneeled beside the couch and embraced Sir Ewaine about the body with his arms. And the tears ran down King Arthur's face and wet the face of Sir Ewaine that was beneath him. And Sir Ewaine said, "Art thou there, my king? For I cannot see thee, and yet meseems I feel thee weeping upon me." And King Arthur said, "Ewaine, it is I."

Then Sir Ewaine said, "Sir, send for Sir Launcelot to aid thee in this war. For Sir Launcelot is the best of all thy knights and he has with him *Sir Ewaine* several knights that are very good and strong. These will *biddeth King* come to thine aid if thou wilt ask it of them, and so thou wilt *Arthur to send* *for Sir* easily overthrow Sir Mordred. For many of the knights also *Launcelot.* are friends with Sir Launcelot who are now in the army of Sir Mordred, thinking that thou art at enmity with Sir Launcelot. But if

Sir Launcelot cometh to thee, then will those knights quit Sir Mordred and will cleave to thee. But if thou dost not send for Sir Launcelot then it may be that Sir Mordred will overthrow thee. Wherefore I beseech thee to send for Sir Launcelot and for his knights to aid thee."

Quoth King Arthur, "How shall I send for him? And by what right shall I ask him to come to mine aid? Sir Launcelot is my foe, for he took from me my wife and held her from me for several months. And he hath slain my nephews and he slew Sir Gawaine, who was my best beloved of all. How, then, shall I now ask him to come to mine aid?"

Quoth Sir Ewaine, "Give me parchment and ink." So they brought ink and parchment to Sir Ewaine and they propped him up *Sir Ewaine* upon his bed. And with that his wounds burst out bleeding *writeth a letter* afresh, so that he wist that he had but a short time to live. *Launcelot.*

Then Sir Ewaine wrote to Sir Launcelot and he said to him, "Sir, this day hath been fought a great battle upon Baremdown, and King Arthur, mine uncle, won that battle. But many knights have died in that battle, and I in it have received my death-wound. Sir, I pray you let all by-gones pass and be done betwixt you and King Arthur. And I pray you to forget and forgive any injury you may have received or given; for in this war King Arthur is put to such a pass that maybe he shall win and maybe he shall not win; wherefore I pray you to come to him without any delay, and so make his winning this war a certainty.

"Sir, I myself have been sorely wounded and am dying, and in an hour I shall have passed and gone from this earth. So, with my dying strength I write you to come to the aid of your king who made you a knight some while ago."

Such as this was Sir Ewaine's letter, and after he had written it he signed his name to it.

This letter King Arthur sent by a messenger to Sir Launcelot of the Lake in France. There Sir Launcelot received it and paid heed to it. For he summoned his knights about him and he read that letter to them, and he said to them, "Messires, such as this is the need of King Arthur. Now who will go with me to Britain and do battle in this for the King of Britain?" And those knights said, "I will go!"—"And I!"—"And I!"— "And I!"—until they all of them agreed to go to Britain and fight for King Arthur.

Now return we to King Arthur again. For there was he left kneeling beside the couch of Sir Ewaine. And so he continued to kneel and pres- ently Sir Ewaine said, "Good, my Lord, are you there?" For *Sir Ewaine* Sir Ewaine's eyes were now darkening in death and he could *dieth.*

not see anything.　And King Arthur said, "Yea, I am here."　And he took Sir Ewaine's hand in his, and Sir Ewaine's hand was cold and very heavy, like to lead.　And Sir Ewaine said, "Hold my hand and do not let it go." So King Arthur held the hand of Sir Ewaine.　So Sir Ewaine lay for a little while, breathing deep draughts of death; and by and by he sighed very deeply and then he lay still; for his spirit had passed from him with that deep sigh.

Then King Arthur arose and he said, "Alas, that this good worthy knight is gone.　For he was my nephew and he was very faithful to me."　And he said, "To-day we will bury him, and to-morrow we shall follow Sir Mordred, and either he shall die or I shall die.　For so through him and his deeds hath this kind and noble gentleman died; wherefore he must pay the price of that death—he must slay me as well, or else I will slay him."

So King Arthur arose and went forth from that place.　And when the day was come, Sir Ewaine was buried at the minster at that place, and it was said in the history of these things that his skull was to be seen there even to the very day of the ancient writing of this history.

Then after all honors had been paid to the body of Sir Ewaine, King
King Arthur advances against Sir Mordred. Arthur gathered his army together and he arose and pursued Sir Mordred in the direction of Salisbury.　And the next day he came to that place where Sir Mordred was, and there he halted his army.

That night King Arthur lay in his pavilion and he slept very deeply and profoundly, as sleeps the man who is weary of toil and marching.　And anon while he slept he had a dream and the dream was this:

He dreamed that he sat upon his throne, and that his throne was established upon a monstrous wheel.　And the wheel rose high with him sitting upon his throne.　And anon the wheel rose above the rim of
The King hath a dream. the earth, and he beheld the sun shining in all his glory.　And the sun glittered upon him and he felt all the joy and all the delight of that sunlight.　And it seemed to King Arthur that he was a great while in that sunlight, but he was not, for the wheel was turning very slowly with him.　So the wheel reached its highest apex, and then it began to descend.　And the wheel descended more and more swiftly, and anon it descended below the rim of the world, and so the sunlight had left the King.　And the wheel descended more and more swiftly, so that King Arthur began to fear he would be cast out of his throne by the turning of the wheel.　And King Arthur dreamed that he looked down beneath him, and he beheld that the wheel was descending very rapidly to a great pool, as it were a lake.　And this pool was filled with blackness and with blood,

and behold there was no bottom to that pool. And by then the throne of King Arthur was inclining very greatly toward that pool, and the King felt that he was slipping from his throne, and at that his soul was filled with terror. Then he tried to awaken, but he could not. So, in his terror, he screamed very loudly and shrilly, "Save me! Save me, or I fall!" And so shrill was his calling that several knights and attendants ran into the pavilion where he was, and these beheld the King struggling in his sleep. And they cried out, "Lord, Lord! What aileth thee? Awaken!" And with that King Arthur awoke.

And King Arthur sat up upon his couch and gazed about him, as one sunk in great amazement, and he said, "I slept and I dreamed a dream; and it was a dreadful dream." And he said to those in attendance upon him, "Do not go from me yet, for that dream hath affrighted me."

So they all sat near to him and by and by they beheld that he breathed very deeply and softly, wherefore they wist that he slept again. Then all they withdrew from the pavilion, saving only two of his attendants who still sat beside him.

But King Arthur did not sleep, though it was a manner of sleep, for he beheld all the things about him as though he were partly awake, yet he could not move.

Then, while he was in this sleep, King Arthur beheld a vision. For he saw the flap at the doorway of the pavilion that it moved, *The King* and anon it was raised and Sir Gawaine entered the tent. *dreameth again.* And Sir Gawaine held the flap of the doorway aside, and King Arthur beheld that fourteen ladies entered the tent behind Sir Gawaine.

And when these ladies had all entered the tent, Sir Gawaine let fall the flap of the doorway, and so he came forward to where King Arthur lay. And the face of Sir Gawaine was very calm and smiling and cheerful, and King Arthur felt great peace and happiness when he beheld him standing there.

Then King Arthur dreamed that he spoke to Sir Gawaine, and he said, "Sir, how is this? Methought that you were dead, and here I behold you alive. Was it not then you whom we buried in France some while ago?"

Sir Gawaine said, "Nay, Lord, that was not I, that was but my shell— my poor, crumbling, perishable carcass that you buried. This is I myself, and I have come to you from Paradise."

Quoth King Arthur, "Who are these ladies whom you have with you?" To this Sir Gawaine made answer, "These are those ladies for whom I one time did battle. For some of those ladies I saved from grief, some of them from misfortune, some of them I saved from danger, and of some of them I saved their lives. So they have accompanied me hither from Paradise that I might speak to you."

Said King Arthur, "Sir Gawaine, my nephew, what is it you would say to me?" To the which Sir Gawaine made reply, "Sir, I come to you to charge you that you shall not do battle to-morrow-day. For great danger lieth before you, and if you do battle you will assuredly perish. Wherefore I come to you to beseech you that you will not enter into war with your enemies. Wit you that Sir Launcelot will in a little while come to your assistance, for already the letter from Sir Ewaine hath well-nigh reached him, and when it reacheth him then will he come to you with all speed. Wherefore I pray you make such terms with Sir Mordred as you may, but do not join battle with him."

King Arthur said, "How shall I know that this that thou tellest me is a vision of prophecy and not a dream? For if it is a dream, then perhaps it is mistaken, as many dreams are mistaken; but if it be a vision of prophecy, then I shall believe that it is sooth."

"Sir," said Sir Gawaine, "you may believe it from this sign that will remain unto you. And from it you may know that what you now behold is indeed a vision of prophecy, and not a dream."

So with that Sir Gawaine reached forth his finger and touched with it
Sir Gawaine the back of King Arthur's hand. And when the finger of
leaveth a sign. Sir Gawaine touched his hand, lo! upon the hand of King Arthur there was left a spot as white as wax.

Then the figure of Sir Gawaine melted slowly from his sight, and the figures of the ladies also melted away and King Arthur awoke from his sleep. And King Arthur sat up upon his couch and he beheld that the day-light was streaming into his pavilion, for the sun had already arisen.

And King Arthur looked at the back of his hand, and he beheld that there was the spot as white as wax where Sir Gawaine had touched him. Then King Arthur was very much perturbed in spirit, for he wist that what he had just beheld was no dream, but that it was a vision of prophecy.

So King Arthur called at him his knights and gentlemen and yeomen, and he told them to bring to him those bishops who were with him, and also the wisest of his counsellors. When these were come he told to them
The King ad- the vision of his sleep, and he showed them the white spot
vises with his upon his hand, where the finger of Sir Gawaine had touched
counsellors. him. And he said to those counsellors, "Sirs, is it better to treat with these our enemies to-day than to do battle with them? For if it be true that Sir Launcelot cometh to us, then all those knights who for his sake are now in the army of Sir Mordred, will leave that army and will

join them with us for the sake of Sir Launcelot. Thus will many lives be spared and much blood remain unshed, for there will be no battle with Sir Mordred."

Then all those counsellors agreed with him and they said, "That which thou sayst is true. Do not fight with Sir Mordred to-day, but treat with him. For thy dream and thy vision foretell thy death if thou fightest with him."

So King Arthur chose him two of those bishops, and he chose him Sir Lucian the Bottelier and Sir Bedivere, his brother, from all the Knights of the Round Table, and these two knights and those two worthies he sent as his ambassadors to Sir Mordred. And he said to them, "Spare not your promises of land and of estate, but make this treaty for a month and a day; for by that time we will know how Sir Launcelot standeth toward us."

So those two envoys went to Sir Mordred, and they entered into treaty with him and his advisers. And they argued for all that day, *The envoys* and against eventide they had not decided. So the next day *treat with Sir* they went to Sir Mordred, and that day it was determined *Mordred.* that Sir Mordred should hold Cornwall and Kent for his own during the life of King Arthur, and that upon the death of King Arthur all Britain should be his to rule as king.

This treaty they brought to King Arthur, and when he read it he frowned until his eyes were hidden. "Well," said he, "this traitor claimeth much. Let him be thankful that instead of all this land he demandeth, he hath given to him instead only six feet of earth in which to lie."

So it was arranged that Sir Mordred and King Arthur should meet upon the next day at high noontide, at a certain place betwixt the two armies. And it was there arranged that each of them should sign this covenant, and that there should then be peace in all the land.

And the place where this meeting was to be held was a certain smooth and gentle valley, that sloped upward upon either hand. And upon one extremity of the valley one could behold the distant ocean, and upon the other side of the valley one could behold the plains of Salisbury. At this place those two armies were gathered upon the hills looking down upon the middle of that valley.

And in the centre of that valley there was a great pavilion of parti-colored silk erected for the accommodation of the King and of Sir Mordred. And a great banner emblazoned with the arms of the *Of the meeting* King and another emblazoned with the arms of Sir Mordred *of King Arthur* flew from the peak of the pavilion. And King Arthur came *and Sir* with six knights, and Sir Mordred came with six knights, and *Mordred.*

these twelve knights—six upon either side—stood some short distance away separate from one another, and King Arthur and Sir Mordred entered the pavilion.

There upon the table lay the treaty to be signed, and those two drew near to the table to sign it.

Now it was understood that none of those twelve knights who had come with King Arthur and Sir Mordred should draw a weapon of any sort, but that all should remain with sword in scabbard. For King Arthur did not trust Sir Mordred, and Sir Mordred did not trust King Arthur. For King Arthur said, "This man is altogether unnatural. His soul is black and he is full of treason and guile. Wherefore, if you see any of his knights draw a sword, then do you draw your swords and fall upon them and upon Sir Mordred." And Sir Mordred said, "I trust not this King in any way. For he giveth too readily of that which he cannot spare. Wherefore, be you ready, and if you behold any of his six knights draw a sword, draw your swords and fall on, and, if possible, see to it that you slay King Arthur himself."

Now whilst those two parties of six knights each stood talking to one another, it chanced that an adder that lay hidden in a furze bush came *A knight slay-* forth from its hiding. And one of the knights of Sir Mor- *eth an adder.* dred's party stepped back from his place and trod upon the adder, and the adder stung the knight in the heel. Then the knight looked down to see what it was that stung him, and he beheld the adder beneath his heel. So without thinking of those commands that had been laid upon him, he drew his sword to slay that adder.

This the knights of King Arthur's party beheld, and they beheld the knight draw his sword, and they beheld the bright and trenchant blade gleam in the sunlight as the knight swung his sword to slay the adder.

Then the knights of King Arthur's party immediately drew their swords and they shouted aloud, crying, "Treason! treason! A rescue! A rescue!" And the knights of Sir Mordred's party, upon their part also drew their swords and ran so to the defence of Sir Mordred.

But King Arthur heard the outcry of those knights, and upon that outcry he thought that Sir Mordred had betrayed him, wherefore he cried out in a terrible voice, "Hah! Wouldst thou betray me?" And with that he catched Sir Mordred by the throat and as he catched him thus he drew his misericordia to slay him. But Sir Mordred tore himself loose from King Arthur, and he rushed out from the tent, crying aloud, "I come! I come!"

Then King Arthur also rushed out from the tent and he beheld his six knights at battle with the six knights of Sir Mordred, and he beheld his army and Sir Mordred's army rushing toward them. And *The armies* the beat of the hoofs of those approaching armies was like to *rush to battle.* the sound of distant thunder ever coming nearer and nearer and louder and louder. And the cloud of dust behind those armies was like the smoke of a great conflagration rising up into the sky. And in the midst of those clouds he could see the flashing and blazing of polished armor catching the sunlight and flinging it off again as those armies rode rapidly down the slopes and toward them.

Thus those armies came together with great uproar and thunder and a flashing like to flaming lightning in the midst of a storm. And King Arthur ran to his horse and mounted nimbly thereon, and he spurred back to meet his army, and an esquire who rode with that army gave to him a good stout spear of ashwood.

So those two armies met with a shock that might have been heard a league. In that shock of meeting one recoiled from the other by the force of the assault it had itself delivered. And many knights fell in that first assault, and most of those that fell died as they fell. For the horses pressed upon them with their hoofs and many died beneath that pressure. And after the horsemen came the yeomen afoot, and these ran hither and thither and slew many who yet lived.

Then those knights who were still a-horseback cast aside their spears, for they could not longer use their spears in that narrow pass, wherefore they cast them away and drew their swords. And with their swords they hewed about them from right to left, and from left to right. And so, in a while, the ground was littered with cantles of armor and with men lying dead or dying beneath the hoofs of the horses.

So that fierce battle began a little before the prick of noon, and it continued for all that afternoon, and it continued through the twilight of the evening and until the falling of the night.

For that was the last and the greatest battle that King Arthur ever fought, and in it were slain twelve thousand knights and gen- *Sir Mordred* tlemen and yeomen. But as night descended the army of *is defeated.* Sir Mordred broke and fled from the field, and King Arthur was left the victor of that battle.

But when King Arthur sat his horse in the midst of the battle-field, he wept so that the tears ran in streams down his face. Yea, he tasted those tears in his mouth and they were salt to his taste.

For of all those knights who had once surrounded the Court of King Arthur and had made it so glorious, there were hardly any left. And of all those Knights of the Round Table who had once been his crowning honor, there were not twelve who were yet alive. All others had perished, and the ground was sown thick with them as the sea-shore is sown thick with the cobbles that lie upon it.

Wherefore, when King Arthur beheld all this ruin of his life, and when he heard the doleful groans of those who were wounded, and when he beheld those who were dead lying still in death and gazing with sightless eyes up into the sky, the tears ran from his eyes in great streams and traced down his face and into his beard, so that he tasted the salt of those tears.

For now indeed the glory of his reign was past, and nothing remained for him but an empty kingdom devoid of all honor and all that was of worth. "Alas, and woe is me!" cried he, "for my fate hath now overtaken me and my day is done."

The Passing of Arthur

Chapter Ninth

How King Arthur slew Sir Mordred, and how he himself was wounded so that he was upon the edge of death. How his sword Excalibur was cast away, and how three queens came from Avalon and took him away with them.

SO that night, after the battle afore told of, the moon arose very full and round, and very clearly shining. What time King Arthur rode across the field of battle, with intent to discover what friends and what foes had been slain. And the King discovered many *The King* knights lying there who were friends and many other knights *rideth upon* who were foes. *the battle-field.*

For at that time the sky was without any cloud at all upon it; and the light of the moon was as clear and bright as though it were daylight, wherefore one could see all things upon the earth and to a great distance away upon all sides of the earth.

And with King Arthur there rode Sir Bedivere and Sir Lucian the Bottelier, who was brother to Sir Bedivere. And Sir Lucian was very sore wounded, even to the death; but of this he made no mention nor any complaint whatsoever, but ever he rode with King Arthur and his brother, and neither of those two wist that he had any wound whatsoever.

And amongst many other knights that lay there dead upon the field of battle, they discovered Sir Mador de la Porte lying dead. Then King Arthur pointed his finger at the body of Sir Mador and he *He perceiveth* said, "See you that man, Messires? That was once a good, *Sir Mador de* strong and very valiant knight. One time he was my friend, *la Porte dead.* but then he accused the Queen of treason, and so I exiled him from me and from my court. So he took arms against me and now he lieth dead here as you perceive. Ah me! That he should have brought that false accusation, for it was the beginning of the end that hath been my undoing, and woe for him, for he was a good strong knight, and a Knight of the Round Table. And one while he was very dear to me."

237

So said King Arthur and they listened to his words.

Now as they progressed still farther upon the field of battle, they were, by and by, aware of a knight who stood alone beside a bramble bush. And the knight stood very silent and still, like to a statue of iron. And the light of the moon shone down upon him and glistened upon his armor. And at certain places that armor was stained with red, for he had been wounded in several places.

He findeth Sir Mordred standing alone. So they came nearer to that knight, and in a little while they knew him, and they knew that it was Sir Mordred who stood there alone. And all about Sir Mordred there lay several dead knights; for here Sir Mordred had made his last stand with several of his knights. And these were of the dead knights that lay around him, and others of those dead knights were the knights of King Arthur.

But the horse of Sir Mordred had been slain and Sir Mordred himself had been wounded in the thighs so that he could not escape with those of his army who fled away from that field of battle.

Then King Arthur said to Sir Bedivere and Sir Lucian, "Look you! Yonder is Mordred himself. He is the destroyer of all my court of knighthood and of all my joy of life. For through him hath come all this later evil upon me, wherefore he is meet for death at my hands." And the King said to Sir Bedivere, "Lend me thy spear and I will go and slay him."

Quoth Sir Bedivere, "Let him be, Lord, for anon will come those who know him and will slay him even here where he standeth."

King Arthur said, "I will not entrust his death to any other hands but mine own. For as he hath brought all this misfortune upon me, so will I slay him with mine own hands. Wherefore, Sir, give me your sword that I may slay him."

Then Sir Bedivere said to the King, "Look you, Sir, how he stands looking at us in the moonlight, like a wounded hawk looking upon those who have wounded him. Beware, Sir, and remember the dream that you had last night when Sir Gawaine appeared to you in that dream. So far have you escaped all harm, but should you assail this desperate man, who knoweth but that you may yet meet your death at this time and at his hands?"

But King Arthur said, "What is my life to me now, and what have I to lose in losing my life? Have I not lost my Queen, who was the lover of my youth? Have I not lost all these knights, who were the chiefest glory and pride of my reign? What, then, have I to live for, saving it be an empty throne of royalty? Tide me life, tide me death, I will slay this man, so give me your spear, Messire."

Then Sir Bedivere gave his spear to King Arthur and King Arthur took it into his hands. And he set that spear in rest against Sir Mordred.

Now all this Sir Mordred beheld, and he believed that the King was now threatening his life. And he heard all that the King said to those knights who were with him, and he wist that now his life was forfeit to him.

So Sir Mordred drew his sword and it flashed like white light in the moonlight. And he came forward to meet King Arthur and his death, and as he came he whirled his sword on high. And King Arthur drave his spurs into his horse and charged against Sir Mordred. And King Arthur directed the point of his spear against the body of Sir Mordred beneath where the shield sheltered his bosom, and the point of the spear penetrated the body of Sir Mordred and it pierced the body and stood an ell out behind the back of Sir Mordred's body. *King Arthur pierces Sir Mordred through with his spear.*

Then Sir Mordred felt that he had received his wound of death, wherefore he bethought him only of revenge against King Arthur. So he pressed up against the spear with all of his might. And he thrust himself up the length of the spear until he had reached the burr thereof. And when his body was against the burr of the spear, he took his sword in both his hands and he swung the sword above his head, and he smote King Arthur with the edge of the sword upon the helmet. *Sir Mordred smiteth the King with his sword.*

In that blow was all the last desperation of Sir Mordred's life, and so strong was the blow that it sheared through the helmet of King Arthur, and through the coif beneath the helmet, and it sheared through the brainpan of the King and deep into the brain itself.

Then King Arthur reeled upon his saddle and his body swayed this way and that, and from side to side. And he would have fallen from his saddle only that Sir Bedivere catched him and held him up upon his saddle.

And Sir Mordred wist that he had given King Arthur his death wound, wherefore he fell down upon the ground and he laughed and he said, "So I die, but ere I die I have finished my work, for the King also shall die." Therewith he breathed very deep, and it was his last breath, for with it his spirit left his body.

Sir Bedivere said to King Arthur, "Lord, are you hurt?" And King Arthur, breathing very heavily, said, "Sir, this wound is the wound of my death as that knight declared. For the wound, I believe, hath pierced into my brain and I cannot live. Messires, take me hence to a shelter." And King Arthur said, "What building is that yonder?"

Sir Bedivere said, "Lord, it is a chapel upon the field of battle." King Arthur said, "Take me thither and let me be at peace, for I cannot live but a little while."

So Sir Bedivere dismounted from his horse and he took the horse *Sir Bedivere* of King Arthur by the bridle and he led the horse toward *and Sir Lucian* the chapel. And Sir Lucian held King Arthur up upon *bring the King,* *wounded, to the* the saddle, and King Arthur swayed from this side to that *chapel.* side, and he would have fallen only that Sir Lucian held him up in his place.

So they two brought King Arthur to the chapel in safety, and they bore him into the chapel and laid him upon a bench that was there. And in thus lifting King Arthur the wounds of Sir Lucian burst out bleeding afresh. And with that Sir Lucian, after King Arthur had been laid upon the bench, sank down upon the ground and lay there frothing at the mouth, and the froth was red.

Then Sir Bedivere cried out, "Ah, my brother! My brother! Art thou *Sir Lucian* hurt?" And King Arthur said, "Search him and see if he be *dieth.* wounded." So Sir Bedivere examined Sir Lucian and felt his face and his hands, and anon he said, "Lord, my brother is indeed dead. And I knew not even that he had been wounded; for all this while he hath borne his wounds in patience, speaking no words of it, or making no complaint of it. Ah, my brother! My brother! That thou shouldst be dead!"

Then King Arthur groaned very deeply, and he said, "Alas and alas! So hath another of my noble Knights of the Round Table died and left me!" And then he said, "So would I weep for him, but I cannot weep; for also in a little while I shall be with him and with them who are gone." And he said to Sir Bedivere, "Remove my helmet, and search my hurt." So Sir Bedivere removed the helmet of King Arthur and he beheld the wound upon his head that it was very deep and bitter, so that the brains of his head were exposed in that wound. And Sir Bedivere wept when he beheld that wound; for he wist that of it King Arthur must die.

But King Arthur said, "Weep not, Sir Bedivere, but do straightway as I tell thee." And he said, "Beholdest thou Excalibur strapped about my loins?"

And Sir Bedivere said, "Yea, Lord," and ever Sir Bedivere wept.

King Arthur said, "Take that sword and carry him to the water and cast him into the water: then return thou hither and tell me what thou seest."

Then Sir Bedivere unbuckled the strap from about the loins of King Arthur, and he drew the strap from beneath him. Then he folded the strap around the blade of Excalibur and he took the sword *Sir Bedivere* with him and went away with it. But when Sir Bedivere *taketh* had come out into the moonlight, the moonlight shone very *Excalibur.* brightly down upon the hilt of Excalibur, and Sir Bedivere beheld how that the hilt and the handle of the sword were studded all over with jewels, and the gold into which they were inset flamed and blazed in the moonlight as with a thousand colors.

And Sir Bedivere said to himself, "Why should I cast this splendid sword into the sea? Behold how richly it is studded with jewels so that it flashes and flames with pure light. Certes, the King raves when he telleth me to cast it into the sea! Rather will I keep this sword, to show to those generations who are yet to come how great and how splendid was the estate of King Arthur."

So Sir Bedivere looked about him and he beheld a dead and riven tree that stood there, all stark and leafless in the moonlight. So *Sir Bedivere* he took the sword Excalibur and he hid it beneath the roots *doth not cast* of that tree. Anon he returned to King Arthur, and he said *the sword away.* to the King, "Lord, your behest is done and I have cast that sword into the sea."

Quoth the King, "What sawest thou, Sir Bedivere?"

Quoth Sir Bedivere, "What should I have beheld, Lord? I beheld nothing but the waves beating upon the shore. And the moon shone upon those waves, as it were a path of living and of glittering silver."

Then King Arthur said, "Ah, liar and caitiff knight! I am undone for trusting to thee. For thou hast deceived me, who trusted in thee. For thou hast coveted the jewels set upon the handle of the sword, and hast refrained from casting it into the water of the sea." Then Sir Bedivere said, "Lord, I repent me of this."

But King Arthur said, "Go now, and do what I bid thee do, and see to it that this time thou failest not. For my time draweth near and I have now but a little while to live."

So Sir Bedivere went forth again and he went to that place where he had hidden the sword. And he took the sword from where it lay hidden and lifted it in his hands. And when he again beheld the light of *Sir Bedivere* the moon illuminating its handle of gold and flaming upon *goeth forth* the jewels of the handle, his heart and his purpose weakened *again.* within him, and he said to himself, "Surely, it would be a sin to *He doth not* cast away this sword. For it is the most beautiful and noblest *cast away the* sword in all of the world. Wherefore then should I destroy *sword.* this sword that belongeth not more to the King himself than to the world in which he lives? Certes, the King raved in this, wherefore for the sake of posterity and for the sake of those who are to come after, I will not cast this sword into the sea."

So Sir Bedivere returned to the King, and the King said to him, panting as he spake, "Sir, have you performed that which I have commanded you to undertake?"

And Sir Bedivere said, "Yea, Lord."

Quoth the King, "What saw you in doing this thing?"

Said Sir Bedivere, "Lord, I beheld the moon shining on high, and I beheld the waves of the sea breaking noisily up against the pebbles of the beach; but naught else did I behold."

Then the King was silent for a little while and then he cried out, "Oh, woe is me! that all my authority hath departed from me with my strength! For it was to be supposed that mine enemies would betray me but not that my friends would betray me. But here lie I hovering upon the edge of death, and now this knight who is my sworn knight and vassal will not do that which I bid him to do because of the jewels that enrich the hilt of that sword."

Then Sir Bedivere wept and he said, "Lord, I will do that which thou biddest me to do." And King Arthur said, "Do it, and make haste."

So Sir Bedivere ran forth from that chapel. And he ran to where the *Sir Bedivere* sword was hidden and he took the sword and wrapped the *casteth away* belt of the sword about it. And he ran down the rocks to *the sword.* the sea shore, and when he had come there he whirled the sword several times about his head and cast it far out over the water.

And Sir Bedivere beheld the sword that it whirled, flashing in the moonlight like to pure circles of light, whirling in the darkness. So the sword *An arm catch-* described a circle above the water and it descended to the *eth the sword.* water, and as the sword descended to the water there emerged from the water an arm. And around the arm was a sleeve of white samite and about the arm were many bracelets of gold inset with precious stones. And the arm catched the sword by the haft and brandished it thrice, and then drew it down beneath the water. And the water closed over it and the sword and the arm were gone.

All this Sir Bedivere beheld, and when he had beheld it he returned, musing, to where King Arthur lay in that small chapel above the cliffs.

And when he returned, King Arthur said to him, "Sir, did you do as I commanded you to, and did you fling Excalibur into the water?" Sir Bedivere said, "Lord, I did as you commanded me."

Quoth King Arthur, "And what did you behold?"

Said Sir Bedivere, "When I thus threw that sword into the water of the sea, an arm came out of that water. And the arm had to it a sleeve of white samite and it was enclasped with many bracelets of gold, and the bracelets were set with many precious stones of various sorts. And the hand of the arm catched Excalibur by the hilt and it brandished him three times in the air and then it drew him beneath the water. That is what I saw."

Said King Arthur, "Well hast thou served me in this! But the time groweth short and mine end draweth near. Take me upon thy shoulders and bear me to the sea shore at that place where thou didst cast Excalibur into the sea. There thou wilt find a boat with several ladies in it. That boat is intended for me, and now I know that boat will be there waiting for me since that arm arose and the hand of the arm seized upon Excalibur."

So Sir Bedivere stooped his shoulders. And he drew the arms of King Arthur upon either side of his neck, and the arms of the King were very weak and limp like to those of a litt'e child that is ill. And *Sir Bedivere* Sir Bedivere raised himself and he lifted King Arthur from his *beareth the* couch, and King Arthur groaned when Sir Bedivere lifted him. *King to the boat.* And Sir Bedivere bore King Arthur out of that chapel and into the moonlight. And Sir Bedivere bore King Arthur in that wise down to the cliffs of the sea. And by now a chill was upon the night so that the panting breath of Sir Bedivere came forth from his nostrils like to thin smoke. And ever the iron shoes of Sir Bedivere smote upon the rocks as he walked, so that the rocks rang beneath his tread.

So Sir Bedivere bore King Arthur down that cliff to where the sea splashed and moaned upon the rocks of the sea, and the shadows of Sir Bedivere and of the King were very black and shapeless upon those rocks, and the shadows walked with them down to the sea.

So by and by Sir Bedivere perceived that they were coming close to that place where he had cast the sword into the sea. And as he drew near he perceived that there was there a boat drawn up to the shore at that spot where he had stood to cast the sword into the water. And Sir Bedivere saw that there were several people standing within the boat and that these people were three queens and their attendants.

Two of those queens Sir Bedivere knew, for they were the one Queen Morgana le Fay and the other the Queen of North Wales. *The three* But the third of those queens he did not know. Yet he saw *queens take* that she was very tall and straight and that she was clad in *the King into* garments of green, very thin and glistering. And her hair was *the boat.* black and glossy, shining in the moonlight like to fine and very glassy threads of silk. And her face was exceedingly white, like to wax for white-ness, and her eyes were very black and brilliant, like to brilliant jewels set into that ivory whiteness. And around the neck of this lady were many necklaces of jewels of gold inset with emerald stones, very bright and shining.

This lady stood at the tiller of that strange boat and she was the Lady of the Lake, though Sir Bedivere wist not who she was. And she held the tiller very steadily and so held the boat close to the shore.

And in that boat were several other ladies who stood there very silently and looked ever toward the shore where was Sir Bedivere; but these were the ladies attendant upon those queens.

Then when Sir Bedivere came thitherward carrying King Arthur upon his shoulders, those ladies lifted up their voices in piercing lamentation so that the heart of Sir Bedivere ached to hear that lament. And Queen Mor-gana le Fay and the Queen of North Wales arose and reached their arms for King Arthur; and Sir Bedivere gave King Arthur into their arms and they two took him—Queen Morgana by the shoulders and the Queen of North Wales by the knees—and they lifted him into the boat.

And they laid him upon a couch within the boat, and he lay with his head pillowed upon the lap of Queen Morgana. And Sir Bedivere stood upon the shore and looked upon the face of King Arthur as it lay within the lap of Queen Morgana, and he beheld that the face of King Arthur was white like to the ashes of wood, wherefore he wist that he was dead. And Sir Bedivere cried out in a loud and wailing voice, saying, "My Lord and King, wilt thou leave me? What then shall I do? For here am I alone in the midst of mine enemies."

Then King Arthur opened his eyes and he said, "Hah, Messire, thou hast no enemies about thee, for thine enemies are put to flight, and in a little *The King* while Sir Launcelot comes who will be thy friend. But go *speaketh to* thou back into the world and tell them all that thou hast *Sir Bedivere.* beheld at this place. For wit you that now I know that I shall not die at this place, but that I shall go in this boat and with my sister, Queen Morgana, to Avalon. There in the Vale of Avalon I shall live, and by and by and after many years I shall again return to Britain and no man shall know of my return. But with that return shall come peace and tranquillity. And war shall be no more, but the arts of peace shall flourish. So take that message back with thee into the world, for now I go to leave thee; and so farewell."

Then for the third time those ladies lifted up their voices and wailed in lamentation, and with that lamentation the boat trembled and moved.

And it moved away from the shore; at first slowly, then more and more swiftly until it disappeared in the moonlight of the night. And for awhile Sir Bedivere saw it, and then he was not sure that he saw it, and then it vanished away into the whiteness of the moonlight, and was gone from his vision.

Then Sir Bedivere moved weeping away from that shore and he wept so that hardly could he see what next step he took. And so Sir Bedivere came away from that shore, and in his sorrow he wist not whither he went. But ever he walked forward for all that night, and when the morning was come he found himself to be near to a considerable city. So he went forward to that city and he found that there was a great bustle and turmoil of people coming and going.

So Sir Bedivere entered the city and he said, "Who is here?" They say to him, "It is the Archbishop of Canterbury who is here." Sir Bedivere said to them, "Take me to him." *Sir Bedivere cometh to the Archbishop.*

So they took him to where the Archbishop was, and several other bishops were with him. And when the Archbishop beheld Sir Bedivere he said, "Sir, why are you so pale?" Then Sir Bevidere said, "Sir, I am pale because of all that I have beheld." Then Sir Bevidere told the Archbishop and those who were with *He telleth the Archbishop what hath befallen.* him of that great battle they had fought the day before between Salisbury and the sea. And he told him of all that had happened in that battle and of the knights who were slain therein. And he told him how that Sir Mordred was slain and how King Arthur had been wounded by Sir Mordred and had departed at night in that boat as aforetold of.

To all this the Archbishop listened with great astonishment and he cried out, "How is this, and what is this thou tellest me? Is King Arthur gone, and has that good and wise King disappeared thus mysteriously from amongst us?" And he said, "What next of kin doth the King leave behind him?" Sir Bedivere said, "His nighest of kin is Sir Constantine of Cornwall, who is cousin unto Sir Gawaine."

The Archbishop said, "Him then shall we crown to be the next King of Britain. For so will he succeed in rightful line from the strain of King Uther Pendragon."

And so it was done as the Archbishop said, for shortly after that Sir Constantine of Cornwall was crowned King of Britain at Camelot—which same, saith the history of these things, is Winchester of these present days.

So I have told you of the Passing of Arthur, which in all the other histories of those things is told as I have told it. But of that which happened thereafter there are many distinct and separate histories.

But that history which hath been accepted of old by the people of England is this: That King Arthur did not die, but that he was taken by Queen Morgana le Fay and by those two other queens to Avalon, and that there he was salved so that he did not die. And that history saith that he lives there yet, and that some day he shall come back to Britain as he promised to do, and that when he thus shall come there, there shall likewise come continual peace and plenty and joy and happiness as he promised.

And touching Avalon there is this to say—that it is the dwelling-place of Queen Morgana le Fay, and that it is a strange and wonderful island *Concerning* that floats forever upon the sea to the westward. And many *Avalon.* people declare that they have beheld that land, but always from a distance. For sometimes they call it Fata Morgana, and sometimes they call it Avalon. But always when they see it it is to behold high towers and glittering pinnacles reaching into the sky; and it is to behold the embowerment of trees, both of forest trees and of shade trees; and it is to behold hill and vale of that mysterious country more beautiful than are the hills and vales of the dark and gloomy earth. For Avalon is sometimes called the Vale of Avalon and sometimes it is called Avalon the Beautiful.

There in that pleasant country is no snow and no ice; neither is there the scorching heats and droughts of summer, but all forever and for aye is the tepid warmth of vernal springtime.

And the people of Avalon are always happy, for never do they weep and never do they bear enmity to óne another, but all live in peace and tranquillity watching their flocks, which are as white as snow, and their herds, whose breath smelleth of wild thyme and parsley.

There, people believe, yet liveth King Arthur, and he is not dead nor is he yet awake, but ever he lyeth sleeping as in peace.

But it is believed by many that the time shall come when he will awake again. Then he will return once more to this earth, and all shall be peace and concord amongst men.

And many believe that this time is now nigh at hand. For less and less is there war within the world, and more and more is there peace and concord and good will amongst men. Wherefore, let every man live at peace with other men, and wish them well and do them well, and then will King Arthur awake from his sleep. Then will his dreadful wound be healed and then will he return unto his own again.

Of such was the passing of Arthur.

The Passing of Guinevere :•

Chapter Tenth

How Sir Launcelot came to Queen Guinevere, and how Queen Guinevere remained a nun. How Sir Launcelot went into the forest and became a hermit, and how seven of his fellows joined him there. Also of the death of Sir Launcelot of the Lake.

NOW it hath already been told how that Sir Launcelot of the Lake received the note of Sir Ewaine, and of how he and his knights decided to come to the aid of King Arthur.

So Sir Launcelot and his knights to the number of two hun- *Sir Launcelot* dred and twelve came to England in ships and galleys, and they *landeth at* landed at Dover as King Arthur had done. *Dover.*

And when Sir Launcelot arrived at Dover there came to him a messenger and told him of that battle that had been fought upon the plains not far from Salisbury, and how that Sir Mordred had been slain and how that King Arthur had died of his wound thereafter. And that messenger also told him how that Sir Constantine of Cornwall had been crowned King of Britain, in the room of King Arthur.

All this Sir Launcelot heard and also the knights who were with him. And Sir Launcelot wept a very great deal and several of those knights who were with him wept also. And Sir Launcelot cried out, "Ah, my dear noble and gracious lord, King Arthur! Woe is me that in that first battle I should have slain Sir Agravaine and not Sir Mordred! For it is now upon me to believe that Sir Mordred was the instigator of all this mischief. But now is King Arthur gone and all is turned to ruin and to loss about us. For here be hardly any of the Knights of the Round Table yet living, and many of those who were amongst the best and noblest of those knights have been slain. To wit, Sir Gawaine hath been slain, and Sir Lionel and Sir Ector have been slain, and Sir Ewaine hath been slain, and Sir Gareth who was my dear and loving friend hath been slain, and Sir Geharis hath been slain. All these have died and several others, and had it not been for Sir Mordred and his treachery these would yet have been alive. But all these have died because of the treachery of Sir Mordred. Would that he had died in the beginning, for these would all then have been saved!"

So Sir Launcelot made his lament, and in making it the tears flowed down his face in streams. And Sir Launcelot said, "Who of us can now serve under King Constantine as vassals?" They say to him, "none of us can so serve him." Said Sir Launcelot, "nor can I serve him." Then he said, "Where is now Queen Guinevere?" They say to him, "Sir, she is at this present at the convent of Saint Bridget at Rochester and she is the Abbess of that convent. For since King Arthur gave her to the church she hath taken up the orders of the church and hath become a nun of black and white."

So that night Sir Launcelot took horse and he rode away alone, and he rode to Rochester and to the convent of Saint Bridget. And *Sir Launcelot* Sir Launcelot came into the room of that convent and he said *goeth to* to those who were there, "Let me have speech with the Abbess *Rochester to seek* *the Queen.* of this place."

Then anon came Queen Guinevere to where he was, and Sir Launcelot stood in the middle of the room and looked toward her. And he beheld that her face was grown very white and thin and that she was clad in robes of black and white. And the Queen looked toward Sir Launcelot and she knew him. And when she beheld him she cried out in a very loud and piercing voice, "God save me! Is it thou?" And with that she felt around behind her as though in a blindness. And she felt that there was a form behind her and she sat down upon the form. And she swooned upon that form so that her head fell backward across the back of the form. And Sir Launcelot perceived that she had swooned.

Then Sir Launcelot called to the ladies of that convent in a very loud voice, "Make haste! Make haste! For the Queen hath swooned!" So several of those ladies came hastening and they loosened the robes of the Queen at the throat and they chafed her hands and bathed her temples with vinegar, and anon she awoke from her swoon and found Sir Launcelot kneeling before her.

And the Queen reached out and touched Sir Launcelot and she said, *The Queen* "Art thou real, or art thou a spirit?" And Sir Launcelot *bespeaks Sir* replied, "Lady, I am flesh and blood as thou art." Then *Launcelot.* the Queen said to him, "Sir, what seek you here?" And Sir Launcelot replied, "I seek thee, Lady. For ever thou art present with me by day and by night, and never art thou absent from my thoughts."

The Queen said, "Ah, Launcelot! It is vain for thee to seek me here, for ever my heart is here in this place and here it will always remain. For here have I bethought me of my life and of all the joys and pleasures of my life, and of all the sinfulness and the evil that I have committed. And I wit that my lord, King Arthur, is now ever first within my thoughts and within my heart. For though I fled from King Arthur that time and betook myself with thee to Joyous Gard, yet there at Joyous Gard my heart turned ever to my lord and my King. For he was the lover of my youth, and first and last my heart turned ever to him in all my joys and in all my troubles. So now my King is passed, and my heart cleaveth to him in Paradise, and there I will haply rejoin my King and will dwell with him for aye. For there we shall be together in bliss and naught that is of sorrow or uncertainty shall ever come betwixt us."

Then Sir Launcelot cried out, "And I, Lady, is there naught in thy thoughts for me?"

She said, "Yea, Launcelot, there is great friendship and love for thee, but not that sort of love. So get thee back to Joyous Gard and there take thee to wife some fair and gentle lady of that place. For so thou mayst rear to thee children in the stead of that Sir Galahad who hath departed from thee some while ago."

Sir Launcelot said, "Lady, I can never wed any woman in this world but thee." And the Queen said, "Ah, Launcelot, that is a pity."

So that speech between those two came to an end, and Sir Launcelot rode away from that place with his head bowed low upon his breast. And Sir Launcelot rode ever toward the forest and anon he rode into the forest. And when Sir Launcelot had come to that place *Sir Launcelot* he kneeled down before that Hermit of the Forest and he *departeth from* said to him "Sir, I pray you to confess me and assoil me. *the Queen.* For here henceforth and to the end of my days will I remain a hermit of the forest like as thou art. Several times have I lived here as a recluse, yet have I ever returned by and by to the world. But now will I never return to that world again; for all the pleasure of that world was taken away from me and I am left barren of hope and of joy."

So Sir Launcelot withdrew to another part of the forest, and he took his armor from off his body and hung his armor up upon the *Sir Launcelot* branches of a tree that was near at hand. And he took the *becometh a* harness and trappings from off his horse and he turned his *forest recluse.* horse loose to browse at will upon the grass that grew there at that place. So Sir Launcelot became a recluse of the forest with intent never more to be anything else than that forest recluse.

Now when those knights who were in attendance upon Sir Launcelot at Dover discovered that he had gone from them, they wist not where **he** had gone and they searched for him at all places, and yet they could not find him. So most of those knights separated and divided, each knight departing to his own home. But several of those who were kin to Sir Launcelot joined them together to search for him. And these were the knights that searched for Sir Launcelot: there were Sir Bors and Sir Bleoberis and Sir Blamor de Ganis, and there was Sir Galahud and Sir Galahadin, and there was Sir Villiars, and there was Sir Clarus. These seven knights searched Britain from end to end and all athwart the land, and ever they sought for Sir Launcelot. So, at last, they came to that part of the forest where Sir Launcelot abided.

And those knights beheld a horse browsing in the open parts of the forest, and Sir Bors said to the others, "Messires, yonder an I mistake not is the horse of Sir Launcelot." Then they went a little farther and they beheld the armor of Sir Launcelot hanging upon the branches of the tree. And Sir Bors examined that armor and he said, "This, certes, is the armor of Sir Launcelot. Now he cannot be far distant from this place."

Anon they heard the knelling of a little vesper bell, and Sir Bors said, "Yonder is the bell of the Hermit of the Forest. Let us go thitherward and mayhap we may hear news of Sir Launcelot." So they went in that direction and by and by they came to the chapel of the Hermit of the Forest. And they looked within the chapel door and they beheld the Hermit and another anchorite kneeling in prayer. And there were little birds within the chapel and they hopped about there upon the floor and about those two kneeling figures and were not afraid of either of them.

So, by and by, those two ended their prayers, and they arose. Then *The knights companion find Sir Launcelot.* those knights beheld the face of the anchorite and they saw that it was the face of Sir Launcelot. For though the face of Sir Launcelot was covered with a beard and though it was very thin and peaked from fasting, yet they knew it for his face. For Sir Launcelot had eaten no meat and but little food of any sort, but had deprived himself of food for the betterment of his soul.

Then Sir Bors spake and he said, "Sir Launcelot, is it thou who art here?" And Sir Launcelot said, "Aye, it is indeed I whom thou beholdest." Sir Bors said, "Sir, this life does not beseem thee to lead, wherefore place upon thee thine armor and come forth with us into the world again. For thy life is certes of value to that world." "Nay," said Sir Launcelot, "I will not leave this place, for here I dwell in peace and amity with the world. Why then should I again go forth into strife as of old?" Quoth Sir Bors, "Sir, this life thou art leading is but the neglect of duty, for the duty of every knight is to be within the world and to do the work of the world, be that work to battle or to labor. Why then shouldst thou rest here in this hermitage and without action of any sort?"

"Messire," said Sir Launcelot, "were there a call for me to go forth into the world, then would I go. For my duty would then demand of me to assume again the armor of my knighthood. But there is no such call, nor am I any longer young, as one time I was. Wherefore, now hath come my time for rest, and so I remain here in quiet within the woodlands."

Sir Bors said, "Sir, we are your knights and your followers, wherefore if you remain here within the forest, so also do we remain *The knights* with you. For your life shall be our life and your fare shall *companion be-* be our fare until the end." And Sir Launcelot said, "Let it *come recluses.* be that way."

So all those knights remained there within the forest and all of them assumed the holy orders of hermits. Thus they remained there for three years and in that time they dwelt in great peace and concord. And they disturbed none of those things that were living within the forest, so that the wild creatures of the forest presently grew tame to them. For they could lay their hands upon the haunches of the wild doe of the forest and it would not flee away from them, for the wild thing wist that they meant it no harm.

Thus they lived there in solitude and they cultivated their plots of pulse and barley, and the fame of their virtues and of their holiness spread far and wide, so that many people came thither from the world for the sake of their prayers and of their benediction.

Now one night as he slept Sir Launcelot had a dream, and the dream came to him in the second watch of the night. And the dream of Sir Launcelot was this:

He dreamed that he beheld Queen Guinevere standing before him, and her face smiled and was very radiant as though a bright light shone through her face from behind. For her face was translated by that *Sir Launcelot* light so that it was all of a glorious and rosy pink in its color. *dreameth.* And the Queen was clad all in a very straight robe of cloth of gold and that robe shone with a very singular lustre. And around her neck and her arms were many ornaments of gold and these also shone and glittered as she moved or breathed. And this vision of Queen Guinevere said, "Rejoice, O Sir Launcelot! For my troubles and cares are at an end. For now I am in Paradise and my body sleepeth and is dead."

Then Sir Launcelot awoke and he found that it was morning and that the sun was shining.

And Sir Launcelot arose and went forth and he came to where the Hermit was, and he told the Hermit of that dream. Then the Hermit said to him, "Sir, meseems from this dream that the Queen is no more, but that she is dead and that her soul hath been translated unto Paradise. Make haste and go thither where she is and see if this be so."

So Sir Launcelot mounted his horse and his seven companions mounted their horses and together they rode unto Rochester. And Sir Launcelot rode to the nunnery at that place and he said to them that came to him, "Where is the Lady Abbess of this monastery?"

They say to him, "Sir, she died last night at the second watch of the night." Sir Launcelot said, "Bring me to her."

So they took Sir Launcelot to where lay the body of the Queen, and *He beholdeth* it was in a large upper room and the windows were open *the dead Queen.* and the breeze blew cold through the room. And Sir Launcelot beheld the Queen that her body lay upon a couch of white linen, and he perceived that the face of the body was white like to wax. And he saw that the lips of the body smiled as he had beheld the Queen to smile in the dream that he had had of her the night before.

Then Sir Launcelot did not weep, only he stood with his hands clasped very tightly together, and he reviewed in his mind all that had befallen him and her. And he reviewed the first time that he had come to the King's Court at Camelot. And he reviewed how he had sacrificed the life of his lady for the love of the Queen. And he reviewed how he had done battle for the Queen, and how he had saved her life by that battle, and he reviewed how he had fought and slain his friends that he might bring her away from her trial to Joyous Gard. All those things he reviewed, and some of those things were of peace to him and some of them were of torment. Then he spake and he said, "Ah, Lady! Would that I were lying as thou lyest. For then would I too be at peace, whiles now I am not at peace."

So died Queen Guinevere, and at that time she was in the forty-sixth year of her age and was exceedingly beautiful.

So those eight knights remained there at the nunnery for two days, and upon the third day the body of Queen Guinevere was interred before the altar of the nunnery. And upon the stone that covered that body were these words:

> Hic . jacet . Guinevera . Regina .
> Quondam . Regina . Brittaniæ . erat.

And for many years that entablature was to be seen at Rochester, wherefore it may be known that Queen Guinevere was indeed there buried. For so saith the history of those things and so those things must be.

After all those things had passed, those knights again retired to the forest and there they again took up their abode as of old. And so they lived there for two or three years longer. Then they left that forest as shall presently be told.

For now speak we of the Passing of Sir Launcelot, which was as follows:

One morning all they who were there awoke very early and they went to their matin prayers. That morning was in the May time, *Sir Launcelot* all the trees were in leaf and the apple trees were in blossom. *cometh not to* For whensoever the soft warm wind blew through the trees, *prayers.* then did those blossoms shed their fragrant pink snow until all the grass around about was spread therewith. And the birds were singing in every bush and tree so that all the air was full of their melodious and harmonious jubilation.

That time when they were assembled they looked around and beheld that Sir Launcelot was not there and they said, "Where is Sir Launcelot, that he cometh not to matin prayers?" So Sir Bors went to the cell of Sir Launcelot and he beheld that Sir Launcelot was lying very peacefully upon his couch. And Sir Bors went to Sir Launcelot to arouse him, and he saw that Sir Launcelot was dead. And the hands of Sir Launcelot were folded upon his breast, and there was a smile of great peace and good content upon the lips of Sir Launcelot.

Then Sir Bors went to the door of the cell of Sir Launcelot and he called those others to come thither and they did so. And Sir Bors *Sir Bors* said to them, "Behold! Here lyeth that which was once Sir *beholdeth* Launcelot, but which is that knight no more. But God be *him, dead.* praised that he died in such peace and tranquillity as he hath done."

And all they, as they gazed upon Sir Launcelot, beheld that it was so, and that he had indeed died in great peace and tranquillity with his God.

And Sir Bors said, "Let us take the body of this good knight and carry it to Joyous Gard that it may be buried there. For so would he have it that his body should be buried at Joyous Gard."

So they brought them to that forest place a horse bier and they laid the body of Sir Launcelot upon that horse bier, and they covered the body so that no one might see it in passing. And they bore the body thence and to Joyous Gard, and so, after many tribulations and many sufferings and sorrows, the body of Sir Launcelot lay in peace and quietness at that place.

And those knights who were with him did not return to the forest, otherwise they continued at Joyous Gard. And one of those *He lyeth at* knights always sat at vigil beside the tomb of Sir Launcelot *Joyous Gard.*

and kept burning there seven waxen tapers. And so the tomb was always illuminated with those waxen tapers whiles those knights lived.

And the last of those knights to die was Sir Bors de Ganis, for Sir Bors *Of the death* was over fourscore years of age when he died. For when *of Sir Bors.* the priest came thither one morning, he found Sir Bors sitting beside the tomb of Sir Launcelot, and Sir Bors had died at that time. And one of those seven candles (which same was the candle of Sir Bors) was not lit but was burned out. For so the life of Sir Bors had flickered out, even as the light of that candle had departed.

So with this endeth the history of the lives of those knights, and so I have told it to you.

Conclusion

THUS have I written the history of King Arthur and of sundry of those knights that comprised his Round Table. For so may you see with what patience, what labor and what self-devotion those knights served their king, their Round Table and their fellows.

For those knights were very gallant gentlemen who thought but little of care and trouble and who practised self-denial when that self-denial could be of avail to help their friends or to benefit the world.

For ever they brought aid to those who were in trouble and comfort to those who were afflicted ever they brought food to the hungry and drink to the thirsty; and ever they destroyed giants and monsters and wicked men, and so made the world a better and a comelier place in which to dwell. And wit ye that no man can do better than that in this world: to bring aid to the afflicted; food to the hungry, and a release from trouble to those who are in anxiety.

Yea; for seven years have I been engaged in writing these books, which contain the history of these things. Many other things have I done in that time. For I have painted many pictures besides having written these books and other works of a like sort. And these books are four in number: first, there is the Book of King Arthur; then there is the Book of the Champions of the Round Table; then there is the Book of Sir Launcelot and his companions, and now there is this Book of the Grail and the Passing of Arthur, and this book is the last. For those books comprise a history of all this time; for though there be many things left untold in them, yet those things are of small consequence. For all that is of greater note hath been here told, and that in full.

And I thank God that he hath permitted me to finish this work, for wit ye that when a man taketh seven years of his life to complete an undertaking, he knoweth not whether he shall live to complete that which he hath begun.

But so I have completed it, and for that I thank God who permitted me to complete it. Amen.

Finished at Wilmington, Delaware,
This 16th day of April
in the year of grace
MCMX.